Dearly Ransomed Soul

A Georgia Pattison mystery

Avril Field-Taylor

Published in 2008 by YouWriteOn.com

Copyright © Avril Field_Taylor

First Edition

The authors assert the moral right under Copyright, Designs and Patents Act 1988 to be identified as the authors of this work.

All rights reserved. No part of this publication may be reproduced, stored in a retrieval system, or transmitted, in any form or by any means without the prior written consent of the author, nor be otherwise circulated in any form of binding or cover other than that in which it is published and without a similar condition being imposed on the subsequent purchaser.

All characters in this publication are fictitious and any resemblance to real persons, living or dead, is purely coincidental.

Published by YouWriteOn.com

Acknowledgments

I could not have written this book without help, support and encouragement from family and friends.

In particular, I would like to express my love and gratitude to Paul, my endlessly patient husband, who designed the cover, frequently calmed me down and is one of the good guys.

I must thank Janet Shell, a truly wonderful mezzo-soprano, inspiring teacher and friend, who answered all my queries about the life of a singer with wit, charm and patience.

Thanks are also due to Hornsea Writers for their advice, encouragement and support.

I dedicate 'Dearly Ransomed Soul' to the memory of my mother.

1

I sat there with the bottle of scotch on one side of my uneaten breakfast and the paracetamol on the other. It was Thursday morning. After another sleepless night, I'd decided enough was enough. I'd tried so hard to reason the pain away. I felt tired and helpless and lonely. I'd like to say that my hesitation was due to some higher form of consciousness about the sanctity of life and all that, but in reality it was lethargy and the telephone ringing. Habit made me pick it up.

'Hey there, Georgy-girl. How's tricks?'

'Hi Melanie. It's not a good time right now.'

'Rubbish. It's the perfect time. Linda Sharpe has pulled out of Temingham and I need an early music soprano to do the Mozart Requiem, Vivaldi's "Gloria" and a song recital. How are you fixed?'

Temingham. A late starter as music festivals go, but one gaining ground fast. I liked the Peak District, too, what little I'd seen of it. Melanie heard the cogs going round. She knows which buttons to press for each client.

'All the dailies will be there. This could put you well and truly on the map, George.' She paused. 'George? Are you still there? What are you doing?'

'Thinking.'

Could I be bothered, that's what I was really thinking. Singing was my life but just now, life had raised its ugly head and struck me what old fashioned lady authors used to call a mortal blow.

'George. I need you to think quicker.' Her voice sharpened. 'What's the matter?'

I came clean. 'Mike.'

'Damn him.' She paused again. 'Look, George, I can't tell you to forget him, but it's been over a month now and it's about time you rejoined the human race. It would be far better for you to go to Temingham and sing than vegetate in that dingy little basement of yours. I've negotiated a good fee.'

I bet she had, seeing that she would get ten percent of it.

'Besides, isn't your old flatmate the Temingham conductor's wife now?'

Now how on earth did Melanie know that?

'So instead of feeling sorry for yourself, shift your arse, get in the car and head south. Go via Bakewell and have a tart on me.'

Which is how I came to find myself the next evening in the Maddox Hotel's conference room, glass of Pouilly-Fumé in hand, standing next to Caroline Gardiner at the Temingham pre-festival bash. Her husband, Neil was glad handing round all the guest soloists and the VIPs. I felt Carrie stiffen as Ariana Staithes sashayed through the door wearing a silver sheath dress which left nothing to the imagination. No change there, then. Neil went red, then white and hurried over to greet her as if she was the Queen.

'Met her before?' I muttered.

'No. You?'

'Oh, yes. I worship the ground she slithers on.'

'So does Neil all except for the slithering bit, unless it's slithering all over her, of course.'

'Ah.'

We both shut up when Neil brought Ariana over to meet us. He'd got guts, I'll give him that. Ariana shook Carrie's hand politely enough, but I knew her and her eyes were issuing a challenge. I dare not look at Carrie, so I had no idea if the challenge was acknowledged or accepted.

'Neil tells me you used to dance a little.'

'Neil is understating it, Ariana,' I interrupted. 'Carrie was with the English National Ballet. I'm sure you've heard of them, even in the wilds of Canada.'

The fixed smile grew a little more rigid. 'Georgia Pattison, isn't it? Do I remember you from the Academy?'

'Possibly. Weren't you in the running for the early music prize the year I won it?'

'I'd already decided to give my soul to opera and oratorio. It sits better with my voice.'

She turned to Neil as I muttered 'And your tits' in Carrie's ear. Her mouth twitched.

'Ariana is singing the angel in "Dream of Gerontius" tomorrow night,' said Neil to me, unaware that he was pouring oil on troubled fires.

'How lovely. I'll check my diary to see if I'm free.'

Ariana was about to make some sort of riposte, one of her failings being never to know when to put up and shut up, but just then there was another kerfuffle at the doorway of the room. We all turned. Merlina Meredith was making her entrance, as the song says, with her usual flair. I saw Ariana's lips tighten. They enjoyed an acrimonious relationship and more so since the upstart Canadian had been offered Gerontius' guardian angel. I liked Merlina. More than that, I admired her. Nothing ever appeared to disrupt her outward serenity. I wished I was more like her. The thought of Ariana Staithes singing a part Merlina had made her own for more than twenty years must have set her back almost as much as Mike's defection had me. She swept over to our little group.

'Neil, darling, how lovely to see you. I am so looking forward to the Blount. Georgia. I didn't realise you were joining us.'

'Linda Sharpe has bronchitis, Merlina.'

'Then we are lucky to get you instead, darling. Now,' she said looking round and managing not to see Ariana, 'where does one get a drink?'

After the party, Caroline and I walked back to "Vox Celeste" the corny name of the cathedral organist's house, arm in arm, giggling from the effects of the booze. My first reaction to the house she and Neil lived in was that, if that was the sort of tied house cathedral organists were given, perhaps I ought to bag myself one. It sat on the banks of the River Teming with a view over the moors in one direction and looking into the cathedral close on the other. I think Carrie would have preferred a new detached des-res somewhere out of town, but Neil had to be close to the job. He had stayed behind to see the last of the party-goers out and he came in just as we were finishing our nightcaps. His tie was undone.

'Hi, Neil. You look as if you've been mauled by a tiger.'

He blushed. 'Not a great party person, Georgia. By the way, I have an enormous favour to ask.'

'Ask away. I've had a few so you might be in luck.'

'This flu bug has hit the choir. I'm three sopranos down in the semi-chorus. Don't suppose you'd do a stiffen for me tomorrow night, would you?'

'Not sung Gerontius since I was at college, Neil.'

'They just need a bit of boosting. Please, Georgia. This is my first concert in my first festival and I really need it to go well.'

'You'll have to pay me.'

'I can fix that.'

'In my hand and not a word to Melanie Southall?'

'Scout's honour.'

I thought for all of five seconds. 'Actually it might be fun. OK, Neil.'

The next afternoon, we had the usual ripples running through the choir sopranos at the threat posed by a professional singing in their midst. Roughly speaking they fall into two groups, the Fawners and the Footlight Fannies. The former are easy to deal with; you just smile and are meekly modest. The Footlight Fannies can cut up as rough as any seasoned diva and with far less reason. The woman asked to move back to the second row of the semi-chorus to make room for me was a fully fledged Footlight Fanny and did everything bar walk out at the insult of being shifted from the front row. The rehearsal was so-so. The men were horrible at the beginning of the Demons Chorus but then they always are, even in big professional choirs. When we were almost finished, Jamie Topcliffe and Kevin Dace, the bass and tenor soloists slid onto the platform, so Neil did the usual topping and tailing of the crossover bits between solos and choir. It was almost four-thirty before Ariana made her entry. Neil stopped the rehearsal specifically to introduce her to the choir and then introduced Jamie and Kevin as an afterthought. I did not even rate an after-afterthought. When the choir was finally told it could go, I made a point of walking round the edge of the orchestra to speak to Jamie and Kevin.

'Georgia, where did you spring from?' said Jamie, grinning from ear to ear, giving me a hug and bruising my collar bone in the process.'

'Flick Jamie, what have you got in your inside pocket?'

He laughed and pulled out a massive and ornate gold fountain pen. 'Mum's last present. I always carry it for luck. Sorry darling, have I bruised you? What are you doing here?'

'Playing super-sub for Linda Sharpe and stiffening the semi-chorus for tonight.'

'Great. We must get together. You know Kevin, of course.'

'Yes. Hi, Georgia. Darling, what on earth are you singing in the choir for?'

'Favour to Neil, well Caroline actually.'

Neil was making ostentatious consultations of his watch, so I smiled at the guys and tip-toed off the platform.

The time between final rehearsal and performance is always fractured. I spent a good half hour walking round the cathedral looking at the flower displays. I wish I knew how to get them looking like that. The scent of them at close range was unbelievably cloying after a few minutes exposure and reminded me of all the churches in the days after Princess Diana's death. I was a new girl on the block then and singing Monteverdi in Hull, of all places. Everyone wanted to leave a floral tribute to the people's princess. It didn't matter where I stood to sing. That heavy fragrance was everywhere. It was a toss-up as to whether I passed out or threw up.

There weren't that many displays in Temingham, thank God. As I watched, one of the women caught her foot in the base of the stand and the arrangement they were just finishing off crashed to the floor accompanied by the involuntary scream of the woman who got splashed with water and oasis. Nice acoustics, I thought listening to the echo. I heard Ariana on a long top A falter to silence and then Neil's voice demanding to know what the hell was happening. A blonde woman who had been working on another display went halfway up the aisle and explained. Neil grunted and turned back to the orchestra. The woman came back and shot a look at the one who had knocked over the display. I wish I could do it like that. The culprit looked as if she had been caught stealing the family silver.

'I am so sorry, Lady Barbara,' she babbled. 'My foot caught in the curly bit at the bottom.'

'All right, Sarah. I'll repair this.

I walked back down the nave, listening to Ariana and confirming my opinion of the acoustics. Wonderful. More like Worcester than Westminster where all the lumps of marble take five seconds to send you back the notes you've just sung, by which time, you aren't singing them anymore. Lincoln can be a bit like that, too, but the end of the "Praise to the Holiest" in Gerontius sounds wonderful there because the echoes take about ten seconds to stop chasing each other. One of my Elgar enthusiast friends likens it to the heavenly host joining in and forgetting to watch the conductor to know when to stop singing.

I looked at the stage set-up. The whole of the west end of the cathedral had been blocked off and the central section made into tiered seating which stretched halfway up the boarded west window and was for the choir. The orchestra were in front of the seating on a stage a couple of metres above the main floor of the cathedral. There were panels from the stage to the floor across the entire width of the building, with swing doors in the north and south aisles for people to come from the backstage area into the cathedral and vice-versa. I pushed through the door in the north aisle.

The backstage area had a little curtained off dressing room for the soloists and conductor. At ground level underneath the tiered seating, a passage and been constructed in the scaffolding, joining the north and south aisles in a T-shape, the stem of the T leading to the west door. The areas at each end of the passage were big enough for the orchestra and choir to congregate before going up steps at either side onto the staging above. At the moment both areas were strewn with the orchestra's discarded instrument cases.

There was also a huge marble statue of a former bishop, sitting with one arm outstretched as if teaching his flock. Some wit had hung his dress trousers over the bishop's arm and his shirt on the pointing finger. The whole place looked clean and there was none of the dirt and mustiness I sometimes find in churches. I walked through the passage under the seating to the south aisle area and through the swing door into the cathedral proper. Time to get back to Carrie's house.

I went through the cloisters. I saw Lady Barbara, the flower lady, talking to a stooped elderly guy and it was not until they turned the corner near the chapter house that I realised it was Sir Robert Fielding. He had been one of my piano tutors at the Academy and was an absolute sweetheart. I almost went and interrupted them, but thought better of it and went back to the house. I was glad it was so close to the cathedral because our usual English summer was in full swing, with the liquid sunshine hitting the road so hard the water bubbled as if in a cauldron. Carrie was talking to a big guy who looked as if he would have been more at home on a rugby field than anywhere else.

'Georgia. This is Scott Wiley.'

I held out my hand. 'Delighted to meet you. I came to hear you at the Wigmore last February. Are you playing during the Festival?' His eyes were the most intense blue I had ever seen. So blue they were almost purple. On any other occasion, I might have let myself drown a little, but the shock of Mike's treachery was armour against anything.

'I'm playing the Mozart twenty one and the Rachmaninov two. Not on the same night, of course.' He paused a moment still holding my hand and giving me the full benefit of eye contact. 'Excuse me,' he smiled and turned back to Carrie. 'Neil said I could borrow his music room for practising. Is that OK?'

He followed Carrie through to the room next to the dining room. I sped upstairs to change for the concert thinking how beguiling an Australian accent could be, especially when teamed with a voice like wood smoke.

I have to admit that the concert was outstanding and much as I hate to say it, the difference between good and fabulous was solely down to Ariana. The Gerontius angel is a strenuous sing, but she made it sound effortless. Her alleluias were so full of tone but never shrill. They floated round the cathedral. It was a night when you could say in truth that a star was born.

Of course, the audience went wild at the end. Neil, Jamie, Kevin and Ariana bowed and then went down the steps to the back of the platform. There was the usual pause to let everyone catch their breath. Neil came back up the stairs first and took his bow. Bloody well earned it was, too. Then Kevin came up and did his showman bit. Jamie followed him and they both stood there acknowledging the crowd, the choir, the orchestra. It made me wonder if I'm like that after a performance. Had the cathedral cat been there, it would have been acknowledged as well.

So, there we were waiting for the star turn to come up and take her bow. I could tell the audience thought everyone else was a bit of an also-ran. So we waited. And waited. I caught Neil's eye and he jerked his head to one side. I slipped down the steps. I wish I hadn't.

Ariana was lying on her back on the floor with her feet inside the makeshift dressing room, its curtain pulled back. I could see the gold sandals on her feet and the skirt of the gold dress was moving. It took me a couple of seconds to realise there was a draught from somewhere. The upper part of her was grotesque. I stopped short and had to hang on to the stair rail with both hands.

She looked a bit like a pig that's just been put on the spit roast. The lower part of her face was black mixed with red and her shoulders were beginning to char. Low blue flames were licking along the bodice of her dress. Some of her hair was singed but it hadn't begun burning properly yet because she had worn it off her face. Just starting to make itself felt was the nauseating sweet smell of melting fat and barbecued pork mixed with burned hair.

I caught my breath and put my hand up to my nose to try and ward off the stench. I knew I had to move, to get help. I wanted to go and help her, but I stood there like Lot's wife. I could still hear the applause - her applause, but she would never hear it again. It seemed to take forever to make my feet move, but eventually I ran back up the steps and fainted into the arms of a Footlight Fanny.

2

When I came to, I was the victim in the revenge of the thwarted nurse. Some kind soul or let's be generous, some enthusiastic soul who had just failed her St John's Ambulance exam had hauled me onto a seat. When I was in a state to notice anything, all I saw at first were my feet because my skirt was somewhere round my thighs and Florence Nightingale had shoved my head between my knees. I'd lost a shoe but I couldn't see it for the crush of black skirts.

A confusion of voices was coming at me down a long tunnel and the fact that I'd been folded over like a napkin was stopping me from breathing. I tried to push myself up to a sitting position, but my head was held in a vice-lock by somebody - probably the Fanny whose seat I'd pinched. I tried to say 'let me up,' but it came out as a strangled gurgle that not even a dentist would have been able to translate. Had she pushed my head any further, I would probably have been able to see my knickers.

'There, there, dear. You've had a shock. Just stay where you are until the doctor arrives,' somebody said. By this time, my ears were singing because all the blood was rushing to my brain so I don't know if the voice was male or female, but I think it was female.

I was just about to elbow her in the groin when a new voice entered the fray.

'It's all right now, Mrs Richards, I'll take over.'
I've always liked the soft Edinburgh accent, so I allowed myself to be lowered to the floor. I looked up at a man in an evening suit, so I assumed he was one of the choir.

'It's Miss Pattison, isn't it? I'm Doctor Carter. Don't try and talk for the moment.'

I caught hold of his wrist and gestured down the steps. 'She's down there.'

'Yes. I know. Nothing for you to worry about. Now, Mrs Gardiner is here. I want you to lie quietly for a few minutes until you feel ready to get up.'
I tried to push myself up but he tutted at me so I lay down again.

'Let the orchestra and choir get off the staging first, Miss Pattison. No need for you to stir just yet.'

I turned my head to one side. The orchestra were virtually all off although they had left their instruments behind. Members of the choir were lined up on either side of Neil's podium being helped down two ladders. It didn't take Einstein to work out that backstage was out of bounds. I felt slightly drunk. Everything was happening in slow motion and out of focus. Intense weariness and a desperate impulse to giggle vied with each other, but I realised that if I tried to do anything, I would probably burst into tears. The best course of action was to do what the doctor ordered. Strange as it may seem, I was beginning to float away when he spoke again.

'We've found your other shoe. I'll give it to Mrs Gardiner. Now, do you think you could make it down that ladder at the front of the orchestra?'

I looked back up at him and nodded.

'Good girl. Lean on me.'

I'm still not sure how I managed to get down that bloody ladder, especially as the only black skirt I had brought with me was a full three-tiered satin job that I only wear when I'm in gypsy mode and it kept getting tangled up with my remaining shoe. However, some kind knight whisked me off the steps as if I weighed about eight stones wet through. How I wish I did.

Carrie was waiting for me. The doctor gave her the lost shoe and she helped me put it on. Her face was without any kind of expression. I decided that if I looked as white as she did, I must look as if I'd just been dug up. She put her arm round me.

'Come on darling. Let's go back home. I think you could do with a nice cup of tea.'

'Stuff the tea. I want a gin.'

'Doctor Carter says no alcohol.'

'You are joking. Why?'

'Because it isn't any good for shock and the police will have to ask you questions.'

I turned to the doctor who had followed me down the ladder.

'Quite right, Mrs Gardiner. The last thing you want at the moment Miss Pattison is a drink, much as you might think you need it. Besides, if you are three sheets to the wind when the police come, they won't be happy with either you or me.'

I acquiesced with as much grace as I could muster. What kind of Scotsman would stop a girl having a drink? In truth, though, tea sounded fabulous. I was half leaning on Carrie and walking towards one of the doors leading to the cloisters when a sharp female voice stopped us in our tracks.

'Excuse me,' it said. 'Can you hang on a minute, please?'

We spun round. A tall woman in a navy suit was hurrying towards us. Her hair and general appearance looked as if she had just escaped the attentions of an ardent gorilla.

'I'm sorry, ladies,' she said when she reached us. 'Miss Pattison?'

'Yes.'

'I'm Superintendent Michaela Hamilton, Peak District Police. Look, I realise you've had a nasty shock, but if you could just answer a couple of questions now, I can leave you alone until tomorrow.'

'Why can't you leave her alone now, Superintendent? I think finding a body rates as a bit more than a nasty shock, don't you?'

'And you are, madam?'

'I'm Caroline Gardiner, the cathedral organist's wife. Georgia is staying with us.'

'Fine. Fine. Thank you.' She bared her teeth at Carrie. 'Miss Pattison, I only need to ask you a couple of things now.'

I sagged back into Carrie's arm. 'OK.'

'When you went down the steps did you see anything?'

'What sort of stupid question is that? You know what I saw.'

'Sorry, I didn't phrase that very well. Apart from the body, did you see anything else?'

'Like what?'

'Anything which struck you as out of place? Anybody else there? Take your time. Just mentally go back down the steps. Don't look at the body. What can you see out of your peripheral vision?'

I thought. And all I could see was that horrible lump of flesh. I put my hands up to my face. I hate people seeing me cry.'

'I'm sorry, Miss Pattison. I know it is distressing. Can you remember anything other than the body?'

'No. I didn't go down to the bottom step. I think I was about three steps up from the floor. I just saw her. She.....she. Oh my God.'

Hamilton put her hand on my arm. 'That's fine, Miss Pattison. You go with Mrs Gardiner now. I will need to see you again in the morning. Where can I find you?'

'At "Vox Celeste" in the close, Superintendent,' cut in Carrie. 'Now, if you don't mind, I really need to get Georgia to bed with a cup of tea.'

'Of course, of course. Thank you for your time.'

I just about made it out of the cloisters before throwing up by a buddleia. It was still raining, so by the time we got back to the house, I was wet and shivering. Carrie was amazing. When we were at college, she never took the initiative in anything. I was the nutty one with the daft ideas. She fell in with things. Now, she was ordering me about like a drill sergeant.

She left me sitting on the bottom of the stairs and flew into the kitchen to put the kettle on. I just sat there staring into space. I knew who the murderer was. It couldn't be anyone else. What made it worse was he was a friend. I felt detached as if I was seeing everything quite calmly but it was all through an invisible plastic bubble and I was separated by it from everything going on in the outside world. Carrie came back and helped me up.

'Come on darling. Let's get you to bed.'

I pointed at one of her ears. 'You've lost an earring, Carrie.'

Her hand flew to her ear. 'Damn and blast. They were real diamonds as well. Neil's last birthday present. I'll have to go back and look for it. But I'll get you settled first.'

And she did. First of all, she took off my war paint with a tissue cleanser and then wiped my face and hands with a warm flannel. I began to feel drowsy and safe like a little girl inside the circle of Mummy's love and protection. She was even wearing Chanel No 5, my mother's favourite perfume.

After I was settled into bed, she went back downstairs and came up with a small pot of tea sitting on its matching cup and saucer. She talked about her recent visit to Chatsworth until I had finished the tea. Then, out of the blue, I felt as if someone had pulled out my energy plug and everything had swooshed down the plug-hole. Carrie settled me under the covers and turned out the light. I didn't so much fall asleep as become unconscious.

Next morning I was not sure what the atmosphere would be like downstairs so I dawdled about in the family bathroom. Had I not seen the ensuite bathroom attached to Carrie's bedroom, I would have deduced that this one was only used occasionally because of the absence of razors and toothbrushes. Miss Marple, eat your heart out.

I was examining my face for wrinkles, trying to work out how the killer could have been someone other than Jamie Topcliffe when Carrie knocked on the door and asked if I was OK. Time to face the music. I unlocked the door. The sight of her face stopped me in my tracks.

'Steady, girl. Deep breaths and all that.'

She burst into tears. 'George, it's awful. Neil is just sitting there as if his world has come to an end. I think he must have really been in love with her.'

'Well I can tell you she would not have been in love with him.'

'How do you know?'

'How do you think I know?'

'How well did you know her, George?'

'Look, little one. She was known as the town bike at the Academy and with good reason.'

We all called Carrie, little one at college. It was one of those stupid reversal things because, for a ballerina, she was disconcertingly tall, which played havoc with the visuals of the corps de ballet. The use of her old nickname brought a brave attempt at a smile. I put my arm round her shoulders. 'Seven out of ten for effort. Don't worry about Neil. He'll recover.'

'Not if he was in love with her.'

'Daft bat. He's in love with you. He's forgotten, that's all. Carrie, you know what the music scene is. It's all emotion and passion and sometimes that spills over. Look at me with Rudy last year when we were in "Orpheus". As long as he sang to me like that I would have followed him to the ends of the earth. As soon as the production was over, I would have run away from him to the ends of the earth. Neil will be fine and so will you, you hear me?'

'Yes, miss. Do you want any breakfast?'

'Can I start with a coffee and then see?'

We were sitting round the kitchen table. Neil was trying to appear as if his world had not crumbled round his feet. Carrie was tip-toeing round him like a skier not wanting to cause an avalanche and I was struggling with the desire to tell him exactly what I thought of him. Thankfully the doorbell rang.

Carrie preceded Superintendent Hamilton and a male sidekick into the kitchen. Hamilton looked at me eyebrows raised, a smile on her face.

'This is Inspector Stafford. How do you feel this morning, Miss Pattison?'

'OK.'

'Up to a few questions?'

'How many's a few?'

The smile widened. 'Enough so that we don't have to bother you again, perhaps?'

'Sounds good to me. Where?'

She turned to Carrie. 'Do you have anywhere we can chat? If not, I've an incident room in the cathedral library.' She turned back to me. 'Where would you prefer, Miss Pattison, here or there?'

I thought for about three seconds. I desperately wanted to get out of that pressure-cooker kitchen. 'There. It will be easier for everyone.'

'Fine. Would you like to come now?'

The pong told me that the cathedral library had just been repainted. Hamilton had a desk near the window. She seemed impervious to the paint smell and plonked herself in her chair. She saw me look out of the window at the river and the moors.

'I like a nice view, Miss Pattison. It helps me to think.'

I did not reply, but sat on the chair Stafford pulled out for me.

Hamilton turned to me. 'Right. Your full name is Georgia Pattison, yes?'

'Georgia Honeysuckle Pattison.' That made her eyebrows nearly disappear into her hairline.

'Unusual name.'

'A joke. Apparently, my parents had an arbour laden with honeysuckle and there is a chance that I was conceived under it.'

'Not always good to have parents with a sense of humour.'

'Oh, they did it to my brother as well. He's called Finlay. Both my parents are doctors. So is my brother. And you'll notice that my initials are GP.'

I could see her lips fold inwards to stop the smile and she looked down at her desk for a few seconds.

'Finlay Pattison, there's a name to conjure with.'

'No, he's Finlay Allgood. My father's name is Allgood.'

She checked my left hand. 'But your surname is Pattison.'

'It's a family name on my mother's side. I changed it by deed poll.' I could see her confusion. 'Can you imagine the gift it would have been to the critics having a name like Allgood?' I paused. 'All good?'

'Yes, I see what you mean. Yes. Good. Now, as I understand it, you are here because another soprano is ill and you are singing in her place.'

I nodded.

'And you found out you were coming when?'

'Thursday morning. I drove down here on Friday morning.'

'I see. And you were in the choir just to help them because of the flu epidemic?'

'Yes.'

'Did you know the deceased?'

'Not well. I was aware of her at the Academy, but she was a couple of years ahead of me.'

'What was she like?'

I hesitated. She rephrased her question.

'I mean what was she like as a person, not a singer?'

'Ah.' I could see her waiting for an answer, but my brain wasn't feeding any words to my mouth.

'If there's dirt to be dished, Miss Pattison, we'll find out one way or another. Please be open with us.'

'OK. She was known to be promiscuous. If she fancied someone, she didn't stop to see if they were attached to anyone. She just muscled in. Nine times out of ten, she was successful.'

'Ever do it to you?'

'Yes.'

'Serious?'

'At the time. Look, I'm sorry I just have to ask you something'

'Fire away.'

'It seems perfectly obvious to me that the last person to see her alive was Jamie Topcliffe. Why haven't you arrested him?'

'We've spoken to Mr Topcliffe, of course, and to Mr Dace and Mr Gardiner.' She stopped to think. 'It will be public knowledge very shortly if it isn't already so I don't mind telling you, Miss Pattison. The man who guards the west door during the performances was knocked out last night. Apparently he is there to see that nobody comes in and interferes with the orchestra's equipment or gets into the concerts without paying.

She stopped at my exclamation. I told her about the draught moving Ariana's dress. She nodded. 'Good. Now we know that the door was left open before the body was discovered. We couldn't be sure.

We found Mr Gregory outside at the bottom of the steps with a weighted sock next to him. Whoever knocked him out had left a calling card just inside the door. There were a couple of wet footprints with bits of grass adhering to them. There were also signs of grass near the body. Whoever our murderer is, it isn't Mr Topcliffe, Mr Dace or Mr Gardiner.' She paused. 'Or you. When Miss Staithes was killed, all four of you were in full sight of at least a thousand people.'

3

She must have seen my shoulders relax. I suppose they are trained to watch for things like that.

'I take it the three gentlemen are friends of yours?'

'I know Jamie from college. We've been friends a long time. I couldn't see him being a killer, he's such a pussy cat, but it seemed so obvious. I don't know Kevin so well, but we have done a few Messiahs here and there. Neil, I don't know at all but he is married to the girl I shared a flat with when we were at college.'

'Tell me about Mrs Gardiner.'

'What do you want to know?'

'What is she like?'

I concentrated on what she was like at college and tried to forget the previous night's drill sergeant. 'Carrie was with the English National Ballet. She wasn't a principal dancer, but even if you're in the corps de ballet, you still have to work very hard. She worked harder than most.'

'That tells me what she did. What is she like?'

'A follower, not a leader. An English rose with very few thorns.'

'That means some thorns. What are they?'

'Not the sort you're looking for, I can tell you that, Superintendent, but she has her breaking point just as we all do. I've only ever seen her act out of character once. Carrie is allergic to nuts, and someone thought it would be a fine joke to put a few in her salad. Luckily, Carrie saw them before she ate any of it otherwise she might well be dead. She has to carry a syringe thing around you know, just in case she ever goes into anaphylactic shock.

We all knew who had done it, of course. It was someone who, unlike Carrie, was not very popular in the company. Carrie waited until the girl had a performance and put a laxative in her energy drink. It is the only time she has really surprised me, but I expect when somebody does something which might kill you, you would react differently, don't you think? She told me afterwards that this stupid girl had assumed she would just sneeze a lot. She had no idea Carrie could have died.'

'What happened?'

'The girl almost missed the performance. Carrie was hauled over the coals, of course, but the fact that she might have died meant that she wasn't given the push'

'I'm allergic to dogs,' said Hamilton. 'It can make life quite difficult.'

There was an undertone in her voice which I could not fathom. I wondered if it was like me with peaches. I love them but they make me ill.

I waited, but she seemed lost in thought. 'Do you need to ask me anything else?' I asked at last.

She looked at me for a few seconds, her mouth twisted to one side as if she was weighing something up. 'What's your programme for this week?'

'Mozart "Requiem" tomorrow night in the cathedral. Vivaldi "Gloria" on Thursday night, also in the cathedral. And I'm doing an early music recital in a chapel, the Lady Greenwood chapel, I think it's called, on Tuesday afternoon.'

'Fine. Good. Yes. I think that's all.' She looked at her sidekick. 'Do you have anything you'd like to ask Miss Pattison, Inspector Stafford?' I turned round to face him.

'Are you planning to go home after the Thursday concert, Miss Pattison?'

'No. Carrie and Neil have invited me to stay until next Sunday. I plan to be in London on the Monday, so I shall go down directly from here.'

'Where are you based?'

'I have a flat in York, but I spend a lot of time in London. I have a room in my brother's house with everything I need, you know, clothes, and stuff.'

'Can you let us have your York and London addresses, please?'

'Why?'

'In case we need to get in touch with you when you've gone.'

'Oh. OK.' I turned back to Hamilton. 'I hope you manage to clear this up quickly, Superintendent.'

'So do we, Miss Pattison?'

'What will happen about the rest of the festival?'

'No firm decision has been made yet. I'm meeting the festival committee later this morning. We'll make a decision then.'

'I'll keep practising the Mozart then, just in case.'

'Yes. Good idea. Thank you for your time, Miss Pattison.'

I pushed myself out of the chair and walked towards the door. The library was at the top of a spiral stone staircase and I hoped that they wouldn't want to interview anyone who had joint problems or a fear of heights.

I ached and still felt a bit dizzy, but that could have been delayed shock plus the smell of paint. It was not that I kept seeing Ariana's body or anything as hackneyed as that. I could not understand why I felt so shaky. I didn't even like the bloody woman for God's sake. Instead of going back to the Gardiner house, I went for a walk along the river bank. I remember the sun was shining and I thought that was a sort of blasphemy. How could the sun come out when such a horrible thing had happened? How could all these people on their narrow boats chug their way down the river sunning themselves as if nothing had changed from yesterday?

I sat on a bench and tried to reason out why I felt so churned up. My dad once told me when I was in a stew about something that I should sit and make out a mental balance sheet. OK Dad. On one side was the fact that a violent act had deprived someone of life just when they had given the most amazing performance they ever had or probably ever would. The perfection of Ariana's singing last night would stay with me for a long time, probably for ever and the musician in me mourned. What balanced that out? The fact that it was Ariana and I couldn't stand her. She'd taken Pete out from under my nose all those years ago and then dropped him when something better came along two weeks later. Was it that I was still not over Pete? No. Anybody who goes for the stuff in the shop window without trying to find out if there is anything better in the shop is a complete prannock in my book.

So, what was making me feel like this? Was it the worry that I'd thought the killer was Jamie and the relief when I found out it wasn't? Possibly. I'd always carried a bit of a candle for him. He was a year ahead of me at college and very much shielded by Lucy who did the big sister 'get lost' act every time a woman looked at him. She was studying piano at the Royal College. She was also devoted to her brother and Jamie took that on board as his right. She'd accidentally drowned the summer of my first year. I think it must have knocked him for six for a while. His tutor wanted him to battle on and work through it, but his parents needed him so he left. A sad story, but not unique amongst people as temperamental as musicians.

So, it was not solely that causing this feeling of nausea mixed with fright and insecurity. I finally tracked it down, doing the mental balance sheet bit to a desire to rip Neil Gardiner's head off for hurting Carrie the way Pete and Mike had hurt me. What she was going through had stirred my swamp just when I thought those feelings had settled into deep mud.

At this point, I started walking back. I would be polite to Neil, of course I would, but Carrie needed me and there was no way I was going to let her down. If, as I hoped, I had a chance to be alone with Neil, I would tell him what a bastard he had been to his wife by shagging a tramp like Ariana Staithes. But I'd say it politely, of course.

I looked at my watch. Getting on for lunchtime. Time I did the first vocalisation of the day. I lengthened my strides and began some deep regular breathing.

I avoided Neil and Carrie's company by the simple expedient of asking Neil if I could borrow his music room and flitting to it as soon as he said yes. I spent a few minutes making sure that yesterday's choir singing had not strained anything. In a choir, a singer can't hear their own voice, which is such a rare occurrence that the temptation to push so that you can hear it is almost irresistible. All was well, thankfully.

My abiding fear is that one of these days I will open my mouth and bugger all will come out. I don't make a fortune singing. I never will. I'm a good jobbing soprano who still has to do supply teaching when there is too much month left at the end of the money. It's a pain but there are thousands of us to one Renee Fleming and I bet she does her own laundry. I sighed and looked at the music for Tuesday's recital. Fifteen seconds later, I was back in the kitchen.

'Neil, who's playing for me on Tuesday afternoon?'

It took him a couple of seconds staring at me before his brain got his mouth to work. 'Len Morris. Why?'

'When's the scheduled rehearsal?'

'Ah. I should know that. Hang on, I've got his mobile number here.'

I grabbed the phone, praying the guy was in. He was. He was just as fidgety about it as I was. Nobody had thought to keep him in the loop. Did they think we would float into a first meeting ten minutes before the recital and just make beautiful music? Wankers. I asked him to hold on a moment.

'Neil, do you need the music room this afternoon?'

'No. Let me talk to him. Len. I'm so sorry about this. You know about Ariana? Tragic. Yes. Stunning. Yes. Do you want to come over and rehearse Georgia's stuff this afternoon? OK. No problem.' He lifted his eyes to mine. 'Is two-ish OK? Yes, Len, that's fine. See you later.'

He folded the phone up and put it back in his pocket. 'George, I'm sorry, it's just that with everything that's happened, your recital went right out of my head. I ought to get moving and see what the committee have decided for the rest of the festival. It was going to be such a wonderful triumph and it's all turned to dust.' His mouth moved in a strange sideways motion. He looked down at the table.

I put my hand on his shoulder, moved against my will by his distress.

'Neil, I'm sure the committee will find some way of continuing the festival. There's too much money invested in it not to. You need to concentrate on the music.'

He put his hand over mine. 'You're a good friend, George. You're right. Thank you.'

'Don't mention it, and whilst you're about it, you might try and think about what you've put Carrie through just lately.'

His head swung round as if he had been punched. He must have noticed my expression because he most certainly did not say what he was intending to. 'Yes. Well. We all make mistakes.'

I grunted. 'Where is Carrie?'

'Oh, I think the police are interviewing her.' He looked at his watch. 'She's been over there almost an hour. She should have been back by now.'

The sound of the front door slamming made us both jump. Carrie stalked into the kitchen, ignored both of us and started taking stuff out of the fridge. Well, I say taking. It was more like hauling stuff out of the fridge and throwing it on the table.

'Carrie?'

'Don't you Carrie me, you stupid bitch.'

I dropped into a chair. 'Bitch? What the hell's the matter?'

'You may well ask, friend.' She emphasised the last word and spun round to look at me for the first time.

'What have I done?'

'It had to be you who told that Hamilton woman about the laxative in Rachel Watson's drink, yes?'

'Yes, but what has that to do with what happened here last night?'

'I'll tell you. Jesus, how could you be so stupid?'

I was beginning to lose my rag now. 'Well unless you tell me how stupid I've been, I won't bloody know, will I?'

Neil shot to his feet. 'I'm off if you two are going to start a cat-fight.'

'Yes, Neil. Why don't you fuck off?' Caroline was shouting by now.

Neil looked like one of those cartoon characters that has just been clobbered with a club. 'Caroline, I've never heard you use language like that.'

'Then it's about time you did. You prick. Did you think I didn't know what you've been up to for the past three months with that slapper?'

This was the point at which I learned the hard way not to intervene between husband and wife, especially when they are having a domestic.

'Carrie. Calm down. You were never like this in the old days.'

'And you can shut your mouth as well, Georgia.'

'Yes, this is between me and Caroline and nothing to do with you,' put in Neil, possibly hoping that by weighing in with Carrie, he would deflect her rage.

- 23 -

Then the storm died and left the rain. She slumped into a chair, put her head on her arms and sobbed. Neil reached over to squeeze her wrist, but she shook him off like a dog with a rat. 'Leave me alone.'

Neil, stupid man, did just that. He grabbed his jacket from the back of the kitchen chair and walked out. The front door slammed for the second time in less than five minutes. I sat down.

'Come on. What's happened? What desperate clanger have I dropped?'

She lifted her head. 'You know I lost my earring last night?'

'Yes.'

'Well, I thought I must have lost it in the cloisters when I was helping you back to the house. So after I got you to bed, I went and looked for it. There was a policewoman there who asked what I was doing, so I told her.'

I still didn't see the problem. 'Yes?'

'I didn't find the earring. But the police did.'

'Well, that's good, isn't it? You said they were real diamonds. What's the problem?'

She took a deep breath. 'The problem is that they know Neil was screwing that bitch. They know about the laxative in Rachel Watson's drink.'

I could feel the quicksand flowing upwards to my knees and my heart was doing that weird "what-if, what-if" it does when I've forgotten to breathe for a while. 'What does that have to do with your earring?'

'They found it inside the west door of the cathedral this morning. They think I killed her because of Neil.'

'Oh flick. What were you doing inside the west door?'

'I never went near the west door yesterday, or any other day.'

'Hang on. This doesn't make sense.'

'None of it makes sense. But nobody knows the worst bit.'

The quicksand had reached my chest. Breathing was an effort. 'Worst bit?'

'Yes. I'm pregnant. I only found out on Tuesday. They'll think I killed Ariana to stop my marriage from breaking up and my baby being fatherless.'

4

I put the kettle on and stood with my back to her whilst my mind tried to sort out what the hell was going on. I spooned as much coffee onto the work surface as I did into the mugs. Putting one in front of her, I sat and stared. This could not be my friend. My little wallflower friend being accused of murder?

I tried to find something sensible to say and came up with 'Oh this is just plain stupid.'

She wrapped her hands round the coffee cup. She must have been past feeling because when I tried it, I yelped and pulled my hands away.

'Why is it stupid?' she asked. 'Look at it from their point of view. Woman gets murdered. She is known to have been having an affair. The wife's earring is found on the scene. What would you think?'

'I'd want to know how your bloody earring got there for starters.'

'I have no idea.'

'Did you go round there at all yesterday?'

'George, I've never been into the cathedral by the west door. I always use the cloisters and either the Priors Door or the Miserrimus Door.'

I thought a bit longer. 'You're going to have to tell them about the baby.'

Her reaction was not unexpected. 'No way. I haven't told Neil yet and I'm certainly not telling them.'

'Don't be stupid, Carrie. They'll find out in the end and it will look ten times worse if you've kept it back.'

'It's nothing to do with them. I don't want them to know.' She pointed a finger at me. 'And you're not to tell them.'

'Carrie...look..'

'If you want us to stay friends then just mind your own business, George. Why do you always think that you can sort problems out by going at them like a rampant bull?'

'And why do you always think that problems will go away if you stick your head under your pillow and think happy thoughts? You have to meet problems head on. It's the only way to cut through all the crap.'

'You mean like you did with Lucy Topcliffe?'

I looked at her for so long she began to fidget. 'Meeting problems head on is one thing, Carrie. Hitting below the belt is another.'

We sat in silence sipping our coffee. She looked like a panda that hadn't slept for a week. God knows what I looked like. I finished my coffee without saying anything else and then washed the mug on auto pilot and walked out of the kitchen. Once upstairs, I packed my case and rang the Maddox. Fortunately the room allocated to Linda Sharpe was still available, so I booked it until Friday morning and said I would check in later that afternoon. I had what Finlay calls my "defensively justified" head on. I was cold and miserable and in no mood for singing. However, Len was due in less than fifteen minutes. I went out onto the landing to watch for him and hefted my cases down the stairs as quietly as I could. When I saw him walking towards the door I opened it, making sure I left the key Carrie had given me on the hall table.

'Hi, Len. Slight change of plan. Do you know if we can practise in the chapel? I'll get a better idea of the acoustic and it will give me time to work on bits that need it.'

Len threw me a long look and an even longer one at the cases, but nodded. 'I thought maybe it might be better in there, so I rang the caretaker. There's nothing on this afternoon. We can have it until five. It will give me a chance to set up the keyboard. That OK?'

'Fabulous. Let's go.'

It was the best thing I could have done. I checked out the room I would be using as a dressing room. It had a double plug socket and a mirror. Good. Len said he would come in black trousers and a white shirt. He also had a red brocade waistcoat we agreed would look suitably Renaissance. We spent the next two hours concentrating on nothing later than 1720. Len was fantastic. Linda had planned a programme of French and German material, but Len felt that as we were performing in a three hundred year old chapel in an English medieval city, it would be a good idea to include some English repertoire. Luckily I had brought some Dowland, Blow and Purcell with me, so, between us we worked out a recital lasting just under the hour. The programme started in England, moved across the channel through France and Germany and ended up in Italy.

There were a few glitches with my top register, but I wasn't too concerned. I had been through a traumatic time during the past twenty four hours. I decided to finish the whole thing off with Vivaldi's "Nulla in Mundo Pax Sincera" which always goes down a storm. If they wanted an encore, we decided that "O had I Jubal's Lyre" would fit the bill and send them all out into the summer sunshine in joyous mood. I was still feeling churned up when we walked out of the door. We agreed to meet the following afternoon for a quick run through, and then leave it to chance and that indefinable something that runs a thread between singer and accompanist and down which communications fly both ways during a performance. Some people call it professionalism. I call it witchcraft.

My room at the Maddox turned out to be the bland hotel room I always seem to stay in. Cream walls, cream bed, dull carpet. Such a shame for a beautiful old building. The only concessions they make to the fact that it is almost two hundred years old are the stupid uniforms they make the staff wear. The chambermaids even have to wear mob caps for God's sake. The waitresses have those little white caps with black velvet ribbons that are nothing more than snobbish affectation. The poor souls all had my sympathy.

It was not until I was in the shower that I remembered I had just packed and walked out of the house without giving Carrie the least notion that I was not coming back. I chickened out and sent her a text message explaining that I felt she and Neil really needed to be on their own at the moment and telling her where I was and that we would meet up when things had calmed down a bit. I waited half an hour, just to see if there was any response, but either her mobile was switched off or I really had stepped out of line this time.

I remember Finlay telling me when I was about sixteen that, after my sloe-black eyes, my mouth was one of my most attractive assets. He went on in the next breath to suggest that I would have a happier life if I didn't open it so often and put my foot in it. That is the big difference between us. Finlay is all thought and no passion whilst I am exactly the opposite. I am so unlike him, or Mum and Dad, come to that. When I was small, I used to think I was adopted.

I put my brain into gear and reviewed my last conversation with Carrie. In all honesty, I still thought I was right and she was wrong. I sat at the dressing table looking at myself for a long time feeling like the cursed Lady of Shalott . It seemed that whenever I stopped looking at life in the mirror and tried living it, everything fell round my ears. After a while, my natural bloody-mindedness triumphed. I was not about to put myself in a boat and float down the river to the Camelot of "Vox Celeste", so I stopped looking in the mirror and looked out of the window over the green between the hotel and the cathedral. She would need me before I needed her, I decided, which is my usual way of dealing with the fact that I have cocked up another relationship. My stomach was protesting that I had eaten nothing all day, so I decided to put on a happy face or at least some make-up and go down to the dining room.

To my delight, I found Jamie Topcliffe also heading for the dining room. Kevin was nowhere to be seen, so, in unspoken agreement, we headed to the same table and picked up the menu.

'What are you having?' he asked looking through the menu for the third time.

'Something safe.'

'Soup?'

I shuddered. 'No, I think I'll go for the melon medley. Sounds suitably musical.' I changed my voice to a Yorkshire twang. 'And now we 'ave Black Dyke Mills playing "Melon Medley" by Tagliatelle.'

Jamie giggled. 'I always did like your sense of humour, George. I'll join you.'

I finally settled on salmon for the main course, but then spoiled the whole effect by finishing with sticky toffee pudding, which won by a short head over Mississippi Mud Pie. No wine tonight. I was singing tomorrow. So was Jamie, but he still managed to down a couple of pints of Guinness. After dinner, I suggested a walk along the river. It was still light.

'How's Mike?' he asked when we had negotiated the steps from the hotel garden down to the towpath.

'Gone.'

He turned to me with a quick frown. 'George, I'm so sorry. I had no idea.'

'Nobody has any idea except Melanie and she is taking the "better off on your own than with a bastard" line. Besides, she has a vested interest in keeping me singing and earning money for her.'

'Come on. Tell Uncle Jamie. Confession is good for the soul, so they say.'

'Oh yes? What confessions would you like to make?'

His arm tightened into a hug and he dropped a light kiss on my hair. 'When did it happen?'

'Six weeks ago.' I had not wanted to talk about it before, but now it felt right to get it off my chest. 'It was so old hat. I found a letter in his jacket.'

'Serves you right for looking in his jacket.'

'Don't jump to conclusions, Jamie. He told me to look in his jacket for some petrol money.'

'Sorry. What did you do?'

'Made a note of the address and when he went off on one of his buying trips, I went down to see her.'

'Hellcats at dawn type thing?'

'As it happened, no. I saw Mike's car up the street so I knew he wasn't on a buying trip at all. I crept up to the lounge window and took a few photos on my camera phone. Next morning, I followed her husband to the station, and onto the train. I showed him my photos.'

Jamie stopped and turned towards me. 'That was hardly fair, George.'

'It wasn't bloody fair that his wife was having it away with my fiancé,' I shouted at him.

'Calm down. Of course it wasn't fair, but he was just as innocent as you were, so why make him suffer?'

'I didn't particularly want him to suffer. I wanted her and that two-timing bastard of mine to suffer. The only way to do that was to let him know what was going on.'

'You ought to have thought of something else.'

'Well I didn't.'

'No, George. You never do. That's always been your problem. You see something, you react. Immediately. A knee-jerk, automatic wham. You need to add some thinking time in the middle.'

'You mean like you always do?'

'I do think things through, yes.'

'And is that why you let your sister put her oar in when we were at college? Because you thought about it?'

'Lucy always did what she considered was best for my happiness.'

'Yes, and you followed like a tame sheep.'

'At least I'm not like a sheep dog, harrying everybody and nipping their ankles if they don't go in the direction I want them to.'

We stood looking at each other, appalled by the strength of feeling that the old unfinished business still aroused.

'I'm sorry, George. I shouldn't have moralised at you,' he said at last, turning to continue the walk.

'No, it's me. You're right and you're the second person who's told me the same thing today, so it must be right.'

'Who was the other?'

'Carrie.'

'Oh. Tell me how the Mike saga finished.'

'As you might expect. The husband and I arrived back at his house. He used his front door key and opened the door ever ever so quietly and we followed the trail of clothes and grunting. They were doing it up against the washing machine this time.'

'I don't know what to say, George.'

'Neither did they, although I think I heard the word divorce mentioned. Several times. I took off my ring and threw it at Mike, but then thought better of it. Whilst he was bending over to pick it up, I kicked him in a delicate place and snatched the ring back. Then I phoned for a taxi to take me back to my car at the station and I drove home to York.'

'Have you seen Mike since?'

'Not seen. Heard. He came back to the York flat, but by then, Nettie's husband had changed the locks for me and I had put all Mike's clothes in two bin bags on the front door step.'

'Remind me never to get on the wrong side of you. Seriously, are you OK?'

'Bit bruised but I'm coming out of it. Doing the festival is helping. I'm having to concentrate so much harder because I haven't had my usual preparation time.'

He kissed the top of my head again. 'You'll be fine. I'm doing the Mozart tomorrow night, too, so we'll hold each other's hands.'

I laughed and then remembered. 'What's happening about the rest of the festival? Has the committee decided?'

'Yes, they can't afford not to continue, but we won't be able to use the west end. The idea currently, is to use the bit under the tower. They think they can get the choir and the orchestra in there facing west. They are going to have to turn all the chairs round, of course to face east. The cops have screened off the murder scene.'

'Right.' I looked across the river. The sun was setting in one of those spectacular displays that lovers think are just for them. I did not feel a bit romantic and neither, judging from his almost avuncular affection, did Jamie. Perhaps he was over that old trouble. I hoped so. Whilst it had been in no way shape or form any fault of mine, I had been involved on the periphery. I wondered how to broach the subject.

'So, how are you these days?'

He took a few seconds to consider. 'Fine. I think.'

'No romantic tangles?'

'Not since college, no. I've seen where it leads and I don't want to follow. I shall stay footloose and fancy free. It's safer.'

I winced. 'How very sad and what a bloody waste.'

He laughed and squeezed my shoulders again. 'Shall we get back?'

We turned round in contented silence and headed back to the Maddox. As we walked through the door, the dead spit of the jolly green giant, minus the daft costume, was standing at the reception desk. I felt Jamie halt for a moment, then he walked towards the man, pulling me along in his wake. He tapped the newcomer on the shoulder and the mountain turned and looked down at him. Jamie held out his hand.

'Tony. I didn't know you were in the country.'

The other held out his hand with some reluctance, I thought and they shook hands with a brevity that was almost insulting. Jamie turned to me.

'Georgia, you won't know Tony Labinski? Tony, this is my friend, Georgia Pattison.'

'Pleased to meet you, Mr Labinski.'

The mountain rumbled for the first time. 'And you, Miss Pattison. Now, where is crime central in this place?'

'If you ask the receptionist, I'm sure she will put you through. You need to ask for Superintendent Hamilton. She's a woman, by the way,' he added.

I looked at Jamie in surprise. What on earth had made him say that? The other man looked at him in what I can only call a matter of fact way for a few seconds before replying.

'Thanks. Strange as it may seem, we have women police officers in Canada as well. See you later.' He nodded at me and walked towards the lift.

It was an obvious and to my mind, rude dismissal. Jamie steered me through to the bar and, without asking, ordered two gins with tonic.'

'Who is that man, Jamie?'

'That is Tony Labinski, or, put another way, Mr Ariana Staithes.'

5

'Her husband? I thought they'd divorced years ago.'

'You shot off to the Riviera or somewhere the summer Lucy died, didn't you?'

I felt myself turning red. 'You know perfectly well what happened, Jamie. Lucy made it quite plain that she would not allow her darling little brother to be tarnished by the likes of me. It was so unfair. She didn't even know me.'

'I didn't know she'd done that. It explains a lot.'

'I told her it was sod all to do with her who you saw. She told me not to cross her. She was so bloody arrogant.'

'She had my best interests at heart.'

'She still had no right to make your decisions for you. What were you? A man or big sister's apron string?'

'That's not fair, George. She didn't fit in and you know what that's like.'

'No. Never been an issue for me.'

'Well it was for her. Our parents didn't believe in compliments. Lucy was convinced she was an ugly duckling who had grown up to be an ugly duck. She was also shy, which someone as in your face as you would never understand.'

'I am not in your face. You never took the time to find out what I was like. Too busy falling into line with what big sister said. And as for Lucy, she was plain toffee-nosed. It put everyone's back up, you know.'

'And you never did, of course. She was like that because she was shy. Jesus, George, don't you understand the first thing about people? Anyway, if we're throwing brickbats, you didn't put up much of a fight for me, did you?'

'And you did?'

'Perhaps it's a good job we didn't get together. This is our second row in an hour.'

I held up both hands in mock submission. 'OK, let's change the subject. Why are you so wobbly about the jolly green giant?'

'I am not.'

'Yes you are. You wittered at him like some terrified lackey and then ordered me a gin I neither wanted nor asked for.'

'Please yourself. I'll drink it.'

There was a frigid silence for a couple of minutes and there was no way I was going to break it.

'Where did you disappear to that summer?' he asked eventually.

'Well after your shy sister threatened to get my legs broken if I didn't stop "pestering" you...'

'You weren't pestering me and I'm sure she didn't say that.'

'Well, she didn't actually say the word pestering. She called it stalking and she did threaten to get my legs broken, said she knew where to find someone who would do it for sixty quid. So that shows just how well you knew her, doesn't it? Anyway, Mum and Dad were about to drive down to Gourdon so I went with them and spent the summer there alternating between crying over you and being glad I wasn't tied to a wimp.'

He stared down into his glass. 'I never knew, I promise you, George. Lucy never said a word about it and then of course, the end of exams party came round and Ariana brought her new husband along. That's when all the trouble began.'

'What? The jolly green giant?'

'Yes. For Lucy it was love at first sight. And we know how it ended don't we? Can we talk about this at some other time, George? Please?'

'Of course. Sorry Jamie.' I looked at my watch. 'I think I'd better head off for an early night.' I looked back at him when I reached the lift door. His face was set and unhappy and he was picking up my untouched gin and tonic.

I took off my make-up and prepared for bed with none of the usual frisson of anticipation at the forthcoming week's singing. I lay with the covers off and Radio 3 turned low enough, in theory, for me to sleep, but not so low that I couldn't hear it when I woke in the night as I undoubtedly would. Most people assume that the number of different beds I have graced in a ten year singing career have rendered me immune to the "can't sleep in a strange bed" syndrome. How I wish. Sometimes I resort to pills from the chemist. Mostly, I just doze in half hour blocks.

I was thinking about Jamie and me. Whether it would have worked or not. For months after Lucy's intervention, I'd felt like one of those damaged female Alaskan crabs caught by mistake and thrown back to bury themselves in the sea bed. The old attraction was still there, but the years of silt built up by both of us since then would take some clawing through even if we wanted to. I sat up in bed and turned on the light feeling butterflies of panic dancing in my stomach. What on earth was I getting in such a state about? I picked up the score of the Mozart "Requiem" and began to breathe some of the phrasing.

Next morning the night horrors had vanished. I took a long warm shower and washed my hair before sitting in front of the mirror to put on my make up. Usually I just wear a bit of blusher and mascara with lip gloss during the day, but today I did a bit more with my eyes. I kidded myself that, as today was a concert day, this was for my "public". Yeah, right. I was putting on the mascara when my eyes asked my reflection if I missed Mike all that much. It took a couple of minutes of really honest thought, not something with which I am familiar, before deciding that I didn't. I thought that was it, but the next question was whether I cared about keeping Carrie as a friend. I couldn't meet my gaze in the mirror and examined my nails instead, but I knew the answer was yes. Better do something about it then, said the voice in my head. Now is as good a time as any, it persisted. I gave in and texted Carrie a grovelling apology for my childish behaviour and asked if we could meet for coffee. Then I looked back in the mirror and told myself to shut up.

Rehearsal was at ten thirty so I arrived on the dot only to find Superintendent Hamilton's sidekick waiting for me.

'Good morning, Miss Pattison.'

I nodded. 'Good morning..er'

'DI Stafford. Can you spare the superintendent a few minutes, please?'

'What, now?'

'Yes.'

'But the rehearsal is about to start. Can't this wait until after?'

'I'm sorry, this is a murder enquiry.'

My good mood was immediately replaced by anger bubbling up. Then I remembered Jamie's comments about my argumentative nature, so I swallowed the retort which nearly slipped past my larynx.

'Hang on a moment,' I said, holding up my hand.

I walked to the podium where Neil was standing waiting to start the rehearsal. He must have seen me out of the corner of his eye, but continued to turn the pages of the orchestral score. I determined not to speak until he stopped and after a minute's impasse, he slid his gaze sideways and raised his eyebrows.

'I'm sorry, Neil, the police want to talk to me.'

'Now?'

'Yes.'

He looked at his watch. 'Don't worry, I'll rearrange the order until you get back.'

'Thanks.' I was walking away when he called me back and bent over the side of the podium until his face was about six inches away from mine. He smiled. Anyone looking would think we were friends passing the time of day.

'If you ever upset Caroline like that again, I will personally make sure you never sing in Temingham a second time. Do we understand one another?'

I smiled back. 'Perfectly. You can screw who you like, but a girly spat is a hanging offence, yes?' I patted his arm. 'You'll be such a nice man when you grow up, Neil.'

Superintendent Hamilton was staring out over the moors when Stafford and I came through the door. She appeared deep in thought. Now I looked at her, she was not as young as I had first thought. Her skin tone was beginning to fade as was the short mousy hair. I wondered why she didn't rev it up with a bit of colour. With some make up on, she would have been a good looking woman so long as she stuck to wearing trousers, that is. I could never abide thick ankles. We had a teacher like that at school. It was hate at first sight and whenever I think of her now, all I can remember are glasses and tree trunk legs.

Hamilton turned and her grey-blue eyes met mine. 'Good morning, Miss Pattison. I am sorry to interrupt your rehearsal.'

'You said you wouldn't need to bother me again, Superintendent.'

'What I actually said was perhaps.'

I gave in. It was easier. 'Mr Gardiner says he can manage without me for a while. How can I help you?'

'It's about this earring of Mrs Gardiner's.'

'Yes?'

'When did she notice it was missing?'

'I noticed it when she helped me back to the house after I found...you know.'

'What did she do then?'

'She said the earrings had real diamonds, that they were a present from Neil and that she had better go back and look for it.'

'And did she?'

'I have no idea. I was asleep.'

'Tell me about the victim?'

It took a couple of seconds to realise who she meant. 'Ariana?'

'Do you know another victim, Miss Pattison?'

'It's just that I have never thought of Ariana as a victim. You know her husband is here, don't you?'

'Yes, apparently he arrived in the country a couple of days ago.'

'A couple of days?'

She looked up then, interested in my reaction. 'Is there something I don't know that I should?'

'No. It's just that I would have expected him to come to Gerontius.'

'Why?'

I did not know how to answer. Mike had always come to my concerts. I suppose I expected it as my due from the person who was supposed to be in love with me.

'Miss Pattison?' Hamilton was still looking at me, her eyebrows raised.

'I'll try to explain although you probably won't understand it. This concert was being covered by the broadsheets because the festival here is gaining that sort of reputation.' I looked up and she nodded. 'So, really, this was an opportunity for Ariana to get all the headlines if she did a good job.'

'And did she?'

'Yes. She was amazing.'

'No professional jealousy?'

I laughed. 'I didn't like her, Superintendent, but we were not rivals for the same roles. Ariana was a mezzo soprano. She majored in opera and oratorio. I am an early music soprano. Completely different voices, different timbre, different range. I could no more sing the Gerontius angel than she could have sung Gluck's Euridice. I am just a jobbing soprano singing early music. I do not and never will earn mega-bucks. Ariana was headed for the top. She would have ended up on a par with someone like Cecilia Bartoli. A superstar.'

'And you didn't mind that?'

'I do what I do reasonably well. Enough to earn a crust and sometimes a bit of jam on top. I am lucky. My family buy me a car every three years because they know I can't afford one, but I need something reliable. They support me in every way. I wouldn't want to change that for the type of life Ariana was having. Flying here there and everywhere, no home life, at the beck and call of managements, not quite yet being able to call the tune, just dance to it. I like my life. I would have hated hers but it's what she wanted and worked for. She was on the springboard. Gerontius was the bounce.'

OK, so no rivalry, then. And this affects the husband how?'

I leaned forward. 'When I was engaged, Mike came to all the concerts he could. It's a supportive thing. How can I explain this? Look, if the papers had been reporting on the concert, instead of her death, then they would probably have sent Ariana's star flying through the musical firmament - sorry to be so flowery, but that's how the press would have termed it. She will have known how well she was going to sing. You get a sort of high when you know it's all working properly and that feeds on the adrenalin. Chances are you will either sing out of your skin or go over the edge and be all over the place. She sang out of her skin. I just think she would have wanted her husband to share that and I don't understand why he didn't.'

'You weren't aware of any marital rift?'

'I hardly knew her, Superintendent. What I did know of her, I didn't like, musical ability apart. She was not someone I chose to be friendly with.'

'Because she nicked your boyfriend?'

'Yes, if you want to know.'

'Still niggles after ten years?'

I looked at her with my best "which stone did you crawl out from under" look. She was immune. 'I didn't kill her, Superintendent Hamilton.'

'I know you didn't. But you probably know who would want to.'

So that was it. I was being promoted to grass in chief. We locked eyes. This time, she broke first. Well it was her who needed the favour.

'I'll level with you,' she began. I've learned that when people say that they are usually about to lie through their teeth.

'Really?'

She came as near to blushing as I expect she ever does. 'Well, no, not really, but as much as I can. I don't understand the musical world you see. My world is full of druggies and knifings, with a bit of robbery and burglary thrown in. I don't mix with luvvies.'

'Me either.'

She frowned. 'This is serious. I need help. I think this murder was premeditated but you were only engaged to sing here a couple of days in advance. So, quite apart from the fact that you were in plain sight when she was killed, I think I'm safe putting you out of the running.'

'Good of you. Do I get a star for being teacher's pet?'

'If you were my usual type of client, you'd get a thick ear in the back of a police car.' She changed tack. 'At the moment, your girlfriend is well and truly in the frame as we always say.'

'Nothing like a cliché,' I shot back. 'I generally avoid them like the plague.'

'Oh, chuckle. Come on. Will you help me?'

'Can I think about it?'

'Yes, but keep it to yourself, please.'

'One question?'

'Fire away.'

'Why me, apart from the reason you've given?'

'Because of the reason I've given. If I can work out that you are not the murderer because you replaced someone at the last minute and you never left the stage, then everybody else can. So they'll talk to you when they won't talk to me or to any of their colleagues who might have done it.'

I sat silent in the chair. It was a relief to know she was serious when she said she was not considering me a suspect, but I was more than worried about Carrie. Hamilton levered herself up on the tree trunks. 'I'll come down with you. I could do with a break.'

I slipped into the cathedral. The rehearsal was in full swing but Neil saw me and looked pointedly at the chair next to Merlina, the alto soloist. I put my mouth in an "eek" and tiptoed round the orchestra. It was only when I sat down that I noticed Carrie sitting halfway down the nave. I raised my eyebrows at her. She grinned. Thank God for that. A weight slipped off my shoulders, but underneath it was a heavier one I had been unaware of. One that was beginning to panic in case the police did not find out who had murdered Ariana and decided to pin it on Carrie instead. I think it says a lot for the quality of my friendship that I never thought to ask myself whether she was in fact the murderer.

6

The rehearsal that afternoon with Len went well if you ignore the fact that we mucked around with the programme so much it bore very little resemblance to the one we had worked out the previous afternoon. It was only when we started to put things together that we realised it did not flow as seamlessly as we had imagined. It was also bloody miserable.

So we chucked out half the English stuff which seemed to be all about weeping and dying and put in a few fireworks, like the Vivaldi "Alleluia" and the Pergolesi "Salve Regina", which isn't exactly a firework, just lovely. By the time we finished at half five, I was wondering if I'd have the energy to sing that night, but fortunately, the soprano part in the Mozart is not all that strenuous. An hour's rest, a cup of tea and a sandwich and I would be fit for anything. We walked out of the chapel to find Superintendent Hamilton leaning on the wall in the vestibule. I frowned at her.

'I'll catch you tomorrow, Len. Here at two, yeah?'
'OK. See you, George.' I saw him looking at Hamilton and her returning his look with what I was beginning to call her deadpan expression.
The superintendent and I fell into step.
'I liked the last thing you sang. What was it?'
'Handel. Called "Oh had I Jubal's lyre".'
'Liar?'
'No, lyre, the instrument.'
'Right. Tell me, does everyone call you George?'
'Friends do. Why?'
'Because I'm interested. I expect it has more impact for you because you look so feminine and a masculine name emphasises that. My name's Michaela. Everyone calls me Mick, but that probably isn't to stress my femininity.'

There was no answer to that, well not one I wanted to voice. She did a good line in making me feel uncomfortable. I expect that's how they train them.

'I like being called George. The feminine thing doesn't enter into it. Long hair is great for singers. We can do so much with it to help portray the role we are playing.' I looked at her crowning glory. 'I suppose long hair in a police officer could be a disadvantage,' I added. 'Perhaps the startled hedgehog look is more practical.'

'You don't like me, do you, Miss Pattison?'

'Would you like me to be honest?'

'Why not? It makes a change from people who lie to me all the time.'

'It's not that I don't like you. I don't know you enough to like or dislike you. I dislike what you are doing.'

'It's a dirty job but someone has to do it, isn't that what I am supposed to reply? But that's not your main reason, is it?'

I took a deep breath. 'Actually, Superintendent, you remind me what I would look like if I stopped bothering about my appearance.'

I'll give her due credit. She took it on the chin. 'Oh, is that all? Well, you see I don't have to dress up like a dog's dinner to do my job properly. You have to look glamorous in front of all those people who have paid a fortune to hear you sing. I just have to catch villains.'

'Now you sound like something out of the "The Bill".'

She laughed. 'It's what people still expect us to be like. Short hair is practical. When you arrest people, some of them try to grab you by the hair. If you don't have enough to grab, you don't suffer the headaches. So, have you thought about our conversation this morning?'

'I'd like to get the Mozart over with and then sleep on it.'

'Fair enough. Good, here's my lift.'

A blonde girl younger than me pulled up in a muddy blue Volvo. There was a big golden retriever in the back, grinning behind the dog bars. I saw Hamilton flick a glance of dislike at it as she opened the door. The car pulled into traffic and I watched it disappear round the corner heading out of the city. Hamilton was much older than her companion. Or, I wondered, should that be partner? Interesting.

The Mozart was nothing to write home about. The festival committee had decided to dedicate it to Ariana's memory. I don't know what Merlina thought of that. She kept the gracious smile firmly in place. The choir came a little unstuck in the fugue bit of the Kyrie. Neil managed to settle them down again, but it was an edgy performance. No singer is supposed to commit the heresy of disliking Mozart but he has never been my favourite composer. Too smug by half. I'd promised myself one glass of wine afterwards and boy, was I looking forward to it. As I gathered my stuff together, Carrie came and touched my elbow.

'Lovely to hear the voice again, George. It's a bit rounder since I last heard it.'

'Thank you. Did you enjoy it?'

'No, not really. Not enjoying much at the moment.'

'How's Neil?'

'Halfway between guilt and self-justification.'

'Told him yet?'

'No. He must make the decision about whether he wants to stay first.'

I spotted Sir Robert and the flower lady with their heads together near the Priors Door and I asked Carrie about them.

'That's Lady Barbara Royston. She's chair of the Ladies Committee. They organise virtually everything bar the music. She's supposed to be a wonderful organiser, but Neil says she's dropped some real clangers, especially with the catering.'

There was an uncomfortable silence between us, not helped by the orchestra roadies taking out music stands and instruments to put in the pantechnicon. They were off to Liverpool for the next night's performance and the BBC Symphony would be playing at Temingham until Thursday.

I put my arm round her shoulder. 'I'm just off to the Maddox for a nightcap. Want to join me?'

'I shouldn't really. I should get back home.'

'What for?'

She paused trying to think of something and failed. 'OK. Just one then.'

We passed Neil chatting to his assistant organist. He turned a startled face on us. 'I'm just taking Carrie for a drink, Neil. Won't be long.'

I would like to say that I gained no satisfaction from the suspicious look he threw me, but I'd be lying. That was another problem. I wanted to mend the friendship with Carrie. I needed to know she was not guilty of Ariana's murder, so I would have to stay closer to her than I was at the moment. And, for that to happen, it was important that I heal this rift with Neil. On impulse I turned back to the two men and suggested they tag along. We passed Merlina being gracious to an avid fan. I made drinking motions to her behind the fan's back and she smiled and nodded. Jamie had disappeared with the tenor. I thought that maybe he was feeling uncomfortable about our chat the previous evening and was avoiding me.

The assistant organist was called Sebastian, poor sod. Actually he was a working class boy whose parents had called him after Sebastian Coe who must have won his gold medals at about the time this unfortunate lad was born. I imagine he would have needed to be a sprinter to escape from the bullying his name would have attracted at school. The very fact of his being musical would have been held against him by the inverted snob brigade.

I shall never forget coming into the sixth form common room after the assembly during which the head had announced that I had been accepted by the Academy. Celia Braithwaite was wailing like a ruptured pig, which she followed by saying in exaggerated cut-glass Oxford English "I am the perfect divine Georgah and I'm orf to the Royal Academy". I stood in the doorway and suggested she'd be orf to hospital if I caught her taking the piss again, but it rankled. It still does. There's always some less gifted peasant trying to take the shine off.

Where was I? Oh, yes. Neil bought the round and we all sat there trying to come down from the singing even though it hadn't been half the performance Gerontius had been. I meant to just have the one glass and then go to bed. However, I was still undecided about Hamilton's suggestion. So I stayed put in the hope that something would be said that might help me make that decision. In the middle of a discussion about the English choral tradition, Merlina raised her glass.

'To Ariana,' she said. 'I didn't like the mouthy cow, but by God she could sing.'

The rest of us lifted up our glasses with little enthusiasm and a lot of embarrassment. I looked at Neil and was about to make some witty sarcastic comment when he stopped me in my tracks.

'She was a good singer, he said, 'but when you sit and think about it, she wasn't that nice a person was she?'

Lots of things sprang to mind, but I thought better of all of them and contented myself with shaking my head. I think we were all hoping he would shut up about her, but he seemed bent on confession.

'She dazzled me,' he said as if he had forgotten we were there. 'She made everybody else look colourless.'

Things were beginning to get maudlin and I could see Carrie's head down over her orange juice trying not to cry. It was Merlina who, having started the subject, decided she ought to finish it.

'That's because she was one of those people who could light up a room when she came into it. She had charisma. It's something all performers have to some extent. I could have liked her if she hadn't been so damned aggressive to everyone. She knew I was upset about Gerontius but instead of leaving it alone, she had to make a point of asking me when I was going to hang up my larynx.'

I'm surprised you didn't deck her,' said a new voice. We all looked round to see the jolly green- sorry, Tony something or other - standing in the shadows outside our peripheral vision but within hearing distance. Merlina gathered up her bag and music, rose from the seat and faced Ariana's widower.

'English ladies don't do that sort of thing,' she said with a quiet dignity that silenced us all.

Her departure was the sign for what turned out to be a fast exit by all concerned except yours truly. Tony Thingy must have thought he had forgotten to put on his deodorant. We ended up looking at each other in an embarrassed silence I just had to fill.

'Well now you've driven them all away, why don't you sit down,' I suggested.

'Sorry. Can I buy you a drink, Miss Parker?'

'Pattison. Try Georgia.'

'Is that a cocktail?'

'No. It's my first name. I'll have an orange juice. Thank you.'

'Nothing stronger?'

'I'm singing tomorrow.'

'Where have I heard that before?'

When he finally came back, I was wondering what to say, but he opened the batting.

'You knew Anna?'

'Anna?'

'Yeah, her proper name was Anna. I always called her that. It annoyed her.'

'A marriage made in heaven, then?'

'Nope.'

Now I began to understand why he had not been at the performance.

'Do you like music?'

'I like jazz, but not the really modern stuff.'

'Opera?'

'Nope.'

I really must learn to stop asking closed questions.

'How did you meet Ariana..er Anna?'

'In Toronto about twelve years ago. I was in the big city trying to sort out my father's business. We're in lumber.'

It was a few seconds before I clicked. 'Oh, you mean trees.'

He looked at me as if he was unsure about whether I was taking the piss or was just plain stupid. 'Yeah, trees. Big tall things with leaves. Grow in forests.'

'I'm not being thick,' I gabbled. 'It's just that being in lumber in this country means you are in difficulties.'

His face cleared. 'The two countries divided by a common language thing. Right?'

I nodded. 'Did you sort out your dad's business?'

'Yeah. I literally fell over Anna when we were trying to grab the same cab. She expected me to back down. I didn't.'

'That must have gone down like a lead balloon.'

'I think it piqued her interest and after five minutes, I was sure interested in her.'

'So you got married?'

'Nope. She ran off to London singing. I didn't hear from her for almost two years. Then she rang because she was pregnant and the guy wouldn't foot the bill for the abortion.'

'So you did?'

'Nope. I caught the next plane. Two weeks later we were married and she agreed to keep the baby.'

'So you have a child? I didn't know that.'

'Nope. She fell down the stairs during an argument and lost it.'

My feelings for Ariana were undergoing a sea-change. Poor lass. Just starting at college and in a mess like that. Then marrying Tony Nope. He looked at me. His mouth was smiling but his eyes were not.

'Don't get all dewy-eyed, Miss Pattison. She was glad. Let's just say things started badly and then fell away. We hadn't seen too much of each other for the past few years.'

'Did the police contact you to come over after Saturday night?' I asked, knowing that, according to Hamilton, he had been in the country for a couple of days.

'Nope. I came over last Wednesday.'

'Right. I thought you might have been at the concert, you see.'

'I've been through all this with the cops. I came over because I wanted to see Anna, yes. You see, I've met someone back in Canada. Someone who likes living off the beaten track, someone who doesn't die if they are taken out of the city.'

'Right. I see,' I said, although I didn't see at all.

'I'm a catholic,' he continued. 'I've spent ten years trying to think of ways Anna and I could make a go of things. All the time, I knew I was playing second fiddle to her voice and definitely second fiddle in her bed.

About a month ago, I was chatting to Moira. She told me she loved me and wanted to be with me but she wouldn't play bridesmaid to Anna's bride any longer. She said I would have to make a decision. So I made it and here I am. I was going to tell Anna I was divorcing her.'

'Did you get to see her?'

'Yeah. Just after the afternoon rehearsal. We sat in the audience chairs.'

'What did she say when you told her?'

'She was real mad. She said this concert was her big chance and that I'd come on purpose to spoil everything and put her off her stroke.' For the first time, his voice faltered a little. He cleared his throat and stared down into his drink. 'She said I could have a divorce over her dead body.'

7

I slept a little better that night, but only because I'd found the pills in my bum bag. They always make me groggy when I wake up, so for the last minute of the morning shower, I turned the water to cold. I came downstairs to find Jamie Topcliffe red-faced standing with his fists clenched on top of the reception counter. I put my hand on his arm.

'Jamie. What's wrong?'
'I hope you haven't left anything valuable in your room, George.'
'Only my laptop. Why?'

At this point the receptionist, a sharp-faced blonde who looked as if she had been weaned on a pickle, looked at me and turned on her smile so unexpectedly, I thought one of her shirt buttons must be an electric switch.

'Miss Pattison?'

I nodded.

'Mrs Gardiner is waiting for you in the blue sitting room through there.'

'Thank you.' I turned back to Jamie and saw the girl's smile suffer a power cut. 'What's happened, Jamie?'

'My grandfather's pocket-watch has disappeared from my room.'

'Are you sure you haven't put it somewhere else?'
'No, I put my suit out to be cleaned last night and I remember taking it out of my side pocket and putting it on the dressing table thing under the mirror.'

The girl interrupted. 'Mr Winston is in his office now if you'd like to go through, Mr Topcliffe.'

'That's the idiot in charge of security,' Jamie said to me. 'I'd better go.'

'I hope you find it.'
'Heads will roll if I don't.'

- 49 -

I made my way to the blue sitting room, which should really be called the faded blue and slightly tatty sitting room. Carrie was dressed in jeans and trainers. She jumped up when I came through the door.

'Have you had breakfast yet?'

'No. I've only just come down.'

'OK if I join you?'

I nodded. 'Course it is. Why? Have you run out of Weetabix?'

'No. I can't cope with Neil. He didn't come to bed until gone two this morning. He stank of scotch. At five, he was comatose and throwing up. I managed to get him into the shower, but he didn't wake up properly even then.'

'Why didn't you ring, Carrie. I would have come over.'

'You forget ballerinas are not weaklings. I managed. I sat him in the shower tray, turned the water on cold and went to change the bed.'

'I take it he didn't drown.'

For the first time, she giggled. 'No, but he wasn't very happy. I showered in the other bathroom and I've been waiting here since half six.'

I looked at my watch. It was just gone eight. I beckoned her to follow me and walked back to the reception desk. Miss Pickle had the electric up and running again. She agreed that Carrie could stay for breakfast and that I could foot the bill. By the time Carrie had put down a full English and two cups of coffee, that peaked look had disappeared and her cheeks had some colour.

'You look better.'

She grinned. 'Shame really. I can guarantee that by ten it will have come back up.' She stifled a burp. 'Actually, might be sooner than that.'

'What are you going to do now?'

'What, you mean apart from talk to the great white telephone?'

I shuddered. I've always hated that phrase. She saw my face. 'Sorry, I forgot. I shall go back and see if my husband is sober or if he is still sitting under the cold water.'

I caught hold of her arm. 'Before you go, Carrie, tell me about the gorgeous hunk with the blue eyes.' Her own eyes looked blank. 'I mean Scott Wiley. He was at your house on Saturday afternoon.'

'Oh, him. I haven't seen him since I came out for the Gerontius concert. He practised for a while and went off to Tallis Hall for something to eat. Then he came back twenty minutes before I left. He was playing Beethoven, I think, when I went out of the front door. Don't tell me you fancy him?'

'I thought he said he was playing Mozart and Rachmaninov?'

'Do you always sing early stuff?'

'Good point. No, I don't fancy him. Well, I do, but I'm not in the market.'

'So why do you want to know about him?'

"Cos I've got a nose like a coat hanger. Is he married?'

'Don't think so.'

'Attached?'

'No idea. What is all this, George?'

'I'm just interested, that's all. When are his concerts?'

'Haven't they given you a programme?'

'Yes, but I haven't read it.'

She sighed and rolled her eyes at me? 'What are you like?'

'Beautiful? Talented?' We both laughed, then her face changed and she sprinted for the nearest white telephone.

When she came out, the pallor was back. I put my arm around her shoulders and hugged her to me. 'You're going to have to tell him, Carrie.'

'I know.'

'Come on, I'll walk you across. Do you want me to stay with you?'

She hesitated. 'Can you come in just 'til we find out how he is? If he's OK, I'll shake my head at you and you can make your exit.'

'No problem.'

We let ourselves into the house quietly. Carrie glanced up the stairs as she tip-toed to the kitchen. I followed. Neil was up and almost dressed. His shirt was untucked and his feet were bare. I could smell stale man and second-hand scotch from the door. He sat at the kitchen table his head resting on his arms. When he heard us, he looked up. His eyes were red but I think that was because he had been crying. He just held out his arms to Carrie and began to sob. She put her arms round his shoulders and cradled his head, lying her own on top of his. I might as well not have been there. His whole body shook and snot bedraggled tears dripped onto his shirt front. When she finally lifted her head, I could see that she was crying too. I began to edge to the door. She looked at me over his head and shook her own.

It was that vision of Carrie comforting Neil that made my decision for me. No way on God's earth could she have done what Hamilton suspected. I was as sure about that as I had ever been about anything. I went straight to the cathedral library. There was a middle-aged fat man in the office, so I asked if I could see the superintendent as soon as she came in.

'What's it about, miss?'

'That's between me and her.'

He frowned. Perhaps he'd been hoping I would make his morning less boring. He made a note of my name and mobile number and I made another heroic descent of the spiral stairs without a rope or safety net, opened the door at the bottom into the cloisters and almost knocked Hamilton flying. She dodged me with a speed and skill I would not have expected her to possess, especially with legs like hers.

'We can't keep meeting like this, Miss Pattison.'

'I've just been to see you. I wish you had an office somewhere else. I hate these bloody stairs. I reckon the monks must have been mountain goats.'

'Yeah, well monks weren't allowed to run were they? What can I do for you?'

'Yes.'

'Sorry?'

'Yes. The answer's yes.'

Her face cleared. 'Good. Let me think. Your thing's this afternoon, isn't it?'

'Yes. Why?'

She looked round. The tea bar wasn't open yet so the cloisters were practically deserted. 'What time do you need to be back?'

I did a quick mental schedule in my head. 'The recital begins at two-thirty. I need twenty minutes for a warm up, half an hour to change and do the schmoo...'

'Schmoo?'

'Yes, make up, hair, jewellery, you know.' I looked at her. 'On second thoughts, perhaps you don't. Ten minutes to walk to the chapel from the hotel. Where are we? That's an hour. So, if I am back at the Maddox for one, that gives me time to get over there, do everything and still have half an hour to focus on the music.'

'Gordon Bennett, I thought you just slung the dress on and walked on.'

'I like to have mentally sung a couple of things before I walk on.'

She looked at her watch. 'If you take the towpath away from the town, you'll come to a footbridge.'

'Yes, I walked that way on Sunday.'

'Good. Go over the bridge and up to the road. I'll be there in thirty minutes, OK?'

'Why not give me a lift from here?'

'I'll explain. Off you go. And don't tell anyone.'

I walked out of the cloisters and looked up at the sky. There were a few ominous looking black-edged clouds. I trotted back to the hotel. There appeared to be an unusual amount of bustling going on, so I surmised that the search for Jamie's missing pocket-watch was in full swing. When I got to my room, the chambermaid was just making the bed. I smiled at her, grabbed a jacket and slipped down the stairs to the back door of the hotel. There was nobody in the gardens. I let myself out onto the towpath and began to stride out. It took another fifteen minutes to reach the footbridge and cross it.

Hamilton was parked adjacent to a picnic site on the other side of the river, in a mouth-watering BMW 3 Series Coupé. She leaned across and unlocked the passenger door. Without speaking, she gunned the engine and drove towards Glossop. We passed Ladybower and headed up a one-track road.

'Nice car,' I remarked. 'Good engine note.'

'Do you like cars?' Her voice showed surprise.

'Yes, I like the power although I don't always use it, but I have to have something reliable and big enough to transport all my paraphernalia.'

'So what do you drive, then?'

'Saab 95 Estate.'

'Very nice.'

We were driving through some bare looking moorland and I shuddered to think what it was like in winter. She seemed to read my thoughts.'

'Do you know this area at all?' she asked.

'Did the usual school visits to the Blue John mine and I've spent a couple of weekends near Matlock, but other than that, no.'

'I love it up here. It can be bleak and hostile or sunny and soft. It puts things into perspective for me.' We came to a flat area covered with stones overlooking the reservoir. Hamilton pulled the car onto it, stopped the engine and opened the door. 'Just listen to that.'
I wasn't aware of anything at first, but then, I could hear a skylark and nearer the sound of bees. The breeze was swishing through the long grass whispering secrets to the air and I caught the faint scent of clover.

Hamilton sighed. 'This is better than all your Mozarts and Bachs. The sound of nature and no human being to spoil it.'

'Only man is vile, you mean?'

'Pardon?'

'I think it's an old hymn. Where every prospect pleases and only man is vile.'

'I like that.'

She climbed out of the car and half sat on the front of the bonnet, staring down at the ruffled water. I joined her.

'This is lovely, Superintendent, but why am I here?'

She became all business. 'Yes. Right. So, if I understand it correctly, you are happy to ask a few questions and let us know if anything interesting turns up?'

'I said yes back in the cathedral. Why did you have to drag me all the way up here? Did you think I was going to back out of it?'

'No.' She looked directly at me for the first time. 'Are you a good actress?'

'What?' That was the last question I was expecting.

'Can you act? It's a plain enough question, surely.'

'Of course I can act. It was part of the course at the Academy. If you're doing an opera you need to know how to act and how to move.'

'Good. Because you'll need to use that skill.'

I wasn't getting so much irritated as scared now. 'I don't understand.'

'Think about it, Miss Pattison.'

'Please call me Georgia.'

'Fine. Well, Georgia....'

'What shall I call you?'

'Let's keep it to superintendent, shall we?'

'Well, that's nice, isn't it? You can call me Georgia, but you can't possibly dent your dignity enough for me to call you Michaela or Mick or whatever.'

Her voice sharpened. 'It has nothing to do with my dignity. It's more to do with your safety.' She gazed back over the water. 'I'm banking on the fact that these people won't say to a police officer what they will say to you, yeah?'

'Yes.'

'And you all belong to the luvvy set and, of course, you all adore each other, yeah?'

'No.'

'OK. Put it another way, you're a fairly close-knit community.'

'Reasonably, yes.'

'Right. Now you're going to be asking questions within this community of which you are a member.'

'Yes.'

'Then you must see that you will be much safer if you continue to call me superintendent, because if anyone hears you call me Mick, they will twig what is happening and that could be dangerous for you.'

I laughed. This was stupid. 'You mean someone might have a go at me?'

'Have you met many murderers, Georgia?'

I stopped laughing. She looked straight at me.

'If someone even gets an inkling that you are on their track, they won't think twice about eliminating you. I don't want that on my conscience, so tread carefully and back off if you think the great Grimpen Mire is one step away. Is that clear?'

'Yes. What sort of things do you want to know?'

'Start off with general stuff and let's see where it leads us. It might be easier for you if you could write up anything you find out. Would that be possible?'

'Yes, I have my laptop with me. I can do it on that.'

'Good. Make sure you password the file, just in case somebody gets nosy.'

She looked at her watch. 'Just on twelve. I'll drop you back at the picnic site, OK.'

'Fine.'

'There's one more thing you should know and please keep this to yourself because we are not making it public.'

'OK. What is it?'

'We think Miss Staithes was rendered unconscious. The pathologist won't commit himself as to how just at the moment. A long steel pin, like a hat pin was thrust through her right eye into her brain and it is this that killed her. The pathologist says it was wiggled about to cause maximum damage. The killer then poured a small amount of accelerant over her face and chest and set her alight. We think it was petrol but the test results aren't in yet. Whoever did this appears to have left no trace at the scene. We haven't yet found out who the wet footprints belong to, either.'

'How big were they?'

'Size ten.'

'Has to be a man then, doesn't it?' My heart did an octave leap. Carrie only took a size six.

'It could have been a woman wearing big shoes. Sorry, your friend is still in the frame.'

'Why are you telling me all this?'

She looked over the water again and sighed. 'This plan was premeditated as I said before. It speaks of a hatred that runs deep and has remained hidden for quite some time. Don't have any illusions. Behind one of those happy smiling faces that you know so well is someone you do not know at all. What he or she did to Ariana Staithes, could happen to you. Keep that in mind at all times. This is my mobile number. Programme it into yours. Don't call it police or anything stupid. Call it Lizzie.'

'Lizzie?'

'My niece. Nice girl. We share a house. Come on, let's go. Just remember, be careful.'

We drove back to the picnic site in silence.

8

Just as I arrived back at the Maddox, my mobile shrieked. I looked at the screen and cursed under my breath. Melanie.

'Hi, Melanie.'

'Georgia. Been doing a guvvy job then?'

How the hell had she found out about Saturday?

'I did a stiffen for the Gerontius, yes.'

'And the money?'

'Neil is paying me, yes, but you didn't get the booking so you're getting nothing.'

'That's not how it works, George.'

It's amazing how, when your back is against the wall, your brain can sometimes come up with such easy lies. 'I'll send you half the meal, Melanie.'

'Meal? What meal?'

'The meal at the "The Peacock" that Neil is treating me to, to say thank you for singing on Saturday.'

'What? He's paying you in food vouchers?'

'No. In food. I think it will probably be a high class version of surf 'n turf.'

'Oh. OK.'

I decided to go in for the kill. 'Let's get things straight, Melanie. For gigs you find, you are entitled to your percentage. If I find my own gig, you've done nothing to earn the commission and if you think you will get any, then perhaps it's about time we parted company. I don't remember it saying anything about that in my contract, so stop being a greedy bitch and be thankful for what I do earn you.'

'You are feeling better, aren't you? Good. It's the recital this afternoon, isn't it?'

'Yes, and I really need to go and prepare for it.'

'OK, girl. Go give 'em hell. See if you can get a repeat booking for next year.'

'No, Melanie. You see if you can get a repeat booking for next year. I'll just go and sing.'

I folded the phone up on the voice impediment she calls a laugh. I ran up the stairs to my room, let myself in and kicked the door to behind me. Then I spent three minutes kicking the bed to get rid of the burst of temper that threatened. I looked at my watch. Twenty to one. Right. I had to calm down, well, not calm down exactly. I needed to put the last seventy two hours out of my head and think only about the next three hours. I needed yoga.

Thirty minutes later, I emerged from my room, serene and with my mind firmly back in the eighteenth century. The first thing I did when I got to the Lady Greenwood Chapel was hang my dress from a handy peg on one wall, and plug in my steamer. Then I set my hair on big Velcro rollers, wet them with the setting stuff and dried it with my travel hair drier.

I looked at my watch. Half one. I spent the next fifteen minutes warming up the voice starting off with the siren scales which used to make Mike howl with laughter. I tried a few phrases. Sounded good. Felt good. I went back to the dressing room, took the cellophane cover off the dress and began steaming the creases out of it. I decided quite some time ago that for early music recitals, I needed a dress that matched the era of the music. I found this fabulous dark wine taffeta thing, with a low cut square neckline and a few frills and flounces on the sleeves. It looked the part. Best of all, I looked the part, too and it was knocked down in the sale to just over a hundred quid.

The make-up was trickier. I went for pale skin and emphasised the eyes without letting it look as if I had make up on at all. I checked my watch. Almost two. I put the dress on, then undid the rollers. My usual hairstyle for these sorts of recitals is to part it in the middle and put most of my hair into a bun, leaving several long bits near my face. These I make into ringlets. It only takes me about five minutes. I don't use hairspray because it buggers up my voice.

I looked at my watch again. Five past two. Good. I sat down and breathed my way through a couple of songs. At twenty past, Len arrived, panicking slightly because a traffic jam had made him late. The waistcoat looked great. I love it when by sheer accident, I manage to co-ordinate with my accompanist. At half past, on the dot, we walked out, hand in hand, smiling. The chapel was full. Halfway through Purcell's "Evening Hymn", I noticed that Scott Wiley was sitting, arms crossed at the back. He didn't make eye contact at all. His head was sunk on his chest and I wondered if I had sent him to sleep.

The audience was warm and appreciative. They wanted the encore, bless them, so I made a special effort with the fireworks in "Jubal's Lyre". At the end, we took a final bow and headed back to the dressing room. Len followed to give me back my music. Hot on his heels was the gorgeous hunk. He came through the door, just managing to clear the frame and advanced, both arms outstretched.

'Darling, you were wonderful. What a fantastic voice.'

'Thank you, Mr Wiley.'

'Scott. Call me Scott.'

'And you can call me Georgia, although I don't object to darling now and then.'

We both laughed. Len faded through the door. I called after him.

'Len, thank you so much. Will you be around for the rest of the week?'

'Yes. I'm playing for a couple of things. I'll catch up with you.' He shut the door behind him, leaving me and Scott. I wanted to change and comb the Renaissance hair out, but he stood there saying nothing, just staring at me.

'Scott, I really need to change.'

'What? Oh, sorry. Of course. I'll vamoose. Er, what are you doing the rest of the afternoon, Georgia?'

I had been planning to go back to my room, and think out a logical course of action for the investigation, but this could be interesting. 'What did you have in mind?'

'They do a fantastic English afternoon tea at a place just up the valley. Do you fancy going?'

'I haven't had proper afternoon tea for years. Yes, I'd love to. How about I meet you in the Maddox in half an hour?'

'Great.'

Miss Pickle was still on duty. She saw me lug my bag in through the doors, but didn't proffer any help. I'm always drained after a concert, so it felt twice as heavy as it had when I took it out. I hauled it to the lift. A quick change and hair brush out and I was back downstairs.

Scott was leaning on the counter talking to Miss Pickle, whose name I now discovered was Rosemary. I would have discovered it a lot sooner had I bothered to look at the name badge on her 32A excuse for a bust. She was simpering up at him like a coy virgin on fast forward. It's a wonder the draught from her fluttering eyelashes didn't blow him over the other side of the room. He looked up as I approached. My smile broadened in direct correlation with the way hers narrowed. I felt like purring.

'Have you heard Miss Pattison sing, Rosemary?'

'No, I can't say I have.'

'What a pity you were on duty this afternoon. Her recital was stunning.'

Rosemary's smile was definitely slipping now. 'My work keeps me very busy,' she said as if that deserved a gold star. 'But I get off at five tonight,' she added ignoring me and looking at him.

'What a shame, we'll just have finished afternoon tea, won't we, Scott?' I smiled sweetly at her just to prove that I could do it as well as she could. Then I put my arm through Scott's and said. 'Lead on Macduff. I could eat a horse between two bread vans.'

I could feel the daggers between my shoulder blades all the way to the door.

Tea was like going back to the 1930s. The place was called the "Little Black Cat" and had views over the moors. There were three rooms and three sets of tables and chairs in each room. We had one room to ourselves. I slipped off my jacket.

'God, this is wonderful. Where did you find it?'

He went red and muttered something. I asked him to repeat it.

'Rosemary told me about it.'

'Rosemary as in "instant smile on demand" Rosemary?'

'That's a bit harsh.'

'No it isn't. I'd sooner she glared at me than put on that false grin whenever I or any other guest comes within a ten foot radius of her.'

'That will be part of the good consumer experience training, I expect.'

'In that case I shall have to write to the manager. Dear Sir, your receptionist, Rosemary is the epitome of efficiency and good grooming. Please do you think you could now teach her to smile as if she means it?'

'Gosh, you're a little fiery this afternoon. Let's change the subject. Are you hungry?'

'I am, to use my nephew's phrase "exhaustified", but yes, hungry as well.'

We ordered smoked salmon sandwiches, cucumber and cream cheese sandwiches, followed by a melt-in-the-mouth raisin and apple scone with jam and cream and finishing off with chocolate cake. Life would be so much easier if I didn't like food. I took one bite of the scone. It was heaven.

'Quick nurse, the screens, it's happened again,' I muttered through the mixture of scone, jam and cream.

Scott, caught on the raw, almost sprayed me with a mouthful of Earl Grey tea he had just taken to wash his sandwich down. He looked at my plate.

'Do you always eat this much when you've just sung?'

'No. The thing to remember is that I don't have to sing for another forty eight hours, so I shall enjoy my other sensual delights.'

'I like the sound of that. Can anyone join or is it an exclusive club?'

I looked at him for a moment. The blue eyes were laughing into mine, but there was an uneasy niggle at the back of my mind that he was only flirting. Mindful of my recent romantic wreck, I decided to keep it light and airy.

'It's an exclusive club, Scott. I doubt you would qualify.'

His face looked hurt, but I thought his eyes looked relieved. 'Why? What have I done?'

'Nothing, but all my experiences seem to have been with bastards and I don't think you are one.'

He did a quick mock bow. 'Thank you kind lady.'

'Think nothing of it milord; you can wear my favour in the joust next week.'

'Point me at the dragon and I shall slay him.'

We both giggled. I don't know why he did, but the knowledge that I was two concerts down and only one to go was part of it. Ariana had been dead for three days and we were no further forward with the investigation, so there was nothing to laugh at in truth. I shook my head at the tacit assumption I had made that I was part of the investigation and not just a snitch. He saw the shake and frowned.

'What's the matter?'

Quick thinking and lying time again. 'I was just feeling guilty that we are sitting here enjoying tea and cake and Ariana is lying cold in a mortuary.'

'Did you know her well?'

Hang on, I was supposed to be asking the questions.

'I knew her at the Academy. Did you know her?'

'She was at Glyndebourne the other year. It was my first time in England. Friends took me. She sang the boy part in the "Marriage of Figaro".

'Cherubino?'

'Possibly. I don't know much music outside the piano repertoire, of course.'

'Didn't you sing at college?'

'The only singing anyone would want me for would be to scare the birds away.'

'Were you at the performance on Saturday?'

'No, I was practising at Neil's. Have you forgotten already that we met in the front hall there?'

'No. I just wondered if you came to the concert after you had finished.'

'No. I went back to the hotel.'

'What time was that?'

'Why do you want to know?' His eyes narrowed and the cup stopped on its journey to his mouth.

'Because I am always nosy about other performers and their habits. How long do you practise?'

His face cleared. 'Oh, I see. Well, I guess I walked back about a quarter after eight, so that would mean about three hours, if you count the hour or so before tea.'

'Hell, I couldn't possibly sing for three hours, not without a break, well several breaks actually.'

'Don't you do that when you're in a production?'

'No, you tend to sing in five minute bursts during the arias and then only odd lines of recitative until the next aria or duet or whatever.'

'What's it like singing with an amateur choir?'

'Depends who they are. This lot are quite good.'

'Neil still has to mouth the words at them, though, doesn't he?'

I sprang to the choir's defence. 'Well most conductors do that. Watch the Proms sometime.'

'I might be doing a Prom next year?'

'Really? What will you play?'

'Don't know. Probably a Mozart concerto.'

'Do you like Mozart? I have real problems with him?'

'You're joking. He's the best.'

'No he isn't. He's a smug little bastard saying "look how clever I am" all the time.'

'Well he was clever.'

'And smug.'

'Better than Beethoven anyway?'

'He's too late for me so I don't know much.'

'Too macho by half,' he said waving at the waitress for the bill. I took out my purse. He waggled his finger.

'Oh, no. My suggestion. My treat.'

'Thank you. I shall have to return the favour.'

'Shall we get back?'

'Yes. Dinner's at eight-thirty.'

'You have to be kidding. You mean you'll be hungry again in three and a half hours?'

'Possibly.'

We parted in the hotel car park. I fancied I could see Rosemary through the lounge window, so I gave Scott a hug and kissed his cheek. He returned the hug.

'Thank you, Scott. That was lovely.'

'My pleasure. Let's do it again. Soon.'

I waggled my fingers at him in a mock wave and turned to go into the hotel and up to my room. It wasn't until later that I remembered Carrie saying Scott had been playing Beethoven as she left for the Gerontius concert.

9

Once back in my room, I showered again, my third of the day and a bit extreme even for me. I rang room service and asked for a bottle of the house white and a glass. One of the waiters brought it up and obviously expected a tip. He was sorely disappointed. I spent the next hour studying the Vivaldi for Thursday night. Depending on the speed Neil wanted to take the "Domine Deus", there shouldn't be too many problems. Good. Now for the important stuff.

I plugged in my laptop, checked for e-mails and then opened up Word. I hesitated for a moment, but then password protected it as Hamilton had suggested. I typed everything I could remember about Saturday from the time Ariana came into the rehearsal until I went down the steps at the end of the concert. I tried to watch it as if it was a film on the television. Did anyone seem to be put out or acting strangely? No. Apart from the killer the last people to see her alive were Neil and her fellow soloists.

What was my biggest problem? I didn't know anything, that was the problem. Who could possibly be on the suspect list? The husband is always a good bet. I imagined Hamilton was covering the angles where the jolly green giant was concerned.

It was all so easy in books, but books didn't have real live people and the detective never seemed to suffer pangs of doubt or conscience to any great degree. The people under suspicion as far as I could see were Tony Labinski and Carrie. I thought some more and then added the name of Scott Wiley with a string of question marks next to it. The Beethoven thing bothered me. Another problem was that I liked all three of the suspects. One of them was the closest thing I had to a best friend. I didn't want any of them to be the murderer.

This was getting me nowhere. It all came back to the fact that I didn't know enough about anybody in this tangle. The person I thought I knew best was not the person with whom I had shared a flat all those years ago. Carrie was still the Carrie I knew when she was with me, but did Neil know a different Carrie? And why did he always call her Caroline, because he called me George, not Georgia? What did I know about Neil apart from the fact that he couldn't keep his trousers zipped up? Come to that, what did I know about any of them? I'd known Jamie the longest, but Lucy had put paid to any chances we might have had. No, actually, that wasn't fair. My cowardice and Jamie's lack of real feeling for me had done that. When I first knew her Carrie wouldn't say boo to a goose, but she'd been protective enough on Saturday night when she thought that Hamilton was overstepping the mark and hassling me.

So, the first thing I needed to do was an information gathering exercise. No, the first thing I needed to do was go and buy a notebook and pen so that I could jot things down if I wasn't near the computer. I looked at my watch. An early night seemed a good idea. I had a free day tomorrow, with no rehearsals and there was a lot of work to do. I put the cork in the bottle, resisting the urge to have a third glass and climbed into bed. On impulse I rang Finlay. I'm not sure why. I think I just needed to hear his voice. I told him what had happened and he did his usual "not very nice but try to forget about it and it will soon go away" speech. I always make out that it annoys me but in truth, I felt more settled when I folded the phone up. I thought it would take ages to go to sleep, but I actually fell quite quickly and woke to an overcast sky and that cold light that usually accompanies five in the morning.

I was up before six and decided to go for a quiet walk to think through my strategy. That sounds so pretentious, because, really, I had no strategy. My best bet was to ask what I thought were pertinent questions interspersed with harmless ones so that nobody guessed I was anything other than nosy.

On my way back to the hotel, I called in at a newsagent and bought a small notepad that would fit in my pocket and a couple of pens. By seven-thirty, I was back in the dining room. Bingo. Scott Wiley and Jamie Topcliffe were eating breakfast on adjacent tables. I put on my best "what a lovely morning" smile and headed in their direction. Scott saw me first and half rose in that gentlemanly way a lot of Australians possess. His movement made Jamie lift his head. He waved to the seat opposite him. I kissed Scott on the cheek in passing and sat with Jamie.

'Fickle jade,' said the Aussie.

'Ah, well I had tea with you yesterday. It's only fair that I have breakfast with Jamie.

Scott put his napkin on the table. 'If that means you will have dinner with me tonight, then I will forgive you.'

'Actually, I was hoping Georgia would have dinner with me,' interrupted Jamie.

'Guys, you are not dogs and I am not a bone. I'm having dinner with Carrie tonight. We haven't had time to catch up much since I came down. Sorry.'

Honour satisfied, Scott pushed back his chair. 'Let's take a rain check, yeah?'

'Fine. Thanks, Scott. Are you playing today?'

'Yeah. It's the Rachmaninov tonight. I need to go and get the fingers flying. See you.'

Jamie watched him leave the dining room. 'I hope I haven't put a spoke in your wheel there, George?'

'No. I only met him on Saturday. He took me to afternoon tea at a place called the "Black Cat" yesterday, but there's no romantic link.'

'Good. I was hoping to see more of you this week. Besides, I saw you first.'

I felt a little niggled with his assumption of possession. 'Yes, but you didn't do much about it, did you?'

He had the grace to look uncomfortable. 'No. I was too wrapped up in other things. Sorry, George.'

'I think we both were. Tell me to mind my own business by all means, Jamie, but don't you think you might feel better if you told me about what happened to Lucy?'

For a moment, I thought I had blown it. His face became set and still. He had obviously been very close to his sister. It made me wonder what I would do if anything happened to Finlay.

'I'm so sorry, Jamie. Look, forget I asked. Have they found your grandfather's pocket-watch yet?'

'No, but apparently it is the last in spate of thefts at the hotel. They are devastated, of course, but also insured.' He laughed, but he didn't sound amused. 'Look, let me get another pot of coffee.'

He called Samantha, the dark-haired waitress over and asked for a fresh pot. Whilst we were waiting, I went up to the breakfast buffet and grabbed melon, toast and that rarest of things in a hotel dining room, Marmite. The coffee came in record time, so I assumed Samantha was as smitten with Jamie as I had always been. Once we were settled and I had poured us both coffee, he cleared his throat.

'You know it's strange - I was going to say funny, but that would not be the right word at all - but whenever I think about Lucy, my throat closes up and I have to keep swallowing.'

'You don't have to talk about her, Jamie. It was only me being nosy.'

'No, George, you're right. Perhaps it would do me good.'

'Is it very painful? I don't want you breaking down in the dining room, they'll think it's the sausages.'

He smiled lopsidedly, as if to applaud my clumsy efforts to lighten the atmosphere. 'No, to be honest, it isn't painful any more. It was for the first couple of years, but then you get used to it.' He took hold of my free hand. The other one was stuffing toast and marmite into my mouth. 'I feel bad that I never got back in touch,' he said. I squeezed his hand. He put mine briefly up to his lips and continued his story.

'I told you, I think, that Ariana brought Tony along to the end of year party?'

'Yes. I was in the south of France by then.'

'And I think I said that Lucy fell for him in a big way.'

'Yes.'

'Well, I think it was the first time she'd ever been in love, or lust or infatuated whichever one it was. She was in her early twenties and she had never had a relationship before. She fell further than most of us because of that.'

I nodded. 'I fell in love for the first time when I was thirteen. It was agony for at least three weeks.'

- 69 -

'Precisely. You get my drift. Well Tony was embarrassed. He and Ariana had only been married for about two months, I think, and here was this gawky English girl making a dead set at him.'

'Poor girl.'

'Yes. And poor Tony, too. It didn't help that Lucy and Ariana were poles apart in all ways. Ariana had that long chestnut hair and those very green eyes. She would have looked sexy in a black plastic bin liner. Lucy had short dirty blonde hair, and a high colour which always made her look as if she had just come off the hockey field.'

'She always came over as being the head girl at school. I always felt she was a prefect about to give me detention.'

He nodded. 'She was head girl as a matter of fact. She was a great organiser. The problem with Lucy was that she always had to be in control. When she fell for Tony, she was most definitely not in control.'

'From this distance I can sympathise. I felt like that when Mike buggered off, or rather, when I kicked him out.'

'Yes, but the difference is that you did the kicking. Lucy became the kicked.'

'How?'

'Tony sat her down and explained that he thought she was a perfectly nice girl, but that he was married to Ariana and he loved Ariana. That he wanted to be friends with Lucy, but it could never be more than friends. Poor bloke. He thought he was doing the right thing.'

'Did Lucy not take that on board?'

'It was worse than that. She thought that he only felt that way about Ariana because he didn't know what she was like. Lucy thought that if she could show Ariana up in her true colours, well....'

'Ah. Not good.'

'Worse than not good, because when she tried to tell Tony about how Ariana slept around, Ariana went to battle stations. Up until then, I think that Tony had told her not to worry and that he could deal with it. I think she might even have found it amusing. But, when Lucy began her "let's open Tony's eyes to this devious bitch" campaign, it stopped being amusing.'

'What were you doing while all this was going on?'

'I tried talking to her. She did the big sister act and told me to mind my own business.'

'What happened?'

'Ariana got some of her cronies to follow Lucy around college. They laughed at her and did mock faints whilst saying stuff like "Oh, Tony, Tony, come to me". Whenever Lucy came over to the Academy, Ariana would say "oh look, guys, it's the lovesick maiden." And then they would all scream with laughter.'

'She always was a nasty piece of work,' I said. 'You should have seen her when she was convinced she would be the next Emma Kirkby. She sang "Fairest Isle" as if she was bloody Tosca. When I sang "Bright Seraphim" and she finally twigged what an early music voice sounds like, you would not believe the comments as I walked past her.'

'Oh, I think I might. What did she say?'

I put on a mock trans-Atlantic twang. 'Oh my, won't that be lovely when you know it. A bit challenged on the upper register though, don't you agree?'

'Ouch. How did you respond to that?'

'I didn't have to. My tutor was sitting in the row behind. He came up and put his arms round me and said, "George, that was great, just like Handel should be - really beautiful. Well done." And then, of course, I won, so that answered anything she might say with knobs on. Anyway, what happened to Lucy? I had no idea all this was going on.'

'How could you know? She tried to ignore the teasing at first. But after a while it became less teasing and more persecution, I think.'

'Why was that?'

'I don't know for certain but I think that Ariana had been economical with the truth regarding her flings and Tony began to realise that Lucy was telling nothing but the truth. So as things between Ariana and Tony deteriorated, she hounded Lucy even more. It culminated at the student summer concert. Lucy was supposed to be playing Alkan's "Concerto for Solo Piano", which is a pig in anybody's language.'

'Oh flick, I can see where this is going.'

'It was worse than that, George. Not only did she make a dog's breakfast of it, but Ariana and her set made sure they were sitting in the front row. They laughed at her.'

'Where were you?'

'Backstage. She pushed past me, told me to go home and leave her alone and ran out.'

'Jamie, I don't know what to say.'

'The police found her body in the river the next afternoon. My parents never got over it.'

We sat there in silence. I often think the reason I have majored in early music is that there isn't too much obvious angst like there is with Verdi and Puccini. The music I sing was written when the fashion was more towards the stylised and there were no visible hearts worn on sleeves. Yes, a lot of the songs are about weeping and dying with lots of euphemisms for the sexual act which go over most people's heads, but it's all very much in the manner of courtly love. No blood and sawdust stuff like Tosca throwing herself off the battlements. That's not to say I don't get involved with what I sing, but I don't have to stagger round the stage in a blood-soaked nightie having just stabbed some poor unfortunate tenor and squawk out my madness for the next ten minutes. So, in a way, I have escaped the need for histrionics and I wonder if that is why I can sometimes look at things almost without emotion and whether that is a strength or a weakness.

I was aware that the story Jamie was telling was tragic, but a larger part of my consciousness was asking if this was in any way relevant to the investigation, before admitting that my interest had more to do with my own thwarted fancy for him than anything else. Part of me hoped that my role as sympathetic listener might help rekindle our relationship. But his story put a different complexion on Tony Labinski, one which I would have to think about. I put my face in what I hoped was a caring expression.

'You must have hated Ariana.'

'No. Not really. My dad used to say we are what we are and she was what she was just as much as Lucy was what she was, if you see what I mean.'

'Sort of. Did you sing with Ariana very much?'

'A couple of times a year, perhaps.'

'What about Tony?'

'Didn't see him much at all. I think he went back to Canada soon after Lucy died. I got the impression that Ariana cared for Tony but she felt it would be a sign of weakness to tell him so and that's why she was so antagonistic towards Lucy.'

'Stupid bitch.'

'Yes. She always had to be top dog. Look, here's Kevin.'

Kevin Dace had wandered into the dining room and stood looking round. He saw Jamie's waving hand, put up one finger and headed for the buffet. A couple of minutes later, he came to the table with a plateful of what looked and smelled like wet cardboard covered with yogurt.

'Hi Kevin. I had you down as an eggs and bacon man,' I said.

'Not a big breakfast eater, darling.'

I looked at his waistline. 'You surprise me. We were just talking about Ariana.'

Jamie swung out of his chair. 'I must be off. Got to go and get ready to be annihilated by Mr Archer.'

'Who is Mr Archer?'

'An inoffensive, butter-wouldn't-melt old boy who plays the meanest game of chess I have ever come across. I've been playing every day since I got here on Thursday last week. It's now Wednesday and I still haven't come anywhere near beating him.'

I put my hand up to catch his and smiled at him. 'What are you singing today?'

'Oh, it's the English afternoon. Vaughan-Williams' "Five mystical songs", followed by the Finzi Bagatelles and then Walton's "Belshazzar" in the second half.'

' Ooh, nice one. I'll try to make it. Look after yourself.'

I turned back to Kevin. 'Do you fancy a fresh pot of coffee?'

'No ta. I'll get some lemon and ginger tea in a mo.'

I repressed a shudder. 'We were saying how well Ariana sang on Saturday night and what a shock it all is.'

He looked at me over his glasses. Why he imagines he looks good with them halfway down his nose, God only knows. 'A shock?'

'Well, yes. I didn't expect her to be killed, did you?'

'Not at that precise moment, no, perhaps not.'

'So you did expect her to be killed at some point?'

'I'm not too surprised.'

I was and it showed. 'Are you serious?'

'Yes.'

I sat and waited but it was obvious he wasn't going to elaborate. 'Come on Kevin, you can't say something like that and then not explain.'

'She wasn't very nice, you know, George.'

'Yes, I know she wasn't Mother Theresa, but then neither am I. I'm not expecting to be knocked off, though.'

'I don't suppose you go around trying to blackmail people, do you?'

'What?' I began and then pulled myself up short. This was not how I imagined an incisive detective mind gained information. I tried to pull myself back on track. Kevin, watching me, misunderstood my silence.

'See. When you think about it, the thought of her blackmailing someone doesn't shock you as much as it should, does it?'

I decided to play along. 'No, I suppose not. Did she try it on you?'

'Oh yes. You know when I did the Elgar "Apostles" at the Proms?

'Yes.'

'Well at the time I was having a thing with one of the conductors; you don't need to know which one.'

'I don't want to know. What did Ariana do?'

'Threatened to sell the story to the gutter press, but with a few untrue spicy extras, like rent boys and three in a bed.'

'What a cow. Why?'

'Jealousy that she hadn't made it that far, I suppose.'

'What did you do?'

'Told her to go ahead, but to make sure she had plenty of money.'

'This is beginning to sound good. Go on.'

'You know what a steam-roller she could be. Under her usual mode of onslaught, most people just laid down and died. I didn't. I told her that I would sue her arse off. She tried to laugh and ask where I could afford that sort of lawyer. So I told her about Uncle Teddy. He's a QC.'

'Fabulous. How did that go down?'

'She thought I was bluffing until I invited her for morning coffee with him in his chambers. She backed right off. I omitted to tell her that he specialises in product defaults.'

'What are they?'

'Well, for example when someone sues a pharmaceutical company because they have had an adverse reaction to one of their drugs, that sort of thing.'

'Oh, right. Interesting though. If she tried it on with you, I wonder who else she tried it on with.'

'Probably tried to pick her potential victims with care, but, just between ourselves, George, I can tell you one of her targets. In fact, he is sitting over there on the table by the window.'

I looked round and spun back to face him. 'Are you sure?'

'Oh, yes. He and I were at an anti-war concert last autumn. We got chatting afterwards. I think we'd both had a few too many, but it was a case of in vino veritas. I can't remember how we got onto the subject of Ariana Staithes, but I told him what had happened to me. When I had finished he just kept staring down into his scotch. I asked him if he was OK and he looked up and said that I was not alone.'

'You're joking.'

'I am not, darling. It set me back on my heels, I can tell you. I thought I hadn't heard him properly, but he looked up and told me straight out that she'd blackmailed him, too.' Kevin looked at me and then his watch. 'Don't look so shocked, George. She was a grade A bitch. I must go.'

We said our goodbyes. I sat at the table for another minute or so trying to work out what to do next. I knew what I had to do really. I just didn't want to do it. Finally, I took a deep breath in and out, rose from the table and walked towards the one in the window. The man looked up at me with a wide grin.

'Hello Georgia Pattison. We haven't seen each other since the Academy days. How are you getting on?'

I sat down and smiled back at him. 'Hello Sir Robert.'

10

'Would you like a coffee?' he asked pointing at the pot.

'No thanks, sir. I'm already awash.'

'Sit down, child. You're giving me neck ache.'

I did as I was told. 'How are you keeping, sir?'

'Not bad, considering my aches and pains and you don't need to "sir" me. I shall soon be old enough to have that disgusting word "sprightly" attached to my name. More to the point, how are you, Georgia? I've never forgotten how awful you were as a pianist, but what a charming student you made.'

'All I wanted to do was sing. I thought the piano was a waste of time at first. But you have to admit, I did improve.'

'I suppose that's one word for it.'

'Well I can accompany myself now which I couldn't before I went to college, so you must have done some good. What are you doing in Temingham?'

'I'm the Chair of the Festival Committee.'

'So you're the person I should butter up if I want a return invitation, then?'

He laughed. 'I've heard good reports of yesterday's recital. Sorry I couldn't make it. I was on duty elsewhere.'

'You say when you're available and I will sing a recital just for you. I didn't think early music was your bag, though.'

'No, it isn't. That's why it is so nice to hear it. If you eat cake all day every day, sometimes you fancy a bacon sandwich for a change.'

Time to start the Spanish Inquisition. 'Was Ariana one of your choices for the Gerontius angel?'

'Why do you ask that?'

'Because I have the impression that Merlina thinks you ought to have asked her.'

'Yes, but we all know how Merlina sings the angel. The committee thought it would be a good idea to have some new blood, though don't let Merlina know I said that.'

I put my hand up. 'Guides honour.'
His eyebrows shot up. 'Were you a guide?'
'No.' We both laughed. I returned to the fray. 'She was a good choice, though. I thought she was amazing.'
'Yes, she was. Say what you like about her, she had that intangible something which just notched the performance up.'
'Well, she wasn't my favourite person. She stole my boyfriend out from under my nose way back.'
'Yes, she had some....er....unfortunate personal traits.'
I kept my right hand under the table with my fingers crossed. That way, God knew I didn't mean to tell lies. 'You can say that again. She once threatened to go and tell Wharram-Biggs that I had lied on my application to the Academy.'
'And had you?'
I sat up. 'No I had not, but it would have been difficult to prove.'
He looked at me with a faint smile. 'Yes, I know exactly what you mean. I don't think you were the only person she tried that on with, either, Georgia. What did she want from you?'
'You've heard of Merigo Baccini?'
'Who hasn't?'
'When I was fifteen, we were at the house in Gourdon and used to drive down most days to the beach at Miramar. Well, we were there swimming and doing the usual beach things and, to cut a long story short, this man got into difficulties. Daddy ran into the sea and got him out, by which time he had stopped breathing. Daddy brought him back. He was staying in a villa nearby. He refused to go to hospital and asked Daddy to go back with him to the villa. Turns out it was Merigo Baccini, who I had never heard of, but Daddy had. We still see him if he is at his villa when we are at our place. Anyway, as a favour, he agreed to listen to me sing and made a few suggestions. I don't know who told Ariana about it, but she knew. She wanted an introduction and a place at La Scala for a season.'
'What did you do?'
'Told her to go stuff herself.'
'Good for you.'

'You said I wasn't the only one she tried it on with.'

'It's such a shame when somebody with her looks and talent thinks they have to resort to blackmail to get up the ladder quicker. Let's not talk about her any more. What are you doing for the rest of the year?'

'Well....'

But whatever I had been about to say was interrupted by the sound of breaking crockery. Sir Robert half rose to his feet and I twisted round. Across the other side of the dining room, Merlina Meredith was standing with a letter in her hand and the contents of her pot of tea were seeping across the white tablecloth like an incoming tide. She had one hand to her mouth. My feet were already moving towards her but I was beaten by a man in a brown/green tweed jacket. It took a few seconds to realise that this was my saviour from Saturday night, Dr Carter. I reached the table just as he had his arm around her shoulder. He looked at me.

'We need to get her away from all these people staring at her.'

'Come with me,' I said and turned towards the door. He pulled Merlina in close behind me and we walked out like formation dancers doing a very long first section to the Gay Gordons. We had to walk past Rosemary who stood there with her mouth open staring at this strange procession. I was very crisp with her.

'Is the blue sitting room empty?'

'What?'

'I think you mean pardon. Is the blue sitting room empty?'

She caught on quickly. 'I'm so sorry, Miss Pattison. I'll run ahead and make sure it is.'

She was as good as her word. When we pushed the door open, a couple were being ushered out into the corridor. God knows what story she cooked up but it worked. She looked back over her shoulder and I mouthed a "thank you" at her.

'Can I get you anything, Dr Carter?' she asked one hand on the door knob.

'Cup of tea would be good, Rosemary. Thanks.' He flashed her a smile at which she coloured up and made a confused exit. He caught my inquisitive glance. 'I often breakfast here.'

I nodded and knelt next to the chair into which he had just lowered Merlina. 'Darling Merlina. Whatever is wrong?'

She sat staring at me as if I was a stranger, her blue eyes wide with fear. She tried to answer but nothing came out. I put my hand on her arm.

'Come on, darling. You can tell me.'

Dr Carter leaned over and stared down into her eyes. 'You are quite safe Miss Meredith. My name is Tom Carter and, as Miss Pattison here will tell you, I am a doctor. Now, be a good girl and tell us what is wrong. Is it the letter?' His voice was matter of fact without being over-soothing.

She found her voice. 'It's wicked. I didn't do it. I didn't.'

I took the letter from her hand. It looked like a short poem:

"Poor Miss Staithes is here no more
An angel now and not a whore.
Your jealous heart and acid tongue
Will once more sing what she'd have sung.
You left your seat, I watched you go.
You had the time, I'm sure you know.
What's done is done. What's past is past
But where were you when she breathed her last?"

I handed it to the doctor to read. 'That's awful, Merlina. Who would write a thing like that?'

'But it isn't true.' She was beginning to weep now.

'Darling, of course it isn't true, but you know you have to show it to the police, don't you?'

'Oh, no. I couldn't do that.'

Tom Carter took her wrist and checked his watch. 'That's a bit more like it. Now, when the girl comes with the tea, you must drink a cup. You'll feel much better after that.'

She hung onto his arm. 'Do I really have to show it to the police?'

'Tell you what,' he replied. 'Would you prefer it if Miss Pattison went and showed them the letter?'

Merlina looked at me. Her eyes were still beautiful even if she was crying. 'Darling, would you?'

'I thought for a moment. I needed to see Hamilton to tell her about the blackmail stuff. 'Tell you what, Merlina. How about I go and see Superintendent Hamilton and explain what has happened? You stay here with Dr Carter and if she wants to see you, she can walk back with me. How's that?'

'I think that's a fine idea,' said the doctor. 'I will sit here with Miss Meredith until you get back.'

I almost collided with the waitress bringing the tray of tea things into the room. The momentum of sidestepping her meant I had no chance of avoiding a head-on impact with Sir Robert.

'Whatever is the matter with Merlina?'

'Bit of a shock, Sir Robert. Fortunately, the doctor is with her.'

'Do you think I should go in?'

'I'd leave her to calm down a bit first.'

'Yes, all right. Hope she is recovered in time for tomorrow afternoon.'

'What is she doing?'

'"Sea Pictures". We thought if we couldn't give her Gerontius, we'd ask her to do the songs.'

'I expect she will be fine, but just leave her for now.'

I went out of the front door and walked as quickly as I could without being obtrusive to the cloisters. I took a quick look round before I opened the door to that damned staircase. Fortunately, Hamilton was sitting at her desk. She was very interested in the blackmail information and in the note Merlina had just received.

'I'll come back over with you. I wanted a chat in any case.'

'What, another one?'

She waited until we had left the cathedral by the north door. 'I've been thinking of a way for us to communicate without alerting anyone to the fact that you are helping us.'

'You mean without them knowing that I'm Snitch in Chief?'

'If you prefer to think of yourself that way, then yes. Listen. My niece, Lizzie.'

'The one you share a house with?'

'Yes. She's a vet. She decided much against my will that a vet had to have a dog a few weeks ago. I hate the bloody thing. Dog shit all over the garden and fur all over everything else. It even gets in the food, for God's sake.'

'I thought you said you were allergic to dogs?'

'I am but not in the way your friend Carrie is allergic to peanuts. I just don't like dogs. I think they are useless. The thing she brought home is just a useless yellow fluff ball. It doesn't do anything apart from eat, crap and mess up the place.'

'What does this have to do with me?'

Hamilton shook her head. 'Sorry. Yes. Lizzie walks the dog along the river each morning at about half six. I thought perhaps the easiest way for us to communicate would be for you to type up anything you've found out, then go for an early walk by the river and give what you've written to Lizzie.'

'Yes, I can do that. I've got my printer in the car, so that's not a problem.'

'Good. At least it will make the dog useful for something. Look, she is picking me up tonight. We are supposed to be taking the damn thing up onto the moors. Can you be at the picnic site at, say, just before six? I'll introduce you.'

'Yes, OK.'

'Good, now where's this woman?'

I left Hamilton with Merlina and Tom Carter. I heard her trying to persuade him to leave, but Merlina obviously wanted him to stay. I couldn't help grinning as I walked out of the sitting room door. I knew who would win that battle and it would not be the dog-hating policewoman.

I decided to catch a few rays in the hotel garden and passed Jamie in the throes of his chess game with an old man who had to be Mr Archer. I didn't disturb them. Jamie had the look on his face that I have often seen on mine in the mirror when I've placed a note wrongly and I am trying to work out how to correct it. I thought it was nice of him to take trouble with the old man, but, that was typical of Jamie.

I sat down on an ornate bench that was obviously only there for show because it was so bloody uncomfortable. After five minutes, I began to fidget. Finally, I managed to find a position which, whilst not comfortable, was better than any other position. I closed my eyes and reviewed the morning's work. It was just on half past nine and I had already spoken to three people and given Hamilton two leads to follow that would hopefully lead her away from Carrie. Carrie. We hadn't spoken since Monday night. I took my mobile out of my pocket and buzzed her a quick text message asking if she'd like to meet that afternoon.

I spent the next few minutes looking out over the river, wondering what to do with the rest of the day, or rather, how to move the investigation forward. A shadow fell over me and I looked up to see Scott. We both smiled and he took that as an invitation to sit next to me. I wondered if the bench would take his weight.

'Did you enjoy your breakfast with your friend?'

'Indeed I did. Jamie and I have known each other since college.'

'May I ask in what sense you mean the word known?'

'No, you may not ask, but I will tell you that we are and always have been friends, but nothing more than that.' I didn't feel Scott Wiley needed to know the truth. His smile relaxed a little and his shoulders dropped. Whoa. I knew that sign. 'Good,' was all he said.

'I'm just getting a bit of sun,' I said trying to change the subject.

'Good,' he said again. 'Don't spoil that lovely complexion, though.'

'I hardly think twenty minutes is going to make any difference.'

'Perhaps not, but you should see some of the women back home. Their faces are like cured leather.'

'What a horrible analogy.'

'They are a horrible sight, Georgia. Now, what are your plans for the rest of the day?'

At that minute, my mobile trilled. It was Carrie saying that she was busy this afternoon, but would I like to meet in Waterstones in the High Street in half an hour. They had a coffee lounge. We could look at books and have coffee and cake. Good old Carrie. Talk about being saved by the bell. I turned to Scott.

'Sorry, Scott. I have to go and meet Carrie now. I'll catch up with you later.'

'Now you're playing hard to get.'

I stood up and smoothed down my skirt. 'No, I'm not. It's just that Carrie and I go back to college days and we haven't seen each other for a long time.'

He caught hold of my hand and pulled me back down on the bench. 'Try and make some time for me this week, Georgia. Please.'

I squeezed his hand and capitulated instantly. 'Don't worry, Scott. After tomorrow night, I have all day Friday. How about we take my car and go to Chatsworth or Haddon Hall?'

His smile was like the sun coming out. 'I'll hold you to that, fair lady.' He took my hand, turned it over and planted the softest kiss in my palm before folding my fingers over it. 'Take care of yourself, Georgia,' he said so softly I could hardly hear him.

I sat there like a lemon not knowing quite what to do, just staring as if it was the first time I had actually looked at him. I could feel that my breathing was becoming uneven and the scent of his aftershave has stayed with me ever since. He smiled again and then using two fingers of his right hand, he tipped my chin up and kissed me. I could not help but melt into him. There were butterflies fluttering in my stomach. The kiss seemed to go on forever. When it ended, we sat and stared at each other in silence.

'I've been wanting to do that ever since Saturday afternoon,' he said at last. 'Now, go and meet your friend. We will reconvene this meeting on Friday morning.'

'I just have to ask you one question, Scott.'

'Fire away.'

'Do you have a big sister?'

'No,' he said, frowning, 'but I do have a younger brother. He spends his time looking at the stars though a telescope. Why?'

'Nothing. Just needed to know. See you Friday morning. Breakfast at eight?'

'I'd crawl over broken glass to be there.'

I almost danced out of the Maddox. All I could think of were his eyes and that smile. I didn't even have room to wonder if Rosemary had seen us. I hadn't forgotten Mike, not by a long chalk, but that cold lump in my solar plexus when I thought about him had gone. So much for the person I had thought was the love of my life. A stupid childish part of my brain began to weave flimsy dreams about life in Australia.

11

Carrie could see that something had happened before I had even reached the bay in Waterstones where she was rifling through a book on pregnancy. She shut the book and grinned, her eyes bright with mischief. Brighter than I had seen them since I arrived in Temingham.

'Confess. I know that look. Who is it?' she demanded.

I tried to hedge. 'Don't know what you mean.'

'Come off it, woman, you've got that love is a many splendoured thing look.'

'OK, you win. Scott Wiley.'

She whistled. 'Tell me all over coffee.'

I didn't quite tell her all, of course, but I told her enough to keep her from wondering about anything else I might be doing. She seemed very nervous and on edge and kept fiddling with her hair. When she was dancing, her blonde locks had been long so that she could grease them back into a tight bun on stage. I liked her hair in this short bob but realised that the fact that it kept flopping round her face was the reason she kept tucking it behind her ear.

After I had watched her do this at least three times in ten minutes, I began to understand how she had lost the earring. We talked ourselves out for about half an hour and then came the lull that happens in all "what have you been doing with yourself" conversations. We were not as comfortable with each other as we used to be. I asked her how things were going with Neil.

'I think we'll be OK. It's early days, but he is a very penitent husband at the moment.'

'Good. I should think the fright has done that as much as anything. Does he know about the bambino?'

'Yes. He does now. I waited until he had made it crystal clear that he loved me and didn't want the marriage to break up. Then I gave him a scotch and told him.'

'How did he take it?'

'Well, already it's going to be a boy, who will be a world-class organist, of course, or, failing that, a 'cellist.'

'A 'cellist? Why the 'cello?'

'Because he wanted to be one, but somebody persuaded him that the flute was more portable and didn't carry such high insurance premiums.'

'I see. So, everything in the garden is now lovely?'

'I think the storm has passed, George. It battered a few of the flowers, but they are beginning to stand up again.' She looked across at me. 'Would you like to come back to us until Sunday or are you happy in the Maddox?'

'I'd like to see more of you, of course, but I think that it would be better for you and Neil as a couple not to be cluttered up with a house guest. The hotel is fine. Perhaps if I get asked back next year, I could stay with you then.'

I could see she was relieved. 'Don't worry, little one. It will all be OK. No need to feel guilty on my behalf.'

'I expect the food's better there.'

'I'm not even going to begin answering that one, Carrie.'

'If you come next year, the baby will be here.'

'Yes. And with you both being blonde and blue eyed, baby is bound to be beautiful.' Privately I couldn't think of anything worse than living in a house with a squally baby and doting parents who thought it the pinnacle of success when the brat shit its nappy, but, of course, I didn't say so.

'What is Neil planning for after the festival,' I asked.

'He's taken on some part-time teaching at a local school. The hours don't clash with his duties at the cathedral.'

'Oh, God. Teaching? Poor him. Which age group?'

'The older ones. He's trying to come to grips with the syllabus at the moment. It goes from the Beethoven sonatas through some Bartok and jazz to pop music.'

'Flick. Think how cool I would have been studying pop music.'

We changed the subject, talking about the things we had done since college and how the dreams and aspirations we had then had morphed into something between success and failure. I don't think Carrie had ever wanted to be the next Daria Klimentova, but she wanted to get out of the corps de ballet. Meeting and marrying Neil had done that. My ambition had been to be the singer that everyone thought of when they heard seventeenth and eighteenth century music. There was a chance I could still make it but it was a slim one.

We ran out of things to say to each other, so went down into the bookshop. Carrie bought a couple of baby books and a book about the Peak District. I grabbed a thriller and a coffee-table book about Australia. By the time we parted, it was almost lunchtime, but the last thing I wanted to do was eat. I felt as if I had spent all morning talking and eating.

I bought a bottle of water and headed into the quiet of the cathedral to think. I wasn't anxious to be spotted by anyone, so I slipped into a side chapel off the south aisle. Instead of a stone wall separating the chapel from the main body of the cathedral, there were two arches cut out of the stone and filled in with a lattice of wrought ironwork. I sat quietly at the back with the piled up kneelers wafting out that faint scent of damp humanity even the driest of churches cannot eradicate. I sat quite still not wanting to disturb a lady in front of me on her knees, eyes closed and with a troubled expression on her face. It took a few moments to recognise Lady Barbara the flower arranger from Saturday afternoon, the one who I had last seen talking to Sir Robert.

She stayed there for about five minutes, during which my brain was working overtime. Could she be part of the pattern or was she just on the periphery? I wondered how involved with Sir Robert she was. I had the impression he was a widower, but I had no idea of her marital status. The movement of her sitting back in the chair interrupted my chain of thought. She was on the end of the first row nearest the south aisle. From where she sat, she could see into the cathedral and be seen. Something about the set of her neck and shoulders caught my attention. I sat very still and waited.

A few minutes later, Sir Robert Fielding came and stood with his back to the latticed ironwork. He appeared to be looking to left and right. I sat with my head bowed as if in prayer, observing them under my fringe. I was not directly in his field of vision, so if I kept still, I should be all right. They held a muttered conversation and then he walked off towards the Prior's Door. She waited a minute or so, but I was prepared for her to move and was on my knees, my head hidden in my arms. She walked past me. I waited for her to appear on the cathedral side of the ironwork, but she didn't. I scampered out of the chapel and peered round the corner towards the Miserrimus Door in time to see her walking through it. Curiouser and curiouser. Should I follow him or her? Easy. Her.

I made sure I kept a good way behind her as she walked past the tea bar round the corner of the cloisters towards the door into the cathedral close. There was no sign of Sir Robert. Once outside she turned left away from the river and towards the gateway under the Chester Tower which led into town. Just as she reached the other side a car drew up She climbed inside the back door and bobbed out of sight. The car sped off down the road, but not before I had seen Sir Robert at the wheel. Now, what was all that about?

I checked my watch. Just over half an hour before the afternoon concert. I decided to explore the cathedral a little more. I walked back into the cloisters and collided with a stout man holding an umbrella. It was actually the umbrella which caught round my ankles. The ensuing tangle brought him to the ground, too, but he sprang up, helped me to my feet and hurried out of the cloisters into the close. I heard a very Anglo-Saxon oath and looked toward the door to see him turning from side to side. Not even a sorry or kiss my arse that he'd knocked my flying.

I shook myself and continued towards the Prior's Door. I was deep in thought trying to work out what Sir Robert and the lady were up to, so I was not prepared for Merlina and Dr Carter to precipitate out of the door leading up to the cathedral library. They were so busy talking to each other that it didn't cross their minds somebody might be on the other side of the door. I landed on the stone floor with a whump for the second time in three minutes. This time I stayed down. It seemed safer. Merlina was mortified. Once Dr Carter had made sure I wasn't injured he seemed more concerned with taking her back to the hotel for lunch.

Merlina was torn between apologies to me and also wanting her lunch, since her breakfast had been so interrupted.

'Georgia, darling. I am so sorry. You aren't singing today are you?'

'No, don't worry, Merlina. I'm not on until the Vivaldi tomorrow night.'

'Would you like to come and lunch with us?' she asked without consulting the doctor. I took a quick glance at his face. To say it was set was an understatement.

'That's really kind of you,' I replied, prolonging his discomfort, 'but I'm going to catch Jamie's concert. It starts in half an hour.'

I looked deliberately at him and grinned. He smiled back his thanks and went pink. I made my way into the cathedral and paid for a ticket about six rows from the front. Jamie spotted me as soon as he walked on, so I gurned at him a bit and stuck my tongue out. I could see he was fighting not to corpse - oh, bad choice of phrase.

He seemed unduly nervous at the beginning of the "Five Mystical Songs", but that could have been the war we all go through. We study the structure of the words and the music and how they intertwine and yet in the final analysis we must only communicate the marriage of the meaning of the words with the emotion of the music. I have to say that for an agnostic, Vaughan-Williams wrote the most uplifting religious music on the planet, but life is full of these paradoxes.

Here was I, a month out of what I thought was going to be the most important relationship of my life, being pursued by two men, one openly and the other not so openly. I wasn't sure how I felt about either of them. I just knew that the thought of Jamie made me smile and feel that everything would be fine, whilst the thought of Scott gave me flutters where I hadn't had flutters for a while.

Where the concert really caught light was in the second half. I've always felt a touch sorry for the baritone soloist in "Belshazzar". He has one bit which is nothing more than a shopping list to sing and the diction for it needs to be so crisp it almost breaks the tongue, and then there's the amazing bit where he sings about being weighed in the balance and found wanting. Jamie seemed to add weight and darkness to his voice for the latter and it was the most ominous rendition I'd ever heard. It caught the audience as well and his applause was well deserved.

I checked my watch. Four-thirty. I felt a touch peckish so decided to go and see what constituted afternoon tea at the Maddox. Not a patch on the "Black Cat", but more convenient to get to. I'd grabbed a programme so I knew when Scott's concert began. I had plenty of time to go and meet Hamilton.

I went up to my room, had a quick shower and dressed in clean jeans and tee-shirt. I decided to surprise my Aussie pianist by wearing a fitted silk dress in white with a sweep of turquoise flowers going from the waist to the hem in a long curve and a matching turquoise wrap. I laid these on the bed ready to change into when I returned, along with the curling tongs so that I could do a partly upswept style with curls cascading over my shoulders. The make-up would take about seven minutes, putting on the dress about three and doing my hair about half an hour. I would then need ten minutes for my arms to recover from being in the air for so long. Provided I was back at the hotel by 6.30, there would be no problem.

I slipped out of the back door and onto the towpath. Fifteen minutes later I was at the picnic site. It was deserted but had obviously been a busy place during the day because the bins were full of litter and there were a few discarded plastic bags lying around the tables. I didn't mind that too much. The flies were more interested in the discarded food than in me, thank God.

The sun still had a surprising amount of heat in it and I sat on one of the picnic benches with my face raised to the sky and my eyes closed. The sound of a car disturbed the quiet and I opened my eyes to see the same Volvo that had picked up Hamilton from the Lady Greenwood Chapel just pulling in to the side of the road. The blonde girl got out without speaking to Hamilton in the passenger seat and undid the tailgate. The dog jumped out and bounded over towards where I was sitting. For a moment, I felt a warm glow thinking that it was running over to say hello to me, but actually, it started to nose through all the plastic bags looking for leftover food to snaffle. Great clouds of disturbed flies descended on the table where I was sitting. I shot to my feet.

'Jordy, here,' shouted the girl. The dog took no notice at all. She dragged him away from the bag he was currently investigating and came over to the less infested table where I had taken refuge.

'Obedient dog,' I remarked.

She burst out laughing and I just had to join in. 'He's a rescue,' she answered. 'Well, sort of. I rescued him from this stupid woman who fed him everything and far too much of it and who let him think he was top dog.'

'And he isn't now?'

'He tries it on sometimes, but no, I am definitely boss and he is definitely slave.'

'Have you told him that?'

'Several times.' She held out her hand. 'Lizzie. I understand that Mick wants me to act as a go-between.'

The dog had decided that my clean jeans were too good to bypass and came to put his chin on my knee, leaving a trail of excess canine saliva down my jeans. I frowned until I looked into those melting brown eyes.

'Mucky pup,' I told him. He wagged his tail in agreement and grinned in the way that only a few breeds can. An even dirtier paw came up and raked the skin through the denim. I detached it, wincing then watched Hamilton get out of the car and stroll over to us. She blanked the dog. Lizzie's lips tightened. I put a hand each side of Jordy's head.

'You are a handsome boy, but you need to learn a few manners, the first being do not make my jeans dirty when I have only just put them on.'

Lizzie bent down to heave him off. 'He is a darling, but a bit uncouth as yet. I keep telling Mick that in a month she won't recognise him.'

'Can we keep to the point,' said Hamilton checking her watch. 'I've been on the go since six this morning and I want a rest.'

I looked back to Lizzie. 'Where do you want me to meet you?'

'Is here OK? How about seven-ish each morning? Or is that too early?'

I glanced at Hamilton. 'Do you have any other instructions, Superintendent?'

She looked around. 'Just be careful, Georgia. If you even smell trouble or sense that there is a problem, ring my mobile and say so. Don't wait, don't think you are being melodramatic. Just ring and say you're in trouble, OK?'

'You mean like "Houston, we have a problem?"'

'If that floats your boat, yes. This is serious, you know.'

'Keep your knickers on Superintendent. I'm not about to put my life on the line to help you.' I turned to the girl. 'OK, Lizzie, I'll meet you here tomorrow morning. I need to type up the conversations I had this morning.'

'Fair enough,' said Hamilton. 'Did you forget anything when you spoke to me this morning?'

'I don't know. I have the sort of memory that plays like a film, so I need to watch the film and write down the dialogue.'

We said goodbye. As Hamilton wanted a rest, Lizzie had decided that she would walk Jordy in the park near to their house a little later, so she was putting the dog back in the car as I turned for the footbridge. The light was still good. It had that lovely quality you don't get in the morning. The sort of soothing acceptance of a day's work done and the softness of earned rest. There were lots of swallows swooping down near the water to catch flies. I checked my watch. It was only ten past six, so I knew I had plenty of time to dawdle back to the hotel.

I suppose I was about halfway back. The blackbirds alerted me first. Something was disturbing their domain and they were screaming their displeasure for anyone to hear. I looked further up the towpath. Nothing. I checked behind me. Still nothing. I looked across the river. The only person about appeared to be me. Perhaps it was a cat, I decided. I looked at the path about a dozen metres ahead.

There was a trick of the light that made it look wet. Then, as I walked nearer, I saw that it was not a trick of the light. The path was wet and the surface dirt seemed to be churned up. My eyes followed the wet trail to the river and I ran towards it. I had seen a shoe in the water close to the bank. I slid down to the water. It wasn't a shoe. It was a foot attached to a man, face down in the river. Without even thinking about currents or how deep the water might be, I slipped in up to my knees and turned him over. Then I tried to drag him to the bank, but he was very heavy.

By the time I managed to get his head on the grass, I was almost sobbing for breath and the silt of the river clung to my jeans and smelled awful. It's strange how inconsequential things go through the mind in these situations. All I could think about for the next five seconds was to wonder where I had read that river bank mud smelled like plum cake. I gave up in the end and looked down for the first time at the face. Oh no. No. I felt for a pulse but couldn't find one. Flick. Come on, you're a doctor's daughter. Think. Right. Mobile phone. Down to Hamilton's number.

'Houston, we have a problem, a fucking great big one and he isn't breathing. I'm on the river bank halfway back to town. Get help here fast. I will do CPR.'

I'd never done CPR for real, although I've done it on the doll thing and been told off for breathing into it too hard. It is so much more difficult when it is a real human being. I knew I had to keep going until help came. I think it only took fifteen minutes or so, but by the time Hamilton and the ambulance people came running up the towpath, I was almost finished.

The medics dragged him further onto the path and began to do their thing. Hamilton stood with her arm round me. I was bent double with fatigue and shock, crying. Hamilton shook my shoulders and spoke with a gentleness I would never have known she possessed.

'Who is it, George?'

'It's Scott Wiley. Please save him. Please.'

12

I sat by his hospital bed, holding his hand and clenching my teeth so that I didn't cry. The paramedics had taken some time to get a pulse but they found one in the end, at which point, Scott had been placed on a stretcher, his head in one of those helmet things to keep it still and carried the half mile to the ambulance waiting in the cathedral close. I had walked forward to get into the ambulance with him, but Hamilton had pulled me back.

'It'll be better if you come with me. They will want to whisk him straight into A&E. We'll wait in the family room.'

'What about his concert?' There was that old inconsequential thing again, popping up to try to deflect me from thinking about what was happening.

'I will phone Sir Robert Fielding. I don't know what they will do, but that's not our concern right now.'

Once at the hospital, a sister who obviously knew Hamilton, took me by the arm and into the family room. She asked if I wanted a cup of tea and I didn't but I said yes anyway. I've found that people like to be useful and doing when something like this happens. She brought it in to me and muttered the usual things.

I've discovered that nurses tend to have a fund of sympathy without empathy, which sometimes makes them a little difficult to work out as people. I suppose it's a wall they have to put up. If they empathised with everyone in their care, they would probably end up in the nearest psychiatric ward. I still find it a bit weird that they can put this sympathetic persona on like a coat and take it off just as easily. Anyway, the sister came back a while later with some white theatre trousers and I took off my dirty wet jeans and changed into them.

It was almost nine before Hamilton came back into the room. She put the light on and I blinked in surprise. I had been so deep in thought I hadn't even realised it was getting dark.

'They say you can sit with him for a few minutes.'

'Can I stay the night?'

'No. Not a good idea, George. He's in Intensive Therapy, so there will be someone with him all the time. Honestly, you'd just be a hindrance. The doctor says that he won't come round for a while anyway. Would you like to see him and then I'll take you back to the hotel.'

So, here I sat, gowned up like somebody from "Holby City", holding the hand of this man who hadn't even been on my radar until twenty four hours before. They had him propped up slightly and there were more tubes going in and out than on the Piccadilly Line. I could see Hamilton the other side of the nurse station talking to a grey-haired man in a white coat. She beckoned to me.

'This is Doctor Raven, George. He can tell you more than I can.'

I looked at him. He was younger than his hair had led me to believe.

He cleared his throat. 'Yes, well, Mr Wiley has sustained a fractured skull. We estimate he was not breathing for quite some time, although the impact of that is considerably lessened by the CPR you did. Well done on that front, by the way.'

'Her parents are both doctors,' interrupted Hamilton.

'Oh, good. He was lucky you were around, then. Well, he is as stable as we can make him at the moment, but he won't be conscious for a couple of days at least and we have to do further tests.'

'Can I come back tomorrow?'

'What about your concert, George?'

'Oh, yes. I'd forgotten. Well, I'll have to do that of course. Is it OK if I come and see him in the morning?'

I saw Hamilton and Raven exchange glances. 'Is there something you're not telling me?'

Raven hastened to reassure me. 'No, it isn't that. Look, ring the ward first. You see, he may be going down for tests and that sort of thing, so I can't say he will be here if you come on spec.'

'OK. I'll ring.'

'Come on, George, I'll take you back to the hotel. I can get a taxi back home. I think we could both do with a nightcap or two.'

'I thought you didn't want us to be seen together,' I remarked once we were in the car.

'I am just a caring copper who's standing you a drink after a shock.'

'Doctor Carter says you shouldn't have alcohol for shock.'

'You're not supposed to eat a lot of fat but people still do,' she answered. 'I don't know about you, but when I'm told I shouldn't do something because it is bad for my health, I often want to go and do it anyway, even if I wouldn't normally dream of doing it.'

Jamie, Kevin and Merlina were in the hotel bar. They had all heard, of course. The men were torn between false optimism and being too solicitous. Merlina just put her arms round me and gave me the biggest hug. I needed that. It was Merlina who suggested to Hamilton that she would see me to bed and who ordered a huge mug of hot chocolate to be sent to my room. For the second time in less than a week, I found myself being escorted to bed by a female friend.

Merlina was not as motherly as Carrie had been, but perhaps that was just my impression because the shock of finding Scott had been much worse than the shock of finding Ariana. I was back in that plastic bubble of detachment. I took my make-up off and showered the dried river silt off my legs, whilst Merlina turned down the bed and took charge of the chocolate when it arrived. She helped me into bed and handed me the mug.

'I'll give your clothes to the hotel laundry to sort out. These white ones can go back to the hospital. I'm not going to pretend you haven't had a horrible time, but you must put that to one side of your mind and concentrate on getting a good night's sleep. You're singing the Vivaldi tomorrow, aren't you?'

'Yes, but I don't know if I can at the moment.'

'You don't have to sing it at the moment,' she volleyed back. 'You have to sing it tomorrow. Drink up. Don't meet trouble before it meets you. Come on, Georgia, this is the sort of thing that separates the boys from the men. You have to go on to that platform tomorrow and sing. And you will. You are a professional singer. Do you understand?'

'Yes. I am feeling tired now. Thank you, Merlina. I think I will sleep.'

'Good. Scott will be fine, love. In my experience, Australians have very hard heads.'

I smiled in spite of myself and caught hold of her hand. 'What happened about the concert?'

'Robert, Kevin and I gave a scratch lieder recital. The orchestra was given a night off. We had to scamper about a bit to find enough music, but I think it went down all right. We offered people the choice of either listening to us or getting their money back. Only a few left. I sang two songs for Scott, "Du bist die ruh" and "Du bist bei mir". A lot of people asked how he was, but, of course, we didn't know anything. I'll see you tomorrow. You go to sleep now.'

She let herself out and I snuggled down, closed my eyes and cried myself to sleep.

The next morning, I made myself have some tea and toast before I picked up the phone to ring the hospital. They told me he had had a reasonable night and that they would be doing more tests at intervals throughout the day so it might be better if I left it to visit until Friday. I rang off with the sister's promise that if anything happened I needed to know about, she would ring me. I, in turn, promised her I would ring before visiting the next day.

I came off the phone to find Jamie standing behind me, a worried look creasing his face.

'How is he?'

'He had an OK night, but they are doing tests today so, no visitors.'

'What the hell happened, George? Were you out together?'

'No, I'd gone for a walk to let my tea go down. I planned to be back in time to change for his concert, but on the way back, I found him in the river.'

He put his arms round me. 'You poor darling. Two in less than a week. Can I help in any way?'

'Well I have the Vivaldi tonight, so this afternoon and tonight are spoken for.' I hugged him back. 'I don't feel I want to be by myself this morning, Jamie. Can we just wonder round perhaps, or do you have anything planned?'

'No, I'm done here. I was going to leave this morning, but I thought you might need a bit of moral support and they are talking about a memorial service for Ariana so the hotel is letting me keep the room on.'

'Oh, Jamie, that's really kind of you. Thank you. I'm here until Monday at least but if there is a memorial service I shall come back for it. I have to go to London. I'm singing at Cirencester next month and I need to spend some time with Janetta. There's a glitch somewhere in my upper register and I can't fathom out what I'm doing wrong.'

'So, what would you like to do this morning?'

'Actually I was hoping I could drag her away to help me look for some things for the new baby's room at the antique centre in town,' said Carrie's voice behind me. I spun round. 'But,' she continued, 'if you're promised to another...'

Jamie put his hands up and backed away. 'I'm sure that will be far more fun than anything I was going to suggest. I'll catch you tomorrow, perhaps, George?'

'Fine.' Once again he was blowing with the wind. Had Carrie not come up, he would have spent the morning with me quite happily. The minute it looked as if someone else might see us together, he was like a frightened virgin on her wedding night with the lord of the manor about to do his "droit de seigneur" bit. I looked after him and sighed.

'Did I stick my big foot in it?'

'No, Carrie. He was just taking pity on me. Now where's this antique place?'

We spent the morning wandering round a huge warehouse split into small units. Some were devoted to furniture, some clocks, others jewellery. There was a small coffee lounge in one, which served the most delicious carrot cake. Carrie talked about the baby and what sort of nursery she was planning. She wanted an authentic Victorian rocking cradle, which I thought was a daft idea on hygiene grounds alone.

'What happens if it tips over?'

'If they did that, there wouldn't be any, you brainless bag. There's a lovely one over there. It's walnut.'

'It won't be the only nut in the nursery then.'

'George, you are hopeless. Look, you go and ogle the jewellery. I'll come and find you when I'm done.'

Of course, by the time she eventually found me, I had fallen in love with a stunning garnet, pearl and diamond ring, which I just had to have.

'What are you like?' she asked shaking her head.

'A magpie.'

I can't say that Scott had vanished from my mind by any stretch, but I knew that he was in the best place and that the nursing staff seemed to be fairly optimistic. I went back to "Vox Celeste" with Caroline and had salad with her and Neil. Neil was especially tender towards her which cheered my heart. Then he turned to me.

'George, I'm sorry to hear about Scott Wiley. I didn't know you knew each other.'

'We don't, not well.'

'But she's hoping that will change, aren't you, George?'

I pulled a face at her. 'I can't think of anything apart from him recovering from this.'

'What are the quacks saying?' asked Neil.

'They seem reasonably upbeat.'

'Then let's not cross bridges,' he answered, echoing Merlina. 'You must concentrate on the concert tonight. I wasn't going to tell you this, but the BBC is recording it in lieu of the Rachmaninov. You'll be on Radio 3.'

'Nice. I've only done Classic FM so far.'

'Oooh, hark at her,' responded Carrie, trying to lighten the atmosphere. 'Only Classic FM. That gets far more listeners than boring Radio 3.'

'Radio 3 is not boring,' retorted her husband.

'Children,' I interrupted. 'This will not be a good example to set the younger generation.'

After lunch Neil and I walked into the cathedral. I had my mind set firmly on the music and nothing else. Katherine May was the other soloist. She greeted me with a wide smile.

'Nice to see you again, George. Been doing anything interesting lately?'

'No, nothing much.' I was not in the mood to explain the events of the past week. 'Ready for the "Laudamus Te"?'

She grinned again. 'I'll fight you every inch of the way.'

Neil decided to begin at the beginning and go straight through. When it came to the "Laudamus Te", Katherine and I flashed eyes at each other and launched into it. Done at a brisk pace and with a light tone, it can give both singers an incredible amount of energy. When we finished, the choir burst into spontaneous applause and Katherine and I sat down giggling. Neil leaned over.

'Sing it like that tonight and we are onto a winner. Well done. Thank you.'

At the halfway point of the rehearsal, I saw Carrie come into the cathedral talking to Hamilton. They both looked grave and preoccupied. I saw Carrie nod and come up to the stage. She beckoned. I leaned down.

'Which dress are you wearing tonight?'

'Why?'

'I thought I'd go over and fetch it so you can come back to our house to change for tonight. Much better than the hotel.'

'What did Hamilton want?'

'To know how you are.'

'Why?'

'I have no idea, George. Perhaps she is worried about you. Finding two victims can't be easy. Shall I fetch your dress? Which one is it?'

I made my mind up quickly. She was right and I was grateful she hadn't said "finding two bodies". It would be easier to change at "Vox Celeste" anyway. 'It's the black one with the lace bodice and pink leaf bursts on the skirt. The petticoat should be on the same hanger. Can you bring all the make up and hair stuff as well, please?'

'Consider it done. I'll take it all back to the hotel before the concert for you, along with the stuff you're wearing now.'

'Thanks, Carrie.'

The "Domine Deus" went reasonably well, although, as I had feared, Neil wanted it slower than I did. It's a times like these that I wish I had a portable iron lung. We went back to the house. Carrie helped me change after I'd had a tuna sandwich. We all planned to go out for dinner after the concert. Between us we managed to get my hair up. I wore the new ring, of course and the jet and crystal teardrop necklace and earrings Dad bought me from Whitby. I sat and thought only about the music. I don't know if my nerves were because of the concert, the Scott situation or the fact that Radio 3 was recording me for the first time. I could hear Janetta's voice in my ear telling me to focus, channel that nervous energy into concentration, to listen to what I was singing, be alert, stay alive. Alive. Scott. I dragged my thoughts back to the beginning of the focussing process and started again. I promised myself I would sing the best I knew how.

When I walked on with Neil and Katherine, the applause from the audience was warm, but that from the choir was warmer. I realised that they knew the ins and outs of what was going on. That must be Neil. I shot them a glance, smiled and sat down. At the beginning of the "Laudamus Te", Katherine and I smiled and bowed slightly to each other then it was war with no quarter sought or given. As we finished I wanted to laugh out loud just for the sheer joy of singing.

Neil was a sweetheart and took the "Domine Deus" a little faster than he had in the afternoon. I just concentrated on making that lovely legato line on the runs. I'm a visual singer and to do this, I sing the line whilst mentally looking at golden syrup being poured out of the tin. Seems to work. At the end, we all shared in that one thing which helps singers know why they started on this precarious profession. The applause of people who have enjoyed what we work so hard to make seem so easy. Both Katherine and I turned to the choir and applauded them. Everyone was smiling.

I saw Hamilton standing near the Prior's Door. She was watching me without smiling and I felt that first small hiccup of fear. The one that makes you want to rush to the loo. It was as if there were only us two in the building. I stopped seeing anyone else. I stopped hearing the noise. I walked up to her.

'That sounded lovely,' she began.
'What have you to tell me?'
'I think you should come to the hospital now.'

13

'What have you to tell me?' I repeated after she had closed the door on the passenger seat and climbed behind the wheel.

'I wanted you to get the concert over with first. I wanted you to be able to concentrate on your job. You didn't need to know just yet anyway. Why do you think I kept you away from the hotel? I asked Mrs Gardiner to fetch your dress and keep you occupied.'

I could hardly hear my voice, it was quiet with the sort of rage that takes the breath out of the body and leaves every muscle contracted, including the vocal ones. 'If you don't tell me right now, I shall yank the steering wheel over and crash this fucking car. Now, tell me.'

'Scott's parents are at the hospital,' she replied, checking her rear-view mirror, quite unmoved by my threat. 'They arrived this afternoon. Fortunately they were visiting his sister in Wisconsin, otherwise they wouldn't have arrived until tomorrow. I'll be blunt, Georgia, things don't look too good for Scott, although the surgeon told me it is early days and at least he is stable at the moment.'

I stayed quiet for the rest of the journey. Did the fact that his parents were there mean he was going to be OK or not OK? I felt dizzy but realised it was because I had been holding my breath, so I began to concentrate. Breathe in, hold for four, breathe out, hold for four.

We arrived at the Intensive Therapy Unit. Hamilton nodded to the sister and walked past her to the third bed along from the nurses' station. I followed, feeling stupid in my concert finery, but they didn't ask me to gown up this time. I was surprised. I must have been full of bacteria. There was a tall dark man standing at Scott's side, his hand on the shoulder of a seated lady who I took to be Scott's mother. The tall man turned his head to look at me with those vivid blue eyes I knew so well now. I took an involuntary breath in. This was what Scott would look like twenty five years hence. Hamilton introduced us. We shook hands as if it was a social occasion. Then his father went back to his mother. I stood clinging on to the end of the bed.

'How is he?'

It was Dad who answered. 'He's in a coma. His skull is fractured and that's what they seem most worried about at the moment because they've had to operate to give his brain room to swell. The surgeon said something about intracranial pressure.'

Mrs Wiley had not looked at me apart from a quick glance when I came up to the bed. Now she turned and spoke.

'You must be Georgia. He e-mailed us about you. You seem to have made quite an impression.'

I looked at the figure lying in the bed. 'It was a mutual impression, then.'

His father walked round to where I was standing. 'Can I have a word?'

I was a bit startled. 'Yes, of course. There's a family room. Shall we go there?'

We sat down in the empty family room. It smelt of stale tea and despair. Mr Wiley sat looking at me for a few moments and then Hamilton came in with three cups of coffee. There was an uncomfortable silence.

'Did you want to ask me something, Mr Wiley?' I said.

'Yes. Er, yes I did. Can you tell us what happened?'

'I met Scott on Saturday before the Gerontius concert. He came to my recital on Tuesday and then we went out for afternoon tea. Yesterday morning we talked in the gardens. We both acknowledged the growing attraction between us. We agreed to have breakfast tomorrow morning and go out for the day. I left him in the garden. That was the last I saw of him until I found him in the river.'

'Why were you on the river bank, Miss Pattison?'

I looked at Hamilton who nodded. 'Superintendent Hamilton had asked me to try and find out what I could about the circumstances of Ariana Staithes' death on Saturday night. We had agreed to meet at a picnic site not far from here. The quickest way on foot is by the towpath.'

'That's not for public consumption, by the way, Mr Wiley,' said Hamilton offering him a cup.

'And had you met the Superintendent?' he continued ignoring the cup and keeping those blue eyes firmly fixed on me.

Hamilton interrupted again. She was quicker than I was because I had no idea why his manner was so hostile. 'We had just finished our meeting, Mr Wiley. It was only ten minutes later that Miss Pattison found Scott. There is no way she could be involved in what happened to him.'

'Why not? They could have met and argued. She could have pushed him in the river.' He finally took the cup Hamilton was still holding out to him.

'In that case, Mr Wiley, why did she spend so much time giving Scott CPR? I've spoken to the staff here and they all agree that if she hadn't done that, Scott would not be alive now. Besides which, we are almost sure he was rendered unconscious in the same way as Miss Staithes before he was pushed into the water. When we arrived, there were no signs on Miss Pattison's clothes or hands to indicate that she had been in a disturbance of that kind.'

I put my untasted coffee on the table. 'I think I'd better go.'

Mr Wiley held out a restraining hand. 'No. Please don't. I'm sorry. We're hurt and tired and worried sick. We need to blame someone. I accept that you had nothing to do with what happened to my son. Excuse me. I must get back to my wife.'

Hamilton held out a hand to stop him. 'Mr Wily, nobody knows that Georgia is helping us. She could be in danger if it became public knowledge.'

'Don't, worry,' he said, putting his cup and saucer on the table. 'I won't say a word.'

After he left, I sat and stared at the wall. I didn't understand any of this. Hamilton gave me a few moments before putting her hand on my arm.

'Do you want to stay here or go back to the hotel?'

'May I see him again for a minute? Then, if you could take me back, I'd be grateful.'

'Of course. It's always the innocent who get hurt the most in these cases. I'm sorry. I had no idea you were romantically involved with him.'

'I wasn't. Yet. But it would have been easy for both of us and we knew that. We knew there was no rush. We had plenty of time. Life really is a bowl of toenails sometimes, isn't it?'

'Yes. It's one of the reasons I went into policing.'

'I don't understand.'

She paused for a moment as if to gather her thoughts. 'When I was about fourteen, I read an Agatha Christie Miss Marple book. Can't remember which one now. Miss Marple said that in any sort of crime, it is always the innocent who get hurt because, until the guilty party is known, everyone is under suspicion. I think she quoted a cleaning lady who was suspected of destroying her employer's will. It came to light later hidden in a tea caddy or something, but by then the cleaning lady had died with this suspicion still hanging over her. When I was at school, there was a spate of silly thefts. Stupid things like books and sweets and pens. For a while, suspicion fell on me. I wasn't popular or pretty and I didn't mix with the local kids. But I was quite clever, so I was an easy target. Fortunately, they soon found the real culprit, but I won't ever forget what it felt like, everyone's eye on you, all of them thinking that you are a thief. And there you are knowing that you aren't but being unable to prove it.'

I nodded. 'Proving a negative is usually impossible. I used to have a jealous boyfriend. He questioned everything I did and asked about everyone I spoke to. I call it the "prove you've never walked over the Humber Bridge" syndrome.'

She looked at me, frowning a little.

'OK, Superintendent Hamilton, prove to me that you've never walked over the Humber Bridge.'

'Oh, yes. I see. A good analogy. Anyway, that is why I decided to go into the police force. To do everything I possibly could to lift that weight off innocent people.' She sighed and stood up. 'Do you want to go and say goodnight?'

I stood at the end of Scott's bed again. I didn't know if he wasn't moving because he was sedated or because of the deep coma. I thought I would cry but I didn't. I stood and stared for so long that when I came back to myself I found Scott's parents looking at me with puzzled expressions.

'I'll go now,' I said to them. 'But I will come back tomorrow if that's OK with you.'

'Yes, that's fine. We want to see if we can get him moved somewhere more private.' Mr Wiley reached out a hand and I took it. 'Don't despair, Georgia. Scott is a fighter. He's had to be to get this far in his career. He won't give in easily.'

I gave a tight smile and turned away. The last thing I wanted them to see was my lips trembling. The journey back to the hotel was silent. As the car glided up to the hotel entrance, Hamilton turned her head in my direction.

'Let this be a warning to you, Georgia. The person I'm looking for has no regard for any life but his or her own. Be on your guard at all times.'

I climbed out and bent down to look at her through the open door.

'Don't worry, Superintendent. I shall watch my back. But I'm still going to ask questions.'

'It would be useful,' she admitted. 'They will all want to know what has happened. Perhaps you can use that as a cover for finding out where each of them was.'

'What I want to know is what Scott was doing there on the towpath.'

'That's easy. I think he was suspicious of someone and followed you to make sure you were all right.'

That had not occurred to me. I shut the car door and watched her drive off before walking into the foyer. There were a couple of people who had obviously been at the concert and who gushed all over me for about five minutes. The last thing I wanted was to smile and be gracious and humble, but habit and the acting skills kicked in and I don't think they noticed that what I really wanted was for them to piss off and leave me alone.

I asked the receptionist - it wasn't Rosemary - if she could send up a double brandy to my room. It arrived at the same time I did, so the manager had obviously briefed the staff about jumping to it if I wanted anything. There was a sitting area at the end of each corridor of rooms and I noticed a man in his thirties sitting reading a magazine. He ignored me so completely that I was instantly on my guard. Then I looked at his shoes. Right. Hamilton must really have the wind up about my safety.

Once in the bedroom, I saw that Carrie had brought back my day clothes and the bag of makeup and hair stuff. I took the gunk off my face and brushed out my hair. Then I slipped into the shower to try and let the warm water work its usual calming magic on me. Afterwards I stared at my reflection in the dressing table mirror, took a sip of brandy and pulled my laptop towards me.

It had taken the shower to make me realise that my uppermost feeling was not shock and distress. It was anger. Generally speaking, I am quick to anger and it burns out equally quickly. This feeling was completely different. I didn't feel out of control, or want to hit anyone. I didn't want to shout and stomp about like a six year old. I looked into the mirror.

My face was pale, my lips set in a straight line. I didn't recognise the person who stared out of the eyes. Georgia Pattison didn't go in for revenge. She blew like Krakatoa and then forgot about it. The person looking back at me didn't. She wanted to make someone pay. Pay for making two innocent people lose what might have been.

A line from Emily Dickinson came back to me. "You could not come and yet you go." Her poem was about a stillborn child. For me it was about the relationship Scott and I would probably never enjoy now. I wasn't taken in by the medics and their soothing words. As the daughter of two doctors, how could I be? At best Scott was going to die. At worst he would be a vegetable.

The hotel had free wireless, so I zipped onto the Internet and put fractured skull into the search box. It didn't make happy reading and confirmed my fears. There was a chance that Scott would come out of this unimpaired. Looking at it realistically, it was much more likely that, if he didn't die, he would have some brain damage. But sure as God made little green apples, his career was over. And the waste of that made my anger cold and constant. What could I do?

I loaded up the file on the Ariana murder I had already started and reread it. I turned my memory back and squeezed everything I could remember from it. What people had said; what people had done; when they had done it; who had been where at what time.

I sent down for another brandy. When it came, I turned out the room light, opened the voile curtains and looked out over the now dark cathedral. I pulled a chair near to the window and spent a good half hour just watching people come and go. I've always liked people watching. A singer gets to do a lot of it one way or another, mostly during rehearsals. When I had finished the second brandy, I was faintly surprised to find that I was not in the least ratted.

I closed the curtains, turned the light back on and went back to the laptop. I turned on the mental film of yesterday morning and my various chats. As I watched the re-run unfold in my mind, my fingers were busy tapping out what questions had been asked and how they had been answered.

I had a five page report ready for Hamilton in the morning. I was about to turn off the computer, when a thought struck me. I had brought in my printer from the car, but a few moments thought made me reconsider printing anything. I took a memory stick out of my handbag and saved the report onto it. Then, I took the stick out of the machine, put it back in and reloaded the file just to make sure it wasn't corrupted in any way. It wasn't. I unloaded it from the computer again and put it back in my handbag. I would need to find a better place to keep it. Perhaps it would be better if I carried it round with me until I could unload it onto one of Hamilton's computers.

Once I was sure the file was safely on the stick, I deleted it from the hard drive on my laptop and from the recycle bin. If, as Hamilton had suggested, anyone came nosing into my computer, they would not be able to recover it even if they realised it was there, which they wouldn't. I knew it took advanced techniques to get that sort of information off a hard drive.

I shut the computer down and went to bed. I had already agreed to help Hamilton in order to clear Carrie, but really, up until last night, I had treated it as a bit of a joke. Not any more. I was going to find the person who had knocked out the poor unfortunate door keeper, killed

Ariana and possibly done worse than kill Scott Wiley. I would find them with or without Hamilton. And when I did...

14

Next morning, I was up by six-thirty and out on the riverbank by twenty to seven. The memory stick was safely hidden in the recesses of my bra. I power- walked up the towpath as if doing morning exercises and bent down from time to time ostensibly to do some stretches, but in reality to see if anyone was following me. When I reached the bridge over the river to the picnic area, I lingered leaning on the thin metal rail looking down into the water in the direction of Temingham.

I waited for five minutes, but nobody popped their head above the parapet, so I strode into the picnic area and hoped against hope that Lizzie would walk the dog here and not choose somewhere else. My plan was to jog back to the hotel and arrive looking suitably knackered as if I had actually been on a morning run. This plan did have one flaw. Anyone who knew me at all well would know that exercise and I go together like peaches and three tons of semolina pudding.

I had been jigging about, not wanting to sit on the damp benches for about five minutes before I saw the car pull in. Lizzie looked startled to see me.

'Hello, Georgia, I didn't expect to see you.'

I took the stick out of my bra and handed it to her. 'Could you give that to Miss Hamilton, please, Lizzie? I've written down everything I can remember. Can you also tell her that I will keep on asking questions in the hope that I can nail this bastard. Oh and I need another memory stick. What is on this is the only copy, so please take care of it. Tell her I am deleting the files off my hard drive after I've checked they are on the sticks, so I need another stick to play turnabout with if you see what I mean.'

'Yes, I understand. Don't worry, I'll take care of it.'

The dog was fussing round me and I automatically bent down to pet him. Lizzie laughed.

'He's getting impatient, aren't you Jordy?' She turned to me. 'Why don't you walk with us?'

'I'd love to but I really ought to get back. Go on, boy, off you go.'

The dog needed no second urging. He bounced over the bridge and down the towpath the other side in the direction of some swans.

'He's a beauty, isn't he?' I asked.

Her face clouded over. 'Yes, he is and everyone thinks so except Mick. She just hates dogs and says she's allergic to them. She says he makes a mess everywhere.'

'Strange. She doesn't strike me as the fastidious type.'

'She isn't. She just likes her own way. We've been sharing a house for almost three years and it has taken me until now to get her to agree to even give a dog a trial. But I can be just as bloody-minded as she can and she'll find that out if she isn't careful.'

I watched her determined face and thought that if anyone could stand up to Hamilton, it would be this girl. I glanced across the river at the dog, now standing looking at the swans, his ears up and neck stretched out. His head was rocking from side to side as if he couldn't quite work out what sort of dogs floated on water. Lizzie followed the direction of my eyes.

'I'd better get over there just in case he decides to go for a swim and try to make friends with them. Don't worry, I'll give this and your message to Mick.'

We parted on the town side of the bridge and, as per the plan, I jogged back to the hotel. Jamie was in Reception.

'Hi, George. Don't tell me you've taken up running.'

'I wouldn't call it running, Jamie. It's just so I can enjoy a guilt-free breakfast. Besides, I need to tone up a bit. Some of my dresses are becoming a bit tight.'

'Any morning you want to run with me, just put on your shorts and come along.'

'Thanks. I'll bear it in mind. It's all a bit too sweaty really. I think I might prefer swimming, but I'll stick with this for a few days to see if it grows on me.'

I kept my feet moving whilst we were speaking and waved as I reached the lift. He was grinning at me, pointing towards the stairs. I gave him one of my "drop dead" looks. He laughed and waved a dismissive hand.

Once showered and dressed, I looked in the mirror and decided to put some war-paint on. I was technically free now and I needed to decide how I was going to set about finding my prey. I waited until I was sure Jamie had finished his breakfast before I went down to the dining room.

I was glad that I had told Carrie I would not be going back to "Vox Celeste", but staying in the hotel. It gave me more freedom. She thought I was being tactful. I suffered a few guilty pangs, but soon decided I wasn't breaking the Geneva Convention. Her perception of my sensitivity might also make Neil keen to have me back next year, so that would be a bonus. Besides it looked as if she had gone into "ickle wickle" baby mode and I knew I wouldn't cope with that for long. I'd be throwing up as much as she was.

Nevertheless, I had to keep in with her because there was a chance, albeit a small one, that she was the person I was hunting. I munched my usual melon followed by toast and marmite and thought about Carrie. What points were in her favour? I sat there for a good two minutes before acknowledging that the only thing I could come up with was that she was a woman and there seemed to me to be just too much physicality about the way Ariana and Scott had been attacked for it to be a woman.

It took another moment to realise that I had discounted the fact that she was a friend. But then hadn't Hamilton said that the killer was more than likely to be amongst the people I knew? Right. So, what points were not in her favour? What is it the crime writers say? Method, motive and opportunity. OK. Method. Hamilton had said that Ariana and Scott had been incapacitated quickly.

To me that indicated someone with knowledge. Someone who had been trained in unarmed combat or self defence. That let Carrie out. Or did it? What did I know of her activities in the years since we had shared the St Paul's flat. She certainly had motive and opportunity for Ariana's death, but why would she attack Scott? No, I would continue to defend her to Hamilton, but in truth I couldn't rule her out.

I poured myself another coffee and moved on to Sir Robert Fielding. What did I know about him, apart from the fact that he had been my tutor at the Academy? Sweet Fanny Adams, that's what. I needed to know more. He had turned the conversation away from Ariana's blackmailing activities very adroitly, helped by Merlina's little scene in the dining room.

Merlina. She was another suspect, although the same caveat applied to her as to Carrie and Merlina was older and not as strong. Or was that an assumption? She was still on the circuit at gone fifty five so she must have a lot of stamina and you only get that by regular exercise. I needed to ask her how she kept her figure. That would do it and, of course, she was the perfect person to ask about Sir Robert. I wiped my Marmitey hands on my napkin, swallowed the last of the coffee and almost sprinted out of the dining room.

Rosemary was back on duty. The automatic smile won by a short head over the weaned pickle. I decided I had to be nice to her. Well, there was a first time for everything.

'Hello, Rosemary. I don't know whether anyone has told you but Mr Wiley is still in a coma, although he seems to be holding his own. His parents have arrived.'

'Thank you for telling me, Miss Pattison.' The smile faltered a little and went out. 'Have they found the person who did it?'

'No, not yet, but I am sure they will. Did you know him well?'

'We went to the Black Cat for tea and a scone. I thought he liked me, but then he took you so I think perhaps he was just being kind.'

Either that or trying to get into your knickers, dear. 'Yes, he is a kind man,' I said aloud. 'Have Mr and Mrs Wiley booked a room here, by any chance?'

'I'm not allowed to tell you,' she replied looking steadily at me, but her head shook a slow negative. I smiled back at her. 'Actually, Rosemary, the person I am really looking for is Miss Meredith. I want to make sure she has recovered from her upset the other morning.'

'I heard her say that she was going over to the cathedral this morning. She had breakfast with Dr Carter.'

'That's fine. Thank you. I was going over there myself.' I walked a few steps away, then returned. 'I shall be going to the hospital today. Would you like me to keep you posted about Scott?'

She bent down and picked a white envelope from under the counter. 'Oh, yes, please. Could you give him this? It's a get well card.'

I was touched and my throat constricted for a moment. I took the proffered envelope. 'Of course I will. It was lovely of you to think of him. I'll make sure it is where he can see it when he wakes up.'

As I walked out of the hotel, my brain was saying "if he wakes up, you mean" and, once outside I had to stand still, my hand on my chest as if that would stop the bongo drums my heart was playing. It took a few seconds before my inner voice told me to get a grip. This was no good. I couldn't afford to let this happen every time I thought of Scott. I had to put him in a mental box and shut the lid tight, otherwise I would be useless. I've had to do this exercise many times, so before I opened the north door of the cathedral, Scott was safely in the box and the lid was nailed down.

I checked my watch. Just on ten. The choir was already seated. Members of the orchestra were strolling into their designated area under the tower in dribs and drabs. The lead 'cellist was changing a string as if he had all the time in the world, which, in reality, he did. I smiled. Neil was standing on a large box about eight inches high ready to start the rehearsal, but fiddling with his score as if he wasn't ready at all. I reflected that had the conductor been someone else, say of international standing, the orchestra would have been all present and correct and the 'cellist would have been changing his string faster than the speed of sound.

It was a little while before I spotted Merlina. She was sitting with Tom Carter halfway down the nave. I noticed that further down the nave near the Prior's Door, Hamilton was talking with a man I had never seen before. He was gesticulating at the west end staging behind me and I could see that he was wearing a clerical collar. Hamilton saw me but made no acknowledgement. I ignored her, too. I walked up to the row of seats behind Merlina and her attentive doctor. She turned and smiled when she saw me.

'Hello, Georgia. I thought you'd be long gone. You don't have any more concerts, do you? Are you staying for Scott?'

'I want to stay until at least Monday to see how he is. But I don't know if the police will let me go yet. Besides isn't there a memorial service for Ariana in the offing? I ought to stay for that.'

'Why ever wouldn't the police let you go? You're one of the ones in the clear.'

I couldn't fathom why her voice had that bitter edge to it. 'Don't tell me they suspect you, Merlina.'

'I think that stupid Hamilton woman suspects everyone.'

'That's her job. I'm lucky. I was in full view of everyone when it happened.'

'Yes, so I gather.'

There was an uncomfortable silence. 'Well, I'd better get up there and do my performing monkey act,' she said eventually. 'Hadn't you better get to your seat, Tom.'

'When are you going to tell him?'

'This morning after the rehearsal.'

'Do you want me to be there?'

She considered. 'It might help, yes.'

'See you later, then.'

He rose to his feet, nodded to me and strode off towards the choir. Merlina looked after him, smiling.

'Do you mind if I stop, Merlina?' I asked. 'I love "Sea Pictures".'

She looked at me as if she had forgotten I was there. 'Yes, of course you can, darling. Do you know the Rutter spirituals?'

'No, I've not come across them.'

'You'll love them. This concert will be a perfect swan-song. Elgar and Rutter; a lovely combination.'

'I knew there was something in the air. Is it to do with Dr Carter?'

'Yes, in a way. Look, Georgia, I have to speak to Robert after rehearsal, but I shall be free this afternoon. Tom has to do a baby clinic or something. Let's meet up for a cup of tea at the Maddox. I need to talk to you.'

'OK. Fine. How would three suit you?'

'Perfect. Are you going to the hospital today?'

'Probably. I have to ring first to see if it is convenient and he isn't having tests and things.'

Her face clouded over. 'We're haunted by that whore, aren't we. It's as if she is still messing with our lives from beyond the grave. Tangled webs, Georgia. Tangled webs.'

She picked up her score and walked towards the orchestra. I was glad because I didn't have a clue what she was on about. I sat down and looked towards Neil. He was talking in a concentrated way to the man with the dog collar who had been with Hamilton. They both nodded a few times then the dog collar clapped his hands.

'May I have your attention, please, ladies and gentlemen?'

I admired his authority. Silence fell like a blanket of midnight snow. 'I have spoken to Superintendent Hamilton. She has told me that the police have finished with the west end of the cathedral and that we can go back to it, with immediate effect.'

There was a round of applause and a small cheer. Dog collar put up his hand. 'However, because of what happened, we feel the need to cleanse that part of the cathedral. Now, I have spoken to Mr Masterson and we think we can do this quickly and quietly, which I am sure you will all agree would be a good idea.'

There were murmurs of agreement. 'So,' he continued, 'if you would all move back to the west end and take your usual places, we need to sing a hymn and say a few prayers, then I can let you get on with your rehearsal. Does that meet with your approval?' I don't know why he asked because he was going to do it anyway. 'I have asked the stewards to give everyone in the choir a hymn book.' He looked at his watch. 'Ten-fifteen. Can you all be ready to go in fifteen minutes?'

The choir superintendent rose to her feet. 'Of course, Dean.' She turned to the choir. 'Please make your way quietly to the platform. Altos and tenors first, then basses and sopranos. Come along.' She clapped her hands as if they were trained dogs, but I admired her because they all turned round in obedience and started making their way towards the west end. It was Neil who stopped them.

'Just a moment, Helen. Can some of the gentlemen take the orchestra's music stands to the stage, please? They can't carry the stands and their instruments.'

It all looked like chaos for a while. I decided to be helpful and grabbed hold of a couple of music stands and carried them to the stage at the other end of the cathedral. Neil looked a little surprised to see me, but nodded and smiled his thanks. I plonked the stands in roughly the right place and then wandered over to where he was arranging his music on the podium stand.

'Hi, Neil. How's Carrie doing?'

'She's fine, thanks, George.'

'I hope you don't mind me not stopping with you, but I think it's a time when you need to be alone and be able to plan the big event.'

His face had darkened momentarily until he understood that I was not referring to his behaviour, but to his coming child, at which point the smile came out in full force and I began to understand what Carrie saw in him.

'Thanks, George. We appreciate it. But you're welcome to stay with us whenever you want.'

I nodded and smiled. Not the time to push my luck trying to get an invite for next year's festival. 'Sure thing. I'll let you get on.'

'Stay for the first bit, won't you?' He saw my expression. 'You had the worst shock finding her. It might settle a few ghosts if you stay, don't you think?'

'Yes, you're right, Neil. I will. Thanks. Shall I perch with the choir?'

'Might as well.' He called to the sopranos finding their places. 'Ladies, have you room for a little one?'

I looked towards them. The Footlight Fanny who had been forced to give up her seat for Gerontius was glaring at me. 'Don't worry,' I said, waving at her. 'It doesn't matter where I sit.'

I ended up on the second row because of someone who was unable to make the rehearsal. True to his word, the Dean was precisely on time. I was going to say dead on time, but that would be inappropriate. He said a few words about Ariana and we prayed for her and Scott as well as for the cleansing of the building. He talked briefly about evil and the ripples it made and how they could spread outwards if they weren't checked. We said the twenty-third psalm and sang "Thy hand, O God, has guided". I'm not particularly religious, but I honestly felt when I sang the words "They mercy will not fail us, Nor leave thy work undone; With thy right hand to help us, The victory shall be won", that some power beyond my understanding was talking directly to me.

I had not even planned to go into the cathedral until Rosemary said Merlina was there. It was uncanny and more than a bit scary, but I felt somehow that I was being given divine blessing to carry on the quest, find the murderer and deliver him or her up to justice.

15

    As the rehearsal proper began, I slipped down the stairs I had walked down almost a week before to find out why Ariana had not come back onto the platform. I'd already decided that I needed to exorcise that particular ghost.

    At the bottom of the steps there was no sign that Ariana had ever been lying on the floor. It wasn't until that moment that I realised I had been holding my breath. Letting it out slowly, I made my way into the nave of the cathedral where the stewards and helpers were already turning the chairs round to face the stage again and sat on the south aisle side not far from the Priors Door. I stayed long enough to hear the beginning of John Rutter's "Feel the Spirit" and then slipped out of the door and into the cloisters. I had to find Hamilton.

    Fortunately, she was in her eyrie. I asked her if she had found out what hold Ariana had over Sir Robert Fielding.

    'I asked him, naturally, but it isn't anything that's relevant to her murder.'

    'Humour me. I'm nosy. What was it?'

    'Apparently, in her first year, she offered to sleep with him if he would get her the understudy at Covent Garden and when he said no, she threatened to tell the papers that he had seduced her.'

    'Did she really think that anybody would believe that?'

    'A lot of people would. Enough to lose him his job, perhaps.'

    'What happened?'

    'He told her that he had no pull with Covent Garden.'

    'What made her think he had?'

    'I asked him that. He shrugged his shoulders and said he didn't know.'

    'Do you believe him?'

    She looked up at me, face alert. 'Is there any reason I shouldn't believe him.'

    'Plenty. He was a professor in the piano faculty. Ariana would know better than most that he had nothing to do with the Garden. I wonder if he was her piano tutor. If he wasn't, then there would be no reason why they would ever come into contact with each other. I don't think she would even know of his existence.'

'Any way you could find out for me?'

'Possibly. He's on my list of people to have a natter with, go over the old days. Leave it with me. Have you downloaded my file from the memory stick?'

She fished in her jacket pocket and held it out to me. 'Don't go to meet Lizzie every day. Somebody might get wise to what you are doing. Go out every morning at the same time, by all means, but not always in the same direction.'

'What about the reports you want?'

'Write them directly onto the stick and just keep it with you, or hide it somewhere very very safe.'

'Will do. I need to have chats with the jolly green giant and Merlina as well as Sir Robert.'

She stopped what she was about to say and looked enquiringly at me. 'Jolly green giant?'

I blushed. I'd spoken without thinking. 'Whoops. It's what I privately call Ariana's husband, Tony something.'

She didn't smile but I could have sworn her lips twitched. 'Labinski, and I shouldn't let him hear you call him the jolly green giant. Have you rung the hospital this morning?'

She must have seen the alarm spring into my face. 'No, don't worry. He's still the same. I don't expect that will change much, either.'

I bent over putting the memory stick in my bag, my hair falling like a curtain so that she could not see my expression. The lid of the mental box I had nailed down came loose a little and the hopeless misery threatened, but I wasn't going to let it take over. I snapped my bag shut and took a deep breath.

'I can't agree with you there, Superintendent. If I thought that, then there would be no point in any of this, would there?'

'No, I can see why you might think that. It's the difference in our experiences of life, isn't it?'

'What do you mean by that?'

'You probably still think hope springs eternal. I know better.'

I was annoyed and showed it. 'You mean, you think you know better than anyone else?'

'I didn't say that.'

'No, but you meant it, didn't you. Like you know better than to let your poor niece have a dog?'

'I don't think that's any of your concern, Miss Pattison.'

'You're right. It isn't. I feel sorry for her, but even sorrier for you.'

She planted the tree trunks more firmly into the floor. 'And what do you mean by that?'

'You might just find yourself on your own if you're not careful. When people feel strongly about something, it's a mistake to think that you can bulldoze them into your point of view. See you.' I gave her no chance to reply, but turned round and negotiated the steps down to the cloisters.

I pushed open the Priors Door as quietly as I could. There was one bit of the bottom of it which caught on the tiled floor and made a noise like a very flatulent elephant. I slid through before it reached the sticking point and tip-toed to a nearby seat. Merlina had just begun "Deep River" and I let the music wash over me. Generally speaking I am not a fan of spirituals, but this was just wonderful and her voice was so rich and full it carried me away. The choir's rendition of "When the Saints" made me want to get up and dance. I made an instant decision that I had to come to the concert.

At the end, Neil gave the choir some last minute instructions and then asked them to leave as quietly as they could. Merlina came down to where she had left her jacket. I slipped up behind her.

'That was fantastic, Merlina.'

She swung round. 'Told you you'd like them. Are you stopping for the Elgar?'

'No. But I am definitely coming to the concert.'

She caught hold of my arm. 'I'd like that very much. It's the last time you will hear me sing.'

'What? How come?'

'Tell you this afternoon, but, til then, just keep it to yourself. Promise?'

'Of course. I'll see you later.'

I was about to walk away when Merlina looked over my shoulder and put her hand on my arm. I looked round to see Sir Robert Fielding making his way towards us. He was looking at Merlina as if she was a flighty cat and he was not sure if he was about to be clawed.

'Hang on and give me moral support, Georgia, please,' she muttered out of the corner of her mouth.

'Problems?' I breathed back infected by the sudden tension in her voice.

'Could be and Tom was supposed to be here to help. Where are they when you need them?'

'Usually at the pub.'

She laughed. Sir Robert reached us. He nodded to me and turned to Merlina.

'You wanted to talk to me, Merlina?'

'Yes. Do you mind if Georgia stays? And I think Neil needs to be here, too.'

'That sounds ominous. What's the problem?' The old man waved at Neil to join them. He came up to us frowning, his antennae alert for trouble.

'What's wrong? Hi, George.'

Merlina took a deep breath. 'Tonight is my last concert. You'll have to find someone to stand in for the Nelson Mass tomorrow. "Sea Pictures" will be my last public performance.'

To say that they were staggered does not even come close. I was staggered, too. I put my arm round her, but she continued to stare at the two men.

Sir Robert found his tongue first. 'But, Merlina, you're our star turn. You can't let us down like this.'

'I'm not letting you down, Robert. I am retiring as of tonight. And it's nice of you to say I'm your star turn, especially as we all know how much you both championed Ariana. However, the plain fact is that my doctor says it is all too much for me. He won't hear of me continuing.'

'Do you mean Tom Carter?' asked Neil.

'Yes. He and I have been seeing quite a bit of each other over the past few days and he says I am under too much strain to continue. He is quite adamant, but he has consented, with reluctance, to let me go out with the Elgar.'

'Sir Robert tried again. 'But we need your stature and presence, Merlina darling.'

'What a shame you didn't consider that my stature and presence was good enough for Gerontius, knowing full well that it would probably have been my last chance to sing it. You know I would have jumped at the chance. But no, you wanted a jumped-up trollop who hadn't proved herself.'

I squeezed her arm. 'Calm down, Merlina.'

She was glaring at the two men, her fists clenched. She breathed deeply for a few seconds. 'And you were right,' she went on in a more tranquil tone. 'She was very good. She made me realise that I am getting too old and too tired for all this, so, in a way, gentlemen, you are hoist with your own petard. Had I sung Gerontius, I wouldn't have dreamed of retiring, because Ariana would not have had the opportunity to show me so very clearly that I am past it.'

'That's just not true, Merlina,' said Neil quietly. 'How can you say that when you have just sung the Rutter so movingly?'

She smiled at him. 'It is lovely music, but not in the same league as Gerontius is it? I shall enjoy tonight and then I shall retire. And please don't tell me you can't get a replacement because there must be a queue of people ready, willing and able to sing the Haydn at the drop of a hat. The agency will know where to find one. Tell them I must pull out owing to ill health. I am sure Tom will give you a medical certificate if you want one.'

'Of course I will,' said a deep voice. None of us had seen Tom Carter. He turned to Merlina. 'Sorry, I didn't think you were going to speak to Sir Robert until after the rehearsal.'

'No matter, Tom. Georgia was here.'

He looked at me and grinned. 'Ah, another patient. Hope you're feeling better.' He turned to Neil. 'Sorry, Neil, Sir Robert, but Merlina's blood pressure thinks it's the cost of living. It isn't a good idea for her to continue, but if you want to get another medical opinion, by all means, go ahead.'

Realising the futility of argument, Sir Robert shook his head. 'I'll talk to the agency. It really is a pity, though, Merlina. You sang the Blount wonderfully. Perhaps you just need a long rest. You still have a lot to offer.' He stopped in thought for a moment. 'Would you consider coming back to do some masterclasses for future festivals?'

'That's a great idea,' cut in Neil.

'I think I might like that,' replied Merlina.

'You don't need to think about it now,' insisted Tom. 'Have you finished?'

'I just need to run through the songs and I'm done. If it's going to be my last performance, I'd better make it a good one.'

'I'll come back later, then. I don't want to spoil my anticipation for tonight. How long will you be?'

'I think we only need to top and tail and do odd bits, really. It's not as if we don't all know it.'

'I will just need to check your speeds with some of it,' said Neil. 'Let's say, forty minutes. Does that sound OK with you, Merlina?'

She nodded and they walked off together towards the stage, leaving Sir Robert, Tom and I standing in a silent circle. Tom said goodbye to us and walked out of the north door. As if by mutual consent, Sir Robert and I walked back down the nave towards the Priors Door.

'Do you fancy a quick coffee, Sir Robert? The cloisters tea bar does a nice latte. And lemon drizzle cake.'

'I could do with something, certainly, after that shock. I need to ring the agency and get a stand-in.'

'I'm sure that will keep for half an hour. Come on, I'll stand you a coffee.'

'Well that was a turn up for the books,' I said as we sat down with two cups of coffee and, I am ashamed to say, a large slice of lemon drizzle cake.

'You could put it that way. I never thought Merlina would retire.'

'Yes, when unexpected things happen you have to re-jig your opinions on people, don't you?'

He looked at me, frowning a little through the steam from his coffee. 'I don't quite understand you, Georgia. What do you mean?'

'Well, it seems to me that Ariana's murder has brought all sorts of things creeping out of the woodwork, doesn't it? Did you see that note that someone sent Merlina? The one that gave her the screaming habdabs?'

'No. Did you?'

'Oh, yes. It didn't go so far as to accuse her of killing Ariana, but it did question her innocence. I think that the letter, together with Ariana singing so brilliantly and Tom Carter coming on the scene are responsible for her retirement.'

'But that's silly. Nobody with an ounce of sense would think she would kill Ariana Staithes.'

'Everybody knows they hated each other.'

'It's still ridiculous. I'm not keen on some of my fellow professors, but I wouldn't dream of murdering them. I doubt if Merlina would be strong enough, for a start.'

I opened my mouth to say that strength was not an issue, that it was more a question of knowing where to hit someone, but shut it hurriedly. After all, he may have been a sweetheart at college, but he equally might be responsible for killing Ariana and attacking Scott. He saw my hesitation and asked what the matter was. 'If things had gone according to plan, Scott and I would be at Chatsworth at this moment,' I said thinking quickly. 'It's a place I've always wanted to see.'

'Well why don't you save it until he's better and then go? It will give you something to look forward to.'

I was shocked that he'd either not heard or hadn't realised how serious Scott's condition was. 'They can't tell at the moment, but it is likely that he may never come out of the coma.'

'I've never trusted the medical profession and I suggest you don't let them fill you full of doom and gloom. Let's talk about something else.'

'There was one thing I wanted to ask you. Tell me to mind my own business if you like, but why was Ariana Staithes blackmailing you?'

He looked at me for several moments. 'I would like to tell someone and I think I can trust to your discretion.'

'Is it something you are ashamed of?'
'Yes, I suppose I am. I've carried it with me for over thirty years.'
'Only tell me if you want to,' I said, silently praying tell me, tell me.

It would be that moment that Hamilton chose to but in. I don't know how long she had been standing there, but I became aware of a shadow to my left and when I looked round, she had planted herself behind me. Sir Robert looked up in alarm.

'Superintendent, you startled me.'

'Me, too,' I added opening my eyes wide and giving her my best innocent look. She ignored me completely.

'Would you mind coming up to the library, Sir Robert?'

'Yes, I would. Even Edmund Hillary would have thought twice about climbing those stairs. Can't you say what you have to say here?'

I pushed my chair back, but he motioned me to stay sitting. 'I'm sure you can say what you have to say in front of Georgia.'

'I think it might be better if she went, Sir Robert.'

'If it's what I think it is, Superintendent, then I would rather she stayed.'

'Why?'

'Moral support perhaps.'

I butted in. 'I seem to be doing a lot of moral support this morning. If it's OK with you, Superintendent, I'll stay.' And I sat back down and pulled the chair into the table.

Hamilton seemed to find it difficult to make up her mind. In the end, she pulled out a third chair and sat between us. 'We've found a letter in Miss Staithes things back at the hotel.'

He looked at her. 'That's taken you a long time to find.'

'It was in a secret drawer in her jewellery box. One of my officers found it last night and handed it to me this morning.'

'And what does it have to do with me?'

She glanced at me as if still unsure whether to carry on. 'Don't mind me, Superintendent,' I said in my brightest tone. 'At the moment, I think the game is at thirty all.'

'Behave, Georgia,' said the old man.

'Sorry.'

'Go on, Superintendent. You were telling me about a letter.' He said turning back to Hamilton.

'It's from a firm of solicitors. Enclosed in it is a letter from Miss Staithes' mother to her, marked "to be opened after my death".'

'And which you have presumably opened.'

'Yes. I wonder if you know what it says.'

'Oh, I think I can hazard a guess,' he said. His voice was quite even, but his face had lost colour. I reached over and put my hand on his without even thinking about it.

'What is it Alan Bennett's play says about the air being black with the feathers of the chickens coming home to roost?' he said with a deep sigh.

Neither of us said anything. He sighed again and put his napkin on the table. 'I imagine, Superintendent, that it says I am Ariana's biological father.'

16

There are moments when I know what I have heard but I still can't assimilate it. This was one of those. I looked at Sir Robert, not just because it was as if I was seeing him for the first time, but I wanted to see if I could see anything of Ariana in him. I couldn't. He had sagged a little in his chair and his fingers were ghosting a few arpeggios on the table.

'I've known for some time that this would come out sooner or later,' he began. 'I received an identical letter when Ariana's mother died. I knew that Ariana had received one and I'd been expecting some sort of reaction from her. She didn't disappoint me.'

'But you admit that she was trying to blackmail you?'

'Yes.'

'Would you like to tell us about it?'

'Not really, no, but I expect I must. When I was young, just after I came to London to study at the Academy, I fell in love with my landlady's daughter. At that time, I did not have enough money to marry and, well, to be blunt, she was not the sort of girl you took home to meet your mother, but I was in love with her.'

I saw Hamilton frown, but she said nothing and Sir Robert carried on. 'To cut a long story short, Rose became pregnant. She died giving birth to a little girl. Rose's mother took on the child. We called her Hannah. I visited as often as I could. During the birth, something had happened to Hannah. She was severely disabled and in a wheelchair. I would go to take her out to the park every Sunday. Ariana saw us there, Rose's mother, Hannah and me one Sunday about thirteen years ago. She somehow ferreted out the truth. She decided that she needed introductions to people in power. I refused. She threatened to go to the press. But then Hannah caught pneumonia and died.

Ariana threatened me again, but I was past caring and this time I lost my temper. I told her that if even a whisper reached the press, I would contact every opera house in the world and tell them never to hire her.

At that time, I was doing a lot of touring and recording when I wasn't teaching. I told her that managements would accept my word over a nobody like her. She believed me. Then, last year, her mother died and we both received the letter.'

'And that's the truth?' Hamilton was still frowning.

'Yes. It doesn't matter now. Rose's mother died two years ago. The only person who can be hurt by Hannah's story is me and I am past caring.'

I looked at his sunken cheeks and the hand that trembled a little as he lifted his cup to his mouth and wondered. The story seemed very thin and contrived to me. I think it did to Hamilton as well, but she let it go.

'Why didn't you tell me the truth before?'

'Because it has nothing to do with Ariana's murder and nothing to do with anyone but me. Certainly not you, Superintendent.'

'What about you being Miss Staithes' real father? Don't tell me that has nothing to do with me, either.'

He lifted his head. 'Personally, I don't think it does. It's just another unhappy episode in my life and, by the way, my wife knows nothing of it and I would like to keep it that way.'

'Then persuade me that it is irrelevant, Sir Robert.'

I sat as still as I could. The news that he was not a widower put his furtive behaviour with Lady Barbara into quite a different light. I was shocked by how much I had assumed about him and how little I knew, but right now, I was more concerned with making sure that both of them to forgot I was there. It would have been torture to have been forced to leave at this moment. Thankfully, they seemed intent on each other.

'When I received the letter originally, I was unsure about whether or not it was true, but I think it probably was,' he said. 'I need to start with Daniel Wintergreen. You won't have heard of him, and that is the fault of me and Amanda Hughes, Ariana's mother. Dan and I were best friends. I still believe he would have been greater than Dupre or Tortelier. We used to dream.' He lifted his arm as if spelling out the words on a banner. "Murray conducts Wintergreen. The definitive Elgar Cello Concerto."

You see, we knew it would happen. We were so sure. And then Dan went to a party and met Amanda Hughes. She was a singer trying to break into the profession. She sang solos for small amateur groups and local recitals, you know the sort of thing, but much to her chagrin, she had never made the big time as they say. Anyway, back to the party. Dan had never been interested in women before, so he fell from a greater height than most of us. He was besotted by her, but she was just - what's the word? - just entertained by his adoration."

'Like her daughter, in fact,' suggested Hamilton.

'Not in the same way. The daughter was single-minded in that she would bed anyone who was useful to her. She used people quite cynically. Amanda was more like a butterfly. If the man was useful, so much the better, but she never bedded anyone she didn't like.'

'To thine own self be true,' I murmured without thinking.

Sir Robert turned towards me. 'What? Oh. Yes, I suppose so.'

'Please go on, Sir Robert,' said Hamilton, scowling at me.

'Well, to cut a long story short, Dan and Amanda were engaged within a month of meeting. I had been touring with the Chicago Symphony Orchestra that summer, as Assistant Conductor, so I didn't meet her until about a month before the wedding day.

It was at another party, and she looked dazzling. When she heard that I'd secured a five year guest contract with Chicago, she made a play for me. From that moment she worked to add me to her collection. Her passion for Dan diminished by the day and he was so unhappy. He knew, of course, that it was me she had set her sights on, so I told him I would go back to America immediately. I was quite sure that once I was out of sight, I would be out of mind."

'Didn't it work?' asked Hamilton, seemingly caught up in the story.

'Dan begged me to reconsider, but I told him that I knew his happiness was centred in her, and his happiness was the most important thing to me. We hugged. We were both too emotional to speak, you see.'

'How very difficult for you,' I said, squeezing his hand.

'I don't mind admitting that I was attracted to her, but my friendship for Dan was much more important to me. On the night before I flew to the States, she came to me with what she called a proposition. If I would…' Sir Robert's voice trailed off into silence.

Hamilton leaned back in her chair. 'If you would go to bed with her, she would marry your friend, yes?'

'Yes. She was very persuasive. You can guess what happened, can't you? She must have told him. I left on schedule, and the next thing I knew was that their engagement had been broken off. Daniel Wintergreen had retired from his budding musical career, and disappeared from London.

I came home as soon as I could, of course. I traced him to his uncle's farm near Melrose in the Borders. Dan was helping him to work the farm. I tried to persuade him to come back to London with me. He never said a word to me, Superintendent, not one syllable. Instead, he walked into the farmhouse and came out with his 'cello'. He burned it in front of me, kicked the ashes and walked back to the barn. He turned at the door spoke one sentence, and then went into the barn, shutting the door behind him.

We never spoke again. I came back to London and tried to trace Amanda, but the only thing I could find out was that she had gone to Canada. Until I received a duplicate of that letter, I knew nothing more of her, not even her married name.'

There was a small silence after he had finished speaking. 'And do you believe, Sir Robert, that after one night of, shall we say, passion, she became pregnant?'

'Superintendent, I have no idea, but it does happen and, as I say, the dates tally.'

'But surely she was sleeping with your friend as well?'

'Actually no, she wasn't. Dan didn't believe in sex before marriage, and she was so intent on adding me to her conquests, that I am fairly sure she was not bedding anybody else.'

'Ah! I think I see. Well, thank you, Sir Robert. At the moment, I can see no reason why this should be made public.'

The old man rose to his feet. 'Thank you. Now, I must go and get a replacement for Merlina. Really, this festival is jinxed.' He walked off towards the chapter house.

'Poor old bugger,' said Hamilton in a soft tone I had not previously heard.

'Sympathy, Superintendent? That isn't like you.'

'You don't know what is like me, Georgia, so don't tread in places where a mine might blow your leg off.' She pushed back her chair and walked off without saying goodbye.

I sat back and thought over the past ten minutes. Quite frankly, I didn't believe a word of it. So, what was it that Sir Robert was hiding? More to the point, where had he been when Ariana was killed? And no way could I believe that Ariana had not made use of the fact that she was his daughter. Unless, of course, she was saving it for a rainy day.

I pondered how to find out what he was hiding. The lemon drizzle cake was sitting rather more heavily than I had anticipated so I decided to skip lunch and wait for afternoon tea with Merlina. In the meantime, I wondered back through the cathedral and into the shop.

It always makes me smile that Jesus threw the money lenders out of the temple but if the church authorities did the same with their gift shops, most of our cathedrals would be closer to falling down than they are. There was the usual array of postcards, key rings, stationery and the like, but I did come across a couple of really attractive bookmark cross-stitch kits. I don't get the chance to indulge this hobby much, but I could slip these into my overnight bag, do them on trains, although sadly, not on aircraft any more.

With my purchases in a small paper bag that fitted into my jacket pocket, I decided the day was sunny and warm enough for a walk down the river bank, but this time, I decided to go the other way, further into the town and see what delights were on offer. Of course, to get to the towpath, I had to go back through the cloisters. It was only when I was approaching the outside door that I thought again about Lady Barbara's strange behaviour. I swore inwardly when I realised that I had completely forgotten to put it in my report. Subsequent events had wiped it from my memory.

I pulled out the small notebook and pen and made a note to let Hamilton know of it. I needed something to lean on, so I moved to one of the stone carrels that the monks had used when they did their copying.

I was out of immediate sight of anyone. I heard a door open further along the cloister and peeped round the stone pillar. It was Hamilton and a red-faced young man who, by his age, demeanour and uniform, I took to be a lowly constable. Hamilton appeared to be giving him the ear-bending of all time. Her voice remained quiet so I couldn't hear any words, but his face told me that he wasn't the most popular guy on the planet as far as she was concerned. She must have dismissed him because he straightened up and for a moment I thought he was going to click his heels together.

She spun round and marched in my direction. I ducked back out of sight pretending that I had seen nothing. She couldn't help but see me as she yomped past. 'What are you doing here?'

I looked round as if startled and swallowed at her expression. 'I was just writing something down I'd remembered so that I could tell you.'

Her expression changed and the voice softened. 'Something useful?'

'Don't know.' I told her what had happened and I could see that she had mentally filed it under "pending".

'You know him better than I do. What did you think to his story?'

'To paraphrase Gilbert, I thought it was a bald and unconvincing narrative.'

'Inventive, though.'

'Superintendent, Major Armstrong's story of making up small packets of arsenic to kill individual dandelions was inventive but it was still a pack of lies.'

'Major Armstrong?'

'You must know your own profession's history, surely. Do you read at all?'

'Don't find a lot of time for reading.'

'1922. Hay-on-Wye, where all the bookshops are. Only solicitor to have been hanged for murdering his wife. With arsenic.'

'Interesting. What are you doing now?'

'Going for a walk. How about you?'

'Something's come up. I need some wide open spaces. I have to think.'

I walked out of the door and into the cathedral close with her. She stomped off to her car and I turned towards the river. The walk was lovely and I discovered a cotton mill, now converted into units for those quirky new-age sort of things like crystals, aromatherapy and modern silver jewellery.

When I had finished looking round it, it was gone half past two and my stomach was beginning to think my throat had been cut, so I walked back to the hotel and sat waiting for Merlina in the lounge. She came downstairs at three, and did her gracious diva smile to a few of the people in reception who recognised her.

'Hello, Georgia darling. Have you been waiting long?'

'No, not really. I was just people watching. You know, you could teach Rosemary a lot about smiling.'

'Oh, you mean the weasel-faced girl on reception?' She saw the shock on my face. 'Come on, child, she is.'

'Yes, I know, but it's usually me that says things like that, not you.'

'Ah, but I am retiring, so now I can say all the things I think, instead of just smiling and saying nothing.'

'You surprise me, Merlina. I've always seen you as walking around in a cloud of serenity.'

'For somebody as bright as you, Georgia, sometimes you are so blind. I can mix it with the best of them when I need to. I just don't choose to. It's far too tiring. Far better to smile. Apart from causing you less anxiety, it makes everyone wonder what you know that they don't. Keeps them on their toes.'

I was still laughing at this when the waitress came over to take our order. Merlina just ordered tea, but then she'd had lunch with Tom. I had missed lunch, so I ordered a sandwich and a scone. We chatted for a while until the waitress had been and gone with our order. I tucked in. Tuna mayo was one of my favourites, but then quite a lot of things are my favourites. Merlina sipped her tea with the same sort of delicacy that embodied how she moved and even how she sang. She watched me over the rim of her cup.

'Darling, nobody is going to come and snatch it off your plate. There's no need to eat as if you'd been stuck in the Sahara for a week existing on beetles.'

I blushed. Very few people can make me feel like an ignorant schoolgirl, but Merlina did that afternoon. I quickly swallowed the mouthful I was chewing.

'You said you wanted to talk to me, Merlina.'

'Yes, I did. First of all, how is Scott?'

'He was about the same last night. I'm not ringing until later, then I thought if it was all right, I'd go and see him before your concert. Why?'

'You two have obviously hit it off.'

'Yes.' I could feel my back starting to bristle.

'Don't get yourself in a knot, Georgia. You know that Tom and I have also hit it off, don't you?'

I grinned. 'Yes, and I'm really happy for you. Is it the real thing?'

'She considered for a moment. 'Well, don't kid yourself that you don't still get the butterflies you get at your age when you get to my age. But, yes, I think it is. It all seems right, the timing, the feelings, everything. Does that sound stupid?'

'Not at all. Why have you never jumped before?'

'Because I thought my singing career was more important than any relationship and that's really why I want to talk to you. I'm lucky, Georgia. I haven't gone on and on until I'm too old and decrepit to hold a note for longer than two beats and had to be eased out. I'm going out on a high. For someone like Ariana, Temingham was just a stepping stone to La Scala and the rest. To me, it is a fitting place to end my career, singing to people who still think I am good enough to pay the ticket price to hear. Being able to go out with "Sea Pictures" is a bonus.'

'What are you trying to tell me, Merlina?'

'I suppose not to be so focussed on your career that you forget your personal happiness. I've discovered in the last week that I wasn't a complete person. Tom has started that process.'

'Do you think you will do the masterclasses Sir Robert mentioned?'

'Possibly. I shall concentrate on doing the things I haven't been able to for the past thirty odd years. You see, Georgia, what I'm really trying to say is that I think the career would have been enough for Ariana, but it won't be for you.'

'You think she would have gone to the top, then?'

'Oh yes. And I owe her, and Sir Robert a debt of gratitude that they made me see the truth about myself.'

'I don't understand.'

'You know how well she sang the angel. It was better than I have ever done it and for a while I was considered to be the quintessential Gerontius angel. When I heard her sing the "Softly and gently", I realised that I could never sing it again because it would never be good enough. It was a bitter moment, I can tell you. It made me cry.'

'Merlina, how awful. What did you do?'

'I slipped out into the cloisters. I didn't want to be seen blubbing like a child. I sat on one of the stone benches near the Priors Door. I just wanted to be alone, but even that small desire was not to be.'

I pricked up my ears, but kept my tone casual. 'Who was there?'

'That nice wife of Neil's. I saw her walk through the door from the cathedral close into the cloisters.'

'Carrie? I thought she was in the audience.'

'I don't know darling. All I can tell you is that whilst I was snuffling into my handkerchief, she came through the door. I don't think she knows I saw her. I kept my head down.'

'What happened?'

'She stopped short when she saw me and slipped round the other side of the cloisters.'

'So she went past the tea bar?'

'Yes, she must have done. Anyway, I decided there and then that I had to retire after this week. Getting that letter and meeting Tom has just made me more determined.' She drained her cup and rose to her feet. 'Just remember what I've said, Georgia. Don't be like me. Make sure you have a rounded life, not just a singing career. Make time. I hope Scott recovers and that you make a go of things. He is certainly a very handsome young man. Now, I must go and get myself ready for my final appearance. Bye, darling.'

I said goodbye, at least I think I did. My head was watching a film I'd not seen before, one I hadn't known existed until five minutes ago. I was standing next to a weeping Merlina who was sitting on a stone bench in the cloisters. My eyes were not on her, though. They were watching Carrie Gardiner flitting round the other side of the cloisters towards the Miserrimus Door that led directly into the cathedral. And just before the Miserrimus Door was the small door which led out onto the grass and round to the west end of the cathedral. The door Carrie told me she had never used.

17

To say I was stunned didn't quite do it justice. It was as if every molecule in my body had gone into stasis at the same time. Even my brain wasn't functioning. After a few minutes, the waitress came up to ask if everything was satisfactory and I had to make some sort of reply.

'Yes, lovely, but I can't manage the scone, I'm afraid. Sorry.'

'Not to worry,' she said, smiling.

She gathered up the detritus, gave the table a quick wipe and scurried back to the depths of wherever she had sprung from. I sat there. What on earth had Carrie been doing in the cloisters near the end of the concert? If it had been anything innocent, she would have told me.

Perhaps she had told Hamilton, though and that was why Hamilton was so insistent on keeping her on the list of suspects. So, who were the suspects? Carrie, obviously. Merlina's snippet of information had pushed my friend up the list faster than if Rudolph Nureyev had done one of his spectacular shoulder lifts. Now, why did I tag her just then with the ballerina identity? It took a few minutes to track that one back, but I managed it in the end. I could see Carrie in the blue sitting room just along the corridor from where I now sat telling me how she had manhandled Neil into the shower. Oh, God. Please, God. Not Carrie.

'You look a little lost, Miss Pattison.' I looked up to see Tony Labinski peering down at me, a slight frown creasing the skin round his brown eyes. It took a few moments to gather myself and put my sociable head back on.

'Mr Labinski. Hi. How is it going?'

'Tony. It's going OK, I think.'

I wasn't sure how to ask the next bit and thought I might as well say it straight. 'Have the police told you what is happening to Ariana yet?'

'Yes, I had a chat with Superintendent Hamilton earlier this morning. Scary lady, isn't she?'

'She can be, yes.'

'I had to wait for about twenty minutes before she consented to see me, which didn't go down well, I can tell you.'

I stifled a smile. 'No, I can imagine.'

'I was chewing the fat with one of her cohorts, young guy, only been in the force nine months. He's scared to death of her.' Tony's face broke into a mischievous grin and he pulled the chair Merlina had been sitting in close to mine and dropped into it. 'Hey, can you keep a secret?'

I nodded wondering what was coming.

'Do you know what they call her – the Hamilton woman?'

'What who call her?'

'From what young Andy said, pretty much the whole of the police squad here.'

I shook my head. He bent closer. 'Princess Ice-Knickers. Fits her like a glove, don't you think?'

I smiled as if appreciating what he obviously thought was hilarious, but inside I felt the first stirrings of pity for Hamilton.

'I think she's very good at her job,' I replied without thinking and a bit more acidly than I intended. 'And let's face it, some men feel threatened by that, don't they?'

He backed off, hands held up, palms towards me. They were interesting hands, not the hands of someone who made a living handling trees. He saw my interest and turned his palms over to look at them.

'What, have I got dirt on them?'

'No, not at all. I just expected that someone who makes a living cutting down trees would have different hands.....'

'You mean that a thick lumberjack has to have hands to match?'

'No. That's not what I meant at all.' I held out my hands. 'Let me see your palms again.'

'Not going to tell my fortune, are you?'

I put on a rustic accent. 'Cross my palm with silver, sir.' He laughed but gave me his hands. 'You almost have musician's hands,' I said looking up into his face. He smiled back down into mine.

'I played piano in my teens. I used to earn money playing in bars. It bought my course books and helped put a bit of food on the table.'

'Course books?'

He frowned and his shoulders sagged a little. 'Yes. Are you English so insular that you think a lumberjack is a guy in a checkered coat who goes round chopping down trees?'

His voice had risen and for the second time in an hour, I blushed and bit my lip.

'Yes, I'm sorry. I sort of assumed that you'd learned at your father's knee sort of thing.'

He laughed outright at that. 'Hell, no. Dad sent me to college. I have a Bachelor of Science degree in Forestry from the University of Alberta in Edmonton.'

'You were telling me about Ariana,' I replied anxious to change the subject.

'Oh, yeah. They want to do some sort of memorial service to her here next week. Not sure how it will go. I think the Festival Committee guy is sorting it out.'

'Sir Robert Fielding?'

'Yeah, that's him.'

Good, it would give me another chance to have a chinwag with my old piano tutor. I needed to be sure what questions I wanted to ask him first, though.

'What about her funeral?' I persisted.

'Well, she was a Toronto girl, born and bred, even though her mother was English. I've been on the phone to the Archbishop over there. I'm taking her back home as soon as they will let me.'

'I didn't know she was religious.'

'She was a lapsed catholic, but I feel that the way she died was so horrible, she deserves a full mass. Do you think I'm morbid?'

I felt my throat constrict and had a silly desire to cry. 'No, I don't think you are being morbid. I think it is touching. I only hope that when my time comes, there is someone to think about my onward journey.'

'We didn't get on, it's true and hadn't since the early days of the marriage, but she was still my wife and it's my responsibility to look after her now.'

'What will your new lady think. Is it Moira?'

His expression softened. 'Yeah. Moira. I've spoken to her. She is fine with it. She agrees with me.'

He put his hands on his knees and levered himself to his feet. 'Guess I'd better go and see when they will let me take her back to Canada.'

'OK. See you soon. Take care.'

'You, too.'

I had a lot to think about. Carrie, for one. I felt another girlie morning coming on and texted her to ask what she was doing the following morning. Then I needed to plan another session with Sir Robert. How was I going to approach that? And last, but by no means least, the jolly green giant had given me food for thought, too. On the face of it he seemed perfectly sincere, but then I expect George Joseph Smith was sincere when he up-ended his new wives' feet and drowned them. And, of these three, Tony Labinski was the one person strong enough to have incapacitated someone the size of Scott Wiley and thrown him into the river. Scott. I looked at my watch. Just gone four. I pulled my mobile out and rang the hospital. No real change but I could come along if I wanted. I wanted.

When I reached the hospital, I headed for ITU. Mr and Mrs Wiley were still by his bedside, but they stood up when I came through the door. I shook hands with Dad and Mum gave me a quick hug.

'How is he?' I whispered.

She motioned me away from the bed. 'They're quite pleased with him. Tomorrow, they are going to remove some of the tubes and things. They need to see if his kidneys are functioning. If things go according to plan, we've organised a move to a private room and out of here.'

I was delighted and showed it. 'That's fantastic. He must be doing well if they are talking about that.' I looked across at the bed. 'I won't stay long. Can I just stay with him for a while?'

She smiled but her whole demeanour told me she was keeping going on little more than nerves. Dad came up and put his arm round her shoulders.

'If you could do an hour's watch, Georgia, then I'll take Tina back to the hotel for a shower and something to eat. No, no,' he continued as she began to protest. 'That's what we're going to do. You can't wear yourself out like this, sweetheart. When he comes round you'll be fit for nothing.'

Tina smiled at me and they went off arm in arm. I went and took the seat she had been sitting in and held Scott's hand. The nurse came up and started taking notes from the machine readouts. He looked at me sitting there silently.

'You need to talk to him.'

'What do I say?'

'Anything you like. You don't mind what she says do you, Scott? It'll be a lot more interesting than me telling you about Sheffield United, won't it? She's very pretty as well. Aren't you the lucky one, having a pretty girl sitting holding your hand? I'll leave you with her now. See you later.'

Left to myself, I felt self-consciously stupid sitting talking to a man I hardly knew and who probably couldn't hear me anyway, but I ended up telling him about the enquiry and how I was trying to find out who had put him in hospital.

Five minutes before his parents came back, I was saying how sorry I was that we hadn't managed to get to Chatsworth, but that if he ever decided to stop being a lazy oaf and get out of the bed, we could rearrange the visit. His head was facing me, his eyes half-closed, but when I mentioned Chatsworth, his eyes opened and a sound like a muted cough came from him. I called the nurse and told him what had happened. He leaned over and called Scott's name, but there was no response.

'You call him,' he ordered not looking at me. 'Call his name and ask him to squeeze your hand.'

I did just that. I held his hand in both of mine and asked him over and over to squeeze. Nothing. 'Come on, Scott. Stop being so bloody idle. Squeeze my hand.'

Once more his eyes opened and he looked at me. I looked up at the nurse. He was grinning with delight. 'Well done, Scott. Look, here's your mum and dad.'

Tina heard him and almost ran to the bed. I slipped out of the chair so that she could take over. 'What's happened?' she asked.

The nurse answered. 'He seemed to look at Georgia. I think we're making progress. I'll get the doctor.'

Ten minutes passed before the doctor came into the ward. He ignored us completely, but stripped the bedclothes off Scott's feet and scraped across the sole of one foot with his pen. The foot moved and Scott's face grimaced.

'Good,' said the doctor. 'He's doing well.'

'Is he coming round?' I asked.

The doctor shook his head. 'Not yet, but he is responding to stimuli more than he has been. It will be very slow and I can't promise anything. Just keep trying to get through to him. I'll look at him again tonight.'

This was brilliant news and I almost jumped up and down like a small child at Christmas. Tina, too, wore a huge smile. She looked less tired. The nurse included us all when he spoke.

'It's baby steps all the way, and there will be days when he seems to go backwards.'

Mr and Mrs Wiley nodded. I made my goodbyes and danced out of the ward, almost knocking Hamilton for six. She put out her arms to steady me and smiled.

'I take it there is good news?'

'He looked at me, Superintendent. He looked at me and grunted.'

'Is he waking up, then?'

'No, not yet. But the doc says it's a good sign. They keep saying stuff like he isn't out the woods and all that, but he is improving.'

'I'm delighted to hear it. I was going to look in but it seems I don't have to now.'

'You were coming to see Scott? But he can't speak yet. He can't tell you anything. He may never be able to.'

'I know that, Georgia. They have said that even if he makes a full recovery, he will probably never remember what happened. The whole week might have vanished from his mind.'

I stopped walking and grabbed her arm. 'Do you mean that if he does wake up he might not remember me?'

'It's possible.' She looked at my face and used that phrase I was beginning to hate. 'Don't cross bridges before you have to. We none of us know what's around the next corner, otherwise we would have time to prepare ourselves.'

This last sentence was said with such bitterness that the question I had been about to ask died before it reached the open air. She looked round to see what had caused my sudden silence.

'Don't mind me,' she said, answering my look. 'I'm just a tired, cynical old bat getting nowhere fast.'

I resumed walking. 'If you weren't here to see Scott, why were you here?'

'To see Albert. Albert Gregory. The west door custodian.'

'Oh, the poor sod who got knocked out by whoever came in and killed Ariana?'

'That's the one.'

'Is he conscious?'

'More so than your boyfriend. He's a bit groggy.'

'Has he remembered what happened?'

'Not yet. I'm not allowed to talk to him for more than five minutes at a time. He hasn't said anything remotely useful.'

'This man we're after is not afraid of violence, is he?'

'No, the person we're after certainly isn't. I don't know if you know more than I do, Georgia, but I can't say categorically that it is a man yet.'

'You mean Carrie.'

'Amongst others.'

'You mean there's another woman under suspicion?'

'Well, Merlina Meredith admitted that at the end of the concert she was in the cloisters but she can't find anybody to back that up.'

It was on the tip of my tongue to tell her that there was, but I shut my teeth together.

'I understand that Tony is taking Ariana's body back to Canada.' I said instead.

'Yes, but not yet.'

'He seems a nice guy. I've been talking to him.'

'Oh yes. Did you get any more information for me?'

'No, but I don't think he did it.'

'Why not? He admits she wouldn't give him a divorce?'

'Yes, but that's because he's a catholic. They don't recognise divorce.'

'They don't recognise murder either, Georgia.'

That shut me up. I was casting around for something to say when she turned and said. 'I have something a bit more tangible to sort out first.'

'Anything I can help with?'

'I'm beginning to think that backstage on Saturday night must have been like Piccadilly Circus.'

'You'll have to explain that remark, Superintendent.'

'Come and have a cup of what passes for tea out of this bloody awful machine and I'll try and explain.'

We sat down at a tatty table. I have to admit she was spot on about the quality of the tea. Dire didn't begin to describe it. I took one sip and almost spat it out. She was watching me carefully.

'Yes, it is like that, isn't it? I thought the police canteen stuff was rank but this lifts appalling to a whole new level.'

I noticed she still drank it though, which is more than I could. 'What was the remark about Piccadilly Circus in aid of?' I asked.

'Well, let's see if we can reconstruct what happened?'

'Oh, I've always wanted to be in a police reconstruction.'

'Stop being so bloody flippant. Actually, Georgia, when we get a bit further along, a reconstruction might not be a bad idea. I'll think about it.' She lapsed into silence.

I coughed and said 'Piccadilly Circus?'

'Oh, yes. Right. Sorry. I was thinking. Well, we know that someone came up behind Albert and socked him one at some point during the second half of the concert, don't we?'

'Yes. You said there were wet footprints and grass.'

'Yes, I did. Now I wonder what time it started raining. I must find that out. I wonder....'

'Piccadilly Circus.' I said through gritted teeth.

'Yes, of course. Well, this is where it gets complicated. Do you know any of the choir members?'

'Only Tom Carter. The ladies I sat in between on Saturday were called-hang on- one was Sharon something. The other one I haven't a clue.'

'No matter. You've never come across an alto called Grace Aston?'

'No. Is she in the choir?'

'Oh, yes. Apparently they have this rule thing about what you can wear during the concert.'

'Oh, yes. Concert dress code. That's normal in most choirs.'

'What about jewellery?'

'Usually, the soloist is allowed a bit of sparkle, but the choir isn't. They are supposed to stick to gold, silver or pearls, nothing that will reflect off the lights and distract the audience. Why?'

'Well it seems that this Grace Aston decided to wear a diamond and emerald bracelet given to her last week by her husband "on the occasion of her birthday" as she put it.'

'I expect she just wanted to show off to her friends.'

'Yeah, well, the choir supervisor woman saw the bracelet, had a hissy fit and made Mrs Aston take it off and leave it and her handbag backstage.'

'Where backstage?' There were icy fingers playing "Danse Macabre" up and down my spine.

'In the dressing room behind the curtain. We found the handbag, of course, but it's only this morning when the choir were allowed back on the stage that the stupid bloody woman came to us. She had expected it would still be where she'd left it. She's in a right state because we've had the damn thing all week not knowing whose it was.'

'Didn't it have any ID in it?'

'No. It was one of those little bitty scrappy things. You know the ones that hold twenty pence and a handkerchief and are stuffed. No, the problem is that the bracelet isn't in the bag any more. She daren't tell her husband because she knows she shouldn't have been wearing it and she is accusing one of us of having nicked it.'

18

'I still don't understand where Piccadilly Circus comes into this,' I said after a few moments.

'Think about it. I'm bloody sure none of my boys or girls have nicked anything. So what we are now being asked to believe is that a thief who is also a murderer on the side was under the stage at the same time. It isn't logical.'

I thought for a moment. 'Perhaps Ariana saw him stealing the bracelet and he killed her to shut her up.'

'What? And he or she just brought along a hatpin and some petrol – it was petrol by the way – as defensive weapons?'

'I see your point. So now you think there were two people backstage.'

'Yes.'

'Oh, flick. Do you think they were in league or they both just happened along?'

'No idea.'

'Be a bit too much of a coincidence to have two separate people going backstage, wouldn't it? And what about when the second one discovered Albert?'

'Coincidences do happen, Georgia. How many times have you thought of someone you haven't seen for ages and then you bump into them three days later?'

'Yes. That happens quite a lot. Still, I don't think that number two would have gone in leaving Albert lying outside.'

'Why not. Number two didn't hit him. They may have not even known he was there.'

'How could they not know?'

'Well, he was at the bottom of the steps in shadow, but what I really meant was that they might not have known that Albert's duties put him there for the duration of the concert so they would not be expecting to see him. They may have thought that the west door was unmanned.'

'Oh, I see. What I don't see is why the authorities needed it manned anyway. Why couldn't they just lock it?'

'Come on, Georgia. Never heard of Health and Safety? They would have to keep it accessible in case the building needed evacuating in a hurry. So, the best solution is to have someone on duty there, isn't it?'

'Right. This is worse than Mastermind. So, Superintendent Hamilton, you have two minutes on your specialist subject, who was backstage, starting now. Who was backstage?'

'Pass.' It was the nearest I had ever seen her come to giggling. Then a thought popped into my head. 'Why don't you try unravelling it from the other end?'

She frowned and cocked her head on one side, just like Jordy had when he was watching the swans on the river. 'You've lost me.'

'It's a technique I sometimes use to learn songs, especially ones that are tricky or have a big finish. My old piano teacher – not Sir Robert – the one at my school in York – he used to suggest I start at the end and work backwards to the beginning.'

'I don't get how that works.'

'Think about it. If you learn the last eight bars first, and then the eight bars before that, you are always travelling into known territory from unknown territory. So, if you work from where the bracelet might be now, and then work backwards to it being in this woman's handbag, it might be easier.'

'But we don't know where it is now.'

'You're being obtuse. Try and imagine what you would have done with it if you'd stolen it. Why would you steal it in the first place?'

'I might like jewellery.'

'So, we're back to Carrie, are we? Nicking a bracelet because she likes it? She wouldn't be able to wear it, would she? Not here. Not in Temingham. Too many people would recognise it, or know that one like it had gone missing. It would be a stupid thing to do and she isn't stupid. Neither, if you notice, does she wear a lot of jewellery.'

'She wears diamond earrings.'

'Yes, but the diamonds are very understated. That's because she wouldn't wear anything so ostentatious as a diamond and emerald bracelet.'

'So you're saying that I'm barking up the wrong tree with her?'

'I do think so, yes. Carrie isn't like that.'

'How do you know? You haven't seen her for years.'

'Because people may change over the years, but they do not change their fundamental character. She is a follower, not a leader. She doesn't initiate things. She just doesn't.'

'Would it interest you to know that when she was living in London before she married Neil Gardiner, she was mugged and that she managed to fight her attacker off?'

I sat there staring at her, trying to work out how to deal with a curve ball like that. 'I don't understand what you are trying to say, Superintendent.'

'What I am saying is that we've gone pretty thoroughly into her background. She used to go to martial arts classes. The instructor says that her ballet training gave her superb balance and strength. She was one of his best pupils.'

'Are you telling me that you think Carrie knocked out Ariana and Scott?'

'I'm telling you that she knew how to, not that she did.' Hamilton put her head on one side and I opened my mouth before I could help it.

'You look just like Jordy when you do that.'

'What do you mean by that?' Her voice had gone very quiet and had an overtone of menace I felt I could have cut if I'd had a knife. I swallowed.

'I didn't mean to upset you. It's just that when I gave Lizzie the memory stick, Jordy ran over the bridge and was looking at some swans with his head on one side just like you do when you are contemplating something. How is he getting on, by the way?'

She wrinkled her nose. 'I am sick of having yellow fur all over my suits. He isn't allowed in my room, but I'm still covered in bloody dog hair.'

'I can help you with that. Take a roll of Sellotape. Reverse it and wind it round your right hand, sticky side up. Then simply pat the dog hair off your suit. If you do it first thing in the morning when you arrive in the office, you will be dog-hair free all day.'

Her eyebrows lifted and her expression returned to its normal one of faintly cynical boredom. 'And that works?'

'Certainly does. It even works on black velvet evening dresses if you are careful. Finlay has one of those scruffy-looking bouncy terriers. He's lovely, really, but he does think the whole house is his territory and I had laid the dress on the bed to put on after my shower. I came out of the shower, put on my make up and went to put on the dress to find that Satchmo had decided my dress was a lovely new bed for him. So there I am, less than an hour before the concert with a dress that looked as if a herd of buffalo had trampled it.'

'Shit. What did you do?'

'Kate, my sister-in-law got their iron out and we steamed the creases out with that and a boiling kettle and I did the Sellotape trick. Took twenty minutes and the dress was on. Bit damp from the steaming, but it looked OK. Try it.'

'I will, thanks.'

'Is that your only objection to the dog? The mess?'

'Why do you ask?'

'You're older than I am, Superintendent. But even I have learned that people don't respond to threats well, only to encouragement.'

'Your point being?'

'That if you like Lizzie living with you and you both get on, then why not try to accommodate her? Otherwise I think you may find yourself living on your own.'

'What do you mean by that? Have you been talking to Lizzie?'

'Not in the sense you mean, no. But I do know from the little that she has said, and she is very loyal to you, that you could well be up against an immovable object here. She really wants Jordy to stay and I think that if the bond with him grows much more, you are likely to find that she has moved out rather than part with him.'

She grunted, but her mouth had tightened. 'Let's get back to the bracelet. If it isn't your girlfriend, then who?'

'We aren't trying to think of who, we are trying to work out what we would have done.'

'So, if it had been you, what would you have done?'

'Well, I move about the country quite a bit, so I might have kept it to wear for singing. If I was a magpie who liked glittering things, I might just have kept it to take it out in private, wear it and gloat over it, but I don't think that is likely. I would possibly take it to either sell it or pawn it.'

'Now that isn't a half bad idea, Georgia. Take it one step further.'

'You mean, you don't want to pawn it or sell it?'

'No. Let's say you are someone with a quick brain. What other things could be done with it besides pawning it, selling it or keeping it to gloat over?'

I rubbed my chin on the back of my hand as if that was going to make my brain work more effectively. 'You'll have to give me a clue,' I said eventually after about thirty seconds silence.

'OK. Look at it logically. This person is not stupid. We know that. We know quite a lot about them.'

'Do we? We don't even know if it's a man or a woman.'

'It could be a man and a woman, if my theory about there being two people backstage is right.'

'Are we assuming that they are working together?'

'We might be.'

I sat forward. 'But if that was the case, surely one of them would be providing the alibi for the other?'

'A good point. Don't think I hadn't thought it. No, it might have needed two people, working together. Number one takes hold of Ariana. Number two renders her unconscious and then goes to work with the hatpin. Meanwhile number one is ready with the petrol and the match. Remember the timings, Georgia. How long was it from the time Mr Topcliffe came back on stage to the time when you went down to see what had happened?'

I thought back to that night. I could see Jamie in the film in my mind. He did the usual things. Came to the top of the steps and held out both arms to the audience. There was a crescendo of applause. He walked through the orchestra. They were also applauding. He shook hands with Neil and then with Kevin. Then he turned to the audience and bowed, then swung back to the orchestra and applauded them and shook hands with the leader. Then he, along with everyone else turned towards the top of the steps expecting to see Ariana. I was mentally counting in thousands, trying to get the timing accurate.

'About half a minute until they turned towards the steps,' I said finally. 'Then about another ten or so seconds until Neil motioned me to go down and see what had happened. Say possibly forty five seconds, fifty at most.'

'So, our duo would have about half a minute of safety. What does that tell you?'

My brain was beginning to hurt. 'Don't know.'

'It tells you that they are familiar with what happens after a concert.'

I sagged back in the chair and just said 'oh.' It was such an obvious conclusion, but one that had not occurred to me. Hamilton was watching me closely.

'That hadn't crossed your mind, had it?'

'No. Not for a moment. I wonder what else hasn't crossed it.'

'I'm treading on delicate ground here, but you started it.'

'What do you mean?'

'Your comments about the dog.'

'He does have a name, Superintendent. Ever tried using it?'

'No.'

'Might be an idea if you did. It might ease the tension between you and Lizzie.'

'What goes on between Lizzie and me is nothing to do with you.'

'Well, it looks as if you're about to get your own back, so shoot.'

'Has it occurred to you that one of the people backstage could have been your boyfriend?'

For a moment I thought she meant Mike, then I realised she meant Scott.

'That's ridiculous. Why would he want to go backstage, and, if your supposition is correct, who was he in league with?'

'Don't get your knickers in a twist. I'm not saying it was him. What I'm trying to show you is that there are several people who don't appear to have an alibi for the time of the murder.'

'It can't have been Scott. If it was, then why was he knocked out and almost drowned?'

'Never heard of thieves falling out?'

'Besides, he hardly knew Ariana. He only saw her last year in "Figaro". He didn't know her.'

'And how do you know that?'

'Because he told me..... oh.'

'Always believe everything you're told?'

'Usually, yes.'

'Perhaps that's why you don't have a good track record in the romantic stakes.'

'And you do?' I asked, stung by the tone of condescension.

'No. I know better than to get tangled up in the first place. What is it the song says? Love changes everything, all your wisdom disappears.'

'You might be a better person if you weren't so cynical. Tell you one thing, Superintendent, if you'd ever suspended your sense and fallen in love you'd understand why Lizzie wants to keep Jordy.'

'We're getting off the point.'

'You mean I've just scored one you can't argue with.'

'Oh, I could, and don't think I haven't ever had a fluttering in the dovecote. I just choose not to flutter it again. Where were we and why do you have to argue so bloody much?'

'Because I can't stand people who think they know all the angles about everything and that's how you come across. Cold, unfeeling, dedicated to the task in hand and stuff the feelings of those around you.' I was well into my stride now. 'Do you know what they call you?'

'What who calls me?' The menace was back in the voice and she had a look on her face that would have shrivelled Satan at thirty paces.

'Never mind. We were talking about who could have been backstage.'

'OK,' she replied after a pause, but I could see we would be coming back to this conversation at some time of her choosing in the future. I cursed my stupidity at riling her. However, it was done now.

'Let's get back to your theory about the bracelet and what might have happened to it,' she said. 'Can you think of any other reason why someone might steal it?'

'It's difficult because they would have to know it was there.'

'Not necessarily. How many times does a sneak thief find a window left open and, before he is even aware of it, he is in and out. It was an opportunity and whoever it was, took the opportunity and the bracelet.'

'I can't think of any other reason why.'

'I can think of at least two more points. Firstly, he or she might have stolen it to put the blame on someone else.'

'What? You mean plant it on them?' I asked, frowning.

'It's a possibility, yes.'

'And the other?'

'How could we go about detecting who might have the bracelet or who might as you suggest, pawn or sell it?'

'You mean find out if someone has money they didn't have last week?'

'Yes, that's a good idea. I'll follow up on that, but that wasn't my point. Let's look at another scenario. Let's say you don't want it for yourself but to do something with it.'

I scratched my head. ' OK, do I want to give it to someone as a present?'

'Could do. What sort of someone?'

I sat up a surge of excitement coursing through me. 'A girlfriend? Perhaps a girlfriend in another country where it wouldn't matter if she wore it?'

'Do we know of anyone in that category?'

I clapped my hands. 'The husband, of course.'

'Well done, Miss Marple. And don't forget, the husband has a girlfriend who wants to get married.'

19

'You mean....'

'Exactly.'

I sat and waited for this to sink in. It changed so many things. If Moira was in Temingham, then she certainly wasn't staying at the Maddox. Or was she? How did I know? How did anybody know? We had no idea what she looked like.

'How are you going to find out if she is in the country?'

'We'll need to check arrivals from Toronto called Moira. Or I can ring my opposite number over there and ask if they can find her.'

'She might have come into the UK by a roundabout route.'

Hamilton sat quiet for a minute. 'That's not as daft as it sounds. This might take longer than we think.'

'So, meanwhile....?' I felt a stupidly warm glow at the reference to "we".

She looked at her watch. 'Just on six-fifteen....'

I jumped up. 'Flick. I have to get back for Merlina's concert.' I began running out of the hospital. Hamilton followed me pretty closely. Just as I reached my car, she grabbed my arm.

'Ring me tomorrow morning. We'll need to get some plan of action going.'

I opened the window as I put the car into gear. 'Will do.'

'And don't break the speed limit,' I heard her yell as I accelerated towards the exit.

I flew through the hotel and up the stairs because I didn't think I had the time to wait for the lift. I beat my own record for getting ready. Twenty five minutes from jumping into the shower to walking out of the door and that included putting my hair up and using the tongs to pull out odd bits and make them into ringlets. I decided to honour Merlina with the Indian silk I had been planning to wear for Scott.

The new garnet ring did not go with the turquoise on the dress, so I wore a silver pendant with a single crystal drop and matching earrings. When I looked in the jewellery roll, I cursed. I could have sworn I had brought the aquamarine solitaire Mike had given me for Christmas. It must still be on my dressing table in York. Too late to fiddle now. I walked out of the door.

Jamie spotted me from his seat at the bar as I emerged from the lift. He slipped off his seat and came through. He was still twenty feet away when he did the loudest wolf whistle I have ever heard. I started to giggle but the girly part of me was preening herself.

'You look good enough to eat,' he said taking hold of my hands and kissing them.

'Don't mention food. I haven't had anything since three and I'm starving.'

'In that case, would madam like to join me for dinner after the concert?'

'Madam would. Very much. Thank you. Are you going to Merlina's concert, too?'

'I certainly am, but if you are going dressed like that, I had better sprint upstairs and smarten myself up. I'll be five minutes.'

It's one of the things I like about men. If they say they are going to be five minutes, they usually are. I suppose it's part of the testosterone thing, whereby woman are supposed to be able to multi-task and men be more spatially aware.

Jamie obviously had a goodly supply of testosterone because he was back down in exactly five minutes. Gone were the chinos and open necked shirt. In their place was a dark lounge suit with a white shirt and gold waistcoat. He looked yummy but then in my book, he always had. I slipped my hand through his arm and we processed over to the cathedral.

'Is it true she's retiring?' he asked as we approached the north door.

'Yes. I think she's realised that there is more to life than being a wandering minstrel. Tom has had a big influence as well, but I think Ariana's death was also a contributing factor, shall we say?'

'But they didn't like each other.'

'What does that have to do with the price of fish?'

'What I don't understand is...'

'Let's talk about it afterwards, Jamie. Look, do you want a programme?'

The concert started in the usual fashion. The audience obviously had no idea about it being Merlina's last appearance. I had mixed emotions. I was trying to concentrate on the Rutter spirituals and I have to say that she put every ounce of feeling and technique into them. The most compelling moment, for me, came when after a typical Rutter introduction, Merlina sang unaccompanied, "Sometimes I feel like a motherless child. Sometimes I feel like a motherless child. Sometimes I feel like a motherless child. A long ways from home. A long ways from home."

It spoke straight to my heart. I felt goose bumps coming out on my arms and legs and a frisson went up my spine as if someone had run a feather up it. Jamie felt the electricity run through me. He put a hand on my arm and squeezed. It was a fabulous performance. Merlina might think she was over the hill, but I doubt if anyone in the cathedral that night will ever hear a better rendition of that particular spiritual.

There was the usual interval. I could tell with "Sea Pictures" that Merlina was saying goodbye to an old and much-loved friend. The audience loved it and her. She received the bouquet of flowers and the smile on her face was not that of the dignified professional singer, but one which made her look younger as if a tremendous weight had fallen from her and sheer happiness had replaced it.

She looked a little taken aback when the Dean appeared at her side and waved his voice for silence.

'Tonight we have been privileged to hear one of the great voices of our time use the instrument God gave her to give us a feast of musical excellence.'

The audience agreed and erupted again, only to be quietened by his hand. Some people just have a natural authority. Had I done that, they would probably have ignored me, but because it was him waving his hand, they shut up.

'You will be sad to learn that tonight was Merlina's last appearance on the concert platform. Due to ill health, she has taken the difficult decision to retire. I hope you will join with me in wishing her a speedy recovery and a long and happy retirement.'

There was an audible groan from the assembled masses, spoiled in part by the discreet but noticeable vision of quite a few people checking their watches and making a runner for their buses. However, Merlina had her gracious face on again and made out that she didn't see them, especially as the majority gave her a standing ovation. She had a huge queue of fans waiting for her on the cathedral side of the double doors, so I decided that I would pay my tribute to her privately, perhaps tomorrow when the reality of her retirement might be beginning to sink in. I turned to Jamie.

'Wasn't she fantastic?'

'Seems a shame she is retiring. I get the impression you know more about that than I do. Let's discuss it over dinner. What do you fancy?'

There were several answers to that one, but we finally settled on Indian. Jamie knew of a small restaurant which specialised in the food from the southern states and Goa. We both decided on the minced lamb cutlets with almonds and sultanas to start with, then I had salmon and okra in coconut curry and Jamie had something called Shakoothi, which looked like roasted chicken with chilli in a thick sauce. Of course, we each had a bit of the other's main course. He finished off with a coconut ice cream and I had a platter of exotic fruit. We had planned to share a bottle of wine, but I wanted something white and crisp and he wanted something red and heavy, so we threw caution to the winds and had a bottle each. What the hell, it had been a roller-coaster of a week and it didn't look as if it was going to get any easier.

'How's Scott?' he asked whilst we were waiting for the starters.

'Still in a coma. They think he might come out of it one day, but it seems reasonable to assume that even if he does, he might be a vegetable.'

He reached over and put his hand on mine. 'George, I'm so sorry. This has been a rough week for you, hasn't it?'

I could feel the tears threatening at the back of my eyes and my throat started to constrict. 'I've had better. I just wish I knew what Scott was doing out on the river path in the first place.'

'Perhaps he was taking a walk. What time did it happen?'

'I found him just before six. Why?'

'I just wondered where everyone was when it happened. Hamilton must be checking everyone's alibi, surely.'

'Don't know. I expect so, but she wouldn't tell me in any case.'

'Well, I might be able to help. I know Merlina was in the hotel because I was playing chess with Mr Archer and she was reading a magazine a few tables away. Kevin had gone to London earlier, so that lets him out as well. Who else is there?'

'Do you know, Jamie, I'm not in the mood for puzzles tonight. I just want to enjoy myself.'

'Fair enough. What are the doctors saying about Scott?'

'Well the doctor says that even in the event of him making a full recovery, there's a very high possibility that he won't even remember being in Temingham, let along remember what happened on the river path.'

'Ain't life a bitch? I can't help being glad in one respect, though and I hope you can forgive me for it.'

I frowned at him. 'What do you mean?'

'It means I might have a second chance, George, or rather, we might have a second chance.'

'Oh, Mr Rochester, this is so sudden...'

'Don't joke, George. I'm serious. What about it?'

I didn't want to muck this up so I was very careful how I answered. 'I can't deny, Jamie, that I've always held a candle for you. It wasn't the right time at college and just at this moment, there is so much batting round in my head that I need time to sort it out.'

He looked down at his plate and I saw him bite his lip. It was my turn to put my hand on his. 'If we're going to have a second chance, it has to be right and there has to be closure of a few things before I can even think about there being an us. But, and I am deadly serious, please just give me time. I'm sure it will all turn out right in the end.'

He looked up and gave a tight little smile. 'Right, as usual. I do need you to know that I have very strong feelings for you, Georgia.'

The fact that he used my proper name convinced me. 'Same here, pal, but I need to be less.....distracted than I am now.'

'I understand. Now, tell me about Merlina.'

So I told him what had happened that morning. He whistled and agreed with me that he hadn't ever expected Merlina to retire either.

I stared into my glass. 'It seems strange losing Ariana and Merlina in the space of a week.'

'Strange that both of them were mezzos, too,' he agreed.

'Do you have any theories about who could have killed Ariana, Jamie?'

He looked a little startled. 'I hadn't thought about it, really. It was a shock because the concert had been so good and she sang better than I have ever heard her.'

'Really? How often did you hear her?'

'Like I said before, we shared a platform a couple of times a year. You know how it is, though, George. Usually there is one thing, however small, which you kick yourself for afterwards. Sometimes, you're late on the entry or the note isn't in the right place, just something to mar it. Saturday wasn't like that for any of us, and certainly not for her. She didn't put a foot wrong.'

'It's tragic, really. Just about to hit the big-time, too.'

'Who told you that?'

'Sir Robert seems to have thought so, and I think so, too.'

'Well, you know what she was like. She would have fallen out with somebody once too often and scuppered herself. Were you around after the rehearsal on Saturday?'

'No, I was with Carrie. Why?'

'Did you know that she told Tony she'd give him a divorce over her dead body?'

'Yes,' I replied as casually as I could. 'Tony told me himself.'

'I bet that snotty bitch with the fat legs doesn't know that.'

My mind went into overdrive. Jamie was not known to have the tightest tongue in the world, so although I was tempted to tell him that Hamilton already knew, I held back. The last thing I needed now was to have him blab all over the place that I was feeding information to the police. I always find it disconcerting that it is possible to think out a whole line of reasoning in a nano second.

'That's her lookout,' I said. 'She's done nothing but hassle me, firstly because I found the body and then because I found Scott.'

'Well they do have this inbuilt belief that whoever finds a body has to be the murderer, you know that, surely.'

'I do know that after her latest little interrogation, I exploded at her,' I said making it up as I went along. I didn't like the gleam in Jamie's eye, so I thought I'd better play the innocent bystander caught up in things they don't understand.

'Knowing your explosions, it must have been a sight to see. I wish I'd been there.'

'Ah, well, I can tell you one thing.'

He sat forward. 'Ooh, this sounds good. What?'

'It is good. Did you know that the only people not being suspected are Neil, Kevin you and me. So there. My temper does have its uses.'

'That's not news, George. She told us that as well.'

'Oh, flick. I thought I'd been clever. What I don't understand is why she took so long to come up the steps. After all, she should have followed you straight away.'

He held his hands up. 'I think that might have been Kevin and me, actually.'

'Really? How?'

'Well you know the sheer elation at the end of a brilliant concert, don't you? And it was a brilliant concert.'

'I'll agree with that, it certainly was.'

'Well, we sort of danced her about a bit when we got backstage. Kevin will tell you, we were all on such a high. Some of her hair came down and she was pinning it back up and swearing at us. I just followed Kevin up the stairs and left her to it.'

I sat up. That was why Ariana never saw her attacker coming up behind her. Because she had both hands over her head sorting her hair out. How many times have I had to do the same thing after an energetic sing. Not to mention the on stage wig disasters. But I won't go into them.

We lingered over coffee discussing various things, including plans to meet up in London the next week. By this time, we were both feeling the effects of the wine. I was definitely on the way to being completely ratted. We walked outside in as dignified manner as we could muster. Arm in arm, we turned up the street towards the Maddox, only to be stopped by a police constable who looked about twelve.

'I do hope neither of you are planning to drive,' he said in a surprisingly deep voice.

We both put our hands up as if he was holding a gun on us and assured him that we were gently staggering back to the Maddox on foot, and would collapse into our separate beds when we arrived there. He grinned and gave us a mock salute.

'Take care.'

We did. We swam through the door of the hotel, just managing to keep our feet. Jamie asked if I would like a nightcap but I shook my head and made a great play of getting my key out.

'See you in the morning,' I said and headed for the lift as he walked towards the bar. Once in my room, with the door locked, I kicked off my shoes, took off the finery and the make-up and then cleaned my teeth. I drank at least a pint of water after washing my face in equally cold water and then shook two ibuprofen out of their blister packs, grabbed a bottle of lemonade from the room's mini-bar and downed the tablets with it. Finally, I opened the window to let in the cool air and breathed deeply before pulling back the covers and sliding into bed.

Next morning, I lifted an experimental head off the pillow. Good, the usual remedy had worked. I had a longer shower, just to wash off the final effects of the booze. I find I can always smell it on my skin the morning after. I hung up the silk dress and put away the jewellery.

It was then that I missed the garnet pearl and diamond ring. I had the jewellery roll out and emptied it completely. Nothing. Then I upended my make-up bag. Nothing. Same with the evening bag I had taken out the previous night. Nothing.

I sat on the bed, closed my eyes and began to think. I had been in a hurry to get ready last night, yes. I remembered looking in the mirror and seeing how out of place my new ring was with the dress. I remembered taking it off and putting it on the top by the mirror. I looked in the drawers under the mirror. No, it wasn't there. And then, quite out of the blue, I remembered grabbing the aquamarine ring off my ring-tree at home and putting it in my jewellery roll. More slowly, I emptied the jewellery roll again. I noticed my hand shaking a little as I lifted the phone and asked for the manager.

20

The manager, Mr Fletcher, asked me to stay in my room and promised he would be there within ten minutes. I phoned Hamilton on the mobile and told her what had happened.

'You know that the case isn't mine, Georgia, so I can't interfere. But, I'm quite happy to have a chat with the officer in charge if you think it would help.'

'I don't know. I didn't ring you to try and get preferential treatment.'

'Why did you ring me?'

'I don't know. Perhaps you're becoming a habit. One I will have to break.'

I could hear her chuckling. I knew she didn't smoke, or at least she never had in front of me, but she had one of those sixty a day voices that went into a basso profundo when she wasn't expending too much breath on a laugh.

'Don't worry, Georgia. I'll have a word with Jethro. When you've seen him or his underling, call me again and let me know how you've got on.'

A few seconds after I had folded up the phone, there was a discreet knock at the door and Mr Fletcher and another guy were there. The other guy turned out to be called Winston and I remembered the name from the morning Jamie had lost his pocket-watch. I invited them in. Mr Winston spoke first.

'When did you miss the rings, Miss Pattison?'

'I missed the aquamarine last night. I wanted to wear it with the dress I wore to the concert, but I thought I'd left it in my flat at home.'

'And the other ring?'

'That was most definitely there under the mirror last night. I checked myself in the mirror and the gold and red looked awful with the white and turquoise of the dress, so I took it off, tried to find the aquamarine and then gave up because I was late.'

'So you now say that you remember putting the aquamarine in the jewellery roll before you left home?'

I picked up the roll and gave it to him. 'Yes. It was right there, in that zipped bit.'

'Is there any way you can check that it isn't at home?'

I thought for a moment. 'Yes, of course. I'll ring Nettie, my landlady and ask her to go and look in my box and on the ring tree.'

'You are sure you haven't just forgotten it?'

Now I was beginning to get a bit miffed. I took a deep breath and looked him straight in the eye. 'The aquamarine was a Christmas present from someone who meant a lot to me,' I began. 'So I can assure you, Mr Winston, that if it isn't in that jewellery roll and Nettie can't find it at home, then it has been stolen.'

'I don't suppose you have photos of the rings, do you?' he asked in a tone that didn't hold out much hope.

'Actually, yes, I can.' I found my wallet purse. There was a photo in it of Mike and me, with my right hand in plain sight and on the third finger a pale blue stone ring. I handed the photo to him. 'You can have this if it would help. I don't know if your people can blow it up or anything.'

'Thank you. That will be really useful. And the other ring?'

'I only bought that a few days ago. Here is the receipt. And here,' I said, unfolding the mobile and pushing a few buttons, 'is a picture of my hand wearing it.'

He took the phone without a word and stared at the picture. 'Strange thing to do, surely, take a picture of your hand?'

I coloured up a little. 'Not really. I was with a friend and it was one of those silly girly moments.' I looked at the expression on his face. 'You can ask her if you like, Mr Winston. Her name is Caroline Gardiner. She is the Cathedral Organist's wife.'

His eyes fell first. 'Yes, all right, Miss Pattison. We'll take this photo off the phone camera if we feel it necessary.'

'Have you called the police yet?'

Fletcher interrupted whatever Winston was going to say. 'I shall do that as soon as I get back to my office.'

'Well can you please let me know what you need me to do as soon as possible?'

'Yes, of course. Have you had breakfast yet?'

'No. I was just coming down when I noticed the theft.'

'Perhaps you'd like to come down with us.'

'Yes. Good idea. I need some sustenance after the shock.' I used the word shock to them, but anger was more like it. They obviously thought I was jumping on the theft bandwagon, probably to claim the insurance money, but, of course, they were too polite or unsure of their ground to actually come right out and say so. It took until the end of the silent descent in the lift to realise that they also wanted me under constant surveillance so that I could not ring Carrie and ask her to corroborate my story about the girly morning. That would have made me laugh if the anger hadn't been slowly burning away under the polite facade I had put on. Did they think I was so stupid that I wouldn't have already worked this out with Carrie before I even phoned to report the thefts? Honestly, some people are so stupid and they are supposed to be the intelligent ones.

I didn't hold out a lot of hope of ever seeing my rings again and at the thought of that, I found myself standing at the buffet with a plate in one hand, a spoon in the other and tears coursing down my cheeks. An arm went round me and Merlina's voice was quiet as she spoke.

'What's the matter, darling?'

'Two rings have been stolen from my room and I don't think the management believes me.'

The arm tightened. 'Just grab some toast and follow me to my table. Keep your head down and nobody will think there is anything wrong.'

Once at the table, she poured me a coffee from her pot and signalled to the waitress for another. I had stopped crying by now, but the tears were not far away. She only had to say a few kind words and I would be off again.

'Now,' she said briskly. 'Stop the tears. It's bad for the voice. Take a sip of coffee and tell me all about it.'

When I had finished, she asked if I had phoned Nettie and tutted when I hadn't.

'Not my fault,' I replied. 'They hustled me out of my room as if it contained state secrets.'

'Do it now. Go on.'

'I'll go outside to do it. I can't stand the "I'm just on the train" people who let you know all their business at the tops of their voices.'

I slipped outside and made the call. Nettie promised to ring me back within twenty minutes, so I went back to Merlina and for the first time noticed how pale she was.

'Are you all right, Merlina. You look a bit tired and washed out.'

'I am tired, love. Tom wants me to have some tests.'

I sat up straighter. 'What sort of tests?'

'Don't get your corset unlaced, Georgia. He wants a blood test. He thinks I might be a bit anaemic, that's all.'

'Oh, right,' I said, following Tom's lead. It wouldn't do to let Merlina know that anaemia could be a sign that something more serious was going on. I would cross my fingers and hope that it was just anaemia. At the same time, I made a mental note to ring Mum and ask her what it might portend. Now that I looked more closely, Merlina's skin was far too pale and her hands appeared almost bloodless.

She looked at me through narrowed lids. 'Go on, doctor's daughter. Tell me.'

I had to think really fast because rule number one is never, never put the wind up anyone without good cause. 'I really can't say...' I leaned over and put my hand on hers. 'I mean that. I can't say because I don't know. But my best guess is that you have spent so much of your life rushing round and trying not to put on weight so that you look good in the frocks, that your red cell count is low and you simply need an iron supplement and to eat more iron-rich foods.'

Her face cleared and I felt like a traitor, but this was really an SEP case – some else's problem. Not mine. Knowing that Tom had a vested interest, I could guarantee that the blood tests would be given absolute priority. I would still ring Mum, though, or, I wondered if Finlay would be better. He was more likely to keep up with the latest thinking. Mum and Dad were winding down to retirement and these days, Dad was more likely to pick up "Golf Monthly" than the "Lancet". Mum was probably too busy looking after Dad. Finlay was the obvious choice.

I was in the middle of this train of thought when my mobile shrilled and I jumped up and walked as fast as I could out of the dining room, unfolding the phone. I still caught some dirty looks from the other diners, though. It was Nettie. The aquamarine solitaire was most definitely not in my jewellery box, but she had rescued a mouldy half-eaten sandwich from the kitchen table, and put it and the contents of the kitchen bin in my dustbin. I apologised profusely, but Nettie isn't one of those gimlet landladies who want to know everything about their tenants. She just laughed and asked me if I needed anything getting in, which was her way of wanting to know when I'd be back. I told her I'd ring a couple of days before and she said that she'd wash my curtains if that was OK. It was more than OK with me.

I folded up the phone and headed for the manager's office. When I knocked on the door, he was with a gloomy looking man who could only be called cadaverous. He was introduced to me as Inspector Jethro Smithson, who asked me if I minded waiting until he could see me. The manager suggested that I wait in the conservatory, and said he would send out some coffee. I asked for biscuits, too. I'd only had one piece of toast.

I thought the conservatory was empty when I walked into it, but out of the corner of my eye, I saw a movement. When I looked it was Mr Archer, playing chess with himself. Jamie had obviously not taken the same remedy I had and was more than likely either still asleep or holding his head in his hands. I walked over to the old man.

'Mr Archer?'

'Hello, dear. Don't suppose you play chess, do you?'

'No, but I know you've been beating seven bells out of my friend, Jamie Topcliffe.'

He laughed. 'Indeed. He plays a solid game, but he doesn't have the killer punch you need for chess. He's far too concerned about hurting my feelings than winning.'

'That sounds like Jamie. I love your chess pieces.' I picked one up. They were very unusual, made of bronze and onyx. The green onyx ones were depictions of the good characters from the Sherlock Holmes stories and the black onyx ones were the baddies. They stood about four inches high and the one I picked up weighed a ton.

Mr Archer picked up the black king, or in this case, Professor Moriarty. 'My darling wife gave them to me a year before she died. I play with them every day, so, in a way, I am in daily touch with her.'

I felt the tears pricking behind my eyelids again. 'That's lovely. I hope they give you comfort.'

'Indeed they do, young lady. Especially when I can sweep people like your Jamie off the board.' He chuckled and I joined in.

'Are you waiting for Jamie now?'

'Not especially. If I'm on my own, I play myself, but it isn't very satisfactory.'

'It's just that I led Jamie astray last night and we both looked on the wine when it was red. I don't think he is up yet.'

'Oh, well, never mind. Do you think you could pass me the newspaper, please. I'll catch up with the latest mayhem and murder.'

I winced at his choice of words, but walked across to the rack. 'Daily Telegraph OK?'

'Perfect.'

Just as I picked it up, Inspector Smithson came through and asked if I would go to the manager's office with him. I passed the newspaper to Mr Archer and saw him slip a magnifying glass out of his pocket. Just like Uncle Ted, I thought. Too bloody proud to get proper glasses.

I sat down in the office. Mr Fletcher had disappeared, but a waitress with a tray of coffee came in. There was also a plate of biscuits. Goody.

'Now, Miss Pattison, I understand from Superintendent Hamilton that you are helping us.'

'I'm not helping you with your enquiries in the sense you usually mean.'

He grinned. 'Sorry, bad choice of phrase. No, Mick says you are being helpful to her investigation of the Staithes murder.'

'And the attempted murder of Scott Wiley.'

'So, you're not averse to jumping in on the side of the angels?'

'I always wanted to be an angel, ever since Mrs Herring told me I had to be one of the sheep in the nativity play at school when I was six.'

He laughed. Saints be praised. This one had a sense of humour.

'I can do better than that,' he replied. 'I was a turkey on the jury which found Toad guilty in "Wind in the Willows". I think I was about nine.'

'Is that why you went into policing?'

'No, not really.'

There was a short silence. 'So how can I help you?' I prompted. He ran through my conversation with Winston and the manager. I nodded and added the news from Nettie. He seemed to be struggling with a decision so I sat and waited.

'I'll tell you this in confidence, Miss Pattison. We think we know who the culprit is but we haven't been able to catch them.'

'Clever use of language. Man or woman?'

'Don't want to say at the moment. Winston wants to put cameras up, but it is difficult to do that without everyone knowing and we think this would drive the thief underground, so to speak.'

I looked at him and sighed. 'So you want me to be a guinea pig?'

He grinned at me again. 'You're very quick on the uptake.'

'Only sometimes. What do you propose?'

'If we give you some flashy jewellery, and ask you to accidentally leave it somewhere, are you willing to do that?'

'Don't you think the thief would think twice before stealing something from me again?'

'Possibly. We are thinking that this time, it could be left in a more public place. Perhaps.'

'What happens if a member of the public finds it and hands it in?'

'Yes, we realise that there is a chance of that happening, but if we time it right, then we think we can catch the thief red-handed.'

'What's to stop them saying that they were about to take it to Mr Winston?'

'That's down to the timing as well. Are you game?'

'Why me? Just because I'm helping in the other case?'

'Not completely, no, but if you don't mind, I'd like to keep that one to myself.'

I sat and considered. Perhaps if I was going to snitch on a regular basis, I should put in an invoice for services rendered. Finally, I looked up at him. 'I'd like to talk to Superintendent Hamilton first, if you don't mind.'

'I don't mind at all. If you make a decision, it might be as well to send it to me via her in any case.'

Here we were, back to the personal danger thing again. 'I have to ask, Inspector, am I going to be at risk doing this at all?'

'Not if we get it right, no. If our quarry susses you, then, yes, perhaps.'

'So, you're asking me to run the risk of getting bumped over the head for a few little bits of jewellery.'

'There are a few other things besides jewellery that have disappeared, and, yes, we believe that if cornered, this person could resort to violence.'

'OK, I'll do it. I may have split up with my fiancé, but I love that ring and I want it back. What do I have to do?'

'We'll be in touch. Just leave me your mobile number as well.'

I walked out of the office and straight across the road to the cathedral. I felt almost soiled being a sneak twice over to two different coppers. I thought I would go and see Carrie. Besides I hadn't done any vocalising since the Vivaldi concert and it isn't good for a singer to take days off. I'd kill two birds with one stone - borrow Neil's piano for twenty minutes just to keep the engine ticking over and catch up with Carrie.

It was still early on Saturday morning, but Neil was already in the cathedral getting ready for the final concert of the festival that night. We waved to each other and I went straight through the cloisters into the close and walked to Carrie's front door. I rang the bell, but nobody answered. She must be upstairs, I thought, so I rang it again and then I looked through the side window to see if she was coming downstairs. She wasn't on the stairs, but the door to the kitchen was open and I could see a pair of feet.

For about three seconds I wondered why on earth Carrie was lying down on the kitchen floor, but then sense prevailed. Dropping my handbag, I turned and sprinted back through the cloisters almost knocking one old dear for six. Just inside the Priors Door, I opened my mouth and screamed Neil's name.

21

I have to say I was getting sick of the sight of that bloody hospital. I was seeing more of it than I was of the cathedral. I was sorely tempted to ask the matron or whoever they have in charge these days whether we could just put everyone in the same ward. It would make Hamilton's job easier, too. She wouldn't have to traipse from Albert to Scott to Carrie to ask her questions.

Neil was in a complete panic. When I screamed at him, he hadn't bothered with the stairs from the platform. He had simply vaulted over the top of the podium like an Olympic steeplechaser, landed on the floor some eight feet below and sprinted to where I was standing. Everything was just too much for me and I was crying so hard he couldn't get any sense out of me, but then he shook me very hard and I managed to say Carrie's name and that I couldn't get in the house.

He shouted at me to follow him. I was quite sporty at school and I'm no mean slouch now when it comes to a short dash, but he already had the door unlocked and was running into the kitchen when I reached the front door. By the time I panted into the kitchen, he had turned Carrie over. Her face and lips were swollen.

'She needs the EpiPen,' he yelled looking frantically round the room. 'Where's her fucking handbag?'

I took a quick look in the hall and then galloped into the lounge, tearing cushions off the sofa and moving the armchairs to see if it was behind one of them. Zilch.

'Try the bedroom,' Neil shouted. He was already speaking to the emergency services on his mobile. I flew up the stairs and there, thank God, on the bed, was her bag. I grabbed it and ran downstairs and emptied it out on the kitchen floor next to Neil. He grabbed the pen and administered the injection.

'I'm glad you did that and not me,' I said in a shaky effort to restore the jokey status quo.

'I've been taught how to do it for precisely this situation.'

'Will she be all right?'

'Where's the fucking ambulance,' he shouted, rocking her in his arms. She was beginning to make little sounds and movements now and, above the sound of his voice telling her to hold on and stay with him, I could hear the sirens. I went to open the front door. The police had arrived as well as the ambulance. Hamilton came running and grabbed my arm.

'What happened?'

'She's had some sort of allergic reaction.'

'What to?'

'Has to be nuts in some form. Neil might be able to give you a better clue, or her GP.'

Hamilton managed to get the GP's name out of Neil, then when the ambulance had departed leaving me stranded at the house, Hamilton declared the kitchen a no-go zone until she had talked to the medics and been given the score. She sent me away after I'd told her briefly what happened.

I ran through the traffic earning some honking from irate drivers, hurried into the hotel car park and drove to the hospital. Neil was pacing up and down A&E. When he saw me, he came over and steered me to a chair.

'Tell me what happened.'

I told him. He sat quietly for a few moments. 'This can't be right. We are both so vigilant about it. Did she ever tell you about the time I kissed her when we'd just started going out with each other. I'd had a packet of nuts about an hour before and I just didn't think. Her face swelled up like a balloon. It scared the hell out of me. Ever since then, we have both read labels sometimes two and three times over to make absolutely sure that there was never a trace of nuts anywhere in the house. I don't understand it.' He shook his head.

I collected a cup of the god-awful tea from the machine and both of us drank it, which is an indication of how distracted we were. After about six hours, well, actually, it was only about half an hour in reality, it just felt like six, a white coat came and found us. We both stood up.

'Er, Mr Gardiner?'

'That's me.'

The doctor looked at me, his eyes asking the obvious question.

'I'm Georgia Pattison, Carrie's friend.'

He eyed me suspiciously. I couldn't work out whether he thought I was Neil's bit on the side or he had seen me before and was trying to remember where.

'How is my wife?' Neil brought him back to the present.

'Her blood pressure is lower than we are happy with at the moment, so we're working on that. She is awake, but we need to monitor her closely for the next few hours.'

'Has she had the chance to tell you she's expecting our baby?'

'Yes, don't worry, Mr Gardiner. She'll be fine. We're helping her with her breathing and giving her medication for the low blood pressure. We only want to monitor her because occasionally the reaction can worsen after a few hours and we want to make sure that doesn't happen.'

'Is it OK to stay here and wait?'

'Yes, of course. As soon as we are happy with her, you can come in.'

I touched Neil on the arm. 'I'll just slip up to ITU to see Scott, OK, Neil?'

The doctor's face cleared. 'Ah, now I know where I've seen you. You're with the young man who nearly drowned, aren't you?'

'Yes.' I felt a bit awkward. 'I came here to sing, but I've seen more of your hospital than I have the concerts.'

'Come on, I'll walk you through. I'm due a break. Just let me tell Megan where I'm going.' I saw him talking to a nurse who had just emerged from the ward, then he walked back to me.

'You're having an exciting time at the moment, aren't you? Did you kill a Priest in a previous life?'

I wasn't in the mood for jokes so I just gave him a brief smile. 'It's a bit more hectic than I'm happy with, let's leave it at that. Carrie really will be OK, won't she?'

'Yes. You caught her in time. She might feel a bit wonky for a day or two, but she and the baby will be fine. Trust me, I'm a doctor.'

'Neil was magnificent. He just grabbed the pen thing and didn't even hesitate.'

'Good job, too. That's why we train the nearest and dearest to give the injections, because sometimes the patient can't reach the EpiPen and need help.'

'I think I feel a bit sick.'

'That's shock,' he said. 'Look, here's a loo. Go and take a load off your mind, as we say.'

I reached the loo just in time and after a couple of minutes I was rinsing my mouth out at the taps, but I could see my hands were shaking. I tottered back outside. The doctor was still waiting for me.

'Does that feel better?'

'Yes, I must stop drinking that bloody awful tea in your machine.'

'That's the spirit.'

When we arrived in ITU, I did feel better. Dr Raven was there and greeted me cheerfully until he saw my face and heard his colleague's story. I had to scrub my hands all over again. When I walked to Scott's bed, it was as if his parents hadn't moved since the previous night. His father turned a tired red-eyed gaze on me.

'Hi, Georgia. Come to take a turn?'

'If that's OK. My friend's just been brought in, so I thought I'd slip up and see Scott.'

'Good. Tina and I will go and have a coffee. How long can you stay?'

'Long as you need me to.'

'I'll take her into town, I think. Change of scenery. Hope your friend is all right.'

This time, Tina put up no arguments at all and within a couple of minutes, I was sitting holding Scott's hand telling him all about my horrible morning so far. After about ten minutes of this downbeat stuff, I decided that it wasn't the sort of thing someone trying to come out of a coma might want to hear. So, instead, I told him that I had a few plans for when he had a room of his own.

I stood up and stroked his hair back from his forehead. 'Oh, Scott, please wake up. I need you. I'm so scared and I don't know who to talk to.'

He frowned, like someone in a drunken stupor when someone else has said something that they are trying to take on board. 'I know you're in there somewhere, Scott. Perhaps I should sing, or do you think the other patients would object?' His head rolled towards the sound of my voice and his hand squeezed mine. I looked around for the nurse who hurried over when she saw my expression.

'Is he responding?' she asked quietly.

'Yes, I told him perhaps I should sing to him and he rolled his head towards me and squeezed my hand.'

'Excellent. Let's try his drinking reflex. It hasn't been too good so far, but it's worth another go.'

She held up a sort of baby cup to his mouth. A lot dribbled down his pyjama jacket, but we both saw him swallow. She was nearly as excited as I was. Dr Raven came across and began his tests again. He swiped his pen across Scott's feet and this time, as well as pulling his legs up, he made an angry grunt. His parents arrived back in time to see their son open his eyes wide and look at them. His mother began to cry and Scott turned his head and grunted again.

Dr Raven put his hand on Scott's shoulder. 'That's it for now, Scott. I'll come and see you later on. Your parents are here.' He motioned to me with his head and as I slipped into a walk beside him, I looked back to see Tina smoothing her son's hair and kissing his forehead.

'That's a good sign, isn't it?' I asked. 'He's waking up.'

'I need to do an MRI, but I think he is less deeply unconscious than he was. It's only a couple of days since the accident, so don't think you're going to see him do the hokey-cokey up and down the ward for a while. Keep your chin up.'

I said goodbye and headed back down to Neil. By this time, Carrie was in a small ward of four people in the bed next to the nursing station. Hamilton was standing by the bed. When she saw me, she said something to Neil and walked to meet me, taking my arm.

'Just a quick word.'

We went to the tea machine. Its fame had obviously spread because there was nobody within sight of it. Hamilton leaned against it. I stood there with my arms folded as if waiting for another blow to fall.

'Don't look so scared, George. I just need to know why you went there this morning. Did Mrs Gardiner know you were coming?'

'No.' I looked up and down the corridor. It was practically deserted. 'I'd just finished speaking to your Inspector Smithson.'

'Yes. He's spoken to me, by the way. I'm not overjoyed about what he wants you to do, either. You've got enough on your plate helping me.'

'Whatever. Anyway, I decided that I needed to clear my head and I also have to confess to feeling a bit tarnished on account of being a supergrass.'

'He isn't asking you to be a supergrass. He wants you to act as an agent provocateur and I'm not happy. Anyway, leave that for the moment. Carry on, you wanted to clear your head.'

'I haven't sung since Thursday night and I know that when I do my exercises and all that, it clears my brain, gets the old endorphins racing about and generally makes me feel better. Besides, I wanted to talk to Carrie again.'

'What about?'

I hedged. I couldn't possibly tell her that Merlina had seen Carrie in the cloisters on Saturday night because she'd have a constant police presence at the poor girl's bedside before I could sing "with the tip of the tongue and the teeth and the lips".

'We were best friends at college and we haven't seen enough of each other since then. I just wanted a chat and a coffee and to sing for twenty minutes.'

'OK, fair enough. Tell me exactly what you did.'

I explained everything from leaving Smithson to looking through the window next to Carrie's front door and seeing her feet.

'And then you went and told her husband?'

'I think screamed for her husband would be more accurate.'

'Now, George, think very carefully. When you left the cathedral, when you were walking through the cloisters, when you came into the close, did you see anyone? Anyone at all.'

I thought back. 'No, not a soul.'

'Bollocks. I was hoping you might have.'

There was a short silence. By the look on her face, I guessed she was either trying to think something out, or trying to think of some way to say what she wanted to say. I couldn't stand the suspense. 'Come on, Superintendent, out with it.'

'I was just wondering if Miss Staithes had ever been in Mrs Gardiner's kitchen.'

This one really did come from left field and it took me a couple of seconds to work out what she meant. 'Do you mean, it might have been Ariana who brought nuts into the house.'

'It had crossed my mind.'

'But why?'

'She was having an affair with Neil Gardiner, wasn't she?'

'Yes, but it wouldn't have been serious.'

'How do you know?'

'Because I know...knew Ariana. She would only go to bed with someone if they were useful, and presumably she found Neil useful before the festival. I can promise you this, Superintendent, she would have dropped him like a hot potato at the end of it and floated back to London. She knew that after this year, Temingham wouldn't have been able to afford her. Besides, what good could he have done her? He's a provincial cathedral organist. He has no influence where she would have wanted it.'

'But maybe he knows people who do have influence.'

'Yes, but...' I stopped to reorganise my thoughts. 'Look, if there were people of influence to be known, Ariana wouldn't have used a go-between. In the musical world there are quite a few strong women, but most of the plums still go to men. She would have gone to the source of the influence, not someone who might know him.'

'You're sure of that?'

'Yes, I am.'

She sighed. 'OK, I'll bow to your greater knowledge.'

'Isn't that partly why you asked for my help in the first place?'

'Touché.'

I drove back to the hotel and asked room service to send up a sandwich and a pot of coffee. And some soup. And a slice of carrot cake. As I sat in front of the laptop, tapping in my latest report, my mind continued to range over the possibilities. How had nuts come to be in Carrie's kitchen was question number one. Question number two was who could have put them there. I could hear Ian Carmichael acting the part of Lord Peter Wimsey saying "when you know how, you'll know who". I ate my lunch and drank two cups of coffee reading a biography of Joan Sutherland propped up by the mirror.

With a sigh, I closed the book and turned back to the computer and then it struck me. There were only two people who, in reality, could have put nuts in the kitchen. One was Neil and the other was Carrie herself.

22

What I couldn't work out was why Carrie would endanger her life and the life of her baby. Surely if it had been her, then she would have made sure the EpiPen was at hand. She could have administered the injection and called her GP. Because of her pregnancy, her doctor might still have admitted her to hospital for observation.

So what reason could she possibly have had for putting herself at risk like that? The lost earring, of course, my inner voice declared. She wanted to deflect attention away from herself as a suspect by making herself a victim, it whispered into my ear. But I had believed her when she said that she hadn't been anywhere near the west door. In that case, I argued, how come Merlina saw her heading that way on the night Ariana died?

I decided that what I really needed was fresh air. The weather wasn't overly sunny, so I put a windcheater on and headed out of the hotel and down onto the tow path in the direction of the picnic site. I was trying to reconcile my memory of the desperation and sheer bloody panic in Neil's voice and the picture of him adding nuts to.... Yes, that was partly it, wasn't it? Adding nuts to what? What could hide the look and texture of them so that Carrie wouldn't be alerted? And, more to the point, why would he want to get rid of Carrie, not to mention his child now that Ariana was dead?

Surely if he had sabotaged the whatever it was the nuts were in, then knowing that he had made a mistake with Ariana and that he really loved Carrie and knowing that his firstborn was on the way, surely he would have got rid of the whatever it was? I needed to know what the nuts had been hidden in before this one was going to be sorted out.

I was about to cross the bridge over to the picnic site when I saw a big golden retriever bounding across it. I looked further back and saw Lizzie crossing the picnic area. I stopped and waited for her which is more than Jordy did. She was slightly out of breath by the time she reached me.

'Hi, Georgia. As you see, I am being taken for a walk. Do you want to tag along?'

'That would be great. Yes, please.'

'How is your investigation going?'

'Not smoothly.'

'Ah, sorry to hear that.' She cupped a hand to her mouth. 'Jordy, here.'

The dog stopped and looked back almost as if he was measuring the distance and wondering whether it was worth pretending to be deaf. Lizzie yelled again.

'Here. Now.'

I could almost see him sighing, deciding that perhaps it might be better if he obeyed. He began to trot back to her. She put a hand in one pocket and brought out a small biscuit. 'Here you go, good boy, Jordy.'

'Where does this path go to?' I asked.

'It just follows the river. I was going to take him up on the moors, but I don't like going there by myself.'

'I'll come with you.'

She turned. 'Really? Do you want to go now?'

'Why not?'

She whistled the dog and turned round. Within five minutes we were in her car and heading out along the same road I had travelled with Hamilton just a few days before. There were a few large informal scrubby areas which people used as car parks and we pulled into one of these near a rock stack that looked so perilously balanced I asked Lizzie to park well away from it. She laughed.

'They've been like that for hundreds of years. I think you're quite safe, Georgia.'

The walk was just what I needed. Clear open space. Clean fresh air. Lovely views back towards Temingham. I could see the cathedral tower which brought back to me the horror of recent events, but I disciplined my mind to forget about that and just enjoy the beauty. True, it wasn't the loveliness of green rolling hills, but it had a savage splendour which made my heart glad to be alive.

'Do you come up here often?'

'Mick likes to come up here when she's on a difficult case or she is feeling troubled.'

'I can't imagine anything troubling her. She is so task driven, it's scary. Somebody told me her nickname is Princess Ice-Knickers.'

'You don't surprise me. That's because they don't know her. She is just as vulnerable as the rest of us.'

'Forgive me if I say I haven't seen any sign of that. Is she getting used to Jordy yet?'

'She actually called him by his name this morning, which I thought was a promising sign.'

'Why doesn't she like him. He's gorgeous.'

The gorgeous one was at that moment trying to lever himself down a rabbit hole. All we could see was a wagging tail looking like a politician trying to work out which way to face. Lizzie ran forward and hauled him out. His face was filthy but he was grinning, I swear he was. I couldn't help but laugh.

'You stupid wombat, look at you. Mucky pup.'

He came bounding over towards me. When I realised that he wasn't actually going to stop, I leaned forward and waved my arms in front of my legs. At the last possible moment, he veered off to the left. I laughed again.

'I wish I could have a dog,' I said as Lizzie walked back to me.

'Why can't you?'

'Too peripatetic a lifestyle.'

'Nobody at home to look after him?'

'No. I live in a basement flat. My landlady, Nettie, has the rest of the house. She and her husband are both in their seventies but you wouldn't believe it. They go all over the place. A dog would cramp their life too much, so there's no prospect of even having one in the house.'

'Shame. I've been banging on about getting a dog for about three years with Mick. She says she's allergic, but she isn't.'

'Perhaps she just likes her life the way it is.'

'What about my life?'

'Well, it must suit you or you would have moved out by now, wouldn't you?'

'It suits her, too, George. Mick's problem is that she views things as being her way or no way.'

'Well, at work, that is how it is, don't you think?'

'Suppose so. She's a funny old stick. She has nightmares, you know.'

'You surprise me. She always strikes me as being, not unimaginative exactly, just someone who is very practical and doesn't think about the whys and wherefores of life.'

Lizzie turned to me. 'That is precisely the problem. She is unhappy but doesn't realise it.'

'Oh no. Surely you know when you're unhappy.'

'Not if you don't let yourself think about it, George.' There was a short silence. 'We'd better get back to the car. Where's the dog?'

Jordy had disappeared behind some rocks, something we only found out when we heard children's voices yelling at something to go away.

'Oh, no,' said Lizzie beginning to run. 'Odds on they've got a picnic and Jordy thinks it's for him.'

We found a group of four children with their backs turned to the dog, trying to save their sandwiches. Jordy, of course, thought this was all part of the game. Lizzie apologised and gave them some money for ice creams. Jordy was put on his lead and frog-marched back to the car in disgrace. He didn't look in the least bit repentant, but I laughed more than I had done for weeks.

I arrived back at the hotel feeling better for the walk but at a loose end. I rang the hospital to find out how Carrie was. She was much improved and providing she showed no adverse reaction, they said she might be allowed to come home later on. When I transferred to ITU to ask after Scott, I was told that he had tried to pull his tubes out, but was fine. They said the doctor would reassess him the next morning.

I put the phone in my pocket and wandered downstairs. Rosemary was on duty again. I wondered if she ever had any time off. She asked me how Scott was.

'I know you gave him my card, but they won't let me see him. They said only family and close friends.'

'I suppose that's usual in this circumstance. He is very ill, but all we can be is optimistic.'

'Do you go to see him a lot?'

'Every day. I just talk to him, really and he is showing some signs that he can hear.' I put my hand on her arm. 'Don't worry, Rosemary. It was very kind of you to send the card. I'll make sure I keep you up to speed.'

She smiled her thanks but looked a little paler than usual. Mind you, I'd be pale if I had to sit in a hotel reception every day watching people enjoying their time off. I walked into the bar. Jamie was chatting to Kevin Dace, who, I realised, I hadn't seen for a couple of days. I walked up to them.

'Mind if I join you, boys? I'm feeling a bit lonely.'

Kevin immediately made room on the bench seat and waved at the barman for a large dry white wine. It was probably my imagination, but I fancied that Jamie was less pleased than Kevin to see me.

'Have I interrupted something?' I asked. 'If so, just tell me to push off.'

Jamie smiled. 'No, you're OK, George. We were just talking about this.' He handed me the local paper. 'Just look at the headlines and then the editorial comment.'

The headlines were all about Ariana's murder and the attempted murder of "internationally renowned pianist, Scott Wiley". It was strange being almost an insider and reading the spin the journalist had put on it. I thought he or she went overboard on the "stain on Temingham Music Festival" bit. I looked at the bye-line. It was a she, and a she who obviously knew more than I did or, rather, more than Hamilton had told me because there were all kinds of theories being put forward, from the usual mad tramp to a sophisticated drug ring. I wondered if the local library would file it under "Fiction".

Sighing and shaking my head, I turned to the editorial. I don't know who the editor was, but I sent up a prayer that he never encountered Hamilton on a dark night. He wittered on about "the incompetence of the police allowing such things to happen in such a law-abiding community as ours when the eyes of the world were upon our Peak District town". He wondered if it was time to call in bigger guns to investigate such a high profile case and that we had to safeguard the considerable income the town earned from tourism. His final sentence said "After all, our local officers, though worthy and competent are hardly likely to have come across such a scenario before and there is no shame in admitting that and asking more experienced hands for help."

I winced. Jamie grinned. 'Doesn't like your friend Hamilton much, does he?'

'She isn't my friend.'

'I thought she was. You seem to spend a lot of time talking to each other.'

I looked at him as if he was a slug I had just found in the lettuce. 'Really? And how do you know how many times Superintendent Hamilton and I have spoken?'

His face was a fiery red by this time. 'Sorry, George. Didn't mean to tread on your toes.'

'You aren't, but I imagine that she has spoken to a few other people a lot more than she has to me.'

'Oh, this sounds good,' put in Kevin. 'Shall we play who dunnit?'

'Is it compulsory?' I asked.

'No, but it might be good fun. Now who are our suspects?'

'I sighed again. 'Miss Scarlett in the conservatory with a candlestick.'

I've often thought the study of people's laughs would make a good subject for a doctorate. Kevin's was less a laugh and more a asthmatic truffle pig snuffle. Then my brain kicked in and decided that, actually, this might be a cracking opportunity to discuss the whole thing and get some ideas.

'I thought you were always supposed to go for the nearest and dearest,' I offered as my contribution.

Kevin put his head on one side and thought for a moment. 'Yes, I can see what you mean, but surely if the lumberjack wanted to get rid of her, he could have made her disappear in a wood-chipper or something, don't you think?'

'Might be difficult and too obvious,' put in Jamie.

I took a sip of wine and looked at him over the rim of the glass. 'Who do you go for, then?'

'I have no idea.'

I decided to put a toe in the water. 'Have you heard what happened to Carrie Gardiner this morning?'

Both their heads swivelled towards me and shook in a negative, so I told them the bare bones of what had happened. I could see that Kevin was trying to fit this into some private mental jigsaw, but Jamie's mouth dropped open.

'Is she going to be all right?'

'The doctor says so, yes. In fact, if she improves this afternoon, they might let her out tonight.'

'Who will conduct the final concert?'

'If she is OK, then Neil will do it, I'm sure. There's been so much disruption because of the Ariana and Scott thing that I'm almost positive he will want to keep the festival boat floating and not drive another hole through its keel.'

'I don't know if I would be able to do that,' said Kevin in a quiet tone.

'How do you know until you've been in the situation?'

'True. Well, children,' he said, getting to his feet. 'I must away. Are you both going to the concert tonight?'

Jamie and I looked at each other, eyebrows raised. 'I think it might be good to show some solidarity, don't you?' I asked. He nodded.

'Good,' replied Kevin. 'I'm going, too. What about we all meet here at seven and I'll ask the dining room to keep some food back for us.'

'Will they do that?' I asked. 'Most hotels are really strict with their eating hours.'

'Don't worry, I'll manage it. Is that all right with you both?'

'Fine. Yes.'

I watched Kevin make his way to the dining room. 'Is he always this sure that people will do what he wants them to?'

Jamie laughed. 'Well, you know, he comes across as a bit bossy and managing, but when he wants you to do something, it is almost impossible to say no to him.'

'What is the concert tonight anyway?'

'Janacek's "Glagolitic Mass"'

'Oh, you're joking.'

'No I'm not, George. Why? What's wrong with it?'

'You mean apart from the fact that it's bloody awful?'

'No it isn't. Your problem is that you are so stuck in the seventeenth century, you can't cope with anything remotely modern. How many times have you sung it?'

'Er..none.'

'All right. How many times have you heard it?'

'I've heard bits of it on Classic FM. Does that count?'

'No, it doesn't. Tonight will do you good, young lady. You are coming and you will enjoy it if I have to beat it into you.'

'Yes sir,' I replied with as much meekness as I could muster without laughing.

'Good. Now go and make yourself beautiful. Go on, George. Seriously, it will do you good to do a bit of pampering and get dressed up without having to sing.'

I gave him a mock salute. 'Certainly, sir. Whatever you say, sir. See you down here at seven, sir.'

I was still smiling when I reached the lift and looked back. I couldn't see Jamie, but Rosemary caught the smile and returned it. I kicked off my shoes when I reached my room and looked at my watch. Almost five. Right, two hours of schmoo. Which dress? I looked in the wardrobe. Ooh, yes, the purple chiffon with the handkerchief hem. Perfect. I'd wear the jet jewellery and my black strappy sandals, which meant I'd have to get a move on because I needed to paint my toenails.

I had a shower first and washed my hair, leaving some gunky conditioner in it whilst I then ran a bath, complete with bubble bath. I must have stayed in it for all of ten minutes before showering the gunk off. I never have been very good at taking time out. I like the idea, but I am far too fidgety to do anything for as long as the instructions say.

First job was painting the toenails, which was necessary because of the time they would take to dry but bloody irritating because it meant I had to walk around like an Egyptian mummy from a horror movie so that I didn't smudge them. My hair was roughly dried and I put it in a braid whilst it was still a bit damp. Make up next. I made myself take twenty minutes instead of my usual seven. Then I sat on the bed reading until fifteen minutes before zero hour. The dress looked good and with the jewellery even better.

I went hunting in the depths of the wardrobe for my sandals and frowned. I was sure I hadn't left my shoes in this mess. I always like my dressy shoes on one side and my everyday ones on the other. But my Ecco walking shoes were piled on top of the silver sandals I'd worn to Merlina's farewell concert. I picked them up making a mental note to have a serious word with Ellie, the chambermaid. The shoes rattled as if they were full of stones. I couldn't see properly in the recesses of the wardrobe, so I stood up straight a shoe in each hand, walked over to the bed and tipped them upside down.

I stood there completely gobsmacked as out tumbled a pocket-watch, an aquamarine solitaire ring, a gold locket, a man's signet ring with a good-sized diamond in it and, last but by no means least, a gold bracelet set with emeralds and diamonds.

23

I stood transfixed for all of half a minute just staring down at the things on the bed. I put my hand on the phone to call the manager, but revised that idea. Instead, I unfolded my mobile and scrolled down to the name "Lizzie". Hamilton answered on the second ring.

'Are you on your own?' was my first question.

'No. Why? Trouble?'

'You could say that. Look, Superintendent, is there any way you can get up to my hotel room without anyone seeing you.'

'Yes, I think so.'

'How soon can you be here?'

'Ten minutes.'

'I'll be watching for you.'

I put my wrap over the treasure on the bed, picked up the room phone and pressed the button for Reception.

'Hi, is that Rosemary?'

'No, she's gone off duty. I'm Becky, can I help?'

'Yes. This is Miss Pattison in 327. I am supposed to be meeting Mr Dace and Mr Topcliffe in reception in five minutes. Please could you tell them I am unwell and apologise for me?'

'I'm sorry to hear that, Miss Pattison. Is there anything I can do? Do you need a doctor?'

'No, I think I may have caught a chill on the moors this afternoon. I think an early night will see me OK, but thank you.'

'If you need anything, just ring. And don't forget room service can bring you a meal up.'

'No, I won't forget. Thank you.'

I had just put the phone down when there was a knock on the door. There was no doubt about it, Hamilton could move when she wanted to. It was less than seven minutes since I'd rung her. I opened the door and she slipped in.

'Did anyone see you?'

'No. Now, what is all this?'

I swished the wrap off the bed like a conjuror. I was too rattled to say abracadabra. Hamilton stood stock still, frowning.

'Precisely the reaction I had, Superintendent.'

'Where did you find these?'

I explained. She rubbed her mouth with her fingertips and then rang Smithson on her mobile. I think Smithson jumped to the conclusion that I had stolen the things but Hamilton reminded him that I wasn't even in Temingham when the first things had gone missing. There was a bit of verbal to-ing and fro-ing. When Hamilton ended the call, she asked me if I had an envelope. There were several in the drawer. She pulled on latex gloves and carefully put each piece into a separate envelope, which she then sealed, adding her signature and the date across each seal.

'Do you have a handbag or something I can put these in?'

I looked around and upended the leather briefcase I carry my laptop in. 'Here use this.'

'We'll need a statement from you, of course.'

'You do know that I've never seen those things before tonight, don't you? Apart from the ones that belong to me, that is.'

'Oh, yes. I think we can agree on that. What were you planning for tonight?'

'I was supposed to be going to the final concert of the festival with Jamie and Kevin. Why?'

'I think you should still do that.'

'But I've just told the girl on reception that I'm ill.'

'Then go out of the back door so you don't see her.'

I looked at my watch. Ten past seven. 'I'll just say that it was a dizzy spell and I feel better. If I run, I can probably catch them up.'

'And for the next few days, just go about as if you hadn't found this little lot, all right?'

'Yes, OK.'

'By the way,' she added as we approached the door. 'There were ground almonds in your friend's ground oats. She was apparently going to make some sort of quiche.'

'Do we know how they got there?'

'No, not yet. Come on. I'll see if the coast is clear.'

As we slithered out of my room, I thanked God that there was nobody watching. They would have seen something out of a bad gangster movie as we flitted down the corridor Hamilton slid through the door to the back stairs. I rode down to reception in the lift. The first person I saw was Jamie.

'I thought you were ill,' he said, frowning.

'I felt dizzy, but it's worn off now, so I thought I would come to the concert after all. Why are you still here?'

'Kevin left his wallet in his room. He'd better hurry up or we'll be late.'

Kevin hurried through the lift door a couple of seconds later and we all rushed over the road to the cathedral. It seemed quite a few of Temingham's inhabitants shared my opinion of Janacek's choral masterpiece because we managed to get three seats together adjacent to the aisle about ten rows from the front.

The citizens of Temingham missed a spectacle. The choir sound was literally thrilling. Sebastian, bless his socks, did wonders with the organ part and the whole ensemble was electrifying. At the end, all three of us stood up our arms above our heads applauding. Neil, saw us and grinned. What a roller-coaster of a day for him. Nearly losing his wife in the morning and a triumphant end to the Festival in the evening.

I turned to the boys and told them I would have to find out how Carrie was and that I'd be over to the hotel in about fifteen minutes. Kevin frowned and told me not to be long because he'd only just persuaded the Maître d' to keep the dining room open for us.

I pushed my way through the departing audience and managed to catch Neil as he was making sure the soloists were being looked after. I caught his arm. 'That was brilliant, Neil. Well done. How's Carrie?'

'She's OK, George. A bit shaken and I've told her she must stop in bed for a couple of days which isn't going down too well.' He broke off to say cheerio to the leader of the orchestra. I turned to go, but he grabbed my hand.

'Don't go for a minute, George. I've an enormous favour to ask. When are you planning to leave?'

'Well I was going to go to Finlay tomorrow and then I need to see Melanie next week and there are a few irons in the fire I should keep a check on.'

'Can you do it all by phone or are you actually singing next week?'

'I'm singing in York on Saturday with the Bach Choir, but I'm supposed to be seeing Janetta this week in London as well. And I have to sort out Cirencester with Melanie and see if she has anything for me or whether I'll have to do some supply teaching to pay the bills this month.'

'I never have understood why professional singers still need lessons. Surely you know all you need to.'

'Never say that, Neil. Nobody stops learning if they are sensible. There's a glitch somewhere and she will spot it within about three seconds, but I can't sort it out by myself.'

'Well surely this week will have augmented the bank account?'

I wasn't prepared to start discussing my financials with Neil Gardiner and I was also aware that Kevin's admonition to be quick was making me fidget. 'What was the favour?'

'Will you stop on, with us, of course, and look after Carrie for a few days, please?'

I thought for a few seconds. 'Can I give you my answer tomorrow, Neil? I need to sort out exactly what needs doing and if I can do it from here or if I need to be there. I'll ring you after morning service tomorrow. Are you doing it, or Sebastian?'

'I ought to, really, but Seb is champing at the bit to have a go. Anyway, that's my problem. Ring me about midday. I should be back by then. Oh, and George,' he added as I turned to sprint over to the hotel, 'thanks. I really do appreciate it. I just think it would do Carrie good to have a close woman friend with her at the moment.'

I nodded and pushed my way back through the still departing throng. It seriously annoys me when people gather right in the middle of a thoroughfare chatting as if there was all the time in the world. I was panting slightly by the time I made it into the dining room.

Kevin looked up at me, then at his watch and scowled. 'Typical bloody woman. Late for everything.'

I'm afraid, I lost it. I walked over to his side of the table and grabbed his tie. 'Look you lard-arsed excuse for a man. This week I have found a dead body, barely rescued someone from the river and we still don't know how brain-damaged he is going to be, found another close friend in anaphylactic shock, been to the hospital more times than I have eaten in this room, and been grilled by the police.

In addition I have sung two concerts and one recital I didn't know I was going to have to until just over a week ago. Don't push your luck, sunshine, or you could find yourself in hospital and I can guarantee you'll be singing soprano for the rest of your life. So back off.' I poured out a glass of water, preparatory to throwing it in his supercilious face, but Jamie's hand caught my arm and grabbed the glass. I stood there out of breath.

'I expect you feel better after that, don't you?' replied Kevin, not turning a hair. 'Why not sit down and we'll eat. Simon would very much like to take our order, deliver our food and then go home. Don't heave your bosom at me, George. I'm not that way inclined.'

Totally bemused I did as I was told. He beamed at me. 'Now, are you hungry?'

'Yes,' I snapped.

'Good. I suggest orange and chicken liver pate to start, followed by fillet of sea bass and marmalade bread and butter pudding. That sound all right to you?'

I nodded. He called the waiter over and we let Kevin order for all of us. After about three minutes, Simon brought the wine menu. From his countenance, anyone would think he had screaming divas in his dining room every night.

Jamie and I left the choice of wines to Kevin as well. I was in that awful state between anger and frightened tears, I don't know what Jamie was thinking. Ten minutes later we were tucking into the pate and drinking a heavy red. The sea bass came with a dry New Zealand white and after that, I didn't much care. We were well into the sea bass and Kevin and Jamie were talking quietly to each other. I just sat and ate, feeling miserable and saying nothing. Kevin turned to me as I was finishing the main course.

'I'm sorry I upset you. I hadn't quite realised how much you've been through this week. I was down in London until yesterday afternoon, so I've missed a lot of it. Are you feeling a bit better now?'

'Thank you, yes.'

'Good. Try the bread and butter pud. It is sensational.'

I did. It was. We had coffee afterwards and Kevin then ushered us to the bar and ordered three large brandies. It was almost eleven and there weren't many people around, so we chose a dark corner.

'How is Caroline Gardiner?' asked Kevin.

'She's at home but in bed. Neil wants me to stay for a few days and look after her.'

'And will you?'

'I don't know. I need to see Melanie and Janetta. I don't know what to do.'

He put a hand on my arm. 'Speaking as a lard-arsed excuse for a man, have you actually stopped to think what you would like to do?'

'I can't make up my mind. I feel I ought to stay, but part of me wants to run away.'

'If I were you, I wouldn't think about it until tomorrow, then just let your mind say yes or no, whichever it comes up with first and go with that.'

I smiled for the first time in a couple of hours. 'Thanks. Sorry I was so bloody rude to you.'

'Darling, compared to some of the tantrums I've had thrown at me, you are a complete amateur.'

I was about to open my mouth and say something else conciliatory when my mobile tinkled in the depths of my bag. It was Hamilton.

'On your own? Careful how you reply.'

'No, not at all, don't worry about it.'

'I'm in the car park. Can you come through?'

'Yes, that's fine. Thank you for letting me know. See you. Bye.'

I folded the phone up. 'Sorry about that.' I turned to Kevin. 'I think you're right. It's been a long day. It's been a long bloody week. I'm cream-crackered. Do you mind if I go to bed now? Thank you for a lovely meal and I really did enjoy the concert.'

They waved me to the lift. As soon as I reached my room, I slipped out of the dress and into my discarded jeans and a black jacket. Five minutes later, I was peering out of the door from the back stairs towards reception. Not a soul. I slid through the door into the car park. Hamilton leaned over to open the passenger door. She was moving before I had the door shut.

'What's the rush. Has something happened to Scott?'

'No. If it had, I would have come into the hotel to tell you. Everyone knows you visit him. No, it's Albert.'

'Albert?' My mind had gone blank.

'The doorkeeper. Another victim of our murderer. He's woken up enough to talk to me.'

'And?'

'And what?'

'And what does that have to do with me?'

'I want you to hear what he says first hand. I want to make sure he really has remembered and he isn't simply confused.'

'I don't understand what this has to do with me?'

'You will.'

We reached the hospital car park. I was sick of the sight of anything connected with the hospital. We walked through the main doors and up the stairs.

'By the way,' Hamilton said. 'They think they might be moving Scott to a private room in a couple of days. He seems to be improving quite a bit.'

'Thank God for that.' The tears were very close again.

'You'd better not tell anyone else for the moment, and neither can you tell them about Albert.'

'I don't suppose anyone will be interested in Albert, but there are a lot of people interested in Scott. Why can't I say anything?'

'Use your brain, George. If whoever clobbered him gets a hint that he might be compos mentis enough to tell us who it was, they might just have another go.'

'But the doctor said it's very unlikely he will remember, even if he does come back with no brain damage.'

She looked at me and shook her head. 'Would you take the chance?'

'Ah. I see. OK, I'll keep it zipped.'

We walked into a ward. On the right between the nurses' station and the ward proper, there was a partitioned off bit. Sitting by the bed was a policeman in uniform and in the bed was an elderly white-haired man with a bandaged head. Aided by a young student nurse, he was drinking a cup of tea through a straw. He reminded me of granddad after his stroke, vulnerable and frightened. I bit my lip and stared at the wall behind his bed.

'Hello, Albert,' said Hamilton. 'I don't know. The lengths some people will go to, to get a pretty nurse to feed them a cup of tea.'

The nurse smiled and took the cup away. Albert also smiled but he looked very tired. 'I am honoured. Two visits in one day.' He looked at me. 'Who's this? Your daughter?'

'No, she isn't, you daft bugger. This is Georgia. She is helping me find out who hit you.'

'Good. I suppose it's more questions, is it?'

'Sort of. Mind if we sit down?'

'Be my guest. You're better looking than this bloke any road.'

Hamilton nodded dismissal at the uniformed guy who shot to his feet and strode out of the ward. Hamilton sat down in the chair he had vacated and motioned me to the one on the other side of the bed.

'Now, Albert. I just need Georgia to hear the answers to my questions. Is that OK?'

'Yes.' He looked troubled. 'Do you want me to tell you what I told you before?'

'No. I have some different questions. Now, what made you go outside in the first place?'

He leaned across to her. 'You won't get me into trouble, will you?'

'Why would I want to do that?'

''Cos I'm not supposed to leave the door, but I wanted a smoke.'

'Ah. I see. No don't worry, Albert. Your secret is safe with me.'

'Good.'

'So you went outside and lit up?'

'I never got the chance. I walked to the top of the steps down to the grass and I saw that some careless beggar had thrown one of those plastic holders for tins of beer on the grass at the bottom of the steps. You know what I mean, they look like four plastic rings.'

'Yes, I know. Go on.'

'My memory's a bit fuzzy, I think I need to sit a bit more and let it come back, Miss Hamilton.'

'Don't kid me, Albert. You know perfectly well what happened next. Come on, spill it, or I'll eat all your grapes.'

'Who could refuse such a gracious invitation? OK, I started down the steps to pick it up and put it in a bin. They can get tangled round the swans and ducks, you know. If they're not removed, the poor little beggars die.'

'Yes, I know. What happened then? What did you see?'

'I can't say I saw anything. I was aware of a movement and a swishing noise. I half turned, but something hit me and I remember thinking how daft I was going to look falling down the steps.'

'So you didn't see who it was who attacked you?'

'No, well, not exactly.'

'So, tell me, exactly, what you saw. Nothing more, nothing less.'

It was a woman, Miss Hamilton. A tall woman. As I fell, I got a whiff of her perfume. It was real strong.'

24

We were walking back through the silent corridors.

'What am I supposed to make of that, Superintendent?'

'I was going to ask you what you did make of it.'

'You're trying to pin it onto Carrie again, aren't you?'

'I'm not trying to pin anything on anyone. I just want to get to the truth. And don't forget the earring.'

'Well, I still don't think it was Carrie.'

'Had it occurred to you, George, that she might have arranged her little medical emergency?'

'I did think of it, yes. But it doesn't make any sense at all.'

I went through the arguments I had presented to myself that morning. 'What you need to find out from Albert is what he considers to be tall.' I concluded.

She nodded. 'I'll get onto that first thing in the morning.'

'Look, Carrie has just been through almost losing her husband. She is pregnant. It is all OK again, now, but they have both had a real fright. I am bloody sure she wouldn't risk any harm to her baby.'

'Perhaps you're right.'

'Why did you really bring me here tonight, Superintendent? It must be important. You know the day I've had.'

'Yes, and I know how much you drank tonight, too. Are you close-mouthed in your cups, George?'

'I never get that much in my cups that I need to worry about it. Is that it? You were afraid I was going to blab to Jamie and Kevin, so you pulled me out of the bar like a naughty schoolgirl?'

'Not exactly. I did want you to hear, first hand, what Albert said, so that you couldn't accuse me of twisting his words, but I was a bit startled when ...someone.. rang and told me you were putting it back like there was no tomorrow.'

'Who?'

'Nobody you need to worry about?'

I stood for a moment and thought about that. 'You either have a spy or, more likely, spies at the hotel, or....or' I was groping a bit here. 'Or, you have somebody watching over me. Which?'

'Not your problem. Now, let's get back to business. Is there any way that you can prolong your time here?'

'Neil has asked me to stay for a few days and look after Carrie.'

'And are you going to?'

'I need to speak to my agent and my singing teacher first. Then I'll tell you. And Neil. I can ring tomorrow morning.'

'Does your agent work on Sundays?'

'No, but I do have her home number for emergencies and I can make this sound like one, if you want.'

'It would be handy. I've heard, by the way, that they are definitely arranging the memorial service for this coming Tuesday at seven-thirty. You'll be there, of course?'

'Of course.'

'I don't know what form it will take. I'd better drop you back in the hotel car park.'

The first person I saw when I came back through the back door was Jamie. It was almost as if he had been waiting for me.

'I thought you were going to bed.'

'I needed some fresh air.'

'Don't lie, Georgia. I saw Hamilton pick you up. Was it her who rang just before your sudden urge for an early night?'

For a few moments, I couldn't think what to say, so I just came out with the first thing that sprang to my lips. 'You sound almost jealous, Jamie. That isn't like you.' This gave me time to think of a good excuse. 'Yes, it was our delightful Superintendent. She was going to the hospital and wondered if I wanted to accompany her.'

'Is that the truth?'

'Absolutely, it is. Why would I lie?'

Jamie put his hands on my shoulders. 'Sorry, George. I have a confession to make.'

'What about?'

'You.'

This was a real surprise. 'Me? What about me?'

He looked at his feet and mumbled something.

'Jamie, I have no idea what you are on about. Look at me and speak clearly, for God's sake, or I am going to bed.'

'I said that I had hoped we could try to get to know each other better this week, but you seem to have fallen in a big way for Scott Wiley.'

I gave him my best glare. 'I have known Scott for just over a week, met him twice, rescued him from a watery grave and spent the last four days visiting someone who looks like him but who is probably never going to be anything other than brain-damaged.' My voice was rising with every sentence but I couldn't stop myself. It was as if all the horror and unhappiness had finally bubbled to the surface and poor old Jamie was copping the lot. 'And you have the nerve to stand there, whole and healthy and tell me you are jealous of someone in a coma. For God's sake go into a corner and have a word with yourself. I've known you over ten years, but it's only when someone else shows any interest in me that you decide you want me. Is that it?'

'No. No it isn't. You're being unfair.'

'Well you'd better tell me what it is then, because that's what it looks like standing in my shoes.'

'Please, George. Please. Look, over the past ten years, we haven't met that often. When we went for that walk by the river, it was the first time I had really been able to chat with you properly.'

'Yes, and I remember we had a row then.'

'Yes, but that was my fault. Look, all I am trying to say is that I thought we might have a chance of making a go of it and then this thing happened to Scott and suddenly, you're right over on the other side of the fence.'

He looked really miserable and I felt so guilty because I realised in a split second that I had made him initiate the chase because of the hurt he caused me all that time ago. 'Look, Jamie. I'm sorry. I do still care for you. I think I always will, but this week has been such a runaway train of a journey that I don't really know whether I'm on this earth or Fuller's.' I put my arms round his waist and hugged him to me. 'I need some quiet time, to think. Can we meet for breakfast tomorrow and perhaps by then, I'll be a bit more settled in my head about where I am and what I want. Is that OK?'

He hugged me back. I could feel his chin on the top of my head and caught the faint whiff of his aftershave. 'Of course, it's all right, George. Take all the time you need. We have to get it right this time, don't we?' He leaned back and took hold of either side of my face looking down into my eyes.

'Absolutely.' I said trying to keep to some level of decorum. 'I'll be down about eight-ish. Is that OK?'

'I'll see you then. Goodnight, Princess.'

'Goodnight, Jamie.'

We went up in the lift together and he gave me a very chaste kiss on the cheek as it stopped on the third floor. I walked out, turned round and waved as the doors closed on him. Back in my room, I kicked off my shoes and decided I needed a shower to clear what passed for my brain.

Lying in bed with a cup of tea, I sat and tried to concentrate on what it was I wanted from life. I was thirty three. Where did I want to be and who did I want to be with by the time I was forty? Did I want to be with anyone?

I sat back against the headboard and felt completely alone. It was gone midnight, so I couldn't ring anyone. That old familiar running away feeling was there with its insidious voice telling me that if I just upped and left, then I wouldn't have to face anyone, answer any more questions, or make any decisions. I could just go on flitting through life, doing what I was good at and loved but never having to commit to anyone, just like I always had. The old responsibility conundrum. But wasn't it time I changed my usual reaction to situations? What was it the psychology people say? If you always do what you've always done, you'll always get what you always got.

I only had one question to answer, really. Kevin had sussed it. What did I want? No ifs or buts. What did I really want for me? I put the light out and hoped that by the morning, I would have an answer.

I would love to have been able to say that by next morning, my mind was clear and my objectives in focus. I felt as fudged as ever and, because I woke up early with a dry mouth and dull headache, I decided that the only remedy was a pint of water, two ibuprofen and a walk before breakfast.

I walked along to the picnic site breathing deeply and trying to sort out what I did want for my life. There is a lovely interval, early on a summer Sunday morning, when the world is at its most beautiful. The sun was just beginning to shine, the dew made the grass look newly washed and the river flowed serenely on as it had for hundreds of years and possibly would for hundreds more. I paused halfway across the footbridge to lean over and gaze into its depths, clear enough to spot a few fish although I have no idea what they were. I had half hoped to bump into Lizzie and Jordy and I wasn't disappointed. The Volvo drove up and Lizzie emerged. The surprise was that Hamilton also emerged. She hurried over towards me.

'Anything wrong?'

'Not unless you count a slight hangover and a confused brain.'

The dog bounded up to me, tail wagging as usual. Hamilton's expression didn't change much, but at least she didn't look as hostile as she had previously.

'Looks like you're the new best friend.'

I bent down to stroke the silky head before patting his rump and telling him to get on with his walk. 'I think you're lucky, Superintendent. I had dogs when we were young, and my parents still have an ancient lab/collie cross. I'd love to have a dog.'

By this time, Lizzie had reached us. She nodded and smiled but followed Jordy, whether to prevent any mishaps with the swans or because she thought that Hamilton and I were discussing something confidential, I don't know. Her aunt and I fell into step.

'I have to admit that if you can get past the fur and the mess, he can be quite amusing,' she admitted.

'Gundogs have a tremendous sense of humour. Has he made you laugh yet?'

'Lizzie made him lay down last night and then came and sat next to me on the settee. But the dog wanted to be with us, so he started to get up at which point she made him lay down again. So he realised he had to stay down, otherwise he would be in trouble, but he also still wanted to be at the other end of the room with us, so he compromised by commando walking the length of the room without actually getting up.'

I laughed. 'What did Lizzie do?'

'We both started to laugh and by the time we stopped she said it was too late to do anything, so he stayed where he was. With us. I still can't get used to all the bloody dog hair, though.'

'Don't worry, you will. And look at it this way. When Lizzie is out, he will be company for you and vice versa.'

'She usually takes him with her.'

'That's probably because she still thinks you dislike him.'

'I don't dislike him, really. I just think he is superfluous.'

'Sometimes it's good to have something superfluous in your life.'

She grunted. 'You said your brain was confused. Why?'

'Oh, just the usual, you know, trying to sort out where my life is going. Don't you ever do that?'

'I used to, I suppose. When you've had a few knocks, though, you learn to be satisfied with what you have.'

'What? If you can't have the one you want, love the one you have type of thing?'

'I suppose so. I don't think about it much.

'Have you ever been in love, Superintendent?'

'None of your business.'

'Don't be so prickly. It was an innocent enough question.'

'I'm not being prickly. My life is mine and sod all to do with anybody else.'

'I can understand that. My problem is that I fall in love too easily but shy away when it gets serious.'

'How can you say that when you've just had a broken engagement?'

'Because, Superintendent, if I'd really wanted Mike, I would have gone the extra mile and sorted it out, not just flounced out and run away like I did.'

'Running away never does any good, George. You take it with you.'

'Thus speaks experience.'

'You'd better believe it. Now, to business. Have you decided whether or not you are staying and if so, will you be moving in with the Gardiners?'

'I know I can talk anything through with Melanie on the phone. That isn't the issue. What is the issue is that I have a gig next Saturday and I must get to see Janetta before then and fix this problem with my voice.'

'I see. So, if you need to go down to London to see this Janetta, would you come back the same day?'

'Probably not. I'd stay over with Finlay and come back the next day. Why is it so important that I'm here?'

'Because things seem to happen when you are about. You found Ariana Staithes. Scott Wiley was either following you or there was some connection to you and our man – or woman – tried to kill him. Your best friend is mysteriously stricken with her allergy. Do you see what I mean?'

'That makes it sound suspiciously as if everything is connected to me.'

'I think it might be.'

I stopped walking. 'Do you mean that you think I am responsible for all of this?'

'No, I don't think that.'

'But you could make a case for it being me?'

'Yes. I could do that easily.'

'How?'

'You don't need to know that. But I could. And if I could, so could other people. Has it occurred to you that someone might be trying to make sure you are involved in everything to deflect suspicion away from them?'

'We're back at Carrie again now, aren't we?'

'Not entirely. Look who we have on the list.' She ticked them off on her fingers. 'Your friend, Carrie, whose earring was found inside a door she maintains she never went through. Sir Robert, the father of the victim and your old tutor. The husband, who might see in you someone with a grudge against his wife and who then manufactures events so that you are always on the periphery. Merlina Meredith who had a grudge to pay and who has suddenly decided to retire, but who admits she was in the cloisters for the past part of the concert. It wouldn't be the first time a whole bundle of circumstantial evidence had been fluffed up into a solid conviction.'

'So you think that someone might actually be after me?'

'No. I think that they might be after framing you. Then we have to take into account the fact that you found stolen jewellery in your room. Was it planted by the enigmatic X, or are we supposed to think that you were the thief all the time?'

'But you said that some of the thefts happened before I came.'

'Yes, they did. All I am saying is that there is a possibility that someone is out to muddy the waters by involving you at every touch and turn. So I will reiterate what I said at the start of this. Be bloody careful. All the time. Trust nobody.'

I remembered last night. 'You need to be more careful, too.'

'She shot me a quick glance. 'Why?'

'Because Jamie Topcliffe saw you pick me up in the hotel car park.'

'And what was he doing watching the hotel car park?'

'He's jealous of Scott.'

'Jealous of a man in a coma?'

'Yes. Because I am spending more time at the hospital with Scott than I am with him.'

'You didn't tell him that you didn't see Scott last night, then?'

'No. I told him you had picked me up to go to the hospital. He assumed that it was Scott I was visiting.'

'Well, keep it that way. Are you seeing him today – Jamie, I mean?'

I looked at my watch. 'I'm supposed to be having breakfast with him in half an hour.'

'Better get back then.'

I turned to go just as Lizzie and a decidedly wet Jordy came back to us. The dog shook himself. I managed to avoid most of the drops but Hamilton hadn't been prepared for it at all. Lizzie and I burst out laughing. Hamilton looked at us as if we had come out from under the nearest stone.

'Oh, Mick, I am sorry. He is such a butter-brain. He saw a stick floating in the water and before I could stop him, he was in and swimming.'

'I suppose that means that as well as me being wet and dirty we'll also have the stink of wet dog all the way home, then.'

'That's exactly what it means. Hi Georgia. Everything OK?'

'Yes, but I'd better go. I'm having breakfast with someone.'

'Just a minute,' she said stopping me. 'Turn round, the label on your jacket is hanging out the back.'

I obligingly turned my back on her and felt her tucking it in. 'Thanks, Lizzie. I'll ring you later, Superintendent and let you know what I am doing this week.'

Hamilton made no reply. She stood quite still staring at me, but I don't think that she was seeing me at all.

'Superintendent?'

'Mick, are you all right?' Lizzie put a hand out towards Hamilton.

'Yes. Yes, I am. Lizzie, just tuck Georgia's label in again.'

Lizzie and I stared at each other and then back at Hamilton.

'Please,' she said. 'Just do what you just did.'

Without saying anything, I turned and again, I felt her fingers on the collar of my jacket. We both swung round to face Hamilton.

'Why did you do that?' she said to me.

'Do what?'

'Turn round.'

'So that she could tuck my jacket label in. What is all this?'

'If a stranger told you to turn round because your label was out, would you?'

'I don't know. Probably not, especially if it was a man.'

'So what does that tell us. Come on, both of you. Think.'

'That you've worked out something we haven't, or that you are in the first stages of early dementia.' I replied trying not to feel scared.

'No idea,' said Lizzie. 'I'm a vet, not a puzzle solver.'

'It means that Ariana Staithes must not only have known her assailant well, but she also trusted him or her, don't you agree? If it had been a stranger, she wouldn't have turned her back, would she?'

'Probably not,' I agreed. 'She would have challenged him. Or her. And, it also means that it must have been someone she either knew well, or she would not have expected to see them there. So that means it has to be someone in the music world.'

'Right. Or, perhaps she did expect to see them. Perhaps she had found a new blackmail victim. Perhaps she had told them to come and see her after the concert. Perhaps they turned up a little earlier than she expected. She would think that they were nervous and didn't want to be late. It wouldn't occur to her that they would kill her.'

'I see where you're going with this.' I said slowly, trying to visualise the scene. 'You mean that the victim decided to stop the blackmail permanently. And to do that, he or she plumped for murder.'

'Yes. That's exactly what I mean.'

25

'Surely that lets Carrie out?'

'Why?'

'Well, Ariana wasn't blackmailing her, was she, so Carrie would be the last person she would expect to see.'

'She might assume that Mrs Gardiner was waiting for her husband.'

'If I was having an affair with someone and his wife turned up unexpectedly, I don't think I would be comfortable enough to turn my back on her.'

'No, true, but we're dealing with someone who everyone tells me was self-centred and contemptuous when she felt like it. So perhaps she might have turned round to show that she thought your friend was of no account. All the same, if another woman told you your label was showing, wouldn't it be natural to turn round without thinking about it?'

'I really don't know.'

'Didn't your Jamie say that he danced her about and mussed up her hair a bit. Well, perhaps another woman might offer to pin it back up, especially if Ariana was in a hurry to get back on stage.'

'That's possible, I suppose. I still can't see Carrie in the guise of First Murderer. And are you trying to tell me she knocked out the doorkeeper as well? She's a pregnant ex-ballerina, not a hit man for the Mafia. I think there are more likely people on your list, like the husband, for one. You've already said it would have to be someone she knew well. And if your theory about Moira being over here is correct, the perfume Albert could smell might belong to her.'

'Possibly. Remember, Georgia, Ariana had just told him he could have a divorce over her dead body. What would she think if he then appeared unexpectedly backstage? She would be on her guard, don't you think?'

'So you think we can cut Tony out then?'

'No. Not at all. He could have said there'd been an emergency. All I'm saying is that it had to be someone she knew and trusted because they had to be able to get behind her without her suspecting anything.'

I paused to gather my thoughts. 'But if the Moira theory is right, surely Ariana would have kicked up a fuss at the sight of her?'

'She might have kept in the shadows, out of sight, until the vital moment, at which point, Ariana wouldn't have been in a position to kick up anything.'

'So, really, we're no further forward. Or are we?' This was making my head worse.

'Possibly. I need to ask a few more questions. Look, you get back for your breakfast date with the jealous one, and ring me when you've sorted out what you are doing.'

I was five minutes late into the dining room. Jamie was looking fidgety, but his face cleared when he saw me.

'Hi. I thought you'd stood me up,' he said kissing my cheek.

'What? Miss the opportunity of you and food? Never.'

Samantha came over and asked if we wanted tea or coffee. We both plumped for coffee and I was aware of her sour glance at me. Honestly, what with Rosemary holding a candle for Scott and Samantha doing the same for Jamie, I had better watch my step. Perhaps they would club together and push me down the stairs. As it was Sunday, I opted for my once in a while full English with all the trimmings breakfast. I have no idea why I always let myself get conned into it because it is never as good in reality as it is in imagination.

Jamie was nearly as interested in my plans for the forthcoming week as Hamilton had been, but only because he wanted us to spend some time together and see if the smouldering embers could be rekindled.

'I have to ring Melanie and Janetta soon. Then I promise I will tell you what I am doing and we can make some plans. Yes?'

'Yes. Great. What are you doing for lunch?'

'Depends on Melanie and Janetta, I'm afraid. Let's take a rain check on it. If I'm here, I'll be here about twelve-thirtyish. If I'm not, then I'm not.'

'Fair enough. See you, George.'

I climbed back into the lift, a tenuous plan to take the first train out of Temingham bound for London surging in my brain. I looked at my watch. It was just on nine. Once in my room, I rang Melanie on the mobile. She voice sounded even more like a basso profundo than it normally did.

'Shit, Georgy-girl. It's still the middle of the night.'

'No it isn't. Look, I need an excuse to come up to London today and stay over. I want to see if I can fit Janetta in as well.'

'Why? Are the rozzers breathing down your neck?'

'No. It's more complicated than that. I could do with a chat, actually, Melanie. Any chance?'

'I've got guests for lunch, but I'm free this afternoon. Ring and tell me what time. Seriously, George, is everything all right?'

'Everything is far from all right, but I'll be able to tell you properly when I see you. I must phone Janetta.'

Janetta was giving breakfast to her brood of three. Tim answered the phone and I could hear all sorts of screams and laughter in the background. There was a laugh in Janetta's voice when Tim finally managed to get her to the phone. I explained about the glitch and she was immediately all business.

'I don't have anyone tomorrow morning. What time can you make it?'

'I'm coming down to London now. I'll leave my car here and catch the train. It's more convenient. How about ten?'

'Fine. I'll block out two hours.'

'Perfect. Then I can catch a train back up here.'

The next call was to Hamilton. She offered to pick me up and drop me off in Sheffield and then have someone pick me up on my return. 'There's a train at eleven thirty to Kings Cross. Can you be outside in ten minutes?'

I could. I was. I explained to Rosemary that I wouldn't be back until the following afternoon, but that I was leaving my car in the car park. Then I walked through the main door carrying my bum bag and my overnight case and climbed into Hamilton's car. Neither of us appeared to want to discuss the investigation, which left very few options for conversation. I could see she was one of those people who don't speak all that much when driving. The ones that look so at home behind the wheel that you know they are brilliant drivers. I like to think I look the same.

'Did the police teach you to drive?' I asked when I thought the silence was getting oppressive.

'I've done the training courses, yes, but I was driving a tractor on my father's farm when I was nine.'

'How exciting.'

'It is when you're nine because it makes you feel grown up. It's not so good when you're older and want to go and hang about with the other kids but you can't because your father doesn't have enough manpower to do what needs doing, especially at harvest.'

'Does he still have the farm?'

'Good God no. Dad died when I was in my twenties. He was only fifty four. Mum followed him the next year. Margo said that she died of a broken heart, but Margo always was the soppy one.'

'Margo?'

'Elder sister. Mum and Dad always called her Mags, but that wasn't posh enough when she went to art school, so she reinvented herself as Margo.'

Then the penny dropped. 'Lizzie's mum?'

'Yes. Lizzie, thank God, is more like Gareth than Margo. Knows what she wants and keeps to the essentials. Perhaps that's why she and I get on so well.'

'Didn't Margo have to drive tractors?'

'What, and ruin her nails? No fear. Dad said I was as good as a boy and when I was nine, I thought that was brilliant. I wasn't so sure when I was sixteen.'

'What happened to the farm?'

'We always lived hand to mouth. Dad's problem was he thought he was put on this earth to help people. Other people always came before we did. A generous man, my Dad. So bloody generous he'd give his arse away and shit through his ribs.'

I sat there, not just appalled by her unexpected descent into obscenity but also by the feeling behind the words. My silence made her look at me to find out why I had stopped talking.

'Sorry,' she said. 'It was a long time ago. In my mind what happened to Dad is rooted in the time when I was working in Birmingham. City coppers see things differently. Everything is so much more urgent in a city location, mostly because of the number of people crammed in together. Police in urban areas have their own vocabulary to match the environment.'

'What happened to your father?'

'Let's just say that my parents had to take a very sudden early retirement without benefit of a pension.'

'You mean he lost the farm?'

'Bankrupt. Had to live on the state. They never got over it, which is why I take issue with Margo on the broken heart thing. If anything broke my mother's heart, it was my father's stupidity. That and the shame.'

I'm better at reading sounds than I am expressions, so I was careful not to look at her all through this startling family history. I could hear in her voice that there was more to it than just going bankrupt.

'Is that the expurgated version?' I asked after a moment.

'You are sharp, George., I knew you were, straight off. That's another reason I asked you to help us.' There was a short pause before she continued. 'There are only five people who know the whole truth. Dad went missing about six months after they had to leave the farm. The new tenant happened to be a friend. Paul found Dad in the barn, blood all over the shop. He'd sat with his back to a straw bale and with the door open so he could see over the hillside and then he slit his wrists.'

'Oh flick. Your poor mother.'

'Selfish bugger, when it finally came down to it. Not a thought for Mum. Paul called me at work. I drove like the proverbial bat out of Hell from Birmingham. We made it look like as if Dad had had an accident. Managed to fool everyone, including the Coroner.'

'But that's illegal.'

'You don't say.'

'But why?'

'Because we knew Mum could not have coped with the pitying looks and the wagging tongues. It made no difference to anyone else, but it meant the world to her.'

By this time we were threading our way through the city streets heading for the station. Hamilton pulled up outside the entrance and checked the clock on the dash.

'How about that for timing? You've fifteen minutes to get your ticket and catch the train. What time do you want picking up tomorrow?'

'The train gets in about ten past four. Thanks ever so much, Superintendent, and don't worry, I won't breathe a word to anyone. I'm honoured that you think I am worthy of the confidence.'

She nodded briefly and her mouth twisted into what might just be construed as a smile. Then she was pulling out into the traffic. I stared after the car for a few moments before going and joining the queue for tickets.

The train was pulling out of Sheffield when I remembered that I hadn't called Neil, or Finlay. I called Finlay first seeing that I was going to drop on them without any notice at all. I'll say this for my brother. Years of being a doctor have taught him how to listen to what is behind words as well as the words themselves. I told him I would be gracing them with my presence that evening and returning to Temingham tomorrow afternoon. He listened without any interruptions and then said quite out of the blue.

'What's really wrong, George? Why are you coming today?'

'I've just told you why.'

'Yes, but that isn't the whole truth, is it?' My silence told him what my words could not. 'Kate is out tonight,' he said after a pause. 'We'll have a chat over a glass of wine and the sausage casserole she is leaving me. I'll make sure there's enough for two.'

'Thank you, Fin.' I didn't need to say any more.

'What are brothers for?' he asked as he disconnected the call.

I also called Neil to explain that I would return tomorrow night.

'You'll come and stay with us, won't you?'

'Are you sure you can cope with me?'

'Of course. I just don't want Carrie to be on her own at the moment and I am too busy to take any time off.'

'That's fine, then.'

'You're a star, George. Would you like me to get the staff to pack up your stuff and move it all over here so you don't have to go back there?'

I had to think for a moment. I had no idea what Smithson intended for the entrapment of the hotel thief. 'No, that's OK, Neil. It won't take me long and I have to pay my bill and all the rest of it. I'll stay there tomorrow night and come to you on Tuesday if that's OK.'

'Of course. Hope you get yourself sorted voice-wise. Sir Robert is already making noises about a return visit next year.'

On that happy note, we ended the call. I had the rest of the journey, apart from the sprint across Doncaster station to catch the London train, to just sit and think about the crossroads I had reached and which road I was going to go down. When I looked at it, I knew I could probably be happy with either Scott or Jamie, but there was a huge question mark over Scott's prognosis and that was one of the things I needed to talk to Finlay about. I knew he wouldn't pull any punches, not like the hospital doctors who always want to keep things as upbeat as possible.

I also knew that a chat about my musical future with Melanie would help me make my decision. There had been a few notably happy marriages where both partners were in the musical world, but I also knew quite a few which were disastrous. If I was going to make this giant step with whoever, then I had to know the odds.

The taxi rank outside Kings Cross was about three miles long, so I trotted along to St, Pancras about six minutes walk away where, as usual, there was no queue. It pulled up outside Melanie's three-storey Victorian terrace twenty minutes later.

By the time I came out of the bathroom and down into the kitchen, ten minutes later, she had a glass of something white and cold sitting on the table. It looked like Sunday was not going to be an alcohol-free-day, after all.

'So,' she said when we were both sitting at the table, 'what's the problem?'

'I need to talk about anything in the offing, of course, but I also want to ask you about where you think I might be headed, realistically, that is.'

She picked up her glass and motioned me to follow her. 'Let's go and sit on the patio. I can have a smoke then without feeling guilty about your voice.' We settled ourselves into the padded cane chairs, I made sure she was downwind so that the smoke didn't come anywhere near me. She picked a bit of tobacco off her tongue. 'Have you seen the crits of the Vivaldi in the "Telegraph"?'

'No. Any good?'

'Very complimentary. There's one on the kitchen table. Go and have a look before you go. Right. Now, as to what's in the offing, there's the Cirencester thing, of course. You're doing the Bach Choir next Saturday, aren't you?'

'Yes.'

'What are you singing? I've forgotten.'

'Bach.' I looked at her face and stifled a grin. 'Matthew Passion.' I added.

'There's a possibility of covering Dido at the Garden next Spring. How do you feel about that?'

How would anyone feel about the possibility of singing at Covent Garden? Unless it was La Scala or The Met in New York. 'Yes, I'd love to. When?'

'The audition is in about a month's time. There was also a possibility of a cover in "Don Giovanni" but I know how much you love Mozart. Not.'

'Perhaps if I knew him better, I might get to like him. You never know. Yes, I'm definitely up for Dido. I'm happy to have a go at the Don, but I don't think they'll want me.'

'Fair enough. There are a few cruises coming up early in the New Year. There's a round the world one. They want an ensemble, but that's not a problem. I'm sure I can find three other voices. You'd only be on one leg of it, of course, not the whole four months.'

My stomach started to churn with a mixture of excitement and fear. 'I could ask Jamie Topcliffe for the baritone.' I said trying to keep my voice neutral.

She twisted round in her seat to look at me. 'Oh, yes. And is he part of the reason you want a chat? I can feel the vibrations from here.'

'He might be. Can I tell you about it all? You'll be the first outsider I've been able to speak to. I am so confused.'

'Go ahead. I am all ears.'

I spoke for about twenty minutes, which is quite tiring for someone not used to it and the emotion of the whole thing kept making me want to cry. Melanie didn't interrupt once, which just went to show how important she thought it was, or how important she thought keeping me happy was. I have no idea which. At the end, she sat sipping her wine, lighting another cigarette from the butt of the last one and staring out over her garden.

'I think there is only one question to answer,' she said at last. 'Can you envisage yourself either married and juggling two sets of engagements, or seeing your husband jet off round the world whilst you stay at home with the babies?'

Now it was my turn to be silent. I had never thought of the situation in terms like that. I'd only ever thought about me and Scott or me and Jamie. Could I see myself playing second string to their bows, staying home and doing the domestic bit, or, possibly worse, accompanying them but being nobody, only an extension of them? I had no idea. She looked at me through narrowed eyes.

'I suppose the question is, Georgy-girl, do you want to keep singing, or do you want to do the marriage and babies bit, because it is incredibly difficult, not to say tiring to do both. In the end one of them has to give. So what you need to ask yourself, my love, is would you give up your singing for a man and his children? Or, would you give up the man and his children for your singing?'

26

'I don't know.'

'I can keep you in work for as long as you want me to. There is a revival of early music and your sort of voice is not common. I don't think you are ever going to hit the big time, but I do think you have enough of a reputation within the business to keep working for as long as you want to. If we can pull off the Covent Garden covers, that can only be to the good.'

'I can see I have a lot to think about. Thanks, Melanie. You've cleared the mist a bit.'

'George, you're a singer. You emote, otherwise you wouldn't be able to do what you do as well as you do it. But when it comes to decisions like these, emotions need to be discarded. You have to sit and think clinically about where you are headed and who, if anybody, you want to go there with.'

'You're right, of course.' I finished my glass and rose to my feet. 'I can see I have to do some hard thinking, but I definitely want to try for the Dido cover. See what they think about Mozart.'

'I'll put you forward. You have the right voice for Dido, no problem. You may not be what the director wants visually, though. They usually want somebody a bit more ethereal than you. However, we'll cross that bridge when we come to it. I'll make noises about the Mozart.'

I read the crit. in the newspaper and felt a warm glow. My voice was described as bright and focussed and the reviewer had enjoyed the duet as much as Katherine and I had.

I took another taxi and arrived at Finlay's house in time for homemade biscuits and freshly ground coffee. Kate, as always, met me with a smile. She is so laid back she is almost horizontal. Satchmo, the terrier gave me his usual grumbling welcome. I told him he was a git and he wagged his stumpy tail and went back to his bed. My eight year old nephew, on the other hand, always greets me as if I have just returned from three years in the wilds of the Amazonian jungle.

'Auntie George, Auntie George. Come and look at my new train.'

I picked the little boy up. He was a late child and all the more precious for that. The only one of four pregnancies to go full-term and live. 'Hello, Chrysalis. Give me a few minutes to sit and catch my breath and I will come up and see your new train. Which one is it?'

'Duchess of Montrose. Built 1938, taken out of service 1962.'

'Fabulous. I'll be up as soon as I've drunk my coffee and tasted Mummy's gorgeous biscuits, OK?'

The afternoon progressed much as usual after that. Kate, Finlay and I chatted about nothing in particular for half an hour and then, in response to the shouting from upstairs, I laughed and headed up to Christy's room. When Kate had been in hospital a couple of years before, he had come to stay with me in York for almost three weeks. One of the first places we visited was the National Railway Museum and from that day Christy was hooked on trains. But not any old trains. He was very contemptuous of Thomas the Tank Engine. Hence the excitement over his latest acquisition. I was given chapter and verse.

'She's one of the Princess Coronation locomotives.'

'Gosh.' Actually I was more interested than I let on. 'Is she still around?'

'No. I think the Duchess of Sutherland is, but not this one.'

'Right. That's sad.'

We chatted about school and how next term he was going to join the chess club. I went back downstairs twenty minutes later mentally exhausted.

'Honestly, Kate, I don't know how you manage to find the energy for him. He's knackered me and I've been up there less than half an hour.'

'You get used to it, George. I've got to go now, but I should be back before ten. Finlay is responsible for putting his nibs to bed tonight. Why don't you go and have a swim?'

'That would be lovely. Can I?'

'Yes, I'll just put the lights on.'

It sounds as if Finlay has stacks of money and indeed he has, in contrast to my ever-present empty purse. Finlay works very hard as he is fond of reminding me, but only because he wants to. His wealth is down to Great Uncle Charlie, may his knickers rot in Hell. He was Daddy's uncle, a lifelong bachelor who thought that women were the spawn of Satan. I don't know how he imagined he entered this world. He was a bad-tempered, smelly old man who never spent tuppence when a penny would do. When the old sod died, he refused to leave any money to Daddy because he had committed the ultimate sin of getting married. So he left it all to Finlay.

It has been a bone of contention between us since I was twenty. I think Mum tried to persuade him to share at least some of it with me, but Finlay has always thought that singing is not a proper job of work and compared to the hours he works, it isn't. He accepts that I love what I do, though and he does help me from time to time. His house is my house when I'm in London. He thinks that if I had money I would sit at home all day employing someone to peel grapes. He's right too. I probably would. Anyway, Finlay paid cash for his house, built the pool in an old conservatory just off the side of it and built a new conservatory coming out from the dining room into the back garden. The pool isn't Olympic sized, but long enough.

He can be generous, of course. When my old car kept breaking down a couple of years ago, Finlay paid for the Saab. I've become used to being the poor one of the family. I don't know what will happen when I do decide to put down permanent roots and actually buy a house myself. In fact, this was the subject of my thoughts as I ploughed up and down for the next forty minutes. Was I ready to settle down? Answer, yes, it felt right to do it now. Did I want to settle down with anyone in particular? No answer. Oh well, give it time.

By the time I had sorted out my hair and put on some old jogging bottoms and a tee-shirt, the infant prodigy was in bed. I offered to read the bedtime story, an offer Finlay accepted with gratitude. Kate might not find it difficult to keep up with her son, but Finlay occasionally finds Christy's intellectual capacity a bit daunting. Most eight year olds would love a Narnia story, but not Christy. He was into the exploits of brave knights of old. Kate had read "Ivanhoe" to him and I know Finlay had bought him a book about King Arthur and the Round Table after finding him trying to decipher Malory's "Morte d'Arthur" on the Internet. I decided to read him some of my favourite Tennyson, so, of course, it had to be the "Lady of Shalott" and I gave full vent to the actress within.

'Why does she die?' he asked at the end.

'Because she loves Sir Lancelot, but he loves only Queen Guinevere. You must know that from the book Daddy bought.'

'Yes, but it doesn't actually say that in the poem, does it?'

'No, it doesn't,' I agreed. 'You have to think about it and then you realise that the Lady of Shalott was OK until she saw Sir Lancelot and you put it together from there. You can't know everything all at once, otherwise you would never learn how to think things through.'

'You mean a bit like when Tom Dunstan started behaving badly at school and it only made sense when we found out his daddy had moved out of the house?'

'Yes. Poor Tom must have felt that if he did something bad then his parents would get back together to help him, but it doesn't work like that, does it?'

'A bit like a jigsaw?'

'Yes. When you have all the pieces, you can see the picture, but even if you only have some of the pieces, you can sometimes work out what the picture will be, can't you?'

'I shall have to think about it.' He answered, a frown clouding his face.

'Well, don't think about it for too long, then. Night, night.'

Promising to put his light out soon, I left Christy thinking about the complexities of life and went back down to the kitchen. Finlay dished up the casserole and opened a bottle of Pouilly-Fumé

'They had this at the reception before the festival,' I told him.

'Blimey. Who was paying?'

'No idea.'

We ate and chatted about our parents and what would happen when they retired. I think it's half in Finlay's mind to take over from Dad, but whether Kate would wear that is another matter. The one certainty is that they would make a financial killing on the property market with the house in London. I suggested that the way to sell it to Kate would be to emphasise the benefits for Christy. Better air, more room to move about in, all that sort of stuff. Then move on to the benefits for Kate. Bigger house, bigger garden, bigger pool, probably, too. He listened, his head on one side, looking steadily at me.

'You know, sometimes, George, you are just so clear-sighted about things. Why do you allow yourself to get into the tangles that you do?'

'For the same reason that you can't work out how to sell the moving up north idea to Kate. Melanie put her finger on it this afternoon. We both let emotions creep in. I am far worse than you and I accuse you of having no emotion, but we both know that isn't true.'

'What is your emotional tangle at the moment? This patient in the coma?'

'Yes, partly. Do you remember Jamie Topcliffe?'

'No. Should I?'

'Probably not. We almost got it together in my first year at the Academy, but he backed off and I ended up going to Gourdon with Mum and Dad.'

'Oh, hang on. I do vaguely remember Dad saying you were getting over a chap at college. Was that him?'

'Yes, well to cut a long story short, he is up in Temingham as well and is showing interest.'

'And your problem is?'

'I don't know what to do.'

'What do you want to do?'

'That's just it, Fin, I have no idea.'

'Which one makes you hot under the duvet?' he asked, grinning.

I considered. 'At the moment, Scott does, but is that because I've only just met him and what about the coma?'

'Since your call midweek, George, I've had a chat with a chap I was at medical school with. He is now a neuro specialist.'

'What did he say?' I wasn't all that sure I wanted to know, but I knew that until I did, I couldn't make any meaningful decisions.

'The long and the short of it is that nobody can tell what will happen. He may come out of the coma and be exactly as he was. He may come out and have motor problems, or he might be subject to seizures, or he might just not be the person he was before. He might have red hot fits of rage, for example.'

I rubbed my eyes. Tiredness had just dropped on me. 'So your advice would be to stay well clear, then?'

'My advice would be to not make a decision at all. Let's look at it quite coldly. You have on the one hand, someone who blew hot and cold a few years ago and might still do the same. On the other hand you have Mr Unknown Quantity, who might be the most perfect man for you, or might never wake up again. It's too soon to decide what you are going to do. If I was an agony aunt, I'd say you didn't want either of them because otherwise you would know. Just carry on doing what you are doing. How does that sound?'

I got up and hugged him. 'Oh, Fin, you're a gem. Thank you.' And I put my head on his shoulder and cried my heart out. I think he was a bit embarrassed but he put his sympathetic doctor head on and coped.

The next morning, I felt as if a weight had been lifted off my chest. I didn't have to make a decision yet, so I wouldn't make one, or, at least, I wouldn't make one about my love life. I was playing, very tentatively as yet, with the idea of buying somewhere to live in Temingham, though. I'd been in London less than twenty four hours, but already I felt stifled. I wanted to be out on the moors again, preferably walking a dog. I'm not given to envy, but I had a couple of twinges where Lizzie and Jordy were concerned. Lizzie was so lucky she worked in the Peak District. I decided to have a chat with Carrie tomorrow.

Meanwhile there was my lesson with Janetta to look forward to. I came down to breakfast to find Finlay by himself eating some disgustingly healthy-looking cereal. We greeted each other as I grabbed bread and put it in the toaster.

'Meant to ask you last night, George. How are the old finances?'

'About the same as usual. The money from Temingham will help, but it will probably be about a month before I get it.'

'Got enough to manage?'

'Just about. Actually, Fin, I wanted to ask your advice about buying a house.'

He looked up in alarm. 'I thought you weren't going to make a decision.'

'No, I'm not, but I think I've fallen in love with the Peak District. I want to do a bit of scouting round, of course and ask questions, but if I decide to take the plunge and buy, will you help me, please?'

He considered. It was the normal procedure for him to offer and me to accept. I'd just changed the rules. 'Depends what it is. If you go for something sensible and affordable, I don't see why not, but don't do something stupid like live on a narrowboat or in a windmill, will you, because I won't help with that.'

I could feel my temper rising. 'Good old Great Uncle Charles. Thank God you kept Kate hidden until after the old bastard died. I wonder if he was spinning in his grave the day you married.'

'All I'm saying is that I know what you're like, George. Look, a couple of dividends have come in this week. I'll put a couple of thou in your account today. Do your homework on the house front and then come down and we'll talk about it, or I'll come up there and take a look for myself. I can't say fairer than that, can I?'

'You're really good at putting me in a horrible position, aren't you?'

'Yes, well with your track record, I've had plenty of practise.'

I decided to ignore that one. 'Thank you for the money. It will help. And I haven't decided what I am going to do, but I will talk to you about it before I take it very far, OK?'

We finished breakfast in silence. Thankfully Kate and Christy came in and normal service was resumed. I hate it when Finlay makes me feel beholden to him, especially when, had it not been for a misogynistic old bugger, I wouldn't have to come cap in hand to him like I do. He left for morning surgery. I was glad and sorry to see him go, which seems to be the status quo for us. Kate and Christy were doing the rounds of the Kensington museums this week, so there was nothing to keep me hanging round either. I said my goodbyes and grabbed a taxi.

Janetta was all business at once. She had me doing lots of scales and exercises. After about ten minutes we both worked out that there was a hitch in the gear change from middle to head voice. I told her about the cover and she looked out a couple of scores of "Dido and Aeneas", but we both knew the audition piece was bound to be the Lament. It's in my repertoire anyway, but we tickled it up a bit and she gave me some ideas for ornaments that were fun to do and a bit different.

Then, all too soon, it was back to Kings Cross. Back to the maelstrom. Back to danger. But I felt that the break had put a few things in perspective and one thing I did decide on the long journey back was that I wouldn't burn my bridges with either Jamie or Scott. The best thing to do was what my boringly sensible brother had suggested and make no decision at all and the easiest way out of that was to move back in with Carrie straight away. I rang Neil from the train and asked if I could come to them as soon as I was back in Temingham.

'I'm so pleased you rang, George. I think I'm getting on her nerves. Please come as soon as you can. I don't know if it is the aftermath of the nut thing or hormones from being pregnant, but at times this last day or so, she looks as if she'd like to kill me.'

27

Hamilton met me at Sheffield. She'd parked right outside the main door for which I was truly thankful because the weather had definitely taken a turn for the worse. I told her that I had decided to move back to "Vox Celeste" that afternoon. She didn't look at all happy.

'Are you sure that's the right thing to do? She's still a major suspect, you know. Can't you stay one more night at the hotel? I think Jethro has some plan brewing to catch his thief.'

Flick, I'd already forgotten that. 'But I've already promised to go. What can we do?' There was no way I was going to repeat Neil's last remark. I'd tried to end the conversation with him on an upbeat note and told him to hang on in there and that everything would be fine.

Hamilton pulled into the side of the road and took out her mobile. The next few minutes were difficult to follow but I trusted that she would tell me what I had to do, unless, of course, Smithson had already made an arrest. She said goodbye to him and turned to me.

'It's all on for tonight. Is there any way you can ring Neil and tell him you've been delayed? Tell him I need to talk to you, so you'll be with them tomorrow morning. Jethro says he needs you at the Maddox tonight. In fact, we'll go straight to headquarters now and sort out what is happening.'

Which is how I found out they'd roped Jamie and Kevin in, too, obviously to add weight to the plot – very apt for Kevin. So, the stage was set and Act One began thirty minutes later.

I walked into the Maddox, allegedly just back from the train. Jamie met me.

'Hi, George. Have you been invited to the post Festival shindig tonight?'

'Yes. I assumed it was going to be here.'

'No. Lady Barbara is hosting a toned-down soirée in the light of the past week's events. You'll still need your best bib and tucker, though.'

'No hassle. I'm singing in York on Saturday so I brought Granny's treasures back with me. I thought black velvet and diamonds. Good for Bach, don't you think?'

'Perfect.'

Then Kevin came up, a gin and tonic in his hand, as usual. 'Hi Gorgeous George. May I be Prince Charming to your Cinderella for the ball tonight?'

I bit my lip to stop laughing. He made it worse by looking at me with a wide-eyed innocent solemnity that just invited a giggle. I controlled it. 'Alas, sire, this gentleman was before you.'

'Scurvy knave. How about we both escort you?'

'I am honoured gentlemen. I shall appear at eight-thirty.'

'Come and have a drink first.'

So we went to a conveniently quiet corner where nobody could hear us. They wanted to talk about their forthcoming Boys' Own adventure. I wanted to talk about Ariana's murder.

'Have either of you any idea who killed her? I began. They both shook their heads.

'Look, it has to be someone who knows how concerts work, so that means someone in the business.'

'How do you work that out?' asked Jamie.

'Because who else but someone familiar with the procedure and, what's more, familiar with Gerontius would know the rigmarole of going back on stage after you've walked off to get a whole new lot of applause?'

'Someone who comes to concerts,' put in Kevin.

That made me sit up and think. 'So you mean...'

'I mean that it could be anyone who goes to concerts but it doesn't have to be someone in the business, as you put it.'

'You're right. I hadn't thought of that.'

'Why are you thinking about it anyway?' he persisted.

'Because I'm a nosy cow and I want to know. Who would you two put in the frame, then?'

'Nearest and dearest,' said Jamie. 'Isn't that what they say. Where was Tony?'

'Wasn't she paddling with Neil?' asked Kevin. 'What about your friend? She might be worth a look.'

'I don't think Carrie's that sort of person,' I replied.

'Stop being so feeble, George. If you were married to this gorgeous hunk sitting next to me, don't tell me you wouldn't have murder in your mind if someone trespassed. Don't worry, Jamie, you're not my type at all, I'm just being hypothetical.'

'Thank heavens for that. You aren't my type either, Kevin.' They both burst out laughing and I realised that they were very keyed up about what was to happen later.

'Look, behave yourselves. Otherwise you'll give the game away,' I hissed at them.

'Who cares who killed the old cow. She's no loss.' This from Kevin.

'Actually, to the musical world, she is quite a loss,' said Jamie. 'You know how well she sang on Saturday. Just think what she could have done with the angel when she matured up a bit. There's one thing you haven't thought of, my friend.'

'What?'

'We could both lose out on a lot of money because someone knocked her off. Just think about it. It's years since we had the dream team of Tear, Shirley-Quirke and Baker. Don't you think we might have made a whole new dream team of Dace, Topcliffe and Staithes?'

'Hadn't thought of that.'

'No, neither had I,' I put in. The prospect of money seemed to have made them forget I was there for a moment. 'However, surely that gives you both a motive to think about who might have done it, don't you think?'

Kevin looked serious. 'Yes, it does. All right. Thinking caps on. Who?'

I knew I had to be careful not to betray my position as Snitch-in-Chief. 'Well if this was a novel, it would be the most unexpected person without an obvious motive, so I shall plump for, oh, let's say Merlina.'

Jamie spluttered with laughter. 'She had the biggest motive of all. Nobody likes being de-throned.'

'Oh, I don't know. It seems to have brought her surprising benefits with Tom Carter.'

'Yes, but she didn't know that when the murder took place, did she?'

'No,' I admitted. 'OK, then, how about Sir Robert?'

'No chance,' said Kevin. 'He's a careful old boy. I don't think there's anything that would drive him to murder.'

'Isn't anyone capable of murder given the right circumstances?'

'Yes, in theory, but can you see him strangling her or whatever happened? I can't.'

'What do you think, Jamie?' I asked turning to him.

'I keep coming back to Tony. Why is he here? He never came to her concerts. You've talked to him, George. He said he wanted a divorce, but do you think that was a double-bluff to make him look whiter than white?'

'No, I don't think so. He says he's met someone else. I really do think he wanted a divorce.'

'There you go, then.'

'No, think it through, Jamie. If he admits that's why he came back, then he wouldn't say so to us, would he? It would be the most perfect motive and he's no fool. If he was planning to kill her, he wouldn't have told her that he wanted a divorce, let alone us, would he?'

'Like I said. Double bluff.'

'Oh, come off it, Jamie. That sort of thing only happens in thrillers.'

'I still think he had the biggest and best motive.'

'So you don't really think it could be Carrie?'

'I don't know Carrie, but from the things I've heard, it would need to be someone strong.'

'Ah,' put in Kevin. 'But she is strong. She used to be with the ballet. That's what lets Merlina out of it, really. She always looks as if a gust of wind would carry her away.'

'Talking of Ariana,' said Jamie. 'I take it we are all going to the Memorial Service?'

I nodded. 'Yes, of course. Do we know the programme yet?'

'I think Neil and Sir Robert are going to finalise it tomorrow. I'll just put you both on notice, we may get asked to do something at very short notice.'

'What, something specific, or just something suitable?' I asked, my mind going through my repertoire.

'No idea, but I expect Neil will let us know in the morning. Can't say I'm looking forward to it.'

'No,' said Kevin, staring into his glass. 'But I bet we would all like to think that if it was a service for us, our colleagues would make an effort.'

We all nodded, and as it was clear I wasn't going to get anything else from either of them on the subject of the murder, I made an excuse, as they say, and left.

Back in my room, I checked that all was as I had left it. It was, almost. I'd taken all the jewellery with me in my overnight bag, of course, but someone had been rifling through my smalls because they were not how I had left them. I showered in a very thoughtful frame of mind. This was going to be exciting and boring. Exciting that we might finally catch the thief, but boring because I wasn't in the mood for dressing up. The party mentioned downstairs in reception was fictitious. There had been mention of a get-together but that had been cancelled.

However, I had committed to my part, so I twisted my hair up and fiddled with a few ringlets. My slinky midnight blue went perfectly with the fake sparklies Smithson had handed me. I must say they looked impressive. A graduated loop necklace set with what I'll call diamonds for convenience, which ended up with three layers of loops at the front to form almost a bib, with matching earrings. I was about to go out of the room when, as an afterthought, I hid my jewellery roll in the spare blankets on the top shelf of the wardrobe.

I sashayed into reception like Lady Muck. The boys vocal appreciation was quite genuine, I think. Kevin bowed and kissed my hand. He squeezed it and made some sort of joke at which we all laughed. I think both of them knew I was a bit nervous. They both offered their arms and we walked towards the entrance with me in the middle. Jamie was about to reach for the door when I heard my name called.

'Action stations. Go, girl,' muttered Kevin under his breath before we all turned.

'Miss Pattison,' said Becky, the receptionist. 'There's a call for you.' She held out the phone.

I walked over and took it. 'Hello?'

A very quiet Hamilton said 'Can she hear you?'

'Possibly. Is there a problem, Neil?'

'Do your stuff,' came the quiet voice again.

'Oh, no. Is she OK?' Pause. 'I'll be right over, Neil. Ten, fifteen minutes. I have to change. Hang on. I'll be as quick as I can.'

I turned to Jamie and Kevin who looked suitably startled. 'Sorry guys. Carrie is ill again. I'll have to stand you up. Have a nice time.'

I didn't wait for their reply. As if on a mission of mercy, I ran to the lift. Once in my room I undid the ironmongery. That was a relief. The diamonds may have been fake but they weighed a ton. I expected my ears to look like a hobbit's. I dumped the dress on the bed and changed into the jeans and tee-shirt I had put there ready. In less than ten minutes I was back down in reception.

Jamie and Kevin were nowhere to be seen and I hoped they were not waiting outside for that would not have fitted in with my plans at all. I walked quickly through the main door, over the road and down the side of the cathedral to the Chester Tower and through into Cathedral Close. The boys had obviously made for the nearest hostelry. I sniggered to think of the reaction of the locals to two guys coming in for a pint in tuxedos. Knowing the pair of them, I expected the citizens of Temingham would be treated to a full cabaret of witticisms based on each of them tearing the other to shreds.

The drizzle had stopped but the light was fading fast. Bypassing "Vox Celeste", I slipped onto the towpath and back to the hotel through the gardens. Up the back stairs and into my room. This was the bit that frightened me because my instructions had been to go to Neil's house and leave the rest to the boys in blue. I couldn't do that, though. I was a victim of this thief and I wanted to meet whoever it was face to face. I knew Hamilton and Smithson would be outside my bedroom door, so there was no danger.

I slid into the bathroom. I hadn't turned any lights on just in case. I left the bathroom door slightly ajar and tried to calm my breathing down. It was only a twenty minute wait, but it seemed like hours. I was alert, but the intruder was in the room before I had realised. I heard the clink of the necklace and a sigh. That was when I chose to come out of the bathroom.

The problem was the light switch for the main room was eight feet away, but there was enough light coming through the window for me to see the shadowy figure of the chambermaid. She turned and saw me standing there. Whilst I did not expect her to say anything like "it's a fair cop, gov", neither did I expect her to immediately leap towards me, her arm held high. The next thing I knew was a smashing blow on my forehead and she pushed me back into the bathroom. I caught my shoulder on the loo as I crashed to the floor. By the time I had half come to, she was gone.

Ignoring the pain, I scrambled to the door and opened it. The chambermaid was calmly walking down the corridor. She was almost at the other end in fact, her trolley piled high with towels and toiletries. I saw Hamilton emerge from the back stairs door between us. I waved and croaked something. Hamilton saw me and started to run. The chambermaid reacted just as quickly as she had in the room. Once more I saw that upraised hand and this time I saw that it was a torch she held. Hamilton never broke her stride. She grabbed the maid's arm and twisted it. By this time, Inspector Smithson was through the back stairs door, followed by a female uniformed officer I had never seen before. Hamilton thrust her prisoner towards them and came to pick me up.

'You stupid idiot. We told you to stay clear.'
'She robbed me. I wanted to confront her.'
'You could have been hurt.'
'I am hurt.'
'Your own stupid fault.'
'I want to see her.'

By this time I was on my feet and although I'll admit, I felt a bit sick and wobbly, my determination to see the woman who had stolen my jewellery face to face was stronger. We walked up just as the struggle between Smithson and his colleague on the one hand and the chambermaid on the other ended with victory for the law. The maid was red-faced and panting and it wasn't until Smithson turned her to face me and pulled off the mob cap that I recognised her. It was Rosemary.

28

'You?' I gasped. 'Why?'

"Supercilious bitch,' she spat back. Then her voice changed. 'Oh, I brought back Granny's treasures. Why should a useless waste of space like you be allowed to have lovely things, eh? I work all the hours God sends for a pittance. What do you do? Dress up and caterwaul in front of people who should know better. Think you're really somebody, don't you? You're nobody. Just a stupid tart prick-teasing all the men.'

'Keep talking girl, you might eventually say something intelligent.'

'Scott's safely in hospital and what do you do? Start making eyes at those two no-hopers downstairs.'

'That's because I don't have a face like a chewed wasp.'

'At least I'm not a whore.'

I opened my mouth to give back as good as she'd given me, but Hamilton took hold of my arm and marched me to the lift.

'Ignore her.'

'She stole my rings. I want to rip her face open,' I ground back between clenched teeth. Thing was, I wondered how much of what Rosemary had said was what other people thought. Hamilton read me like a pamphlet.

'Don't let her get to you, George. Look, we need to get you to the hospital and get that head wound seen to.

'I'm not going to hospital. I am sick of the sight of the bloody hospital. Doesn't the hotel have a first aid box? I'll patch myself up. I may be a useless waste of space, but I can put a plaster on.'

She tried to persuade me to go to Casualty but I was having none of it. In the end, she patched me up herself. The blow from the torch hadn't broken the skin, but I would have a lovely bruise tomorrow. I was between seething and crying and not at all grateful for her ministrations. When she'd finished, I asked if it was OK to go and get a drink.

'Yes, don't see why not. Just one, though. I'll come and see you first thing tomorrow to get a statement. You'll want to press charges for assault, of course?'

'You bet your socks I will.'

I walked into the bar in a foul temper, one that was growing minute by minute. Not the best frame of mind in which to imbibe alcohol. Tweedle-Dum and Tweedle-Dee were there, still in their tuxedos.

'World war three started, did it?' asked Kevin. I scowled at him. Jamie, who knew me better was making faces at him and I turned just in time to see him changing his expression to one of enquiry.

'Do you want a drink, girl?' asked Kevin, picking up his cue with remarkable speed.

'Yes. A big one, please.'

'Was Operation Thief-taker successful?'

'Yes. It was Rosemary.'

That did shake them. 'But she seemed such a nice girl. Always smiling,' said Jamie. Neither of them had the least notion why I instantly collapsed with laughter, but I have to say it did me more good than anything. I told them of my adventures. Jamie was horrified. 'Honestly, George, you've done it again, haven't you? Rushed in without thinking. Decided that you know better than the police. And look at you now. That's going to be a shiner tomorrow.'

'No problem,' chimed Kevin. 'It'll cover with make-up. You'll not even see it.'

'Why do you always have to whinge at me, Jamie?'

'Because I care, you stupid woman. How do you think I would feel if Rosemary had belted you one on the head and killed you or put you in a coma like Scott?'

There was an awkward silence, broken by Kevin. 'I reckon the hotel can stand us a couple of bottles of shampoo and some food for this, don't you?'

We both agreed with him. He headed into the dining room to commune with Simon. In less than five minutes, Simon himself wheeled out a trolley with a silver bucket full of ice and two bottles of Moet & Chandon, one in the bucket ready to open, and three glasses. A waitress followed him with two plates piled with sandwiches. Simon opened the bottle with a distinct pop but no rush of liquid. Brilliant. I hadn't had champagne in ages. He poured three glasses and then, after putting the bottle back in the bucket, gave us all a slight bow and returned to the depths of his dining room. Predictably, Kevin held up his glass.

'I want to propose two toasts. The first is to our intrepid heroine, who, almost single-handedly, trapped the enemy. To Georgia.'

I giggled and drank half the glass. 'And the second?' I asked.

'To friends, both present and absent.'

I wasn't so sure about this one, but drank the rest of the glass anyway. Jamie gave us all refills.

'Don't swig it back like that, George. It's meant to be sipped, otherwise you will end up as nissed as a pewt.'

This started us giggling and the evening deteriorated from there really. The sandwiches were delicious. Chicken and sweetcorn in tarragon mayo and salmon and cucumber. There was a part of my mind which was coldly calculating how much I'd drunk and how much more I could drink, though, and we were halfway through the second bottle when I decided I'd had enough.

'Sorry, guys. This little girl needs her beddy-byes.' I was horrified to hear that my words were slurring ever so slightly.

The next morning, not even the ibuprofen and fizzy drink remedy had worked as well as I had hoped it would. The bruise on my forehead was promising to make me look like a battered wife and, on reflection, I decided that perhaps the headache was not due to champagne, but the belt with the torch from dear Rosemary.

I drank another pint of water and took two more pills, then decided to head out for a walk and clear my head. I had just managed to get onto the towpath when I tripped. To stop me from falling, I held out my arms and ended up clinging to one of those concrete rubbish bins. The smell of dog shit mixed with mouldy food was too much for my delicate stomach. I added to the bin's contents. However, after that I felt much better. The weather was cool and crisp and as I came back into the hotel, I was shivering slightly. Neither Jamie nor Kevin were in evidence at breakfast and I could only assume that they had not only finished the second bottle of champagne, but, knowing Kevin, probably a third as well.

I made my usual breakfast of melon and toast and decided that, if I was ever flung onto a desert island, I would be well able to cope so long as there was a plentiful supply of toast and butter. And Marmite. And perhaps some lemon drizzle or carrot cake. Or both.

After breakfast, I rang Hamilton to tell her I was decamping to "Vox Celeste" and then I asked the girl on reception to make up my bill. The manager came out of his office, looking as miserable as a pimp with no tart.

'How are you, this morning, Miss Pattison?' he asked eyeing my bruise.

'I have a headache,' I replied quite truthfully.

As I hoped, he assumed that it was the bruise causing it and I didn't disabuse him.

'Could you spare me a few minutes?' he asked. Once in the confines of his claustrophobic little office, he offered me the seat on the opposite side of his desk.

'I've been talking to the owners of the hotel,' he began. 'Naturally, we are devastated by the fact that the thief was a trusted member of staff, but my principal is more concerned with the fact that you were injured.'

I felt sorry for him. He was such an inoffensive little man and I imagine that his principal had given him hell. 'Don't worry, Mr Fletcher. I'll live. I just need to cover this up with make-up and I will be fine.'

He cleared his throat. 'It's very good of you to be so understanding, Miss Pattison. My principal has asked me to tell you that the cost of your stay here will be taken care of. He also reminded me that as part of the company chain, we also own a Health Spa not far from here in Warwickshire. I have been asked to offer you a luxury four day stay at Quasham Hall at a time of your choosing, for you and a friend, again, on the house, as it were.'

I was astonished and goggled. 'That is very generous of your...principal, but really there is no need. I'm not going to sue you or anything.'

The way his face relaxed gave the lie to his words. 'Nothing was further from our thoughts, I assure you, Miss Pattison. However, let us say that the Quasham Hall break is our way of saying thank you for helping to trap a thief. One who, had she been allowed to continue, might have ruined the reputation we have worked so hard to build.'

A health spa. Wow. Who would I take? Sort that out later. Close the deal first. 'It is very kind of you, Mr Fletcher. Please tell your principal that I accept your offer with delight and thanks.' See. I can be gracious when I feel like it.

We chatted a little more, but he had done what he set out to do, namely, effectively prevent me from bad-mouthing the hotel. After that he wanted me out of his sight. The fact that I wouldn't have said anything about how stupid I had been was irrelevant. I almost skipped into the conservatory. Mr Archer was hunched over his chess pieces, as usual. He saw me and waved, so I went up to say hello. I felt sorry for him in a way. He must be missing Jamie.

'I don't think Jamie will be playing you today, Mr Archer. I think he might have a bit of a headache.'

'Never mind, young lady. I can't stop long this morning anyway. My daughter is coming to pick me up at nine-thirty.'

I looked at my watch. 'It's only nine now. You have half an hour's grace.'

He looked at his watch and nodded, but I had spotted someone on the towpath and I didn't have time to chat any longer. Coming into the hotel was Sir Robert, very solicitously holding the elbow of Lady Barbara. They stopped short when they saw me. She blushed, I'll swear she did. He kept his nerve. I pretended not to see their mutual confusion.

'Good morning,' I called in a bright tone.

'Good morning, Georgia. Barbara, I don't think you've met Georgia Pattison. She's an ex pupil of mine.'

I held out my hand, which she took with some reluctance, gazing instead at my head. 'Miss Pattison, what have you been doing to yourself?'

'Long story, but, if you can keep a quiet tongue, then I'll happily tell you over coffee.' There was no way I was going to let them out of my sight. They were both behaving as if they had been caught in the act, and I wondered just what the act was.

It was plain that they didn't really want me along, but equally plain that they could not offload me. Sir Robert put the best face on it he could.

'Do you mind if we don't have coffee in the hotel, Georgia? There's a small coffee shop in the arcade. It's only about five minutes walk away. I see so much of the hotel, I'd sooner go elsewhere. That all right with you?'

'Of course, Sir Robert.' In that case, I thought, why were you heading back into the hotel in the first place. 'I'm actually moving out today. I'm going to stay with Carrie and Neil for a few days.'

'How is Mrs Gardiner,' asked the lady. 'Rob tells me that she has been in hospital. Is she better now?'

'I shall find out a little later. Do you mind if I just pop back into the hotel for a moment? I'll be right back.'

I flew into reception, startling the girl behind the desk. I asked if Mr Fletcher would extend me the enormous favour of having the housekeeper pack my things because I had an unexpected meeting and I wanted to vacate the room. She assured me that this would cause no problem and that she would personally see that my room was emptied and put my luggage in store for whenever I wanted it. I sprinted back outside. The knight and his lady were in deep conversation, but stopped as I trotted up.

'Sorry about that. Now, where is this coffee shop and I will tell you all my adventures.'

The coffee shop was just how Sir Robert had described it. It had yellow and blue curtains and tablecloths that reminded me of Provence. The coffee was to die for and even though it was less than an hour since I'd downed three pieces of toast, I managed to force down a toasted teacake. I told them all my adventures. Well, not all, but certainly the one involving Rosemary and the smack on the head. Lady B winced.

'You need to cover that up with make-up.'

'Yes, problem is I don't know how to cover it up. I only ever wear sheer stuff on my face.'

She delved into her handbag. 'Here,' she said bringing out a Boots bag and pulling out a tube. 'Just paint this on the bruise and finger-tip it in. Then carefully cover it with your usual foundation.'

'That's really kind of you, but I can just as easily go to the chemist and get some now I know what to get.'

'No, it's all right, honestly. Take this one.'

I wondered if I was being buttered up for something. Sir Robert was watching my face closely. He laughed.

'Now you've awoken all her suspicions, Barbara. Well, Georgia, we have a secret, too.'

'Ooh, exciting. Is it a good one?'

'It might be.' He leaned over the table and put his hand over Lady Barbara's. She smiled back at him.

'And it's all because of Barbara. Do you mind if I tell Georgia?'

'Not at all, Rob.' She turned to me. 'It isn't really a secret, Georgia. He's just excited.'

I looked from one to the other. She saw the look and burst out laughing. 'No, dear, it isn't anything like that.'

'Oh, damn. I was hoping it would be.'

'Anything like what?' he chimed in.

'Honestly, Rob. Men are so obtuse. Go on, I'll give you three guesses what secret Georgia thought we meant.'

He thought for a few seconds and I saw the light dawning in his eyes. 'Oh, Georgia. It's nothing of that kind. I'm very happily married.'

'I'm sorry. What else did you think I would think, especially after...?' I stopped not wanting them to know I had been spying on them, but it was too late. She picked it up much faster than he did.

'After what, Georgia?'

I decided to come clean. 'I saw you behaving very suspiciously in the cathedral the day Scott was pushed into the river,' I began. 'I didn't mean to spy on you, but you were acting like something out of John Le Carré.'

'And what, exactly, did you see?' Her voice was very quiet.

'I saw you two, looking like Pyramus and Thisbe, holding a muttered conversation through a wall. Then you walked off in two different directions. As all my friends will tell you, I am very nosy. I followed you, Lady Barbara, just in time to see you climbing into the back seat of Sir Robert's car and zooming off.'

'Ah.' Her voice became softer. 'Did you see anything else?'

'No. Should I have?'

'Perhaps I should re-phrase that. Did you see anyone else?'

I thought back and my eyes widened. She saw it immediately and put her hand on Sir Robert's arm. 'Told you, Rob.' They both turned to me.

'I fell over someone hurrying out of the cloisters. I got tangled up in his umbrella, but you'd already gone in the car by then. Why, who was he?'

'Ah, time to come clean, Rob.' She turned to me. 'I'm not proud of this, but I suppose it is time for it all to come out. A long time ago when I was a teenager, I was a bit of a rebel. My parents were wealthy and you know that stage you go through when you abhor everything that they stand for?' I nodded.

'Well, I rebelled to the extent where I discovered I was pregnant. Forty years ago, that was quite a stigma, but my stupidity brought me to my senses. I agreed to have the child and then give it up for adoption. It was a boy, but because I had tried so hard to hide the pregnancy, they had to deliver him by Caesarean section. I was in such a mess that it meant I couldn't have any more children.'

'That's awful,' I said. 'What happened?'

' A few years later, I met Geoff. I didn't tell him about the baby but he knew I was unable to have children. Last year, I was contacted by Social Services. A man called Nathan Gilroy was looking for his birth mother. He was looking for me.'

My mouth opened. 'Flick. What did you do?'

'I didn't know what to do. I kept getting telephone calls and eventually I agreed to talk to my son. But, Geoff was the fly in the ointment. I've spent almost thirty years effectively lying to him. Unknown to me, he heard some of the telephone conversations, got hold of the wrong end of the stick and started recording all incoming calls. Fortunately, Nathan hasn't rung me since the monitoring began. I've always rung him. Now, judging by what you say, Geoff has also put a detective on my tail. I suspected as much, but you've confirmed it. The day you saw us, Rob was taking me to meet Nathan for the first time.'

'What are you going to do about your husband?'

'I don't know yet, but please keep all this to yourself.'

'Of course. But this isn't your secret, is it, Sir Robert? What is?'

He leaned forward. 'Do you remember me talking to you and the Superintendent about my friend Daniel?'

It took me a few seconds to remember. You mean the one who burned his 'cello after you slept with his fiancée.'

He winced. 'You always did call a spade a spade, girl. One of these days it will get you into trouble.'

'Sorry. I didn't mean to put it as baldly as that.'

'Well, after telling you both what had happened all those years ago, the next person I met was Barbara. She could see I was upset, so I told her, too.'

'Does your wife know about it now?'

'Yes. After talking to Barbara, I phoned home straight away.'

'How did she take it?'

'She said the past is another country and not to be so stupid.'

'I'm so glad. Ariana has a lot to answer for.'

'Yes,' he replied softly. 'I wonder if she is answering as we speak.'

There was an embarrassed silence, broken by Lady Barbara. 'He told me about everything, and about Daniel Wintergreen.'

'And?' I prompted.

'I've known Daniel for a long time. He moved here about eight years ago. He writes articles for the musical press under the name Cecil Green. The minute Rob told me the name of his friend, I was certain that it was the same person.'

Sir Robert was looking very pink. 'Barbara has spoken to him. We are going to meet him in the cathedral in half an hour.'

This was one meeting even someone as nosy as me knew needed to be private. I wished them well and waved goodbye after thanking them for the coffee. On my way back to the hotel, Hamilton appeared from nowhere and fell into step with me. I asked her if they had extracted a confession from Rosemary. Apparently, yes, they had. Good. She had admitted that she had planted the missing jewellery in my room because she was jealous about Scott. Hamilton said that Rosemary had thought Scott was far too good for the likes of me. Where had I heard that before? I told Hamilton about Lady Barbara's long lost son and Daniel Wintergreen.

'That's interesting. Where are they now?'
'Meeting in the cathedral.'
'I might look in on them.'
'Why?'
She looked at her watch. 'When are you moving out of the hotel?'
'As soon as I get back.'
'Meet me at the usual spot at six.'
'Can't. It's the memorial service for Ariana tonight. Besides, I can't move to Carrie's house and then swan off somewhere, can I?'
'Damn. I think we do need to have a meeting, though.'
'I agree. Look. How about tomorrow morning. I'll ring you after breakfast.'
'Yes, all right. I'd better make tracks to the cathedral to meet the mysterious Mr Wintergreen.'
'Make it seem as if it's an accident, then. Please.'
'Don't panic. I shall be walking through on my way to the incident room.'
She started to walk off, but a thought struck me and I just had to know the answer. I grabbed her arm.
'When you were talking to Rosemary.....'
'Yes?'
'The emerald and diamond bracelet in the stash in my room....'
'Yes?'
'I take it that it was the one the choir woman had lost?'
'Yes, it was.'
'Then how did Rosemary come by it?'
Hamilton hesitated. 'Keep it to yourself, won't you?'
'Have I let you down yet?'
'No. All right. She says she stole it from Tony Labinski's room.'

29

There are some journeys I've driven, usually quite long ones, when I know I must have gone down a certain road or through a particular place, but at the journey's end, I can't remember doing so at all. This is what happened now. I found myself back in the hotel but with no memory of the streets I knew I had to have walked along to get where I was.

My head was still aching from Rosemary's ministrations. It seemed that just when I had everything sorted and mentally filed, something came along and pulled open all the drawers, scattering my theories. Tony Labinski. It looked as if Hamilton had been right all along. He had seemed so sincere when he told me about the funeral service in Canada, but he would, wouldn't he, my inner voice answered back. I sighed. I was no good at this game.

My cases, overnight bag and laptop were stacked in a small room off the hotel lobby. I flicked open my phone to ring Neil and checked my watch. It said nine o clock. I shook it and heard a faint rattling sound. Damn. I must have broken it when I landed on the bin just before being sick. Bollocks. It had belonged to my grandmother and was one of my prize possessions. In the middle of all this, Neil answered my call. He sounded frazzled in the extreme. The hotel found me a taxi in record time and within fifteen minutes, I was ringing the door bell at "Vox Celeste". When he answered the door, I discovered he looked frazzled, too.

'Thank Christ you've come,' he said sotto voce.
'Why?'
'I don't know how to cope with her.'
'Where is she?'
'Sitting room.'
'Leave me to it.'
'I'll take your stuff upstairs.'

I walked into the sitting room. Carrie was slouched in one of the armchairs, still in her nightdress and dressing gown. I put my hands on my hips.

'What on earth are you doing still in your nightie?'

She scowled at me. 'Don't you bloody start. I've had enough with him.'

'Him happens to be worried sick about you.'

'You mean like you've been? Not seen hide nor hair of you since the hospital and you didn't even come in to see me properly then.'

'I'm sorry, Carrie, but I really haven't had a chance.' I walked up to her and took one of her hands. 'You aren't the only person who's been in the wars, little one.'

She looked at me and saw the bruise for the first time. 'What happened?'

I stood up. 'Tell me what's for lunch. I'll go and make it. Into the shower and dress, madam, and I will fill you in whilst we eat.'

'Including the gory bits.'

'Including the gory bits.'

She giggled and rose to her feet. I put a hand on her shoulder. 'What's with all the wilting camellia bit? You know Neil is going spare.'

'Yes. I decided he deserved it.'

'Not fair, Carrie. If it hadn't been for him, you would be dead.'

'Indeed. But have you stopped to ask who else but him could have put the nuts in the oats.'

'Yes, I have, and he isn't the only one who had the opportunity.'

'You mean...'

'Yes. Did Ariana ever come into the house?'

'Yes. She came for a piano rehearsal, only I couldn't hear much piano playing going on.'

'Where were you?'

'I went upstairs.'

'Is that the only time she came?'

'There were some bits Neil wanted to go through on the Friday before the party.'

'You mean the day before the concert?'

'Yes. He said he wanted to try some new ways with the soloists bits.'

'So, she came here twice.'

'Yes. Once by herself and the second time with Kevin Dace and Jamie Topcliffe.'

'Did she go into the kitchen?'

'I don't know. I expect they all did. Neil won't allow anyone to take drinks into his study.'

'Then, don't you think it is more likely she put the nuts into your oats and not Neil?'

She took a few seconds to take this on board. 'Yes, I see what you mean. Oh dear. I'd better go and shower. There's some salad stuff in the fridge, or, if you prefer, we could have the salad tonight and the casserole now. It just needs heating up.'

'You go and ablute, little one. I will sort out lunch with Neil.'

We opted for the casserole and I did my quick garlic herb roasted potato slices. Neil was as fidgety as someone bouncing on hot knives, so I tried to reassure him and explain Carrie's behaviour away as raging hormone syndrome. When she finally came downstairs, she looked like the perfect English rose. The white sundress was covered over with a flimsy pink cardigan. She walked straight up to Neil and took his hands.

'I'm sorry, darling.'

Whoops, she was about to spill the beans. I glared at her behind Neil's back. 'Carrie, I've just been explaining to Neil that women in the first stages of pregnancy can be unpredictable because of their hormones batting about.'

She picked up the cue bloody quickly, for which I was very grateful. The last thing we needed now was for her to blab my theories about Ariana and the ground almonds just when things seemed to be settling down. Lunch was really enjoyable. I hadn't felt that relaxed with Neil since I'd met him, but in the intervening ten days or so, he and I had come to some sort of understanding which both of us were happy with.

Carrie, on the other hand, looked tired. On close inspection, she had panda eyes and I surmised without needing to be Sherlock Holmes that she hadn't been sleeping for at least a fortnight. After lunch, I banished her to the hammock in the garden, making sure that the garden umbrella shaded her from the sun.

'Leave everything to me,' I ordered. 'By the way, how do you fancy a four day break, all expenses paid at Quasham Hall?'

I walked away smiling at her excited face and telling her to calm down and sleep.

Neil came out just as I had settled her down. 'George, the Dean and Sir Robert need to see us.'

'Now?'

'Yes. I gather it's about tonight.'

We both looked down at Carrie. Her eyes had opened again, but she waved a hand to us. 'Go on, both of you. I'll be fine. I'm just going to have forty winks.'

Neil knelt by her side. 'I'll be back as quickly as I can.'

She looked at him and stroked his cheek. 'I know,' was all she said.

The chapter house seemed quite crowded when we arrived. There was the Dean, of course. Then Sir Robert and Lady Barbara with a man I hadn't seen before, but assumed to be Daniel Wintergreen. Merlina, Jamie and Kevin were all there, too, as was Katherine May who I thought had gone back to London. And, on his own looking like Daniel in the den of lions, Tony Labinski stood leaning on one of the pillars. Merlina pounced on me as soon as I came through the door.

'Georgia, darling. They want us to sing a quartet at the memorial service tonight.'

'Which one?'

'Still arguing about it.'

'Better be something I know, then. I haven't sung since last Thursday.'

'Tell me about it.'

Neil shut the door and the noise reverberated through the room. Everyone fell silent. The Dean took centre stage.

'As you all know, Ariana Staithes' memorial service is tonight. Following representations from her husband, we have decided to change the programme a little and I would be extremely grateful if you would all concentrate.

The cathedral choir is going to sing "In Paradisum" from the Faure "Requiem" and Franck's "Panis Angelicus". Sebastian will also play "Nimrod" and Pachelbel's "Canon". However, Mr Labinski has asked that we include some of his wife's favourite music, and although this will be a little unusual for a cathedral, I think it right that we try to accede to his wishes.' He turned to Tony, who drew himself up and took a deep breath.

'Anna wasn't into miserable music. She liked Gershwin and Gospel music as well as her operatic stuff. I wondered if you could incorporate that aspect of her into the service, that's all.'

'I'm sure we can do something, Tony. Neil?' The Dean was a past master at the art of delegation.

'I have "Down in the river to pray" in four parts. I'm sure we can do that. As for Gershwin, I'm not sure.'

'I have a Gershwin songbook, Neil. How about "Someone To Watch Over Me"?' Jamie offered. 'It wouldn't be suitable for me, but perhaps Merlina or Georgia could take it on.'

Neil looked at Tony. He nodded. 'I don't suppose you could do "Somewhere Over The Rainbow" could you?'

I couldn't decide whether he was serious or just wanting Neil to squirm. Neil was up for it, though.

'Yes. Actually, the cathedral choir did it on their German trip earlier this year.'

'Do you want me to do anything?' Katherine stood looking more than a little fed up that she was being ignored.

'Yes, of course. I was just coming to you, Kathy. Merlina, are you up for a duet with Kathy?'

Merlina nodded and smiled. There was another short silence.

The Dean, used to gathering up stalled meetings, took up the reins. 'So, we can do the gospel song the Gershwin and the rainbow, yes?'

There were nods all round. The meeting broke up, but Neil asked the professionals to stay behind. 'I was going to suggest you did "Jesu, joy" he said, but I'm sure we can sort "Down to the river". Who wants to do the Gershwin?'

Merlina and I looked at each other and grimaced. 'You'd be much better doing it than me, Georgia, honestly.'

I looked at Kathy. She shook her head. So I glared at Jamie, instead.

'Trust you to open your big mouth. Where is it?'

'Back in my room. Shall I....?'

'No,' cut in Neil. 'I'll send one of the choir boys to the hotel. Where's your key?'

'Here.'

The gospel song was catchy but very repetitious, which was all to the good, I suppose because it meant I only had to learn four lines. Neil had both Merlina and I try the Gershwin and I lost. 'I hope you don't expect me to learn the words before tonight,' I told Neil.

'No. But you have the better voice for it. Think of it as yet another favour to me.'

We practised for about half an hour. We'd done everything I was involved in, and as I'd had enough, I walked out clinging to the Gershwin. Despite my moaning, I'd already decided I was going to learn the words. The three girls agreed to wear black, so it looked as if the black velvet would get an outing after all. As I came out of the chapter house, I was aware of a waving hand from the door further up, the one leading to the library. Hamilton. I followed her up the stairs. She seemed taken aback at the music in my hand.

'Gershwin?'

'Apparently, she liked Gershwin. Who am I to question?'

'I thought I'd let you know about Mr Wintergreen.'

The memorial service was instantly forgotten. 'Yes? Could it have been him?'

'I asked myself the very same question, but, no. I'm afraid that years of working on the farm have given Mr Wintergreen arthritic hands. He can hardly hold a pen, let alone a pin, but, he assures me, he can type.'

'Bugger. He seemed too convenient to be true.'

'What, you mean somebody nobody knew?'

'Yes. What about the bracelet in Tony's room?'

'He says he has never seen it before.'

'Well he would, wouldn't he? Especially if he wanted it for his bride-to-be.'

'The only print on it is a partial from Rosemary,' she pointed out.

'And what does that prove?'

'I have absolutely no idea.'

I hit the desk with my clenched fist. 'I just want all this to end. Temingham is such a beautiful place. I haven't had a chance to tell you, but I am seriously thinking of buying a house here. The countryside is lovely, but it's all being spoiled by this awful thing. This hate that someone has brought here. I just want it all to stop.'

Hamilton's voice was very gentle. 'What you have to remember, Georgia, is that this is real life. And real life stops where it wants. Don't cry. Apart from changing nothing, it will ruin your voice for tonight, won't it?'

I nodded. That old familiar tight feeling in my throat was back and I didn't trust myself to speak.

She let the silence go on for a few seconds. 'You've had a rough ride one way and another. I'm very happy but very surprised that you would consider settling down with us. Why don't you go back to Mrs Gardiner and do what you normally do on a singing night, eh?'

I nodded again and shuffled down the stairs. They were a bit safer if taken slowly but it made the journey longer. Sir Robert pounced on me the moment I stepped through the door.

'Georgia. Come and meet Dan. We're in the tea bar.'

The man I had noticed earlier in the chapter house was chatting to Lady Barbara. He rose to his feet as we came up and held out a hand. One look at it confirmed everything Hamilton had said. I think that when I saw his curled up paw, I finally accepted that she had been right all along. Ariana's murder had been committed by someone I knew and knew well, and I could hear Hamilton's voice telling me so.

I looked at Sir Robert with renewed interest. He had the opportunity and the motive. After all, we only had his word about what Ariana had or had not said. Knowing her, I found it very difficult to believe that she wouldn't try a bit of extortion, given such a heaven-sent opportunity. He was also very pally with Lady Barbara. Could she be his accomplice? Whilst I went through the motions of accepting a cup of tea and another slice of that fabulous lemon drizzle cake, my mind was wondering if her story could be true or whether it was something she and Sir Robert had cooked up. Had they been stringing me a line? Even I thought that a bit far-fetched, but it was clutching at straws time. Sir Robert brought me back with a bump.

'It seems that I was under a misapprehension, Georgia.'

'Misapprehension?'

Dan Wintergreen chuckled. 'Yes. Poor Rob has spent the last thirty odd years thinking that he deflowered Ariana's mother and must, therefore, have been Ariana's father. If that isn't penance enough, I don't know what is.'

It was time for my confused look. 'Sorry, I don't understand.'

'Let's just say that it is far more likely that I was her father.'

'You mean she lied? About sleeping with you?'

'Yes. From about a month after we met until Rob went to America, we...er...how can I put this?'

'You don't have to. I've got the picture. How do you feel about that, Sir Robert?'

'Why don't you call me Rob like everyone else does?'

'It doesn't feel right. Perhaps, in time...'

To be truthful, I feel a whole lot lighter, George. I hadn't realised what a heavy weight I had been carrying until twenty minutes ago when Dan told us the truth.'

'I'm glad it's sorted at last.' I said but I was only being polite, really.

The truth was I just wasn't in a socialising mood. I made smiley faces and looked interested, but after about half an hour, I said I had to get ready for the memorial service.

Carrie was looking much better when I returned to the house and was putting the salad together for tea. I slipped upstairs for a quick shower and put my black velvet dress on the bed. If I could have climbed into my car and driven to York, I would have done it without a second thought. The last thing I wanted was to sing a memorial service for Ariana Staithes and I had to have a stern word with my image in the mirror. Part of me knew that once I was up and singing, everything would be fine.

The Dean had split the service into roughly two parts. The first consisted of a couple of hymns, a psalm and the cathedral choir singing the Fauré and the Franck. Then we said some prayers and the Dean had included a prayer for the murderer as well, which I thought was questionable to say the least.

Anyway, the second part was a lot more upbeat. We started it off with "When I went down in the river to pray". The arrangement started with me singing alone and unaccompanied, then it built and built as each verse progressed with the others coming in one by one until at the end, the cathedral choir joined us and it sounded more like a jam session than anything else.

Kevin sang "E Luceven le stelle" from Tosca. He is such a showman. There were a few hankies in view by the time he'd finished. Jamie and Kevin sang the duet from the "Pearl Fishers" and Merlina and Katherine the "Evening Hymn" from "Hansel and Gretel".

The cathedral choir sang a complicated but beautiful arrangement of "Somewhere Over The Rainbow" and I finished off with the Gershwin. As a finishing touch, Neil had the boys sing "When the Saints" from the Rutter spirituals. Everything went down very well, but it all seemed to be a bit of a mish-mash to me. God knows what Ariana would have made of it.

We came off the stage to the usual fawners. It was very hard to smile and make positive noises. I felt so tired, all I could think of was getting to bed and taking one of the pills. Jamie swam through the crowd and grabbed my arm. I fended off some old dear who wanted to ask me what to do with her daughter who apparently had a voice like an angel and how much were singing lessons.

'Georgia, you've moved back to Neil's I hear?'

'Yes. Why? Is it a problem?'

'Well, now that we've got the memorial service out of the way, we can concentrate on us, can't we? How about joining me for breakfast tomorrow morning?'

I thought quickly. Carrie would probably stay in bed and I didn't fancy a hugger-mugger breakfast with Neil. 'I'd love to. Half eight OK?'

He gave me a bear hug that just about knocked all the breath out of me. 'See you then, George. Sweet dreams.'

Life wasn't so bad after all, I decided. I was humming to myself as I walked out of the Priors Door and into the cloisters. Hamilton was waiting for me. Blast the woman. Did she never sleep?

She looked unusually serious. 'A word?'

'I'm tired, Superintendent. Can't this wait?'

'No. Sorry. Let's walk round the corner where we can talk in peace.'

I swept ahead of her feeling nothing but irritation. The cloisters were dim and gloomy so on impulse I headed through one of the arches and walked into the central garden where it wasn't so dark. I halted by the fountain, turned and looked at her. 'Yes?'

'There's no easy way to say this,' she began.

'Is it Scott?' All my anger had vanished.

'In a way. You see, we decided to give Mrs Gardiner's earring back to her today and I noticed that one of the diamonds was missing. Well, you know what a rumpus there was the last time some precious stones went missing, don't you?'

'What does this have to do with Scott?'

'I had a hunch a couple of days ago. I didn't say anything because, well, strictly speaking, it was nothing to do with you, but mostly because I needed to test it out.'

'And?'

'The earring has bothered me right from the start. If you look just at the evidence and nothing else, then it puts your friend in a place she says she's never been.'

'But you think she's lying.'

'I didn't know what to think. So I decided to test all hypotheses. One of which involved examining the clothes of all those who could have been backstage on that Saturday. We've just had the results.'

I waited saying nothing.

'A small diamond, which fits the missing place on the earring was found in Scott's trouser pocket.'

'So you think Scott stole the earring and planted it?'

'Yes. Yes, I do.'

30

'But why?'

'To take suspicion away from him.'

'So, you're saying that it was Scott who stole the bracelet and murdered Ariana?'

'No. If it he had been the murderer, then why was he pushed into the river and left to drown?'

'So you think there were two people backstage that night. Scott and the murderer?'

'Yes.'

'And you think that Scott is a thief?'

Hamilton looked round. 'Here isn't a good place for an in-depth discussion. Do you want to go to the hotel?'

'No.'

'Cathedral library, then?'

'No. Not with those steps and this dress. Let's go back into the cathedral.'

We sat in the choir stalls near the high altar. I don't know how she had managed it but the place was deserted apart from a couple of uniformed constables standing by the north door. Hamilton sat waiting for me to ask what I so needed to know.

'So you don't think Scott is a thief?'

'No, not exactly. I had a long chat with his parents this afternoon whilst you were rehearsing. Apparently when he is under pressure and by that I mean pressure that has nothing to do with his playing, he develops a kind of kleptomania.'

'And he has been under pressure?'

'Yes. Apparently, his agent has absconded with all the money in the client account. At the moment, Scott is virtually penniless. His father said it came as a tremendous shock to them because the agent was also a close friend.'

I sat and digested that in silence.

She continued. 'It came out about two days before he was due to fly here, so he knew he had to play, if only to earn some money.'

'What will happen now?'

'They are going to take him back to Brisbane and set up a trust fund for him. I think you might get asked to go over there and sing a concert to raise funds. How would you feel about that?'

'I don't know. I find it difficult to think of him being a thief.' I paused for a moment. 'Hang on. I can't get this straight in my head. Where does the earring come into it?'

'I've noticed that Mrs Gardiner has a habit of tucking her hair behind her ear.'

'Yes, she does.'

'Well, this is only surmising, but I think that the earring fell out in the house and Scott noticed it when he left to go back to the hotel.'

'So he picked it up, crept up to the west door, socked the doorkeeper, stole the bracelet and dropped the earring?'

'Yes. His parents think that he may have picked up the earring to sell it and then thought that there might be better pickings backstage. Apparently, all kinds of things are left there during a performance.'

'Yes, that's true. Especially if it is known there is someone looking after it, or the room is locked.'

'So he may have been hoping to pick up, say a wallet that one of the orchestra might have left hanging around in a discarded jacket?'

I nodded. 'Yes, that's more than possible.'

'I'm sorry, Georgia. I know he is special to you.'

I didn't answer. I couldn't. I didn't feel anything. Just numb. So much for castle in the air dreams of life in Australia. It seemed that there were no honest men around any more. Only bastards. I looked at Hamilton.

'What happens now?'

'Well, Scott is still coming out of his coma, little by little. Dr Raven says that he is growing more aware, even though he is still asleep. We can't know anything for certain until he wakes up.'

'And if he never wakes up, or he wakes and can't remember, what then?'

'We keep going until we either reach a conclusion or the case goes cold.'

'You mean we might never know who killed Ariana?'

'We can be sure that it can only be between about four people, one of whom I have to say is Mrs Gardiner.'

'Still? Even though you know she didn't drop the earring?'

'Yes. Just because she didn't drop the earring doesn't mean she wasn't there or that she didn't kill Ariana. And we know she took self-defence lessons, so she could have knocked Scott out.'

'But that doesn't make sense.'

'Yes it does. However you look at it, your friend had motive and opportunity.'

'But I can't believe that she is strong enough to have knocked Scott out and put him in the river.'

'Desperation lends strength. How many times have you read about somebody doing something that was beyond them simply because their desperation gave them the strength to do it?'

I gave up. I was tired arguing. 'So, where do we go from here?'

'Well, if you want to go back to York or London, that's fine. What are your plans?'

'I hadn't made any, but I shall probably stay until Friday and just make sure that Carrie is OK. You never know, Superintendent, I may find a clue which will make sense of all this.'

'I hope so, Georgia, but don't forget to take care. The murderer is still out there. He or she will be starting to relax now. If they think you're on to them, The shock will make their panic all the greater. My advice is let it rest and leave it to us.'

'But you've just admitted that you don't know anything apart from the fact that it seems to have been Scott who dropped Carrie's earring.'

'True,' she admitted. 'I shall probably take myself for a long tramp on the moors tomorrow and see if the wind can blow some sense into my brain.'

'Why don't you take Jordy?'

'Will you stop going on and on about the sodding dog.'

'Don't be so bloody rude. It's time someone told you how many beans make five.'

'And you think you know, do you?'

'I know that if somebody wants something long enough and badly enough, they will have their own way in the end. Lizzie loves having the dog. He makes her happy. Your problem is that you are too selfish to realise that you're cutting your nose off to spite your face.'

'Really?'

'Yes. Really. Face it. Lose the dog and you'll lose Lizzie.'

She stood up. 'Perhaps we both have to face things, Georgia. I'm glad mine is only a dog problem.'

We called it a day then. I knew what she meant. If I was really stupid, then I'd keep holding out for Scott. But, my inner voice protested, just because she thinks Scott is a lost cause doesn't mean he is. What does she know of love? I dragged my feet back to "Vox Celeste". Neil and Carrie were in the kitchen. Carrie took one look at my face and walked round the table to put her arms round me. I must have looked so miserable. I needed the hug, though, even if the brooch she had been wearing scratched my chin when I dropped it onto her shoulder.

'Come into the sitting room,' suggested Neil and without asking he poured me two fingers of scotch whilst Carrie put me into one of the armchairs.

'Do you want to tell us what's wrong?' she asked, holding one of my hands.

So I told them. Not everything, of course. Not the bits where Hamilton and I had entertained the idea that Carrie was a killer. But enough. I told them about Scott and how Hamilton had asked me to find out a couple of things and glossed over the other bits. They were both silent when I had finished.

'You poor girl,' said Neil. 'No wonder you seemed so fiery all the time.'

'She's like that anyway,' replied Carrie trying to raise a smile.

There was one thing I had to know. I looked directly into Carrie's eyes. They were only about a foot away from mine. 'Merlina told me she came out towards the end of the concert and saw you coming into the cloisters from the close. She says you saw her and went round the other side towards the Miserrimus Door and past the door out to the area by the west door. Hamilton doesn't know that little snippet or I think she would have been beating your door down and carting you off in handcuffs. I need to know what you were doing there, Carrie.'

'I don't understand why it's important.'

'The fact that she even considered you is what made me decide to help her, Carrie. Don't you understand, if you had never been under suspicion, I would have told her to take a running jump. But I couldn't because whilst there was a chance that she might pin this on you, I had to try and prove her wrong.'

'It wasn't me, George. I have to ask you to believe that.'

'Why were you there, then?'

'I was in two minds about whether to go t the concert at all. But I decided I ought to go. When you all started singing the end bit of the first half, the volume of sound that swept down the nave was tremendous. I was already feeling a bit iffy. I slipped out and back here so that I could throw up in private. I lay on the bed for about forty minutes or so and then I felt better.

I wanted to be there to support Neil. It was, as he said, his first concert in his first festival. So I drank a glass of water and came back into the cloisters. I could see Merlina Meredith crying, well, that's not true. Her posture told me she was crying. I didn't want to embarrass her, so I walked round the other way. When the applause started, the steward let me in the Miserrimus Door.'

We looked at each other. 'I promise you by everything that I love, George, that I never went near the west door.'

I wished I could believe her. I wanted to so desperately. She could see that I was only half convinced. Neil said nothing. I think he had learned the hard way that some things were better left alone. After half an hour of ragged conversation, I could hardly keep my eyes open. The last twenty four hours had been interesting in the same way that Confucius is supposed to have cursed people by wishing that they might live in interesting times. I didn't drink all the scotch.

'Sorry, folks. I am just so tired I don't know what to do with myself. Do you mind if I go to bed?'

Carrie came up with me. She helped me out of the dress and hung it up whilst I cleaned off my war-paint. Then she brought up a glass of water and put it on my bedside table. 'I am telling you the truth, George. I didn't kill Ariana. I was too busy trying not to feel sick.'

'I know little one. Goodnight.'

'Goodnight, George. Don't worry, things will look different in the morning.'

I waited until she had gone back downstairs and then tip-toed to the bathroom with the glass of water, washed out the glass and refilled it. Then I went back to bed, hating myself for not trusting her, but refusing to leave anything to chance.

My sleep was fractured by horrible dreams. I must have woken up five times. I remember my final dream so very clearly. I was standing in a round room. There was a mirror behind me but I was looking out of the window trying to find something. I knew it was there somewhere, but I couldn't see it. I saw Scott walking past waving an earring at me. Then it dissolved into a nightmare where I was floating down a river in fog. I could hear people shouting at me and I knew I was still looking for the thing I had been searching for earlier. Or was it someone?

I was gazing into the depths of the river and saw a body rolling over and over in the water raising one arm like a signpost and I knew it was Scott drowning. I tried to scramble up in the boat but by the time I had found the oars, the body had disappeared. I could hear Carrie's voice saying "things will look different in the morning" but I couldn't see her for the fog. Then Hamilton's voice floated over the scene "I'll see you in Piccadilly Circus" it said and I found myself reading to Christy. He was shouting at me telling me I didn't have time for this and pointing to his watch, but when I looked at him, he had turned into Ariana with her skin charred and burning. Thankfully at that point, I woke up drenched in sweat and with the bedclothes looking as if I had been intent on destroying them.

I swung my legs over the side of the bed panting and feeling scared. I'd already finished the glass of water, so I took it to the bathroom to get some more. I was hot and uncomfortable. In any other circumstances, I would have had a shower, but I didn't want to wake Neil or Carrie. I contented myself with a cool splash of water on my face and looked into the mirror to see a dark worried expression. I had thrashed about so much, the cut from Carrie's brooch had opened up again and blood was oozing. I mopped it up and stared at the scarecrow in the mirror.

Then, like one of those shafts of sunlight that sometimes come through the clouds without warning, I remembered the thing that had been niggling at me, the thing I had been looking for in the dream. I went through the dream again. All the pieces were there. And once I realised that, all those floating disparate bits of the jigsaw settled into one coherent picture. And I didn't like it one little bit.

I've heard it said that people with certain sensitivities can go from a hypothesis to a foregone conclusion without going through the interim stages to test the feasibility of the hypothesis. That's what happened to me now. I knew. By "knew", I mean that I knew who the killer was. I didn't know all the hows, whys and wherefores, but I knew the who. I didn't want to believe it. My brain was still arguing the toss, but cold logic had no chance against my gut feeling.

I also knew that there was no way I could persuade Hamilton of my certainty because I had no proof and didn't even know if any existed. I was fairly sure that the killer could have no idea that I had worked it out, but one thing was for certain and that was that I would need help. I did what I normally do when I'm troubled. I had a shower, not caring whether it disturbed Neil and Carrie. I also put some make-up on to armour me against what I knew I had to do. Then, with dragging, almost unwilling steps, I walked across to the Maddox and Jamie. I was really glad he had invited me to breakfast, because, if I was right, I was going to need him.

31

I could see Sir Robert having breakfast with Lady Barbara. I hoped she would decide to stay on the committee because Temingham needed someone of her organising ability, not to mention her social status and clout to survive what had happened this year. It had become very important to me that Temingham should survive and what I was about to do could swing the balance either way. That would depend on others.

I was aware of a waving hand flapping in my direction. Jamie, a welcoming smile lighting up his face, pointed at the empty chair opposite him. I smiled back and went to sit down.

'You looked a bit lost, darling,' he said. 'Everything OK?'

'No, not really.' I bent forward and dropped my voice. 'I think I might have worked out who the killer is and I need help. Will you help me, Jamie? I don't know what to do.'

His face stiffened and after a moment, he put his hand on mine. 'Are you sure?'

'Yes and no.'

'Shouldn't you go to that woman policeman? What's her name?'

'Hamilton. No, I can't, because you see I have no proof, but I thought if we could go over to the cathedral together, we might find some. Will you help me?'

'Who is it?'

'I can't tell you that. Not until I know absolutely.'

'What? Not even one clue?'

I thought frantically. 'Do you know what happens to babies born in prison?'

'What?' His face had gone white. 'You mean...'

'Are the mothers allowed to keep them, or do they have to go into homes or something?'

'George, I have no idea. You think it's Carrie?'

'I have absolutely no proof, but there might be some backstage. If you could come with me, then I stand a better chance of finding anything there is to find.'

- 261 -

'Won't they have started taking the scaffolding down now?'

'No. There's a concert in three weeks, so they thought they'd leave it up until after that. It doesn't need to be up again until Christmas, according to Neil. Oh my God, Neil. How the hell is this going to hit him?'

'Don't you think you'd be better going to the police? If there's anything to find as you put it, then surely they are the ones to find it?'

'No, I can't go to Hamilton. I've seen quite a bit of her since Scott was almost killed and she may look like a woman, but I'm not sure she is one.'

He looked down at his plate. There was something about the set of his jaw that suggested he was keeping some deep feeling in check. 'I'd be much happier if you left it to the cops, George. If she has killed once and intended to kill twice, then she won't think about adding you to the tally.'

'Don't you see, Jamie? That's why I need you. Please. This festival is important for Temingham. If we can get the proof, whatever it might be, then we can go to the police. Then Hamilton will have to listen, won't she? Do you see?'

'Yes. All right, George. I'll help, but we'd better be bloody careful.'

'I can't see that there will be a problem if there are two of us. It isn't as if the cathedral will be deserted.'

'True. When do you want to go?'

'Let's just grab some coffee and toast first. Then, I think it's a case of the sooner the better.'

Within twenty minutes, we were heading out of the hotel's main door and over the road to the cathedral. It was before nine, but the early service had just finished and we mingled with the outgoing worshippers and sat down in one of the aisle chairs. Five minutes later, all the people had gone and although there was the occasional cleric in a cassock, to all intents and purposes, the building was empty, awaiting the influx of tourists.

'Off you go,' said Jamie. 'I'll be right behind you.'

If anyone had been looking we must have looked like a pair of furtive burglars as we tried to saunter casually towards the double doors leading backstage. I took a quick look round before going through them. Nobody in sight. I was more conscious of my heartbeat than I am before a concert. This was it. We slipped through the doors.

'What are we looking for?' whispered Jamie.

'There's no need to whisper. Just keep your voice low. I have no idea. Just anything that's out of place. You start on the south side, and I'll do the north.'

'How do I know if anything's out of place?'

'Use your third eye.'

'What?'

'Your third eye. The eye of the mind, if you like. Come on, Jamie, you're a singer. We major in imagination. Use your imagination and if anything looks a bit iffy, call me over.'

I watched him walk down the passage under the scaffolding to the south aisle. I looked up at the statue of the bishop, remembering the first time I had seen it on the afternoon before that first fatal concert. In spite of my fear, I smiled at the memory of the trousers over the arm and the shirt hanging from the outstretched finger. I walked behind the statue and looked around in a desultory way waiting for Jamie to come back from his side. Ten minutes later, he appeared with the remnants of a spider's web hanging from his jacket sleeve.

'There's nothing there apart from dust and a few spiders,' he complained, rubbing the web off his sleeve. 'What about your side?'

'No, nothing. I think we'll have to try and follow what happened and re-enact it.'

'You mean do a reconstruction and see if it leads anywhere?'

'Yes. Until now nobody has had any idea who we were looking for. Now we do. And also, we have our imaginations to work with, whereas I think Hamilton thinks imagination is the name of a rock band.'

'All right. What do you want me to do?'

'You stand on the steps as you did on the night of the concert when you came down immediately after the end of Gerontius.'

He walked to the bottom of the steps leading to the stage. 'Fine. What now?'

'Well, we know now that Scott Wiley was probably standing about where I am, hiding behind the bishop here.'

'Scott was?' His voice had gone up about half an octave.

'Oh yes. Didn't I say. Sorry. Hamilton told me yesterday. It's a long story but you already know about the thefts in the hotel and it being Rosemary, one of the receptionists. Well she told police she stole the bracelet from Tony Labinski's room. But the bracelet had itself been stolen from one of the choir members. She was made to take it off and leave it in her bag backstage on the night of the Gerontius concert.

This is where it gets a bit complicated, so concentrate. Scott had stolen one of Carrie's earrings and they found a stone missing out of it in Scott's trouser pocket. So, it had to be Scott who knocked out the doorman and came here, backstage, to see if anyone had left anything worth stealing.'

'Where does the earring come into this?'

'Scott dropped it just inside the west door.'

'So where do the bracelet and Tony come into it?'

'Scott planted the bracelet in his room.'

'How do you know all this?'

'I think Hamilton thought I was getting too fond of him and wanted to warn me. Apparently, his parents told her that when he is under stress he resorts to a kind of kleptomania.'

'Jesus, are you sure of all this?'

'It's what Hamilton said. He has been under pressure because his agent back in Australia has decamped with a whole load of money and Scott is penniless.'

'And she told you all this?'

'Yes. Shame, isn't it? Still, let's get back to business. So, we have Scott crouching here, watching you all as you come down the steps. The next bit has to be conjecture, doesn't it?'

'Don't ask me, George, this is your show.'

'Yes, and you're supposed to be helping. Now, we know that Carrie knows Neil is playing away with Ariana, yes?'

'Do we?'

'Yes, bumble-head. She told me on the Friday night at the reception party thing. You could try to be a bit more proactive and not so reactive, Jamie.'

'Sorry. Do you want me to stay here on the steps?'

'No, I want to be Carrie, now and you have to be Ariana. So, I'll go to the West Door, where the police found her earring. That's really what set me on the right road.'

'Oh, I didn't know that. So, what do you want me to do?'

'You stand in the little dressing room and pretend to be putting your hair back up.'

He made a face at me and we both giggled. I walked towards the West Door and then turned round and stepped quietly up towards the dressing room. I reached the door. 'OK, this is where Carrie gives her the chop, literally, then turns her over, pushes the pin through her eye, pours on petrol and lights it, then scarpers. I want to time this.' I looked at my watch, waiting for the second hand to come up to the twelve. 'Go.'

I touched the back of his neck and he fell onto the floor. I mimed the pin thing, unscrewing a bottle, pouring out the contents and striking a match. Then I ran for the West Door. When I looked at my watch. The second hand was just coming round to the six. Less than thirty seconds. I walked back to where Jamie was just picking himself up.

'Less than half a minute. Yes, it's feasible.'

'But what sort of proof do you think you'll find?'

'I don't know.' Now that I had come to it, I was reluctant to progress further. I realised that, far from being the intrepid detective, frightened of nothing and nobody, I was shaking with fear. Jamie mistook my expression.

'This is hard because she was your best friend, wasn't she?'

'Oh, yes. But then, what is it William Blake said? "It is easier to forgive an enemy than to forgive a friend". I think that's true, don't you?'

'I have thought of one thing which might put a spoke in your wheel, George.'

'What?'

'Wouldn't I have seen her as I went up the steps?'

I took a deep breath. 'Oh, I don't think that's a problem, is it Jamie? Because you know better than anyone that Carrie wasn't anywhere near here. Don't you?'

His smile faltered a little but his face took on that quizzical expression I knew so well. 'Now I'm completely lost, George. What do you mean?'

'I wanted to do the timing thing. Just to make sure you had the time. It was you, wasn't it?'

'Don't be daft. I was on stage when she was killed.'

'No you weren't. You watched Kevin go to the top of the steps, knowing that he would be concentrating on playing to his adoring public. I mentally timed the gap between him coming on stage and you appearing. It was less than forty seconds. Plenty of time.'

He walked towards me and I backed away down the passage. 'You're talking nonsense, George. How did I do it?'

'Let me answer that question with another. The first time we encountered each other on that Saturday afternoon, I almost bruised myself on your gold pen when you hugged me. Where is it now? When you hugged me last night at the memorial concert, it wasn't there, or I would have felt it. Carrie hugged me last night and I got snagged on the brooch she was wearing. It wasn't until this morning that I realised when you gave me that hug last night, I should have felt the pen, like I did on the afternoon of the concert. So I got to thinking. And I thought, what if it wasn't a pen at all? What if it was a holder for a steel pin?'

'Oh, George, if only you hadn't said that. You do know I can't let you go to the police, don't you?'

'Well if you're going to add me to your list of victims, I think you could at least tell me why. Did Scott try to blackmail you with what he had seen?'

'Clever you. Yes, he did. And yes, the pen was holding the steel pin. The pin was made by my father. He was very clever with his hands, you know. Mum and Dad knew that I was the only one who could avenge Lucy. They made me promise. When I saw the setup here, I knew it was the perfect time. You have no idea how often I have visualised it. That's why it didn't take long, I suppose. I had practised it so often in my head that when it came to it, I just did what I had trained myself to do, quickly and efficiently.'

'It can't have been easy.'

'No, it wasn't. It was much harder to push the pin in than I'd thought and, of course, I had to be so careful not to get splashed with any blood or anything, but luckily, there wasn't very much. I must congratulate you. You got the timing spot on, by the way.'

'And what about Scott?'

'Well, you seem to know all the answers. You tell me.'

'I know you told Mr Archer the wrong time to give yourself an alibi. His eyesight is so bad he just accepts whatever people tell him. I told him yesterday that it was nine when in reality my watch had stopped. He looked at his watch and agreed, but it wasn't until much later that I found my watch had stopped. It was late morning and my watch still said nine. So, knowing that the old man couldn't actually see the time on his watch, I think that you told him it was later than it was to give you an alibi for the time of Scott's attack. Right?'

'Very good, George. He hates anyone see him use his magnifying glass. I told him I had to pop to the lavatory but I wouldn't be long. He was so engrossed in the game of chess, he didn't realise how long I was away.'

'What did you say to Scott to lure him to the river? That you were going to give him the blackmail money, but it was better to do it where nobody would see, perhaps?'

'No. I actually told him that I thought you had a little love-light on the side and suggested he follow you. As soon as I saw you go out of the back door and down to the river, I knew where you were going. He was so trusting. He just looked at me and then followed you out.'

'And what did you do?'

'I legged it over the road and through the cathedral close to the gate by the towpath. You'd already gone past, but he hadn't. It wasn't difficult to follow him. I kept dodging behind trees but he never looked back. Then, when we were out of sight of the town, I just came up behind him and, well, you know the rest.'

'You hit him over the head and stole his room key. Then you came back and searched his room, found the bracelet and decided somehow to plant it on Tony Labinski. Am I right so far?'

'Spot on, Sherlock. How did you know about the room key?'

'It sort of came to me when I remembered you taking your key out yesterday afternoon to give to the boy to go and get the Gershwin book.'

'Quite the little detective aren't we? I needed to get into Scott's room just to make sure he hadn't written anything down. The bracelet was a bonus. It was one of those times when some things are meant to be. It meant I didn't have to put suspicion onto Labinski another way. I put Scott's key on the Reception Desk when the girl went through to the office.'

'But why incriminate Tony?'

'The revenge we planned was only complete if he went down for killing his wife. Poetic justice. A nice balance. I like balance. Do you know what's really stupid?'

'Tell me.'

'I didn't even realise that the bloke on the west door stayed there for the concert. I thought that as soon as everyone was in, he shut the door and went.'

'Hamilton tells me it's a health and safety thing. I must ask you one thing. Did you write that charming little verse to Merlina?'

'Yes. I saw her scurry out. I knew that the police wouldn't consider her otherwise. I was muddying the waters, that's all.'

'And the ground almonds in Carrie's kitchen?'

'She was the perfect jealous wife. Neil screwing Ariana. I remembered you telling us about her allergy at college. I slipped them into the oats when I offered to make us all coffee the day before the concert. I thought the police would put it down to her guilty conscience about killing her husband's bit on the side.'

'So, Jamie, what happens now?'

'You come for a little walk down the river path with me. Let's face it, you're deeply in love with Scott and the knowledge that he will be a cabbage forever and a thief into the bargain is too much for your small woman's brain to cope with, isn't it?'

'I am to be victim number three?'

'Yes. Oh, and don't try to call for help because as well as having a nice steel pin for Ariana's brain, I also carry this and I can get to it in less time than it would take anybody to rescue you.' He pulled up his trouser leg. There was a very efficient looking stiletto type knife in a holster strapped to his ankle.

He held my arm, pulling me close to him. We walked into the cathedral and turned towards the Miserrimus Door. As we stepped out into the cloisters, Hamilton stood there blocking our path. Without even breaking step, Jamie reached down and slid the knife from its holster.

'Don't try anything, or, I promise you, she will get it before you can reach me.'

'Don't be stupid, Mr Topcliffe. Just put the knife down and let Georgia go.'

'I don't think I have "mug" tattooed on my forehead, Superintendent. It's a lovely day and Georgia and I are going for a walk. If anyone comes within ten feet of us, I shall slit her throat. Do I make myself clear?'

Hamilton turned her attention to me. 'Do exactly as he says, Georgia.'

I just looked at her, then Jamie was pulling me down the cloisters with his back to the wall.

We walked out into the close and brilliant sunshine. The light was dazzling and for a moment, I thought I could break free, but when I tried, he was ready for me. I felt the knife pierce my throat and a trickling sensation, which I knew was blood running down my neck. I half screamed.

We swung round to face Hamilton had followed us out of the door. I saw her look beyond us, her eyes widening in surprise. Jamie laughed.

'You can't catch me like that, you stupid fucking woman. It's such....'

His words were cut off as something collided with his back. He gave a sort of scream, let me go and turned to deal with whatever had attacked him. I saw Hamilton put out a hand and I instantly ran towards her. She grabbed hold of me and put me behind her. I turned to see what was happening.

There were two sounds. The first was Jamie screaming. He was on the ground now and in falling, his knife had dropped from his hand. The other sound was a deep snarling. Standing on top of him, his front paws on Jamie's shoulders was Jordy, but not a Jordy I had ever seen. This one was showing just how long his teeth were and I swear the grooves in his uplifted lips were so deep they could have been planted with potatoes.

Running up to this tangle was Lizzie, looking horrified. We all knew that Jordy was within seconds of ripping Jamie's face apart. Lizzie shouted the only command she knew the dog would obey.

'Sit, Jordy. Now.'

And Jordy sat. Well, that doesn't describe it really. His rump smacked into Jamie's groin and I heard several of the male officers behind me wince. Hamilton stayed where she was. She gestured to Stafford and one of the uniformed guys to go and rescue Jamie and arrest him.

The last I saw of him was being led away, handcuffed and not so much walking as hobbling. Snarling dog with huge teeth a few inches away from his face was one thing, but the way Jordy had crunched into Jamie's delicate bits was quite another.

Hamilton touched my arm. 'You OK?'

'Yes. Bit shocked, of course.'

'Why didn't you come to us?'

'I knew because of the pen and Mr Archer, but there was no real proof.'

'So you thought you'd act as bait?'

'Well, I had a suspicion that you might be keeping tabs on me, at least, I hoped you were.'

'Good job, too. I got a frantic call from one of my lot to say that you and Topcliffe had come over to the cathedral and that something wasn't right with the look on your faces. We were about to come in and see what the hell was going on.'

I was aware of being very tired and almost tearful. 'Well, I saved you the bother, didn't I?'

'Yes, but you were bloody stupid. Again. I was closing in on him.'

'Were you?'

'Oh, yes. When we learned that it was Scott Wiley backstage, then it became clear. Take away all the dross and what you had left was that the last person to actually be seen with Ariana Staithes was Jamie Topcliffe. The fact that Scott was later attacked using the same method as on Ariana meant that Scott couldn't be the killer. I'll need a statement, of course.'

Lizzie came up. 'George, are you all right. Jordy heard you cry out and I couldn't hold him.'

Her aunt looked at her. 'Damn good job, too. Nice to know he's useful for something.'

'Does that mean he can stay?'

'I don't have a leg to stand on, do I?'

Lizzie's smile was brighter than the sun. 'No. Not one. Thanks, Mick. Shall we all go and have a coffee or something?'

'I can't, Lizzie,' Hamilton replied. 'I need to go and question my prisoner.'

They both looked at me. I shook my head. ' Actually, I'd like some time on my own. Is that OK? I'd like to just sit in my room for a while.'

All the noise had brought out people from the houses in the close, including Carrie. When the show was over, they turned and went back into their houses. Carrie came up to me after Hamilton left, took my arm and started walking me back to "Vox Celeste".

'George, darling, I won't ask if you're all right. Can I do anything?'

I hugged her. 'Could you get me a really big gin and tonic and then just leave me alone for a while, please?'

I hauled myself up the stairs, with what looked like half a pint of gin and tonic. I didn't feel anything except a deep sadness. There were tears, of course. I'd spent most of my time in Temingham see-sawing between two men, both of whom had betrayed me. I had done exactly what Pete had done to me all those years ago. Gone for what was in the shop window, without waiting to see the quality of the goods in the shop.

I turned my head to the window, staring out at the cathedral. My internal voice told me that, in truth, the only betrayal had been by Jamie.

I needed to see Scott. I was not in love with him, I decided, but I needed him to know I was his friend. I needed to know he would be OK. Perhaps that would bring back a bit of balance. I put down the drink, made running repairs to my make up and drove to the hospital.

I walked into ITU. He wasn't there and for a couple of seconds, I feared the worst. Then a nurse recognised me and took me to the private room his parents had organised. For the first time, they were not standing vigil by his bed. I looked round and noticed that someone had brought in an electric piano. I hadn't known that his parents played but it seemed a good idea to try in the effort to wake him up.

I walked over to the keyboard and began for the first time in years to play some Mozart. It was that boring sonata in C major that everyone knows. I had to learn it for one of my piano exams. I hated it then and I still hate it, but perhaps whilst Beethoven would not chime a chord in the depths of Scott's coma, Mozart just might. I'd got to one of the endlessly twiddly bits, when there was an angry noise from the direction of the bed. I stopped and spun round towards him. The voice was indistinct, but the words were intelligible if very slurred.

'For Christ sakes, not like that.'

I laughed. The world had just become a happier place.

Printed in the United Kingdom
by Lightning Source UK Ltd.
135382UK00001B/253-267/P